# A VEILED & HALLOWED EVE

SOULBOUND VII

HAILEY TURNER

©2021 Hailey Turner
All Rights Reserved


Cover design by AngstyG LLC.
Professional Beta Reading by Leslie Copeland: lcopelandwrites@gmail.com
Edited by One Love Editing
Proofing by Lori Parks: lp.nerdproblems@gmail.com
Proofing by Jenni Lea at LesCourt Author Services


Don't miss out on sneak peeks, exciting news, and more!
Sign up for Hailey Turner's newsletter
to stay up to date on her upcoming books.

# WELCOME TO THE WORLDS OF HAILEY TURNER

**Urban Fantasy**
Soulbound

**Science Fiction Romance**
Metahuman Files

**Steampunk-inspired Epic Fantasy**
Infernal War Saga

*To my mother
for being the strongest person I ever knew.
I love you and I miss you.*

1

SOA Special Agent Patrick Collins woke up before dawn on a Tuesday in October with his hands wrapped around his lover's throat.

"*Fuck*," Patrick rasped out, body shaking as he jerked his fingers away from Jonothon de Vere's warm skin.

Jono, his own hands already locked around Patrick's wrists, didn't let go. In the dull gray darkness of their bedroom, Jono's wolf-bright blue eyes reflected what little light was coming through the edges of the curtain.

"It's all right," Jono said, his voice quiet and calm.

Patrick could barely hear him over the pounding of his heart. Leaning over Jono, the blankets twisted around them and pulled up from the mattress, he had no recollection of moving, of reaching for Jono.

Of choking him.

The cold sweat sliding down Patrick's skin made him shiver as he tried to pull away, the lingering traces of his nightmare still trying to take root.

"The fuck it is. I've hurt you enough."

Jono made a wordless sound that vibrated through his chest. He let go of Patrick's left wrist to reach for the small lamp sitting on his nightstand. Switching it on illuminated their bedroom with a soft glow, and Patrick blinked hard, turning his face away from the light. Jono gently pulled Patrick closer. He stiffened, unwilling to be moved, but Jono was nothing if not determined. Patrick soon found himself lying on his side, wrapped up in Jono's arms, trying to calm his breathing.

"You had a nightmare," Jono murmured, searching Patrick's eyes.

"No shit."

"You didn't hurt me."

Patrick barked out a harsh laugh, dragging a hand over his face to wipe away some sweat. "I had my hands wrapped around your throat."

"Barely. You couldn't hurt me like that, and you didn't, so stop bloody thinking you did something wrong."

Patrick shifted in Jono's arms to lie on his back, staring up at the ceiling. Jono settled his right hand over Patrick's scarred chest, fingers splayed wide. He could only feel portions of Jono's touch, the scar tissue and nerve damage inflicted by a soultaker all those years ago never healing all the way despite Persephone's intercedence.

Fucking demons.

Patrick squeezed his eyes shut and carefully curled his hand over Jono's—the one Andras had blown off with an attack spell. Jono could argue all he liked that it wasn't Patrick's fault, but it had been *his* magic the Great Marquis of Hell had used. Jono wasn't an amputee solely because of the werevirus running through his veins.

He took a breath, then another, trying to steady his nerves and shove the traces of that horrible nightmare where Andras was in control to the back of his mind. Less than a day spent with that fucking demon, and the fallout of it was insidiously subtle. Emotional wounds were a lot harder to heal than physical ones sometimes. His VA-assigned therapist kept reminding him of that, but Patrick knew he wasn't really in the headspace to hear it right now.

Patrick didn't think he'd ever stop feeling guilty for what he'd perpetuated against Jono, even if he knew, rationally, it wasn't his fault. But rationality had no place in matters of the heart, and Patrick didn't know how to not carry that guilt.

"Hey, look at me."

Patrick turned his head to the side and looked Jono in the eye. Jono tugged his hand free from Patrick's grip, shifting so he was the one leaning over this time. He dipped his head, lips brushing over Patrick's, the touch gentle, nothing like the horror of the nightmare taking up space in his head.

"I'm right here," Jono murmured. "And so are you."

Patrick chased after Jono's mouth, getting a longer, deeper kiss for his efforts. "Not for much longer."

He had a flight to catch to Washington, DC, at 0900, and Jono wasn't coming with him. He'd wanted to, but things were still a mess with all the packs in New York City. One of them needed to stay behind to handle anything that came up. Samhain was two and a half weeks away, and they were scrambling to shore up their defenses.

"Stay out of the Library of Congress this time," Jono said as he pushed himself to a sitting position.

"Like I have time to read these days."

"Pat."

"Okay, okay. No going back to the scene of the crime."

Back in August, he and Sage Taylor, their god pack's dire, had gone with Captain Gerard Breckenridge to locate and steal a book Ashanti had left behind in some other century. They'd found it, but then soultakers had found them, and they'd only escaped with the help of gods.

Somehow, Patrick hadn't been blamed by the public for that mess.

Patrick ran his tongue over the back of his teeth. He wanted to get the taste of morning breath and toxic guilt out of his mouth. Whiskey would help.

"I'll get your coffee started," Jono said, as if he were reading Patrick's mind.

Patrick grunted and rolled out of bed. He needed to shower off the nightmare and make himself mostly presentable for the joint task force meeting ahead. Since it had been agreed by multiple agencies that Patrick was a designated target of Ethan Greene and the Dominion Sect, he wasn't obligated to wear a suit. He wasn't going to do a media walk in front of cameras when he got there, and suits weren't the best kind of clothing to fight in. The one he'd worn to the Library of Congress had gone into the trash.

Patrick hauled himself under the spray of hot water in the shower and scrubbed himself clean. He didn't take long because he wasn't looking forward to waiting on standby with a teenage dragon if they missed the flight out. Airport food was usually disgusting, always expensive, and Patrick only had so much money in his bank account right now to keep Wade Espinoza fed. At least they had pack tithes coming in every month now to help with that.

After he finished washing up, Patrick quickly got dressed in dark jeans and a black T-shirt that wasn't too wrinkled. He strapped his gods-given dagger to his right thigh before holstering his semiautomatic HK USP 9mm tactical pistol, shoving his badge into his back pocket.

The weight of the handgun wasn't something he thought he'd get back. The handgun and his SOA badge had been taken from him when he'd been accused of Youssef Khan's murder. The return of his job still felt temporary, and Patrick was bracing for the day he'd be relieved of his duty. He didn't know what he'd do when that happened.

Maybe finally take that vacation that was owed to him if he survived.

Once he had his combat boots laced up, Patrick headed for the kitchen, where Jono was pouring just a little cream into a mug for him. Jono had his own mug, that of strong black tea, but he passed over Patrick's coffee with a smile.

"Feel better?" Jono asked.

Patrick didn't have his shields up, so he couldn't lie, but he honestly didn't want to. "Getting there."

Some days, going through the motions was all he could do. Unfortunately, he couldn't be anything but sharp once he got to DC.

Jono tugged him closer, wrapping an arm around his waist. They stood in the kitchen for a few minutes, leaning against each other and sipping their respective drinks. Their quiet moment together was interrupted by the sound of keys jangling in the lock to their apartment's front door. The only people who had access to the brownstone in Chelsea was their pack, so Patrick didn't immediately move.

"Do I smell coffee?" Wade asked as he came inside. "I want some."

"I thought we were picking you up?" Patrick asked as he and Jono disentangled from each other and left the kitchen.

"I was playing video games all night, and then I got bored, so I decided to come over. I texted the group chat."

Patrick groaned. "You're not talking to anyone when we get to DC."

Wade shrugged as he hurried to the kitchen to get some coffee. "Like I want to talk to any of the people there."

Patrick couldn't blame him.

"When is the meeting?" Jono asked as he sat on the couch.

"The afternoon," Patrick said.

"The *afternoon*?" Wade exclaimed. "I could've been sleeping right now!"

"Sleep on the plane."

"That's barely a nap."

"Then maybe next time you'll know not to play video games so late before I need to make face time with the government."

Wade walked out of the kitchen, slurping at his coffee. "Why are we getting there so early if the meeting isn't until the afternoon?"

"I need to look over some files at the SOA headquarters first, and then I need to stop by Arlington."

Jono eyed him. "Arlington?"

Patrick smiled wanly. "I have respects that need to be paid. I'm overdue."

"Steer clear of the bars, yeah?" Jono asked gently.

"Not looking to get drunk."

He had in the past, but that was then, and Patrick needed to be clearheaded today. Besides, Jono had taught him better habits over time.

Jono stared at him, not backing down. "Please?"

"No bars," Patrick promised.

"There better not be any zombies," Wade muttered before swallowing half his coffee in one burning gulp that didn't bother him.

"Don't tempt fate."

"They're assholes anyway."

"Exactly why you shouldn't tempt them."

Wade scrunched up his nose before setting his coffee mug on the low table by the couch so he could tear open his packet of Pop-Tarts. "When are we leaving?"

"Soon." Patrick eyed Wade's jeans and T-shirt. "Where's your jacket?"

"I don't need one."

"It's October. Go grab a jacket from the closet in the guest bedroom," Jono told him.

"I'm not cold," Wade protested.

"You get to pretend it's cold."

Wade groaned but still went to get one. He and Sage had clothes stashed in their apartment for occasions like this. Wade being a fledgling fire dragon had to be reminded to act human some days. He was growing into his heritage and had come a long way emotionally from when he was rescued last year. Therapy and the support of the pack had slowly taught him to trust again, though that trust was limited to exactly three people.

Wade came out in a light jacket that had his favorite hockey team logo patch over the left chest area. His wavy, dark hair peeked out from beneath a beanie he'd found and was now wearing.

"Do they serve breakfast on the plane?" Wade asked.

Patrick sighed. "No."

Jono quirked a smile at Patrick. "Let's get you to the airport. You can feed him there."

"Great. My wallet thanks you."

Patrick drank the rest of his coffee in two big swallows and went to get his leather jacket with its embedded magic. The police had located it in the old god pack's former territory in Hamilton Heights on their crime scene sweep after the challenge fight in Central Park. These days, Patrick wore the charmed jacket like armor, but the best protection he had was his pack. For all the uncertainty ahead, Patrick knew he wouldn't face it alone.

It only took a few minutes to clean up and leave the apartment. Jono was driving, and it was early enough that traffic wasn't too much of an issue. When they finally made it to the passenger drop-off zone in LaGuardia, Jono leaned across the console to kiss Patrick goodbye.

"I love you," Jono said when he pulled away.

Patrick responded the only way he ever did these days. "I'll come back."

It was a promise he refused to break.

2

"Hear me out," Wade said as they trekked over rain-soaked grass. "Hot dogs wrapped in paper American flags and sold from carts."

Patrick shook his head as they walked between rows of white headstones that marked the graves in the section of Arlington National Cemetery for those who had died during the Thirty-Day War. "Food isn't allowed in Arlington."

"But it *could* be."

"You come here to pay your respects, not have a picnic. That's what I'm doing."

"People leave food at graves all the time. It feeds their ancestors."

"You leave food on some altars. You leave flowers at graves in this place."

Wade shrugged but didn't seem put out that his idea had been shot down. "If you say so."

He sounded cheerful enough, even as he constantly scanned their immediate area. Ever since Wade had been left behind when Patrick was kidnapped from the US Attorney's Office for the

Southern District of New York back in August, he'd made it a point to stick close in public. Patrick didn't argue with Wade about staying behind anymore since it was a fight he always lost.

Their morning flight in had been uneventful. Patrick's first meeting of the day with Supernatural Operations Agency Director Setsuna Abuku at the agency's headquarters had run a little long. Patrick had been forced to stop for lunch to feed Wade before coming here. Their afternoon meeting at the Pentagon awaited them, and Setsuna had assured Patrick that Wade would be given a visitor's pass that would enable him to remain close.

"Ugh," Wade said suddenly, lengthening his stride so that he pulled ahead of Patrick. "It's that asshole."

Patrick narrowed his eyes at a figure in the distance, standing within the rows they were walking between. He glanced over at the asphalt road down the hill and the unmarked black car parked there, the only vehicle to be seen.

"Guess our ride is here," Patrick said.

"Could've got a taxi instead," Wade muttered, scowling at the man coming into sharper focus.

"Taxis can't get past the Pentagon's security gate."

They came to a stop at the gravesite a minute later, and the man who waited for them there turned to look at them. Ever since his murder charge had been dismissed, Patrick had been dealing with the judgment of his peers by staring them down until they looked away first. He couldn't do that with General Noah Reed. There was no winning a staring contest with a dragon in human form.

Unless it was Wade, and that was only if they threw food at him as a distraction.

"This isn't where I thought you'd be when you requested a ride," Reed said around the cigarette clamped between his teeth. His field uniform was hidden beneath an ankle-length black wool coat that didn't appear to be military-issued.

Patrick's jaw twitched. He fiddled with the last quarter in his jacket pocket, the metal warmed from being handled nonstop since he'd entered the hushed and warded grounds of the vast cemetery.

"Where did you think I'd be? A bar?" Patrick snorted. "I promised my pack I wouldn't drink while out here."

Reed removed the cigarette from between his lips, puffing out a long line of gray smoke. Patrick's nose wrinkled slightly at the acrid scent that smelled nothing like nicotine which the cool breeze blew his way.

Wade glared at the three-star Army general, standing at an angle to keep an eye on both of them. Patrick could see his brown eyes flashing gold for a split second beneath his beanie. "Put that out. Don't you know it's rude to smoke in a cemetery?"

Considering he'd been contemplating starting up a hot dog cart business in the cemetery, Patrick thought Wade didn't really have the right to complain about what was correct protocol when visiting the dead. He didn't say as much though.

Patrick drew the front edges of his leather jacket closer together in the face of the cool October breeze. The sky was partly cloudy after a morning rainstorm that had thankfully not delayed their flight, the smell of damp earth thick in his nose.

"You didn't have to be the one to come out and get me. You could've sent an aide," Patrick said.

"I told you I wanted to talk to you before the meeting. There are other places in DC we could have had this conversation," Reed said.

"Not comfortable seeing the results of your actions?" Reed narrowed his eyes at Patrick's pointed question but didn't respond. Patrick shifted on his feet, grass tearing beneath his combat boots. "The wards are better here than anywhere else you'd want to talk in public. Besides, we're flying back to New York after the meeting. This is the only time I have to visit. I wasn't going to miss it."

Arlington was filled with the dead and surrounded by protective wards and anti-removal spells, the old magic a weight in the air to those who could sense it. Time was he'd come here and not feel a thing through the heavy personal shields he used to carry. With shield anchors set by a goddess, then removed by a god, the only remnants of the protection that had kept Patrick and the scars he carried in his soul hidden for years were marks on his bones that only showed up in X-rays.

Lack of permanent shield anchors wasn't going to keep him away from here though. Patrick tried to come to Arlington at least once a year to pay his respects to the Hellraisers who'd never walked off the battlefield of the Thirty-Day War some years back. It had been easier before he was transferred to New York City last summer, but he didn't regret that move.

Patrick slipped past Wade and walked over to the grave of his last fallen brother. He pulled the quarter from his jacket pocket, setting it carefully on top of the headstone. It stood out against the white marble, a mark that someone had been by who remembered the dead buried in the ground, who'd been there when they died. Patrick's lips twisted as he stared blankly at the name on the headstone before turning away.

Patrick was one of only a handful of fighters on their old Hellraisers team who'd been alive at the end of the Thirty-Day War. Survivor's guilt was never an easy thing to carry.

He tucked his hand back into his pocket and walked over to where Reed stood on the grass, staring out across the rows of headstones. As the general who had commanded the US forces amongst their allies in the Thirty-Day War, every grave in this section of Arlington was the result of his orders. Patrick wondered if that bothered him or if Reed was too old in dragon years, too inhuman, to care.

Reed didn't put the cigarette out, letting it burn slowly between his fingertips. There'd been a time Patrick had missed the smell of cigarettes, craving the false sense of balance that nicotine offered. These days, he had other ways of dealing with stress.

"So what lies are we telling everyone when we get to the meeting?" Patrick asked.

Because that's why he had come, to sit in on yet another meeting, planning on how to stop the end of the world when they all knew it wouldn't be enough. Plans never were once the bullets started flying and the spells started exploding. The Fates couldn't see the future, death in all its many aspects was nipping at their heels, and government paper pushers wanted to talk about the *cost of logistics*.

Patrick wondered, distantly, where they'd bury him if he couldn't pay his soul debt—here in Arlington or somewhere else. Maybe it wouldn't matter if the world burned into a new hell.

"What makes you think we're telling lies?" Reed replied mildly.

Patrick slanted his former commander a disbelieving look. "My past might be an open book these days, but the gods are still myths to everyone in the government who matters."

Reed hummed thoughtfully before flicking ash off his cigarette. The ground was wet enough that any trace embers wouldn't be a problem. "The Department of the Preternatural's job isn't to make people believe. It's to keep them alive."

Patrick had always wondered just how many secrets Reed knew and kept, because the general hoarded information the way the uber-wealthy hoarded wealth in offshore accounts. "I'm done being everyone's scapegoat."

He'd had enough of it since his case was dismissed and he and Jono claimed the entirety of New York City as their territory. He couldn't help the family he'd been born into, but he was proud of the one he'd chosen as his pack. Patrick had no problems fighting for them, but he refused to duck his head and toe the line for anyone else these days. Not with so much at stake.

"Setsuna has lost standing and support, whether she likes to believe that or not. I'll do what I can to keep you in play, but there are those in the government who want you removed from the

Dominion Sect investigation because of your familial ties to Ethan," Reed said.

"And which god gave you that order?"

Reed brought the cigarette to his mouth and blew a little bit of flame onto it, burning what remained to ash that he brushed off his fingers. "No god."

"Just you being altruistic, hm?"

Reed nodded in the direction of the asphalt pathway, where his car and driver waited. "Let's get going."

The nonanswer made Patrick roll his eyes. "Sure."

He'd laid all the quarters he had wanted to at Arlington, paid his respects in heavy silence. Time to deal with the living. Patrick waved for Wade to follow him to the car, Reed steps ahead of them.

Patrick left his past mistakes resting in the cold autumn ground, hoping he didn't make any more in the month ahead.

---

"Put it out," Setsuna said, not looking up from the file she was reviewing at the large conference table in the heavily warded room they all sat in.

Reed blew smoke out of his nose before dropping his latest cigarette into his water glass. Preternatural Intelligence Agency Director Cornell Franklin made a disgusted face, and he wasn't the only one, but everyone seated around the table wasn't about to call Reed out.

Every agency head present for the meeting might be aware of the danger the Dominion Sect presented, but Reed was the one who'd put the joint task force together in the first place. Created to locate the Morrígan's staff, there was no keeping that godly weapon a secret anymore, not after Paris, not after the threat bearing down on home soil that had become apparent with the surge of hunters and demons in American cities. Now, the joint task force had expanded to outright hunting down and stopping Ethan Greene.

So far, they hadn't had any luck in finding him.

Reed had a better idea of what they could expect on the ground than any of the other heads of federal agencies present except possibly Setsuna. Faced with people in power who didn't trust him, and if Setsuna's damaged standing was true, Patrick hoped Reed had enough clout to keep him in the fight with government backing.

"So you've had no contact with the Dominion Sect since August?" Franklin asked, staring at Patrick.

"If he had, Collins would've reported in about it," Setsuna answered for Patrick.

That had been one of the many dubious requirements set upon him when he'd taken back his badge and gun after the whole mess in August when he'd been framed for murder and his identity had been revealed. Regaining his status as an SOA agent meant being bound by far more rules than he was used to. The restrictions were meant to placate people in government, but the publicity of the action hadn't been accepted easily by the public.

Cries of double standards because he was a federal agent were rife on social media, and Patrick couldn't really disagree. Their nascent god pack had taken some hits due to his job, hits they could ill afford, but so far the damage to their reputation wasn't critical. The contacts they'd kept with other god packs and that support had helped shore them up, but it wasn't a lasting solution. Patrick knew he and Jono would have to prove themselves as fair leaders to the masses, but they couldn't start on that process until they dealt with Ethan.

Most of the restrictions Setsuna had handed down to Patrick were in place to keep him legally in the clear when it came to the cases given him. Others were for his own safety since it had become clear the Dominion Sect wanted him captured alive rather than outright killed. All of them made it exceedingly difficult to follow the orders of the gods who felt they had a stake in the soul debt he owed Persephone.

He didn't have faith in the gods to keep him safe and had even less faith in the government to do the same. Patrick flexed his left hand, remembering the long cut Cernunnos had carved into his skin from elbow to wrist while he'd lain motionless on a pentagram, before a demon took away his bodily autonomy.

It had given him a taste of what his twin sister had suffered through, suffocated by a godhead in her soul. Only Hannah had lived with that horror for over two decades, and Patrick's hours of suffering, locked away in a corner of his mind while a demon controlled his body, didn't compare.

Franklin's expression remained flat. "Are you certain of that, Setsuna?"

"I haven't had any recent incidents," Patrick confirmed, keeping the bite from his tone through hard practice.

A few other people around the table shifted in their seats. Franklin sighed heavily, gaze locked on the large flat-screen television attached to the wall. The digital squares of those videoconferencing in filled the entire screen. Patrick knew all of them by name and rank but not by association.

It was a far cry from the last time Patrick had been summoned to Washington, DC, for a joint task force meeting. He rather preferred the tension he'd sat through back then with a handful of people than the suffocating accusatory pressure filling the room now.

"Ethan hasn't tripped any red flags outside the country, nor has anyone else in his inner circle," CIA Director Erin Batey said, her voice echoing slightly through the speakers.

The screen flickered slightly at the edges. The amount of magic encircling the room here and in other locations meant the electronic connection was on the fritz. Patrick wondered if they should've brought out the scrying crystals.

"That doesn't mean he's inside our borders," FBI Director David Morrison said.

"Disregarding what happened in London and Paris, the Dominion Sect has focused their efforts here in the United States over the last few years." Reed glanced at Patrick, who stared stonily at him. "We have reason to believe whatever they ultimately have planned will happen here."

"Here being millions of square miles with no definitive location in mind. That's a lot of ground to cover."

"Considering Ethan's past history and desires, we believe the Dominion Sect will focus on the Atlantic Seaboard, most likely in the Northeast. New York City is a strong contender for confrontation," Setsuna said.

"And you came about that information how?"

The SOA's in-house problems with Dominion Sect sympathizers had put the agency on the outside looking in for too many years. Even with Setsuna working hard to clean up that mess, trust wasn't easy to come by in the intelligence community.

"The same way all of you come to conclusions. By studying the information at hand."

Morrison wasn't the only person to glance at Patrick. His shoulders tightened beneath their attention, but he kept his face impassive in the wake of their silent suspicions. Being the son of a terrorist wasn't ever a forgivable offense, despite the fact Patrick carried the scars on his body and soul that showed just how little Ethan thought of him.

Patrick was a means to an end for a lot of people—Ethan, government officials, gods, take your pick. Patrick had a soul debt to pay, and what he owed filtered into every aspect of his life. There was no escaping that truth, even after he cast off the lie he'd lived under for so many years back in August.

The people in the room with him saw Ethan as a threat, driven by delusions of grandeur. Of them all, only Setsuna and Reed believed in the truth of Ethan's actions—that he vowed to finish what his family had sought for generations. Turning himself into a god was the stuff of myths, but all myths had been history of a kind at some point in the past, whether humanity deigned to remember them as such or not.

Patrick didn't have a choice in being part of Ethan's story. His soul debt was owned by a goddess whose daughter was dying in Hannah's soul and body. The people sitting in for this meeting might know his history, but they still didn't know all his secrets, and he wasn't about to confess to any of what he'd carried with him over the years.

Reed was right in that they wouldn't believe in myths and legends as fact. Patrick doubted that would change even if they witnessed the presence of gods with their own eyes.

"Your agency's information over the years hasn't been the best, as evidenced by the way you kept your agent's identity a secret," Erin stated coolly.

Setsuna finally set down the report she was reading, turning her head to stare at Erin's face in a square on the television screen. "The SOA isn't the only agency in this room who has made excuses for agents under their command. Don't throw stones in glass houses. Yours will shatter just as surely as ours."

"We brought all of you on board on orders from the president," Reed said, drawing everyone's attention before the argument could devolve. "Your assistance is needed, but not your attitudes. Most of you deal with mundane problems, not magical or preternatural ones. We're the experts here in terms of knowing what the threats boil down to. When we tell you our best bet to winning is sitting at this table, then accept that as fact. Collins isn't going anywhere, and the president is in agreement with that."

"Who asked the president for that clearance?" Franklin demanded.

Reed glared at him. "I did."

Setsuna glanced at Patrick before letting her gaze sweep the room. "We're on the same side here. Our number one priority is the safety and security of our nation. Ethan and the Dominion Sect are a threat that requires support from all agencies. Whatever they are planning, it will end on October thirty-first. That's two and a half weeks away, and we need to be ready."

"For what?" Erin asked.

Patrick thought saying *the end of the world* was a little ridiculous, even if true, so he settled for "To fight."

His words drew everyone's attention. At any other point in his life, he might have wilted beneath the stares of so many powerful people in government, but that was before he'd spent the last sixteen months standing his ground with the support of his pack.

"Ethan cast a sacrificial spell at the end of the Thirty-Day War. Odds are he'll do it again until he gets what he wants. Ilya Nazarov has in his possession a powerful artifact that can raise the dead, as witnessed in Paris. I know what Ethan is capable of. I've fought against him for years. If ground zero happens this time on American soil, then we need to be ready. That means pooling our resources, guarding every nexus, and being ready to move at a moment's notice," Patrick continued.

"And what do you bring to the table?" Franklin asked, shades of derision in his tone. "Your god pack?"

Patrick had to consciously unclench his jaw. "Mine, and others. Werecreatures are better equipped to fight the dead and demons. I saw that when I was in the Mage Corps, and it was a hard fact on the streets of Paris. We've asked god packs across the nation for volunteers to help support our efforts. Reed is aware of the request."

"We're stationing those packs in New York City," Reed said before anyone else could protest. "They're in the process of arriving within the next week or two. We want them in place before the end of the month. Collins will be our liaison with them."

"Of course he will be. And what does he get out of it?" Morrison asked, not bothering to keep the contempt out of his voice.

Patrick brushed his fingers against the hilt of the gods-given dagger strapped to his right thigh, the self-soothing gesture hidden by the table. He opted to ignore the barb directed at his pack and answer broadly. "My life back."

The declaration was meaningless to almost everyone in the room, but it was the truth, and it's what drove Patrick to endure the rest of the meeting where Reed and Setsuna fought to drag support from fellow federal agencies. In the end, communication between everyone would remain open, quick-response teams would be on standby in various cities in the Northeast, with a focus on New York City, but Patrick knew deep down it wouldn't be enough.

Not against the gods and demons of every hell.

When the meeting ended and people started leaving, Wade slipped through the door, walking through the wards Setsuna had set around the room as if they didn't exist. He ignored the frown Franklin gave him on the way out, the PIA director more aware of Wade's background than some of the others. Wade proved immune to Franklin's dissatisfaction.

"You ready to go?" Wade asked. He crumpled up a bag of chips he'd purloined from a vending machine somewhere, proof he hadn't stayed in the empty conference room Patrick had put him in at Reed's order. He must've slipped his military minder as well.

Patrick checked the time on his phone, calculating how long it would take to get to the airport. "Yeah. Let's get out of here."

"Patrick," Setsuna said.

He sighed as he stood, looking over at where she sat, her carved rosewood cane already in hand. "What?"

"Have you heard from Eloise?"

It was just the three of them in the conference room now, which was probably for the best. Discussing Ethan openly among strangers was something he had no choice in doing. Discussing his mother's family was far more personal.

Eloise Patterson was the high priestess of the Salem Coven and his grandmother. The matriarch of a powerful and old family of magic users, Eloise was an activist who hadn't sat back and let life pass her by after her daughter's death and the supposed death of her two oldest grandchildren. She'd spent weeks since the revelation that Patrick and Hannah were alive trying to reach him.

They hadn't spoken, only texted and emailed, because Patrick still couldn't wrap his head around the enormity of being able to make contact with his mother's family after all these years. When the courts had changed his last name from Greene to Collins, it had effectively severed his past. Over the years, Setsuna had made it clear he couldn't contact them for his own safety, and he'd accepted that order.

She had never said why, and he always thought it was at the behest of the gods. Only now he couldn't be sure, and he wasn't in the mood for an interrogation.

"I'm seeing her next week," Patrick said, stepping away from the table.

Setsuna frowned, and he wasn't sure if the worry in her eyes was for him or the situation unfolding around them. "Be careful."

"You should probably take your own advice. You're the one she's pissed at."

Setsuna's signature was on the government documents in his juvenile file, accepting Patrick as her ward. She'd kept silent for over two decades about his status, and from what he'd gleaned by the few interviews Eloise had done over the last month or so where Patrick was concerned, his grandmother's wrath was focused squarely on Setsuna.

Ethan might get her hate, but Setsuna got her fury, which was something to witness in interviews coming from an octogenarian.

Wade tugged on Patrick's sleeve, easily hauling him along. "Let's go. I want to get dinner before we get on the plane. The vending machine choices here were crap."

"You were supposed to stay put," Patrick reminded him.

"I did! I stayed put in the Pentagon."

"There's a car and driver waiting for you out front. Have a safe flight home," Setsuna said.

Patrick nodded his thanks and then spent the next ten minutes herding Wade out of the Pentagon. When they finally stepped outside the main entrance, visitor passes turned in to the appropriate people, it was raining, the late-afternoon sky dark with storm clouds.

"I thought it wasn't supposed to rain again today?" Wade asked as he peered through the downpour for their promised ride to the airport.

Patrick stared at the clouds, unease settling in his gut. "Weather changes."

He could only hope the storm wouldn't follow them back to New York.

3

Jono looked up from wiping down the bar counter as a familiar heartbeat cut through the buzz of conversation. He caught a glimpse of Patrick's dark red hair in the crowd of werecreatures, magic users, and a few fae filling Tempest. He caught Sage's eye and nodded at the seat she'd been saving at the bar for him.

"Pat's here," he said.

Sage lifted her designer tote bag off the seat in question and hung it on the hook under the bar counter. Seconds later, Patrick slipped free of the crowd, hauling himself onto the empty barstool. He and Wade had flown back home from DC last night, and Jono had been the one to pick them up. An early week, out-of-state meeting didn't mean Patrick was taking time off from work. He'd been working out of the SOA field office downtown but had promised to make the Wednesday night pack meeting.

"Hey," Patrick said. "How's it going?"

Jono set a glass of Macallan 18 Year down in front of him. "Busy."

Jono had already presided over nearly two dozen small territory issues amongst the packs. Keeping the boundaries updated between packs that had switched loyalty from Estelle Walker and Youssef Khan's god pack to theirs early on and those who reluctantly came under their protection and command after the challenge fight in Central Park was a headache on the best of days.

Fenrir made sorting out trouble amongst the packs easier. Having an animal-god patron riding his soul and capable of knowing the intent of the werecreatures who showed throat before him made it clear who would ultimately cause trouble in the long run. Jono and Patrick had already barred three packs from New York City after they won the challenge fight. That wasn't even counting the god pack members who had either fled the city or been arrested.

Estelle and Youssef might be dead, and Patrick's ties to the werecreature community might have upended the cases against the pair, but the government was still investigating their mess. Jono had been interviewed half a dozen times since the end of August by the federal government. Sage had worked with Danai Belvedere, their previous criminal defense attorney, to help guide his responses.

They weren't in the clear and wouldn't be for a long while yet. Jono and Patrick might hold New York City as their territory, but that didn't mean all the packs within it *liked* each other or them. Territory disputes weren't just going to disappear because they took charge, but the hostility had definitely dampened a bit in the face of Fenrir's presence.

The traditional god pack territory up in Hamilton Heights remained empty as of now. Jono and Patrick weren't leaving their flat in Chelsea, and in the future, when other god pack members eventually joined them, they'd need someplace to house those members. A four-member god pack, even one backed by a god, wouldn't be strong enough to handle all the problems a territory this size brought. But growing their god pack was at the bottom of their list and would remain there until they dealt with the issues of Ethan, the Dominion Sect, and Patrick's soul debt.

Patrick sipped at his whiskey, turning a little to scan the bar. Jono took a moment to clean up his area while Patrick settled in. They'd agreed some weeks ago to conduct most of their god pack meetings in public. The transparency was needed after the secretive and brutal way Estelle and Youssef had ruled over the packs for years.

It helped that Patrick's past was now out in the open. Some things they still couldn't talk about, like their soulbond, but many of the secrets they'd been forced to keep no longer needed to be hidden.

That didn't make ruling easier.

"I have tacos," Emma Zhang announced as she claimed the empty stool on the other side of Marek Taylor.

Marek kept tapping away at his mobile, scowling at the screen. "Good, because I'm starving."

"Then put away work and eat."

Jono stepped away to pour a couple of drinks for some customers. When he returned, Emma handed him a Styrofoam container, which he took with a quick smile.

"Ta," he said.

Patrick had already demolished one of the street tacos in his container. Jono flipped open the lid on his own dinner and picked up a carnitas one.

"Any new sightings of hunters?" Patrick asked around a mouthful of food.

"New Jersey," Emma mumbled, wiping a bit of salsa off her chin with one finger.

"Eh, it's Jersey. That's not our problem."

"Spoken like a true New York City transplant," Leon Hernandez said as he sidled up beside Jono to pull a beer from the refrigerator under the back counter.

"They'll become our problem soon enough. Bet you anything," Sage said.

Patrick snorted. "I know better than to bet against you."

"The hunters are still a problem we need to keep an eye on," Jono said pointedly.

He'd prefer the bastards all be murdered if they stepped one foot inside their territory. After what had happened to Patrick with Andras, Jono had no interest in mercy when it came to the Krossed Knights and other hunter groups. He was very much in the camp of *kill first, leave the bodies where they lie* when it came to demons these days.

Patrick's scent took a slight dip toward anxiousness before leveling out. His damaged soul and magic left a bitter edge to his scent, one most people didn't like. It had never bothered Jono, but what was new was how the scent was more constant than it used to be.

When Patrick had lost the shield anchors, he'd lost the ability to keep up permanent personal shields without draining himself dry. That meant he only shielded when he had to. The change meant Jono could parse his emotions easier than in months past. Patrick was still uncomfortable with the pack reading his emotional state on a constant basis, and Jono tried not to intrude too much.

When it came to talk of demons and hunters, Jono wanted Patrick to know he wasn't alone. Patrick still blamed himself for the wounds Jono had taken in the challenge ring at Andras' hands in Patrick's body. The distinction there was black and white to Jono, but getting Patrick to believe that was still a struggle.

"We still have our alliances with the Night Courts and the fae," Patrick said.

Sage sighed. "For now."

With only a couple of weeks until Samhain, most of their time was caught up in trying to prepare for a fight they knew was coming; they just didn't know the full parameters of what it would look like. Where and when and how were all terrible unknowns that left everyone stressed-out and trying to guard all sides, not knowing if it would be enough.

Jono was in agreement with Patrick about New York City becoming ground zero. It's why, when they'd asked for support from other god packs, they'd instructed all volunteers to come here and nowhere else.

Leon elbowed him to get his attention, offering up a beer. Jono took it with a nod of thanks, his tacos now finished. He pried the cap off the bottle and tossed the bit of metal into the bin.

"The alliances will hold through Samhain. That's what was promised, and it includes the covens," Jono said.

Emma pointed her fourth taco at him. "I still don't know how you pulled that off."

Jono shrugged. "The Crescent Coven was willing to work with us after the fight in Brooklyn. The Wisteria Coven lost their clout after the bollocks they pulled with the Dominion Sect, so any pushback has been minimal."

They still didn't know what the exact rite was that had been performed in the Ritz-Carlton the night of the challenge fight in Central Park. All they knew was that Cernunnos had stolen Patrick's blood to perform the spell after drawing life out of every park in the five boroughs and breaking through the cliff roses barrier laid down by the Greek gods last year.

The fallout within the covens was a realignment of power that Jono couldn't follow and didn't much care about outside the fact that it gave his pack more support. The Crescent Coven worshipped Hera, and as much as he loathed gods, he at least knew that Greek goddess was on their side of the fight. The Wisteria Coven was not, as proven by their dodgy decisions.

With Patrick's federal standing still on shaky ground, even with his badge returned, he hadn't been able to oversee the Ritz-Carlton case, only review the files after the fact under the auspices of the joint task force. The cleanup by the Dominion Sect that time had been far more thorough than the one that had happened in Chicago earlier in the year. Still, they knew the rite had to be a fertility one, but the underlying spellwork was unknown.

That they'd stolen Patrick's blood to do it was a worrisome connection. Jono knew Patrick's soul was still somehow tied to Hannah's. He'd blocked it as much as he could, unable to risk opening himself up in that way. Jono only hoped their soulbond was strong enough to override a frayed and dying tie to keep Patrick safe.

Trying to plan for the inevitable without knowing the playing field left Jono anxious and worried in a way he wasn't used to. For now, they could only shore up their outside support and hope it would be enough, even if he had a sinking feeling it wouldn't be.

"Any news from the government?" Marek asked, finally putting down his mobile.

"Nothing of note," Patrick said carefully. "Have you seen anything?"

Marek shook his head, mouth twisting wryly. "The future is a black hole right now."

It was a far cry from the time an angel had taken over his mind and used him as a temporary prophet to issue a warning. It cost him every shade of blue, and the vision of a graveyard he'd come away with was a sinister warning Jono didn't ever want to come to pass.

"Wade wanted me to ask about the weather," Sage said before taking another sip of her wine.

Wade wasn't there tonight because he was underage, and there were too many eyes on Tempest these days to sneak him in. Jono was the owner of the bar now and bound by the drinking age laws of his adopted country. Wade couldn't be present for a meeting in Tempest without risking the alcohol license.

"It's raining," Leon said dryly.

"He said it feels off."

Patrick made a face, the expression half-hidden behind his whiskey glass. "He mentioned the weather yesterday in DC. It seemed fine to me."

But Wade was a fledgling fire dragon, sensitive to the natural world in ways he was still learning to understand. If he said the weather felt off, that was another problem they'd have to keep an eye on.

Sage propped her elbow on the bar counter to rest her chin in her hand. "Maybe we reach out to some weather witches, then? See if it's a reactionary storm?"

Patrick shrugged. "The weather would be worse if it was a reactionary storm. Like a hurricane stalled over land."

"Not much we can do about the weather, then."

"Plenty of stuff we can do about everything else." Jono caught Patrick's eye. "When do we meet with the Night Courts?"

"Saturday evening," Patrick said with a long-suffering sigh. "I told Wade he didn't have to go, but he insisted he wanted to be there."

"Are we all going?" Sage asked.

"We can manage that meeting if you'll manage the fae."

"Deal."

Jono gazed at the crowd, noticing the looks thrown their way, which meant people were waiting to come up and chat. He raised an eyebrow at Patrick. "We still have some pack business to get through. You all right with taking over for a bit?"

Patrick nodded. "Yeah. Whoever's next, let's do this."

Someone broke free of the crowd, a tall woman who was almost immediately joined by another woman. They scowled at each other, but when Patrick turned around on his stool to hear their grievance, they kept their voices even.

Jono knew the packs still weren't used to how he and Patrick governed—which was as fairly as they could, and within public view. They didn't play games, didn't play favorites, and absolutely refused to require any pack alpha to fight another to win what they wanted. Every rule that Estelle and Youssef had built up over the years had been immediately jettisoned upon their taking over.

That fairness was a problem for some of the packs, specifically the ones who had prospered under Estelle and Youssef's rule, but

Jono and Patrick weren't changing the way they did things. Anyone who had a problem with their orders could piss off.

Shaking his thoughts away, Jono focused on work. He kept the drinks flowing with his bartenders on shift, stopping to chat here and there with werecreatures who needed his opinion. Both the upper and lower levels of the bar were open, and it was busy for a Wednesday. The crowd started to thin out the closer it got to midnight.

Jono wasn't staying to close up, no longer obligated to now that he owned the place, but he still stuck around on some nights. Patrick had to work tomorrow though, and he'd been hiding yawns behind a water glass for the past hour.

Jono put the last rack of clean glasses onto the shelf and turned around. "Ready to go?"

Patrick shoved himself off the barstool. "Yeah. I'm parked a block away."

Jono made his way to the employees-only room near the back to retrieve the jacket he'd worn to work earlier. He'd taken the subway, despite feeling uncomfortable inside the tunnels. The city was almost finished fixing the span of tracks that had been damaged when a subway train was derailed by demons and magic in August. The notoriety that came with his new position meant getting a taxi or a ride-share pickup was nearly impossible these days.

He shrugged on the jacket, signed off on a couple of restocking forms, and headed back into the main area. Patrick was already waiting for him by the front entrance, mobile in hand as he thumbed through some emails.

"I think we took care of everything that needed to be dealt with tonight," Patrick said.

Jono leaned down to give him a quick kiss on the mouth. "Never thought being a god pack alpha would require giving so much therapy. I'm not licensed for that."

"You're licensed for alcohol."

"That's not a fix."

Patrick smiled crookedly. "I know. It probably wouldn't be like this if we were taking over from anyone else."

The dearth of problems they needed to fix and the people they were responsible for clamoring for attention was exhausting but hopefully not insurmountable.

Jono grabbed Patrick's hand and guided him out of the bar. The cold wind slapped him in the face when they made it outside, and he ducked his head against the strong breeze. The wind had picked up since he'd started work earlier, blowing fiercely over the street and creeping inside his jacket. He followed where Patrick's feet led them, enjoying what passed for quiet in a major city.

"When do we meet with your grandmother?" Jono asked, finally able to broach the subject. It was one thing to chat about pack issues in public, quite another to delve into Patrick's past so openly.

Patrick shrugged one shoulder with a tight motion. "Next Wednesday. We'll need to designate Sage as proxy if you insist on going."

Jono tightened his hold on the other man. "What part of *we* did you miss? I'm going, Pat."

Patrick snorted softly, but he smelled relieved rather than annoyed, and Jono took that as a win. Jono tugged Patrick closer and wrapped an arm around his shoulders. They didn't talk on the walk to the Mustang. Jono had one eye on the street around them when the sharp tang of ozone cut through the air, driven by the wind. It filled his nose, coating the back of his throat, the warning nearly making him gag.

Patrick jerked to a hard stop, body stiffening. "*Fuck.*"

Jono's attention snapped to the pair of large black ravens perched on top of the Mustang, talons scratching the paint, staring at them with eerily intelligent eyes. Corvids weren't strangers to the city's streets, but Huginn and Muninn were something else entirely.

"What do you lot want?" Jono growled.

Muninn spread his wings, head cocked so the immortal could look at the night sky. *Do you sense it, Vánagandr? The end is coming.*

*Are you ready?* Huginn asked.

Odin's ravens launched themselves into the sky without waiting for an answer. Jono followed their trajectory with unblinking eyes. Beyond the shadowy spots of darkness that were the pair of immortals, high above, what looked like sheet lightning flickered in the dark depths of the low-hanging clouds.

Patrick shoved Jono toward the car, fear spiking in his scent. "*Move.*"

"Is that—?" Jono began as Fenrir stirred deep in his soul.

"Yes, so fucking move."

Patrick's curt response got Jono moving. He hurriedly climbed into the passenger seat as Patrick got behind the wheel. The rumble of the engine starting couldn't drown out the warning cries of the Sluagh as the terror of the Unseelie Court crossed the night sky above Manhattan, momentarily breaking free of the clouds before letting the storm hide their presence again.

"We need to meet with the Dagda," Jono said grimly.

Patrick yanked on the steering wheel, pulling into the street, eyes on the sky and not the road. "I'll have Sage get us on the mayor's agenda tomorrow."

"What about tonight?"

Patrick glanced at him, mouth drawn into a grim line. "Text the pack alphas. Tell everyone they need to stay indoors. I'll call Casale and then Henry to let them know about the sighting. Not much else we can do."

"If the Sluagh are here, that means Medb is involved."

"I know."

Jono leaned back and kept his eyes on the sky and the flashes of lightning still burning through the dark. The Sluagh was a sign of war, and he wasn't sure they were ready for what was coming.

## 4

City Hall was a bustle of people who gave Jono and Patrick quite a few double takes when they entered the security area, shaking rainwater off their umbrellas. Jono had quit hiding his eyes behind sunglasses some time ago, and the wolf-bright blue color, a mark of the god strain werevirus running through his veins, always drew attention.

Jono was used to ignoring the stares and the whispers; he'd had years to learn how to turn the other cheek. Patrick's expression wasn't friendly in the least, and Jono wondered if maybe they should've stopped for more coffee along the way. What little sleep they'd gotten last night had been restless, and Patrick was always less murderous with caffeine in his system.

"Might want to adjust your face," Jono muttered, resting his hand on the small of Patrick's back.

"My face isn't the one that needs adjusting," Patrick said, not bothering to keep his voice low.

Definitely should've gotten more coffee.

They passed through the security checkpoint without hassle

and were met by a young man who smelled human and looked as if he'd been impatiently waiting for them, judging by the unsubtle once-over he gave them. At least the bloke wasn't an immortal, which was a welcome change from the last political aide they'd had to deal with when visiting the mayor.

That aide had been Tisiphone, an Erinyes who'd been forcibly removed from the Dagda's sphere of influence by Hermes and returned to face judgment for her actions before Hera and Zeus. Considering she'd been someone who had watched Jono be tortured last year, he had no sympathy for the punishment she most likely endured from the heads of the Greek pantheon.

The Dagda, however, was another problem entirely.

"Ah, there you are," the Dagda greeted them when they finally made it to his spacious office past the receiving room, voice deep and booming in Jono's ears. "You realize I had to rearrange my entire schedule to fit you in?"

In his role as Mayor Doyle Ferbenn, the Celtic god was a tall, broad-shouldered man with curly hair more on the orange side of the ginger scale. His clothes were a flashier style than Jono cared for, favoring prints over dull monochrome colors. In this form, the Dagda was a distilled version of his true self, who had walked across the field beneath the Gap of Dunloe last winter. But gods in any form were dangerous, and Jono didn't trust the immortal before them one bit.

They said nothing until after the aide left the office and Patrick laid down a silence ward. His magic was sharp in Jono's nose, nearly drowning out the burn of ozone that lingered around the immortal.

"Dagda," Patrick said, sounding polite enough. "We wouldn't be here if it wasn't an emergency."

The Dagda leaned back in his plush leather seat, staring at them with inhuman eyes. He didn't offer them a seat, but Jono and Patrick took one anyway.

"We saw the Sluagh riding the leading edge of the storm last night," Jono said.

From what they could gather, if anyone had gone missing last night, their absence hadn't been reported to the police yet. That wasn't to say the Sluagh hadn't dragged unsuspecting citizens into their deadly clutches. The reports would hit the news eventually, like they had last winter.

The Dagda raised one thick eyebrow and made a low sound in the back of his throat. It was difficult to get a read on the god, but Jono thought he sounded curious. "Are you surprised? It is October. Samhain is close. The veil is ever thin at this time of the year."

"It's not Samhain *now*," Patrick pressed.

"You marshal your forces. Why would the same not be said of your father and the hells that follow his lead?"

Jono grimaced, hating to agree with a god. "We've heard nothing about Ethan or the Dominion Sect's movements in recent weeks."

"As you say, that means nothing."

"We know that. But you interceded before—"

"These are not the same circumstances."

"Aren't they?" Patrick shot back.

The Dagda's presence filled the space around them, the sudden pressure a weight against Jono's ribs. He didn't flinch, and neither did Patrick, but he'd be lying if he said his heart didn't speed up a tick.

"Your debt is not paid," the Dagda said in a voice like a storm-filled rushing river, crashing against their ears.

"And when I pay it, what then?" Patrick leaned forward, hands clenched into fists on his knees. "When you stab someone, pulling out the knife doesn't fix the wound left behind."

The Dagda smiled in a way that promised no comfort. "Then make sure the wound is deep enough to kill."

Jono settled his hand over Patrick's fist. "What of the city? Can you issue a curfew?"

"I've issued enough curfews in your favor lately. The public won't appreciate another."

"Is that your polling numbers speaking?" Patrick asked snidely.

"What excuse would I give to corral the public for the next couple of weeks before Samhain that they would believe?" The Dagda spread his hands, looking as far from apologetic as one could get. "We gods you see as myths are not who they believe in. Bring me evidence of a threat, one that the masses will understand, and then, perhaps, I can aid you in my capacity as mayor of this fine city."

Jono glared at the god. The thought of sacrificing people who could've been saved if inaction wasn't the name of the bloody game made him furious. But gods did what was best for gods, and there was no arguing with that sort of stubbornness.

"The Sluagh won't be the last incursion, will they?" Patrick asked after a moment.

The Dagda stared at them, the weight of his presence receding just a little. "What makes you think they were the first?"

"Fuck," Jono muttered, sharing a look with Patrick.

The Dagda reached for his keyboard to tap at it, gaze flicking to the screen and whatever information was on it. "I have another meeting in ten minutes. Will that be all?"

Patrick rolled his eyes and got to his feet. "The PCB and the SOA are aware of the Sluagh's presence. You should probably have a backup plan that isn't ignoring the problem."

The Dagda didn't seem put out by that warning and merely waved them off. Jono followed Patrick out of the mayor's office and into the hallway beyond the reception room.

"Tell me you're not voting for him next election," Jono said as they walked back toward the bank of lifts.

"If he's still around? Fuck no," Patrick replied.

"What do you want to do?"

Patrick scowled. "I'm not sure we can do anything until the

Sluagh strike. Sage still has her meeting with Tiarnán today, so we'll let her bring it up with him."

"All right."

They were waiting for the next available lift when the doors pinged open and disgorged someone neither of them expected. Giovanni Casale, Chief of the NYPD Preternatural Crimes Bureau, was in full uniform rather than a suit, which made Jono think he had a press engagement of some sort.

Jono hadn't seen Casale in person since the fallout from taking over the god pack territory. New Yorkers didn't much care for the civil war that had exploded on their doorstep, but his pack had done their best to contain it with the reluctant help of the PCB, as ordered by the Dagda in his capacity as mayor. Casale's favorability had taken a beating in public polls, but from what Jono had heard, the older man wasn't in danger of losing his position.

Yet.

"Collins," Casale said politely enough. "Jonothon. Fancy meeting you here."

"Casale," Patrick replied evenly. "Here to visit our favorite mayor?"

"I take it you've already spoken to Ferbenn about what you saw last night?"

"Made him move his schedule for us. He didn't care about the sighting."

Casale glanced down the hallway in the direction they'd just come. "Reports of missing people are starting to come into the PCB. I can't say all are attributed to the Sluagh, but it's a good bet some can be tied to the damn things. Does the SOA know?"

"The SOA and some of the other alphabet soup agencies are in the loop."

"We've warned all the packs, and we're talking to the fae today," Jono said.

"Angelina is speaking to the high priests and priestesses of local covens about the problem," Casale said.

Angelina Casale was a priestess for the Crescent Coven and worked beneath Hera, who pretended to be that coven's high priestess while basking in prayers. Jono was fairly certain that goddess was still ensconced in Greece with Zeus. Angelina had aided them briefly with their hunter problem back in August, and Jono was grateful for that. Whether or not she could muster solid support despite promises given remained to be seen.

"That just leaves everyone else in the five boroughs not dialed into the preternatural or supernatural communities," Patrick said. "Millions and millions of people."

Casale grimaced. "You're not telling me anything I don't know."

"And what do you know that you aren't telling us?" Jono asked.

"What makes you think you have the right to be privy to that information?"

Patrick was no longer called upon by the PCB to aid in their cases. What cases Patrick *could* oversee were limited due to his ties to the preternatural community. It meant their information pool had shrunk, and that helped no one right now.

"We'd like to think you know what's at stake."

"Do I?"

Patrick snorted, leaning around Casale to call another lift. "Don't play dumb. You saw what happened in Brooklyn and Central Park. You saw the scene at the Ritz-Carlton. The Dominion Sect is everyone's problem, so don't be a fucking stranger if you learn something before the SOA. We need to know."

The soft chime of another lift arriving prompted Jono to push Patrick toward it, leaving Casale behind. Jono pressed the button for the lobby, both of them keeping quiet until they'd swapped one lift for another to get to the underground car park.

"Will the joint task force do anything about it?" Jono asked once they were driving away from City Hall.

Patrick snorted as the light ahead turned red, braking for it.

"The Sluagh? I want to say yes, but the joint task force is more focused on Ethan and the Dominion Sect right now."

"This involves Ethan."

"Speaking to the fucking choir. Reed could be convinced. Setsuna wouldn't throw up roadblocks. It's everyone else that's going to balk if I report back that there's a bunch of hellish fae running rampant in New York City. They'd want more proof than what we saw."

"Because they don't trust you?"

Patrick tipped his head in Jono's direction in a slight nod, drumming his fingers against the steering wheel. "And they won't trust you."

Jono frowned, turning his attention to the road as the light turned green. "Fuck."

"Pretty much."

Patrick drove toward the SOA field office rather than back to their flat. He was working today, and that meant actually going in for meetings. Patrick double-parked in front of the SOA's entrance when they finally arrived, and Jono leaned across the center console to pull him into a kiss.

"I'm in Queens today," Jono said when he pulled back.

"Take Wade," Patrick said, licking his lips.

"I thought he had school?"

"He's taking a leave of absence for the rest of the month. Sage finally got it cleared with his advisors. She told me last night while you were pouring some drinks."

"Right, then. I'll swing by and pick him up."

"He'll want breakfast."

Jono leaned close and kissed Patrick one more time. "I'll let him clean out a deli."

They both got out of the car and Jono took over the driver's seat, not putting the car into drive until Patrick was inside the heavily warded building. Then he pulled into traffic, already ringing Wade.

"Yeah?" Wade mumbled when he picked up.

"I'm coming to get you," Jono said.

"Uh, now? I'm still in bed."

"Fifteen minutes. No excuses."

"That's not enough time to eat breakfast!"

"It's enough time for you to shower. Clock is ticking. Get up."

Jono ended the call and sighed. It was going to be a long day.

5

Ginnungagap hadn't changed much since the primordial void had slipped free of its walls to be commanded by Fenrir. Lucien's club was still just as popular as ever on the nightlife circuit, even if no one could pinpoint him as the owner. If anyone managed to track a name through the layers of paperwork and shell companies, they'd discover one of Carmen's aliases in lieu of him.

The club was the public heart of Lucien's territory in Manhattan. Patrick still didn't know where Lucien's Night Court rested during the day, and he doubted he'd ever find out. Despite everything going on, Lucien hadn't closed the club for their meeting tonight. Appearances had to be kept up, and dinner had to walk through the doors.

"If he tries to punch you, I'm biting off his hand," Wade said as they approached the club.

Patrick sighed heavily. "That would be considered an act of war by the Night Courts, so keep your teeth to yourself."

Wade scowled, tugging his beanie down low over his ears. "Lucien is an asshole."

"I'm not arguing that fact, but we still need his support."

The three of them weren't so much guests of honor on a VIP list as they were the enemy to everyone who waited inside for them. But war had always made strange bedfellows.

Patrick and Jono had reached out to Ashanti in September about bringing in more vampires for the fight ahead. The mother of all vampires had been mostly agreeable, but Patrick had no idea who she had chosen. They'd had no control over her decision, and he'd known better than to push for that information in advance.

Lucien alone was a nightmare. Patrick knew there were several other master vampires in the country who, while not as historically infamous as Ashanti's last directly sired child, still rated high on the asshole scale.

Patrick shivered a little as cold rain trickled down his neck. They'd been on the go all day before the storm hit, and their umbrellas were back at home. The rain wasn't letting up anytime soon, and he didn't like being out in the open right now, especially not with what might be riding this storm.

"Could've maybe parked closer," Jono mused, head ducked against the wind and rain as they half ran down the sidewalk.

"And let everyone waiting for us know what my car looks like? Hell no," Patrick said.

There was a line of people huddling beneath umbrellas outside the main entrance to the club. A human servant in a heavy wool coat and wide umbrella stood guard at the door beside a tall, blonde vampire, whose lips peeled back in a snarl at their approach.

"Irena," Patrick said in greeting.

"Go to VIP section," the vampire ordered, not bothering to open the club door for them.

Usually, they entered Ginnungagap through the side door in the adjacent alley during hours when the club wasn't in full swing. Entering through the front was a bit of a novelty. Jono got to the door and hauled it open, ushering Patrick and Wade inside.

Crossing the threshold made Patrick's nerves tingle, a reaction to the lingering power in the walls. Ginnungagap might be held between Fenrir's proverbial teeth right now, but the echo of it could still be felt where it once resided in the mortal world.

The security checkpoint where everyone had to give up their holy items was manned by human servants loyal to Lucien's Night Court. They knew Patrick, Jono, and Wade on sight and didn't bother asking them to hand over items which would never leave their possession. Now that they were inside, Patrick could better make out the bass sound of the music being spun by a DJ.

"You three look like drowned rats," Carmen drawled from her spot in front of the counter, glamour dropped in favor of her true form. The dark red pupils of her eyes seemed to glow in the shadows, but her gaze was easy enough to meet.

"Rain isn't going to make us miss this meeting," Jono said.

Carmen tilted her head, long curly black hair falling around the horns of her kind that twisted over her skull. "Our guests await your presence."

Patrick double-checked his personal shields as they followed Carmen deeper into Ginnungagap. The damage to his soul still let him feel the recognition that came when a slew of vampires was in one place. It wasn't quite as bad as what demons from the hells left behind, but it still made him want a shower.

Wade shouldered his way over to Patrick's left, which put Patrick between him and Jono. Wade's eyes had lost their brown coloring and were now a molten gold, though no red scales pushed through his skin.

The dance floor was packed with clubgoers, and the lounges and booths scattered against the wall were filled to capacity as well. If Patrick had to guess, he'd say half the people in the club tonight were vampires, which was far more than the number in Lucien's Night Court. Patrick knew Lucien didn't like sharing territory, so the fact that so many strange vampires were in his club had all the marks of Ashanti.

Carmen slipped through the crowd of dancers, and they were

forced to follow. Jono led the way, his presence clearing a path between vampires and their partners almost as well as Carmen. Patrick stayed on his heels, ignoring the assessing gazes turned their way, while Wade shifted position and took up the rear. They took the stairs up to the VIP mezzanine level, the crowd there smaller but far more dangerous.

Lucien sat on a low-backed couch, the seat beside him empty but soon taken by Carmen. Scattered in the area, taking up every available seat outside the main circle or leaning against the railing that overlooked the dance floor, were numerous master vampires that Patrick didn't recognize and some he did, specifically, the ones claiming Night Courts within the five boroughs. The rest varied in appearance, but all of them had the bone-scraping feel of the undead, recognition slithering through his magic like poison.

Seated alone on a long, cushioned bench was Ashanti, her black eyes like holes in her dark face. The weight of her gaze settled heavily on Patrick as they joined the group. Ashanti gestured casually at the only empty spot, a smaller chaise situated between her spot and Lucien's.

"Sit," Ashanti ordered.

Jono and Patrick sat, while Wade took up position behind the chaise. Patrick glanced back at him, glad to have Wade watching their six. It meant he and Jono could focus on the conversation at hand. Patrick faced forward again, hyperaware of how the vampires around them shifted.

"New friends?" Patrick asked, staring at Lucien.

"I need no friends," Lucien said, disdain curving his lips into a sneer that revealed sharp, jagged fangs.

"Enemies, then. It's not like you're running low on those."

"You're one to talk."

"My children are enemies of no one in this club," Ashanti said, cutting through their sniping.

Patrick's fingers twitched, brushing against the gods-given dagger strapped to his right thigh. None of the master vampires save for Lucien had her eyes, but they'd hopefully listen better than he did.

"Good to know," Jono said as he rested his elbows on his knees, glaring at everyone assembled. "But Lucien's never been the type of bloke who likes sharing, least of all territory, so who did you invite?"

A couple of vampires bared their fangs at Jono's less than respectful tone, but he didn't appear put off by it. If he wanted to give attitude, Patrick would join him.

"You need an army to fight an army. I'm adding mine." Ashanti inclined her head, her bloodred hair styled in Senegalese twists falling over her bare shoulders. "I've called home to me those who claim various cities across this country. More will arrive within the next week."

Patrick's gaze drifted over the vampires who stared back at him with faces as still and cold as marble. While he didn't know any of them, he had a feeling they'd heard of him. Ashanti wasn't one to gossip, only command, but Lucien never could keep his opinion to himself where Patrick was concerned.

Ashanti's plan was similar to what he and Jono were doing within the werecreature community. While they had plenty of packs within New York City, they'd been leaning on their alliances to call in anyone who was willing to fight. They had more control over those werecreatures arriving due to Fenrir's influence. They had no influence with these Night Courts beyond Ashanti's personal desires.

A tall, broad-shouldered master vampire stepped away from the railing to approach the center circle they sat at. Ashanti's gaze shifted to him instantly. He bowed his head in a respectful motion to her alone.

"Mother. You called, and we answered, but I would know what is in it for us to join with these two who have entirely too much government attention on them," the vampire said.

The master vampire's long black hair was pulled back in a

single braid tied off with a strip of leather knotted with beads. The dark blue button-down he wore was embroidered around the pockets and collar with motifs that reminded Patrick of the Native American tribes that called the Pacific Northwest home. If that was truly the place the vampire hailed from, he'd traveled thousands of miles for a war.

"Survival," Patrick said flatly. "You'll starve if the demons take over the world with Ethan at their helm. That's not a hell you'll live long to see."

The vampire turned to face him, lips peeling back over his fangs. "You think so little of us? We who have survived for hundreds, if not thousands, of years?"

Other vampires hissed their wordless support of his statement. Patrick rolled his eyes. "And those long-lived lives of yours are at risk of being cut short."

"Takoma," Ashanti said, her tone not changing, but it was enough to settle the masses.

The master vampire narrowed dark brown eyes at Patrick, as if contemplating the odds of successfully tearing out his throat with Jono sitting right there and Wade behind them. A flicker of fire burned in the air between Jono and Patrick, the heat warming his skin.

"Don't even think about it," Wade warned, sulfur drifting on the air.

Takoma's eyes widened fractionally, but he held his ground. After a moment, he tipped his head in Ashanti's direction again, deference in the motion. "Mother."

Ashanti clacked her iron teeth at him, and Takoma stepped back to his original spot, face once again impassive. More than one pair of eyes were riveted on Wade, and Patrick would've been worried if he didn't know that Wade was more than capable of taking care of himself these days.

"Patrick is right. Living in that hell will grant a true death I want none of you to have. Siding with the heavens was the lesser of two evils," Ashanti said.

Patrick snorted. "Of course it was."

Ashanti stood, the heavy colorful skirt she wore falling all the way to the floor to hide the curved, ironshod bone hooks that were what she walked on. None of the vampires moved, but their eyes tracked her as she approached where Patrick sat.

He watched her come, ignoring the way Jono shifted closer to him, their arms brushing. He knew Jono didn't trust her, but Patrick couldn't find it in himself to doubt Ashanti's intentions.

She came to a stop in front of him, reaching out to place cold fingers against his right cheek, ignoring the rumbling growl Jono let loose. Patrick didn't try to pull away.

Ashanti was beautiful in a monstrous way, the truth of what she was buried beneath the veneer of humanity she carried in her dark skin. She was a goddess, the first of her kind, a legend kept alive in the memory of her children and those who worshipped at her altar. She was dust between the pages of history when she wasn't made whole by prayers whispered in the dark.

But she was here now, after years of being gone, and Patrick was glad for that, even if no one in his pack could ever understand.

"You're not sleeping," Ashanti said.

"He sleeps fine," Jono growled.

"Hm." She gently scraped her sharp nails over Patrick's jaw to rest against his throat for a second longer, pressing against his pulse, before drawing her hand back. "Has your joint task force any word on Ethan or the Dominion Sect?"

Patrick shook his head slowly. "Nothing concrete. The general consensus is that he'll make his move in the Northeast somewhere. Here, or another city."

Ashanti's gaze never wavered from his. "If that is the case, Salem is a possibility."

Patrick tried not to react, but he couldn't quite stop the way his entire body twitched at that city's name. "We know. The SOA has agents on the ground there."

He was proud that his voice didn't crack, that his shields held against the split-second panic that punched him in the gut. But Ashanti, along with Setsuna, had been there to greet him in Washington, DC, when he left Persephone's hands years ago. She knew the horror he'd lived through in that city. Despite the years she'd spent as dust on the wind, her gaze cut right through him, reading him as easily as a book in some ways.

"If you go to Salem, watch your back."

"You don't have to worry about that. I'll be with him," Jono said.

A couple of vampires laughed. None of them were local, which meant they might not know about Fenrir. Either his pack's exploits hadn't traveled far enough, or the vampires present simply didn't believe that Jono carried an animal-god patron in his soul.

Jono ignored the laughter, and Patrick did his best to do the same. They both knew their place, knew what needed to be done before the fighting really began. It was why they were clawing at their alliances, stacking up clandestine meetings like they were going out of style, trying to bring people in now before it was too late.

How it would be too late was still unknown. Patrick just knew they couldn't afford to be caught flat-footed. That meant making deals with the devils they knew and paying whatever price needed to be paid.

"The Sluagh ride the storm line tracking across the Eastern Seaboard right now. They don't discriminate on who they hunt," Patrick said.

"The fae have never been very good at keeping their own in line," Ashanti said with a faint hint of a smile. "Brigid likes to think she is in control, as does Medb. Their squabbles are cyclical."

"Their squabbles are snatching people off the streets."

"Time was you humans knew to stay inside after dark." Ashanti spun on her bone hooks, the heavy fabric of her colorful skirt swishing around her legs. "Let the ones who wish to walk in the shadows risk their lives as they like. We all must feed. That, children, is why you are here. The fight ahead will require all our efforts."

Patrick watched how the group of master vampires, all used to being in control and in power, couldn't meet their mother's gaze for long. He wondered what they saw when looking at her, what the pull was like when she called them to heel, if it was anything like the soulbond that tied him and Jono together.

In the end, they were all children taken to task and made to obey.

Ashanti gestured languidly in Patrick's direction, never taking her eyes off the master vampires surrounding her. "Keep him alive at all costs. You and all those you have sired will live if he does."

Patrick stared at Lucien, arching an eyebrow and putting every ounce of *suck it, asshole* he could summon into his gaze. Lucien's eyes narrowed to slits, but he didn't move.

"None of that," Jono said, nudging Patrick with an elbow.

"I don't know what you're talking about," Patrick retorted, blinking a few times because there was no point in trying to win a staring contest with a vampire.

"Everything's off the table once you pay your soul debt. You'll still need to pass through my streets," Lucien said.

"*Our* streets," Jono shot back.

"The alliance will hold," Ashanti said, cutting them both off. "It will end when I say it ends."

Patrick could only nod at that declaration. The tentative peace between the Night Courts and the werecreature community would break at some point, either when hell burned on Earth or if they survived with the heavens as the victor.

Either way, Patrick could already feel the ghost of Lucien's fangs on his throat.

"I'll keep you updated with any new information the joint task force gives me," Patrick promised.

"It's the least you owe us," Lucien said.

"Did I not just warn you about the Sluagh?"

"Bring better information next time. Preferably Ethan's location. It shouldn't be so difficult for you to find him. You're his son, after all."

"Fuck off," Jono snapped.

Patrick looked at Ashanti, thinking about the book bound in human skin he'd smuggled out of the Library of Congress for her and the blood Cernunnos had stolen from him. "If you're bringing your children here, is this where you think Ethan will show up and not Salem?"

That was his personal assumption, whether everyone agreed or not. Ashanti hummed as she turned to face them again, the sound something Patrick could feel in his bones beneath the bass beat of the music vibrating through the air. "Salem belongs to your mother's family. New York City belongs to everyone."

And all the gods they'd carried to this shore and the iron jungle of an altar built to worship them on.

Her words were a truth and a warning, one Patrick knew they couldn't turn their backs on. "We'll be ready."

"Will you?"

Patrick stood, Ashanti's gaze never leaving his face. "I never forgot what you taught me."

That he was a weapon to be used, in whatever way he could wield himself.

She smiled. "Good."

Jono got to his feet and wrapped his hand around Patrick's elbow, pulling him toward the stairs. Wade stuck to them like a burr. "We'll be in touch."

They walked away from the master vampires and their goddess of a mother without losing a single drop of blood, leaving Ginnungagap behind in favor of the storm outside.

"We could do with less vampires," Jono said on their hurried walk back to the Mustang.

"I could eat some for you," Wade offered.

"Please don't. You'll whinge forever about the taste."

"Could do with a vacation," Patrick muttered.

Jono grabbed his hand, holding on tight. "After we win this fight, we'll go on holiday. Somewhere warm."

Patrick couldn't bring himself to promise an unknown future, but he wanted to believe in it anyway.

6

THE DAYS LEADING UP TO WEDNESDAY WHEN PATRICK GOT TO FACE his past were hectic, full of pack business, long meetings at the SOA, and keeping a critical eye on the weather coming up over the Atlantic Ocean. Being busy should have kept his mind off the day he reunited with his grandmother for the first time since he was eight years old, but the nightmares waking him in the middle of the night proved otherwise. At least he hadn't woken to find himself trying to choke Jono again.

Early Wednesday morning, Jono took the keys from Patrick's hand and said, "I'm driving."

It was a four-hour drive to Salem, Massachusetts. They left Manhattan behind them around 0700, heading northeast along the coast on Interstate 95 before cutting inland through Connecticut on Interstate 91. Once they were past Hartford and on Interstate 84, the cities and towns became outnumbered by large swaths of trees changing color, red and orange overtaking green.

If asked, Patrick would say he didn't remember most of the drive at all.

They veered north around Boston some hours later, bypassing

that city completely in favor of less traffic. Boston was never a city Patrick had been allowed to take cases in over the years when he was part of the SOA's Rapid Response Division. Too close to Salem, to his family, to his past, for Setsuna to allow it once she was in charge.

He felt like a stranger here.

"You don't have to do this," Jono said when they approached Salem's city limits. "I can turn the car around right now, and we'll be back in New York before evening rush hour starts."

"I have to do this," Patrick said through numb lips.

"Bollocks. No one is ordering you to reach out to them. You don't know the Pattersons, and you don't have to if you don't want to."

Patrick clenched his hands into fists over his thighs, trying not to chew his bottom lip to shreds. "I should. They're my mother's family. I'd like to think they're nothing like Ethan, but I won't know that until I meet them."

"Have to wonder why Setsuna and Ashanti keep warning you off about them."

Patrick shrugged one shoulder, keeping his eyes on the road as Jono slowed to the local speed limit. "My guess is because of Ethan. Eloise thought I was dead until I got arrested. She was supposed to."

Because if they thought he was dead over the years, so would Ethan. That lie had been destroyed at the end of the Thirty-Day War, causing Ethan to focus on Patrick to the detriment of those around him. He was done running though, done letting Ethan dictate how he reacted. Standing his ground was always going to be a fight, but facing his past wasn't easy.

Patrick thought maybe it should be. Except he realized, as Jono drove through the historic center of Salem, following the GPS route, that was a lie he'd told himself to get through the days leading up to this moment.

"Don't park in front," Patrick said when they finally turned down a street whose houses were built along the waterfront of a small inlet.

"I don't think we're allowed to park on the street," Jono said, frowning at the narrow road they were on. Every vehicle they passed was parked in a driveway.

"Just do it."

Jono stopped four houses down from the waterfront property Eloise called home. He turned the engine off, leaving them in the quiet, fading warmth of the Mustang. The clouds in New York seemed to have stretched all the way up here, as the day was overcast. It didn't look like rain was in the forecast, but Patrick knew how quickly something like that could change with heavy magic in play.

"We can always turn around," Jono said softly after a few minutes had passed.

Patrick shook his head, finally undoing his seat belt. "Let's get this over with."

The invitation had included brunch, though Patrick wasn't sure who was going to be present or if he'd be able to stomach food. He knew the names and faces of some of his extended family from written reports and news segments. A couple of aunts and uncles, because Clara hadn't been an only child; younger cousins he struggled to recall from a childhood visiting this house, but always drawing a blank where memories were concerned.

He supposed it was time to make new ones.

They got out of the car, the cold, biting wind smacking Patrick in the face and slipping beneath his leather jacket. The warming charms embedded in it kept him from feeling chilly, and his dagger and handgun were a comforting weight within easy reach. Jono's support was what got his feet moving though, the warm hand finding his holding on with a firm grip.

He made sure his personal shields were locked down tight before they started walking. Patrick let himself be led to the house beside the water, the unfenced front yard wilting beneath the autumn season settling over Salem. He could sense the powerful wards laid down on the property before they even reached it, the magic pricking against his shields with a familiarity that felt strange. Blood would always call to blood, and his magic recognized this place even if he didn't.

Curtains on the first-floor window were drawn shut, but they twitched a little as he and Jono came to a stop in front of the house, as if someone didn't want to be seen peering out.

"Do you think it's just the Pattersons inside?" Jono asked.

"The SOA has the house under watch. I'm doubtful Eloise would've agreed to an agent being embedded in her home. They're probably around here somewhere though."

Jono glanced at him, wolf-bright blue eyes full of concern. "Ready?"

*No* wasn't an answer Patrick could give.

Instead, he nodded and stepped onto the cement pathway that led from the sidewalk to the front door. He let go of Jono's hand, wiping his own suddenly clammy ones on his jeans. Heart pounding, Patrick took the steps up to the front door, Jono right behind him. He was reaching for the doorbell when the door opened, and he found himself staring into a middle-aged blonde woman's face, recognition sliding through his magic.

The witch wasn't his grandmother, but the family resemblance to her was strong. Slim and dressed in a dark green woolen coat dress and brown boots, she stared at Patrick with blue eyes that were a little damp.

"Oh," she said, covering her mouth with one hand. "Oh, hello, Patrick. Welcome home."

He stared at her, tongue unmoving in his mouth. It took a few seconds before he managed to shake himself free of his uncertainty and cleared his throat. "Madelyn?"

His mother's younger sister let out a soft, watery huff of a laugh. "Yes, I'm your aunt Madelyn."

Patrick nodded, head jerking a little in Jono's direction. "This is Jono."

"Pleasure to meet you," Jono said, managing a small, polite smile for the both of them.

If Madelyn seemed uncertain about inviting a god pack alpha werewolf into her mother's home, she didn't show it, though Patrick couldn't be sure about scent. "Please, both of you, come in. Your grandmother and the rest of the family can't wait to see you, Patrick."

Madelyn moved back and held the door open. Patrick steeled himself and stepped inside, passing over a threshold that felt more welcoming than any other save the one wrapped around their apartment in Manhattan.

Stairs in the tiny foyer led up to the second floor. French glass doors were opened into an empty sitting room. A second door was partway open to a half bath down the short hallway. A small side table was situated by the front door, but it held no bread or drink.

"Hospitality?" Patrick asked, not sure about the customs the Pattersons or Salem Coven adhered to.

"You're family," Madelyn said firmly as she closed and locked the front door. "There's no need for hospitality."

Patrick thought that was a breach of security, but it wasn't his place to say anything. Madelyn beckoned at them to follow her down the short hallway to the rear of the house. Patrick hesitated and only started walking when Jono touched a hand to the small of his back, leaning down to whisper in his ear.

"I'm right here," Jono reminded him.

Knowing that made it easier for Patrick to step into the open area that contained the home's kitchen and living area, the walls full of windows and glass doors looking out onto a large backyard and the water beyond its shores. Patrick's mind distantly catalogued the dangers the windows provided to someone with a long gun and good aim, but most of his attention was on the people seated and standing in the living room.

Faces that shared bits of his own features stared back at him, some with tears in their eyes, others with frank curiosity. A bolt of recognition burned through his magic, picking out the magic in the room, and he was surprised to discover that everyone present was a magic user of some sort.

Patrick let his gaze drift over everyone assembled before focusing on his grandmother, who sat between two men who had to be his mother's brothers. They looked too much like Eloise and Madelyn to be anything else but family.

Eloise stared at him, blue eyes wide in a pale face that made her minimal makeup stand out starkly against her skin. The tears pooling in the corners of her eyes were carefully dabbed away by the tissue clenched in one wrinkled hand.

"I never thought…" Her genteel voice trailed off, and she swallowed thickly, lips trembling. "Patrick. It's so *good* to see you."

She sounded like she meant it, but some part of Patrick wasn't sure he could believe her. It'd been twenty-two years, after all. Staring at the Pattersons made him realize they had probably spent all that time never forgetting his and Hannah's and their mother's absence while he'd done his best to never look back.

"Sorry, I…don't really remember you," Patrick managed to get out after the silence lingered a little too long.

Eloise sniffed delicately before trying to stand. One of her sons —Finley, his younger uncle—immediately stood and offered his mother a hand. Like Madelyn, Finley was blond, though Grant, now the oldest in the wake of Clara's death all those years ago, was a redhead like Eloise.

Like Patrick.

It was really fucking weird seeing people who looked like him.

Eloise patted her son's arm in a silent thank-you before approaching where he and Jono stood on the outskirts of the group. She was shorter than he was, pale red hair neatly styled, and the pearls around her throat had tiny images engraved on them that he couldn't quite make out but which might have been flowers. She looked at him with wonder and disbelief in her eyes, one hand lifting toward him before she managed to stop herself.

"You remind me so much of my Clara," Eloise said, voice breaking a little on her dead daughter's name.

Patrick wasn't sure what to say to that.

Eloise drew in a breath before carefully placing her hand on his left arm, her touch light. Patrick thought she would try to hug him, and he wasn't sure how he felt about that. He stiffened and forced himself not to jerk away. She must have sensed his unease because she didn't try to embrace him.

Eloise's eyes shimmered a bit with tears that she managed to eventually blink back. "I know this must be overwhelming. It has been for me as well. But I want you to know we are all so, *so* glad to know that you are alive."

Patrick found himself out of his depth as he stared at his grandmother, not knowing what was expected of him in the face of her emotions and his own. He turned his head to look at Jono, trying not to panic and probably failing miserably judging by the way Jono stared back with concern in his eyes.

"Let's sit down for this chat," Jono said, breaking the tableau.

Sitting with furniture between him and everyone else sounded *great*.

Eloise drew her hand back, clearing her throat. "Yes, of course. Please have a seat, Jonothon."

He gave her a gentle smile that didn't show any teeth. "Call me Jono."

"Jono, then."

Eloise stepped back, and Patrick went where Jono led, finding himself seated beside the other man on a love seat, both becoming the center of everyone's attention.

Patrick had felt less like he was about to undergo an interrogation in a federal courtroom than here in his grandmother's home.

"Would you like anything to drink?" Madelyn said, the cheerfulness in her voice sounding forced. "Coffee, perhaps? Tea?"

"A cuppa would be great," Jono said.

"Coffee." Patrick drew in a breath, trying to steady his nerves, and managed a quick flash of a strained smile. "Please."

"I'll help," a slender young woman said, getting to her feet. She appeared to be a couple of years younger than Patrick, most likely a cousin, and shared a resemblance with Madelyn that spoke of being a daughter.

"Thank you, Brittany."

"So." Grant stared at Patrick, taking him in before glancing over at Jono. "You're a federal agent and a god pack alpha?"

"Grant," Eloise admonished.

"It's a fair question, Mother."

"Yes, I'm an SOA federal agent," Patrick said, causing Grant to snap his mouth shut. "And yes, I'm also an alpha of the New York City god pack through Jono. I was with the Mage Corps for almost ten years before joining the SOA. Pretty sure all of that is public record at this point."

"So you really are a mage," one of the redheaded cousins asked, leaning forward excitedly in his seat. He looked more like Finley's son than Grant's, despite the hair, and seemed to be the youngest person there. "You're the only one in our generation who got that rank."

He gestured between himself and the other cousins. Patrick couldn't parse the other man's tone and simply stared at him long enough to make him uncomfortable. The young man coughed and looked away, flushing a little.

"Don't mind Easton," a young woman with strawberry blonde hair said with a quick, nervous smile. "He's studying genetics at Harvard and will talk your ear off about the relations between magic and science if you let him."

Patrick tried not to twitch. "Sounds interesting?"

Maybe if he was drunk. Really drunk.

"The table needs setting," Madelyn called out pointedly.

It seemed to be the siren call for everyone around Patrick's age, because the five twentysomethings all got up and headed for the kitchen to help Madelyn and Brittany sort out the meal. The pretense of privacy didn't really undo the knot of anxiety that had settled in his stomach. He wasn't sure he could choke down the food, but he'd try.

"You're all witches and warlocks in the Salem Coven?" Patrick asked, grasping for something to get everyone else to talk so he wouldn't have to.

"We have members of the Salem Coven who are mundane. We don't discriminate within our coven. Within our family, yes, everyone has magic. As to who are the strongest? Brittany is a sorceress," Eloise said, sounding proud and fond. "Grant is a mage."

"Weather," Grant said with a grunt.

Only in the younger generation, not the older, was what Easton had said. The distinction was noticeable now. Patrick nodded. "That's nice."

Nice, but a little strange that every single member of his mother's family was a magic user. Only a quarter of the world's population was capable of manipulating their soul's energy into magic. Sometimes families had a handful of members over the course of generations with magic, but it was rare for everyone within a family line to have magic.

"She'll follow in her mother's footsteps as high priestess of the Salem Coven when she's older." Eloise offered up a brittle smile. "Clara was supposed to take over my role as the oldest, and Hannah after her. But, well."

Her voice trailed off, and Patrick was grateful she didn't try to explain the obvious.

"Why didn't you ever try to get in contact with us?" Grant asked bluntly.

He didn't sound accusatory, only curious. The question still put Patrick on the defensive.

"I was warned not to for safety reasons," Patrick said.

"Yes, and I know you say you don't remember us as a family, but weren't you curious?"

"Ethan wanted me dead. He still wants me dead. Setsuna told me when I became her ward that I'd be putting all of you at risk if you knew I was still alive."

Eloise's lips pressed into a thin white line. "That woman. She as surely stole you from us as much as Ethan did."

"She was under orders because of the threat Ethan and the Dominion Sect represented."

As much as his relationship with Setsuna was strained these days, he could understand, in hindsight at least, why she'd done what she had all those years ago. Even if the gods hadn't dragged him to her, Patrick thought she probably would've made the same choice to hide his identity.

Madelyn came over with a mug in one hand and delicate teacup in the other. Jono carefully took his tea, hands dwarfing the teacup. Patrick took his coffee from her with both hands.

"Cream and sugar?" Madelyn asked.

"Uh, just cream. Thanks," Patrick said.

"Milk and sugar for me," Jono said.

Madelyn smiled at them. "Coming right up."

The coffee smelled good and tasted even better after a dollop of cream was poured into it. Patrick sipped at it carefully, half watching as his…cousins started setting up the long dining table by the window for brunch.

Eloise smoothed her hands over the soft-looking fabric of her dress pants, prim and poised in a way that made Patrick feel out of place. "Ethan was always a problem, and I regret very dearly that we couldn't keep all of you safe before Clara tried to leave him."

Patrick blinked at her. "She was going to leave him?"

"Divorce papers were drawn up," Finley said quietly. "My sister didn't trust him at the end. We told her we'd go as a family and a coven to move her out, but she was stubborn."

"You wouldn't know anything about being thick, Pat," Jono muttered under his breath.

Patrick politely elbowed him in the side. "Fuck you, I'm a ray of sunshine."

"Not before your alarm goes off. Or after, come to think of it."

"I will throw out your tea when we get back home."

"Got some right here, love."

Jono raised his teacup to show it off before taking a large swallow. Patrick rolled his eyes, trying not to smile, but it was a lost cause. When he dragged his attention away from Jono, he found his uncles and his grandmother staring at him with varied expressions on their faces, but at least none of them looked disgusted. Two of the cousins were whispering in the corner and glancing over at them as well, but the smiles on their faces weren't mocking.

"So you're together?" Eloise asked, gaze flickering from Patrick to Jono. "Not just as alphas, but as a couple?"

"We've been together since last year. We've no plans to separate, no matter what happens," Jono said.

"It's good you have someone," Finley said to Patrick. "I hope you know that you have us now as well."

"It will take time, I know," Eloise said when Patrick hesitated too long, smoothing over the awkward pause. "But we *are* your family, Patrick. We would like to get to know you and—and your pack. We'd invite you into the coven if you would be comfortable with that in the future."

Patrick stared at her. "Uh."

"It's a choice, not a requirement. You will still be family. Always."

Strange to think he had that now outside his pack. He wasn't quite sure it felt real—everyone in this home was a stranger to him, even though they looked like him in some ways. His track record with family was all with Ethan, and it was fucking terrible. Jono would be the first to tell him that side wasn't family in any way that mattered.

Jono settled his hand on Patrick's thigh, fingers pressed over the straps of his dagger's sheath. "It's not something you need to decide right now."

Patrick nodded stiffly, glad to shove that decision off until later. Possibly way later.

Madelyn came over with a tentative smile on her face. "We're ready for brunch. If you'd all like to come join us at the table?"

"Sure," Patrick said.

"Did you get the pomegranates while you were at the store, Maddie?" Eloise asked as she was helped to her feet by Grant.

"Yes, a whole bagful. It's nice that they're back in season again."

"Pomegranates? Are they for a salad?" Patrick asked as he stood, wondering what was on the menu.

Eloise smiled. "No, dear. They're for the family's altar. We worship the goddess Persephone in this home."

The ringing in his ears sounded like a siren, impossible to hear through. His lungs didn't want to work, and he would've spilled hot coffee all over himself and the floor if Jono hadn't caught the mug as it slipped out of his fingers. The nausea that had followed him out of Manhattan and seemed to settle after entering the home earlier crawled up his throat and slid over his tongue, refusing to be ignored.

Patrick clapped a hand over his mouth, choking on bile. He stumbled past Jono and didn't know how he made it to the hallway with the half bath, but he did.

And proceeded to be violently ill into the toilet.

"It's been a stressful couple of months. The whole bloody mess with the trial and his job caused an ulcer he's being treated for. The symptoms come and go," Jono said from the hallway, lying through his damn teeth.

"Oh, if we had known, we'd have been sure to have something he could eat at brunch," Eloise said, sounding distraught.

"We've potions on hand that could help with that," Madelyn said.

"He's being treated back in Manhattan," Jono said.

Patrick spat the last bit of bile into the toilet, glad he hadn't had anything but coffee all day. Ripping free some toilet paper with shaking hands, he wiped his mouth and nose before flushing it all away. Numb, he washed his hands and face, tried to wash the disgusting taste out of his mouth, but there was no hope there.

Maybe Jono would stop somewhere to get a drink after they left.

Because they would be leaving. Right the fuck now.

"I'm not up for brunch," Patrick said when he finally stepped into the hallway.

He wasn't at all surprised to see Jono acting like a living wall between Patrick and his mother's family. His stomach still churned in a threatening way, but he swallowed hard to try to settle it. He couldn't bring himself to smile at the people who worshipped the goddess who owned his soul debt.

Setsuna's careful warnings all these years suddenly, achingly, made so much sense now.

Eloise opened her mouth to speak when Jono twisted on his feet with preternatural speed, body a blur for a split second. The knock that came from the front door just then made Patrick step in front of Jono before he could dart down the hallway.

"Werecreatures?" Patrick demanded.

Jono's nostrils flared on his next intake of breath. "Yes."

"Then stay the fuck behind me, because if they have demons riding their souls, I'm taking off their goddamn heads first."

Patrick turned on his feet, conjuring up a mageglobe, the pale blue sphere burning bright against the palm of his hand. Someone breathed in sharply behind them, but he wasn't going to apologize for the way his magic felt. Patrick expanded his personal shields to protect the people behind him as he walked to the front door. He opened it a few inches, just wide enough to see who stood on the porch.

The woman waiting there had hair more gray than brown, all

of it pulled back in a single braid in deference of the fierce wind. Her wolf-bright amber eyes dominated a heart-shaped face, crow's-feet at the corners of them and smile lines around her mouth. Patrick didn't get a sense of hell off her, but one could never be too careful.

Behind her, scattered on the street, were a handful of men and women keeping watch but staying clear of the property line.

"Yeah?" Patrick asked.

"Alphas of the New York City god pack?" the woman asked.

Considering their faces had been splashed across the media since August, Patrick thought that was a rather rhetorical question. How the werecreatures had tracked them was something else entirely. "We were here for a visit and are just leaving. Didn't think we needed to ask for pass-through rights."

"We've no quarrel with you in our territory, but I would like to speak with you."

The door was pushed open wider as Jono crowded in behind him. Patrick didn't let his mageglobe burn out.

"What for?" Jono asked.

The woman grimaced. "My name is Georgelle. I'm alpha of the Salem god pack, and we've had sightings of hunters in the city."

Patrick heaved out a sigh that made Georgelle wrinkle her nose, probably from the smell of vomit, and let his mageglobe fade away. "Yeah, we've got time to meet with you."

Anything to get out of this fucking house.

7

JONO WANTED TO GRAB PATRICK BY THE COLLAR OF HIS JACKET, HAUL him back to the Mustang, and get the hell out of Salem after that revelation about his so-called family. Instead, he found himself getting through some awkward, terrible goodbyes in order to deal with pack business.

"We can't stay," Patrick said, barely looking at his grandmother in favor of the werecreatures waiting on the street.

"Ta for the tea," Jono said. It had been decent tea, but the taste of it had turned rancid in his mouth once he realized who the Pattersons worshipped.

"Are you sure you don't want a healing potion?" Eloise asked, not quite wringing her hands together but sounding and smelling worried nonetheless.

She stood on the walkway to her home, her three children flanking her. The grandkids were all huddled at the door and on the porch, watching everything going on. The alpha of the Salem god pack had moved off the property after her initial greeting, waiting for them on the sidewalk. Eloise didn't seem concerned about their presence.

Patrick shook his head, finally giving them his attention. Jono couldn't smell anything through his shields, but he knew Patrick wasn't comfortable being here any longer than necessary.

"I'll be fine. This is SOA business." He paused, gaze drifting back to the werecreatures before returning to his grandmother. "You should know the SOA has your home under surveillance as a precaution against an attack from the Dominion Sect. If there's evidence of hunters in Salem, I'm going to request the SOA send a mage with an affinity for defensive magic to ward your homes."

Eloise lifted her chin, annoyance and anger bleeding through her scent. "I want no aid from that agency."

"What you want doesn't matter when it comes to national security. This is about safety, not your pride," Patrick told her bluntly.

She seemed taken aback, and Patrick's aunt and uncles didn't look happy about his words either. Whether the tone or their meaning, Jono couldn't tell. The reunion hadn't gone how they'd probably hoped, but they should've been prepared for that possibility.

"We should go," Jono said, trying to hurry everything along.

Patrick nodded, staring at his family for a couple more seconds before blowing out a harsh breath. "Call me if anything unusual happens. I'll let the agents on the ground here know to stop by."

"When can we expect to hear from you again?" Eloise asked.

"I'll call when I can," Patrick said, not promising anything, which was fine by Jono.

He curled his hand around Patrick's elbow, swinging them both around. "Georgelle? Where should we meet you?"

"We drove. If you want to follow us, we'll take you to neutral territory," Georgelle said.

Jono slid his hand up Patrick's arm to his shoulders, drawing him in close. He didn't ask the questions he wanted to, not out in the open like this, still feeling eyes on his back. Only when they were in the car, with Jono behind the wheel again and a silence ward lining the Mustang's frame, did he speak up.

"You couldn't have known," Jono said.

"Setsuna did," Patrick said through clenched teeth, mobile clenched in one hand.

Jono nodded slowly, keeping his eyes on the car ahead carrying Georgelle. "Probably."

Patrick dropped his mobile in his lap and raised both hands to press them against his eyes once they were out of sight of the house. Jono didn't smell tears; then again, he didn't smell much of anything other than the fading scent of vomit. He reached over and pulled Patrick's left hand away from his face, drawing it closer. He turned his head enough to press a kiss to cold knuckles, holding on.

"It's something we should deal with back in New York, not here," Jono said.

"I know."

"Game face on, yeah?"

Patrick sighed. "And mouthwash. Or whiskey. Something to help me get this disgusting taste out of my mouth."

"We'll find something. I love you, and I want to kiss you, but not right now."

"Ugh. Don't even think about it."

Jono let his hand go and kept driving. What he could see of Salem was quaint, the city extensively decorated for the upcoming Halloween celebrations. It wasn't a holiday Jono had celebrated until he'd moved to the States. Tempest usually had a costume contest on Halloween night, though Jono had a feeling it would probably be postponed until next year.

They ended up at a bar overlooking the Salem Harbor, the waves white-tipped from a strong wind. The sea salt on the wind burned the inside of Jono's nose until he dialed down his sense of smell. The strong scent stemmed not just from the water but the bartender manning the drinks in the Siren's Song.

Her teeth were a shade too sharp, eyes just a little too big in a thin face, and her hair was so black it had a blue sheen to it in the low light. She smelled of the sea but seemed friendly enough toward Georgelle.

"Meeting?" she asked in a distinctly musical voice.

"Usual table if it's available, Saoirse," Georgelle said.

Saoirse waved them toward the back. "Always open for you. Lunch?"

"For mine, yes." Georgelle glanced back at Jono and Patrick. "If you're hungry, they have a menu."

"A shot of Jameson for me. Guinness for Jono," Patrick said.

"We'll take that menu, please," Jono said.

Saoirse tipped her head toward the back. "On the table."

The bar wasn't very crowded yet, though Jono wondered what the lunch crowd was like. They followed Georgelle to a corner booth, she and her dire taking the bench across from them while the rest of her pack members who had been on the street fanned out. Jono didn't like having his back to them, but he trusted in his and Patrick's ability to fight their way out if it came down to it. Besides, from what he'd got off the other god pack earlier, none of them had smelled like lies.

Patrick cast a silence ward over their table before pulling the paper menu off the little wire rack by the wall and flipped it open. "They better have a burger. You can have fish and chips, Jono. Dive into your English roots."

"I'd rather have crab cakes. We're in Massachusetts," he said.

"Good point."

Jono let Patrick figure out their food, turning his attention to Georgelle. For all her kind visage, he wasn't going to outright trust her.

"So. Hunters," Jono said.

"They tried to ambush a member of my pack while she was out for a jog along the harbor last week. Steven here managed to reach her in time when she called for support," Georgelle said.

Her dire was a thin man with dark skin and bleached white-blond hair, about a decade younger than her. While Georgelle was a werewolf, her dire had the distinct scent of a weregrizzly.

"Did your pack member survive?"

"She suffered from aconite poisoning, but she managed to escape. We reported it to the police. After the warnings we heard about London and what happened in New York City, we thought it best to have a paper trail started."

"Were the hunters with any magic users?" Patrick asked, folding up the menu and returning it to the little wire rack.

"She didn't see any, and neither did I once I got there. But more hunter sightings have cropped up since then. The covens have been warned," Steven said.

Georgelle's gaze flicked past them. Jono looked over his shoulder and saw Saoirse walking toward them with a tray of drinks in hand. If she noticed or cared about the silence ward, she didn't say anything.

"Here you are," Saoirse said, passing out beer and whiskey and a fruity-looking drink in a martini glass that she set in front of Steven. "Lunch for you two?"

"Crab cakes, a burger, and an order of fish and chips," Patrick said.

"Got it."

Georgelle and Steven gave their orders from memory. Saoirse left, and Patrick knocked back his shot of whiskey. He coughed to clear his throat, wiping his mouth with the back of his hand. "Better."

"That's all you're having," Jono said.

"Of whiskey. You're sharing your beer."

Jono sighed and nudged his glass over so it sat between them on the table before meeting Georgelle's gaze. "The federal government is aware of the hunter problem. If you've seen an uptick in their presence here, we'll let the SOA know."

Her amber-eyed gaze flicked to Patrick. "No friends of yours, I'm betting."

Patrick smiled thinly. "No."

"But they're here because of you. The Salem Coven wouldn't be a target otherwise. You said you have agents watching out for them."

"Are you happy about that? Or is there bad blood between your god pack and the Salem Coven?"

Georgelle shook her head. "Quite the opposite. We've had good history with them for several generations."

"Preternatural fighting is hell on the tourist industry in this town, and there are some ordinances specific to our community about living here," Steven drawled.

"Would the Salem Coven be amenable to someone from your pack patrolling Eloise's home in conjunction with the SOA?"

"We could come to an arrangement with them," Georgelle said slowly.

Jono nodded thoughtfully. "We'd appreciate it if you'd do that. They're not quite fond of the SOA."

Patrick snorted and reached for Jono's drink. "I can put you in touch with the SOA. The hunters are a problem, but worse is the Dominion Sect threat."

Steven sipped at his drink. "So we've seen on the news."

"We've instructed the packs in Salem to lie low for the next few weeks. Normally this is a time for celebration, but things don't feel right," Georgelle said.

"How big is your pack?" Jono asked.

"We're a small god pack, in a small, if popular town." She didn't give a solid number, but Jono wouldn't hold that against her. "Not as small as yours, but then, ours is not like yours, is it?"

Jono made a thoughtful sound, not taking his eyes off her. "No, it's not, but it's not a competition."

Georgelle smiled slightly. "You'd be one of the few who thinks that. My god pack unfortunately doesn't have that luxury."

"Territory fights?"

"Not within our town's borders."

Jono tilted his head a bit, thinking about the route they'd driven here. "Boston?"

"In some ways, yes. They've been testing our borders for years."

"Massholes," Patrick drawled.

Georgelle chuckled, though it sounded strained. "We all resemble that some days. Look, Salem is filled with all sorts of folks with ties to the preternatural and supernatural communities. We've learned to live with each other without too much fuss. We've had to, if we wanted to stay. Salem isn't like most other towns. Werecreatures who come here looking for a fight are told to move on. Hunters are a different story. There's no talking with them, just fighting, and the Boston god pack didn't warn us the bastards went through their city first before coming here."

"We don't get involved in territory fights between other god packs," Jono warned.

"Ours was enough of a headache," Patrick added.

More like a bloody nightmare.

Georgelle shook her head. "I'm not asking you to fight on our behalf. But I do hope you'll find the information useful and look upon the Salem god pack in a favorable light in the future. We've heard rumors of your patron, and it's been several hundred years since a god pack was known to be blessed in such a way."

Jono tipped his head back and closed his eyes, sending his awareness down deep to where Fenrir resided. The god didn't respond in words so much as a growl, but there wasn't any warning in the sound that echoed through his mind, only an acknowledgment of no threat stemming from the Salem god pack.

"We have alliances with half a dozen major god packs the world over, and that number is growing," Jono said, opening his eyes. "If you aid the SOA with keeping watch on Salem and the Salem Coven, then we'll extend the same courtesy to you."

Georgelle's expression didn't change, but the relief in her scent smelled like truth. She extended her hand across the table. "The Salem god pack thanks you for your trust and will gladly join into such an alliance with you."

Jono reached for her hand, ignoring the kind of electric spark that crackled against his skin when their fingers met. "The New York City god pack accepts your terms and will respect your sovereignty."

A different waitress, probably back from her break, approached their table with a tray holding their food. For a good few minutes after she left, the only sounds at their table were everyone chewing while they ate.

They chatted a little more as the meal progressed, mostly about pack business, the conversation easy enough to get through for the rest of lunch. By the time Jono paid the tab though, he could tell that Patrick was ready to leave.

"You have our numbers, and Patrick will get you contact information for the SOA," Jono said on the way out of the bar.

Georgelle nodded as she followed them out. "We'll be in touch as needed."

Jono ushered Patrick to the car, the wind a cold breeze blowing across the water toward them. Only when they were on the road with Salem's border behind them did he feel safe speaking.

"What do you want to do?" Jono asked.

Patrick rubbed at his eyes, white-knuckling his phone. "I need to talk with Setsuna. In person."

"Okay. We'll fly out tomorrow. Get the tickets."

"Jono—"

"If you think I'm letting you go through this alone, you're off your bloody head." Jono glanced at him, noticing how hard Patrick was clenching his jaw. "That's what pack is for. That's why I came today. You don't have to face all of this on your own. Get two tickets."

Patrick let out a breath before nodding. "I'll text Sage and tell her to get the tickets and that she's playing proxy for a second day. I need to update the joint task force with what we've learned."

Jono flexed his fingers around the steering wheel, pressing down on the gas pedal just a little more. "I'll get us home."

8

Patrick parked the rental car in front of Setsuna's home in Dupont Circle Thursday night, the sun having set over an hour ago. That he found a parking spot in the neighborhood at this hour at all was pure luck. He switched the engine off and sat there for a moment, not in the least clearheaded for the conversation he was about to have.

"Hey." Jono's fingers curled around his chin, turning his head. "It'll be okay. Whatever happens, I'm right here."

Patrick licked his lips and reached out to pull Jono into a quick, hard kiss, drawing comfort from the other man. "Let's get inside."

He'd called Setsuna after getting back to New York yesterday, demanding to see her. Not for an official meeting but a personal one. She'd agreed without hesitation, which told him she'd known what he would ultimately find in Salem.

They got out of the car, locking it behind them. The porch light was on, and he could see the soft glow of more light seeping past the curtains drawn across the living room windows. He knocked loudly when they made it to the front door, the threshold surrounding the home brushing softly against his shields.

The dead bolt turned, and the door opened, revealing Setsuna standing in the foyer without her carved rosewood cane. She was dressed in black slacks and a soft-looking violet sweater, house slippers on her feet.

"Hello, Patrick," she said, stepping aside so they could enter.

Patrick crossed the threshold, letting the familiar magic wash over him. He didn't bother removing his shoes since they were leaving right after the meeting. Jono followed him to the living room, where Patrick made a beeline to the wet bar in the corner and proceeded to pour himself a glass of whiskey.

Setsuna sighed from somewhere behind him. "Please tell me you ate something if you're going to drink like that."

Patrick set the whiskey bottle down on the wet bar with a loud smack, staring at the amber liquid in the cut-crystal glass. "There's not enough alcohol in the world to drown out what I'm feeling."

"Pat," Jono said quietly.

He turned around, holding the glass with tight fingers as he met Setsuna's gaze across the living room. "You knew who they worshipped. All this time, you *knew*."

Setsuna didn't try to deny or equivocate. She only nodded, her eyes filling with a quiet sort of sadness. "I knew."

Nearly every coven in existence worshipped some form of god or goddess, ancestors, or demon—something to pray to, to ask for guidance from, to gain a blessing. Setsuna had always prayed to her family's kami. When visiting her home around his time at an Academy growing up, Patrick had worshipped nothing and no one. He still didn't.

The apartment back in New York had no altar, no physical frame of worship to guide prayers he never spoke. But his mother's family prayed, and who they worshipped was the same goddess who owned his soul debt. Patrick wasn't sure he could ever reconcile the two.

"You always warned me against reaching out to my mother's family. I always thought it was because of Ethan. That you wanted to keep them safe from him. But that wasn't it," Patrick said.

"No, it wasn't. Not completely."

He glared at her, hand shaking so hard the whiskey sloshed against the side of the glass. "You told me to lie, and I did. You told me I had to change my name, and I did. You never told me the *truth*. You let me believe it was just Ethan."

"I never lied about your father. Ethan was a threat back then the same as he is now."

"That's beside the point. I'm talking about my mother's family. Did you think I'd never find out?"

Setsuna sighed, appearing tired, though not unrepentant. "Sit down, Patrick."

"Setsuna—"

"You want answers, and I'll give them to you, but sit down first."

She was already moving toward the leather couch, though Jono remained standing. He met Patrick's eyes before tilting his head at the furniture. Patrick grimaced, taking a large swallow of whiskey before going to sit on the couch, leaving an entire cushion between himself and Setsuna.

She folded her hands together over her lap, sharply cut hair brushing her shoulders as she turned her head to look at him. "Who we worship is private. It is for every family, for every group of magic users that comes together to offer up their prayers."

"I know," he bit out.

"Then know that I would have let your mother's family know you were alive if they had worshipped anyone else but Persephone."

Patrick wasn't sure he believed her—wasn't sure he could. Jono cleared his throat, and Patrick's attention snapped to him.

"She's telling the truth," Jono said quietly.

Patrick swallowed, realizing that while he was shielded in her home, Setsuna was not. She had to know Jono would be able to smell the difference between a lie and a truth, and had kept her personal shields down accordingly. Patrick stared at her, not knowing what to say in the face of her revelation. To know that his life could have been lived in another way if only a handful of choices had been different. That his future maybe wouldn't be *this*.

He didn't know, right then, what he would have preferred.

Maybe the Fates had it right after all, or maybe they were wrong. He would never know.

"I got attached to your mother's murder case after you were brought to me. I was the one who gave Eloise her second interview regarding the sacrificial murder," Setsuna said after a moment of silence had passed.

"She hates you," Patrick said.

"Yes. But I interviewed her to see if it was safe to send you back. She was devastated. They all were. If I could have given them a reprieve from their grief back then, I would have. But when I was in her home, I saw her altar to Persephone, and all I could think about was you in that safe house here in DC and the soul debt you owed at such a young age."

Setsuna's mouth twisted slightly, but she never looked away. Patrick only had dim memories of that time after being brought to her—shock and trauma having eaten away at those moments he'd lived through all those years ago. He hadn't been welcomed to her home until after the legalities over his name change and ward status were finished.

"You asked what I wanted back then. I told you I wanted to go home," Patrick said slowly.

"And I told you it wasn't safe. I didn't lie back then, Patrick." Setsuna sighed, flexing her fingers together. "You were eight and traumatized, and I had no right to send you back to a family who worshipped the goddess who owned your soul. The pressure on you to view Persephone as benevolent, as a savior of sorts, when she held your life and soul in her hand, your *future*, wasn't fair. I refused to put you through that."

Patrick stared at Setsuna, barely able to feel the glass in his hand as he listened to her speak. He knew, rationally, where she was coming from. That yes, he'd been young and just survived a near-death experience at the time. Her decisions on his behalf didn't make it better.

"You didn't give me a choice."

"I told you from the moment you became my ward that you could worship any god or no god, and you chose never to worship anyone. Covens exist to keep the memory of a god alive. Ask yourself if you would you have been allowed that freedom if I had sent you back to Eloise."

Patrick didn't say anything.

"I kept you with me because you would have been made to pray to the goddess you were unintentionally bound to. How would that have been fair to you? Where is the choice in familial requirements?" Setsuna asked gently.

Patrick flinched, knowing deep down she was right, but that didn't make it better. "You and Ashanti made sure I was good at keeping secrets. I could've kept this one."

"You were a child. You had enough weighing on you back then."

"You still should've *told* me. Before I went to the Citadel and the Mage Corps, or even fucking after. I deserved to know."

Setsuna slid across the couch to sit closer to him. "When you came to me, I had no plans for children in my life. I always disappointed my parents in that way, but I never disappointed myself. Not until you became my ward. I knew I could never be your mother, and I didn't want to try because that would've been a lie. But I at least wanted to be someone who put your best interests above as many others as I could. Looking back, I can see the failures and the successes."

Setsuna finally reached for him, curling her fingers over his wrist above the cuff of his leather jacket. Patrick thought about jerking away, but he was the one who'd come here tonight, looking for answers. So he stayed where he was, stiff beneath her touch, and somehow knew that this was growth, bitter as it was.

"I tried to keep you safe the only way I knew how," Setsuna said. "I wanted you to live to see adulthood for *you*, not for what you thought you owed others. You were so hurt as a child, Patrick. I tried to give you space by letting you learn amongst your peers, and I was always here for you when you came home. But you were so standoffish, and I didn't want to push because I was too afraid that trying to break through to you would harm you even more. You'd had enough of other people forcing their wants and desires upon you. I didn't want to add to it."

"I..."

Patrick didn't know what to say to that, not with the sting in his eyes from tears. His stomach twisted, and his face was hot from anger, but beneath it all was the memory of quiet days spent in this house between semesters at the Academy boarding school. Of how Setsuna was so focused on her career back then but made sure to be present when he was around for holidays or the summer break, even if they didn't know how to live around each other.

She'd still tried, in her own way, to care, and he could see that now.

Nothing was ever going to be fair after Persephone dragged him off that spellwork in the Salem basement all those years ago. In that respect, Setsuna was right.

And he'd survived long enough, grown old enough, to understand that.

Patrick set his whiskey glass on the coffee table so he could wipe at his eyes, smearing wetness over the skin near his temples. "Ethan wanted to be a god, and I never wanted to be a hero. Now look at the mess we're in."

Setsuna's fingers tightened over his wrist. "I know. If it was ever in my power to change things for you, I would have tried."

Patrick closed his eyes, sifting through the anger and pain, the heartache tied to the family he'd lost back then and kept losing because of the decisions Setsuna had made on his behalf. But he remembered how he'd felt knowing his mother's family worshipped Persephone, the full-body rejection he'd suffered through.

Persephone owned his soul debt while Ashanti had honed him into a weapon that Setsuna had tried to keep safe and sheathed as best she could.

He'd survived to wield himself in this war, though the cost he kept unearthing seemed impossible to pay some days. But he wasn't alone in this fight and hadn't been in all the years prior since coming to DC as a child. He knew with a certainty that made his teeth ache that if Setsuna had sent him back to Eloise, he'd be worshipping Persephone now, and there wasn't any freedom to be found in the confines of family tradition.

Setsuna had made the best of an impossible choice all those years ago, the same way Patrick was doing now.

Patrick opened his eyes and shifted on the couch, pulling his arm free. Setsuna let him go—she always had—but he caught her hand in his, giving it a careful, tentative squeeze. When he turned his head to look at her, he was struck by how *tired* Setsuna appeared. For the first time in a long while, she looked her years.

"I hate that you lied to me about this for so long. I don't know when I'll be able to forgive you for that. But I'm still here because of you, and I don't think I've ever said thank you for that," Patrick said.

There was a time, he knew, where he would've been furious over this kind of revelation and refuse to listen to reason. But they'd both been dealt shitty hands when it came to his life, and she'd done the best she could with the cards given to her. In the end, her best had kept him breathing.

Setsuna blinked, the corners of her eyes crinkling ever so slightly from the careful smile that curved her lips. "I was never after your thanks."

"I know." Patrick's gaze drifted over to where Jono stood,

leaning against the wall, watching them dig through his past with cut-glass words. "But for this, you have it."

It was the same situation he'd found himself in with Gerard last December in a way. Lied to for his own protection without his knowledge, and he could choose to hold on to that pain and anger and sense of betrayal until it choked him.

Or he could let it go and move on, for however long he remained standing.

He was better at forgiveness now, Patrick realized, staring at Jono. Better because of the compassion Jono always showed him right alongside the support that came with no strings, no quid pro quo of promises. Just the knowledge that Jono would always be there for him, no matter what. That support allowed Patrick to walk through the minefield of emotions that was his past, of everything that made him who and what he was, to come out the other side as whole as possible.

It hit him right then, stealing the breath from his lungs, what he would've lost if Setsuna had given him back to Eloise. He wouldn't be waking up beside Jono every morning, wouldn't be sharing drinks at home or at Tempest. The pack they'd built wouldn't even be a dream because Jono would still be in London, Wade would still be the prisoner of a god, and Sage would always lose the freedom she wanted for herself and other werecreatures beneath corrupt god pack alphas.

Maybe the Fates might have thrown them together eventually, but there was no guarantee they'd be who they were now if he'd grown up differently.

And Patrick, well, he liked the man he'd become when standing by Jono's side.

That tangle of emotion washed through him, forcing out the sting of anger and distress, leaving behind the cool knowledge that he would always choose Jono.

That he would always come back to this, to them.

*Oh,* Patrick thought, holding Jono's gaze.

What a hell of a time to realize he was in love when they were still so utterly fucked.

And he couldn't give voice to that sudden clarity, not when they still had a war to win. So Patrick did what he had always done when there was a fight to be had—he shoved down what made him happy in favor of getting through one more day, one more week. If they could get through Samhain alive, then he'd unravel that knot. He'd stop hiding behind other syllables in favor of a truth he felt down to his ruined soul.

Breathing in deep, Patrick looked at Setsuna, still holding her hand in his, remembering a different time when he'd stumbled into her life and she'd pulled him to some form of safety that he could—all these years later—finally accept.

"Thank you," Patrick said, voice thick in his throat. "For what you did for me."

Setsuna wrapped her arms around him for an awkward hug that left Patrick biting his lip. They hadn't hugged much while he grew up, and he knew now it wasn't because she hadn't wanted to. Patrick's boundaries had been nonexistent back then, and she'd worked in her own way to help him rebuild them. Those barriers had sustained him, maybe even hurt him, but eventually, Jono had taught him how to bring them down of his own volition.

The people in this room had taught him a lot about himself without Patrick even realizing it.

"Do what you feel is right when reacquainting yourself with your mother's family," Setsuna told him after she let him go.

"I will," Patrick promised.

Setsuna patted his knee and rose to her feet. "You don't want to miss your flight home."

Patrick nodded, leaving the remnants of his whiskey on the table as he stood. Jono pushed himself away from the wall, never taking his eyes off Patrick. "Ready?"

He met Jono's gaze and nodded. "Yeah. Let's go home."

"I'll see you out," Setsuna said, ushering them to the door.

She removed her house slippers in favor of a pair of shoes from the shoe rack by the door, following them outside into the cold to stand on the porch to see them off. Jono was already at the car when Patrick made it to the sidewalk, pausing to turn back to Setsuna, lips parting on words he would never speak.

A threshold lived in the framework of a home, guarding the space a person lived in. Where Setsuna stood was beyond its reach, but she wasn't out of reach of the high-caliber spelled bullet that cut through the air—so close to Patrick he felt its passing—and slammed into her chest, finding its mark, or maybe missing it altogether.

He would never know for sure because he'd turned, shifted out of the line of sight, and if he'd stayed put, his own personal shields still in place, maybe things would've been different.

"*Setsuna!*" Patrick screamed.

He slammed his shields outward, covering the area against the sniper staring through a scope somewhere in the dark.

Too little, too late.

Patrick saw Setsuna crumple to the ground, and he couldn't catch her, no matter how fast he moved. When he slammed to his knees beside her on the porch, the growing pool of blood beneath her looked black in the glow of the soft light situated by the door.

"No, no, *no*," Patrick gasped out, pressing shaking hands to the gaping wound in her chest. "Please no!"

Her eyes wouldn't look at him, staring far away at something only she could see.

In the cold, beneath a cloudy night sky, Setsuna's blood slipped between Patrick's fingers, impossible to stop.

9

PATRICK SAT ON A LEATHER CHAIR IN A PRIVATE WAITING ROOM AT George Washington University Hospital, staring at the blood beneath his fingernails.

He couldn't get them clean.

At some point after their arrival, Jono had pulled him into a bathroom and washed his hands for him because Patrick hadn't been clearheaded since Setsuna was shot. The water hadn't washed away all of it, nor his failure.

Fingers trembling, he clenched his hands into fists, fingernails biting into his skin. The sounds of the hospital was dull noise beyond the waiting room where the emergency nurses had ushered them after taking one look at Jono's eyes. The privacy was welcome, considering Patrick had been the one to start notifying people in charge of what had happened.

When EMS had arrived at Setsuna's home, she'd barely been breathing. They'd gotten her in their bus for transport almost immediately, and Patrick hadn't been able to follow because her home was a crime scene and he was a witness to the attack on a federal director's life. He'd managed a bare-bones statement to the police before walking away, pulling the fed card to get to the hospital because that's where he needed to be.

He'd been a combat mage for almost a decade. Patrick knew the damage a fifty-caliber bullet, spelled or otherwise, could do.

Patrick closed his eyes, letting his head fall forward, chin nearly touching his chest. Jono's hand settled on the nape of his neck before sliding down his spine to rub his back. Patrick wasn't comforted by the gesture, not when he had Setsuna's blood on his hands.

"They were aiming for me," Patrick said in a quiet, bitter voice.

"You don't know that," Jono said.

"If I hadn't looked back, the bullet would've hit my shields. I'd have survived." He swallowed hard, opening his eyes to stare at the floor beneath his feet, the light in the waiting room almost too bright. "Setsuna never would've taken the bullet."

"You didn't know this would happen, Pat."

"I *should* have. We're almost to Samhain. We know Ethan is willing to do anything to turn himself into a god. We should have anticipated this."

"You've said it yourself before that plans go out the bloody window all the time. You can't cover every possibility."

Patrick shook off Jono's hand and stood, pacing the small room because he couldn't do anything else. He wasn't a doctor, wasn't a healer. He could do nothing but *wait*, and his powerlessness ate at him.

He was taking what felt like his hundredth turn around the room when Jono's head snapped around, attention on the door. Patrick rocked to a halt, gaze going to the door that was shoved open not even a second later by *Wade* of all people.

"What the fuck are you doing here?" Patrick asked in a strangled voice.

"I told Sage I wanted to be with you guys," Wade said defiantly, an empty-looking backpack hanging from one hand.

"Did she tell you no?"

"Uh. She didn't tell me yes?"

"So you left without telling anyone where you were going when the Dominion Sect is targeting us?" Patrick really wasn't in the mood to explain how incredibly short-sighted and dangerous that was. "How the hell did you even get here so fast?"

Before Wade could answer, General Noah Reed caught the door before it closed and slipped inside the waiting room. "The fledgling flew. I sensed his arrival. You're lucky radar didn't catch him."

"You *flew?*" Jono asked as he stood, scowling at Wade even as he tapped away on his phone, probably updating Sage.

Wade gave him a stubborn look. "I wasn't going to wait on some stupid airplane when I could get here faster on my own. I left out of Central Park, and no one saw me."

"Where the bloody fuck did you even land?"

"Uh, Arlington?"

"I picked him up on my drive over here," Reed said, coming to stand in front of Patrick. "He's growing into his nature if he's able to fly unnoticed by the masses and block radar with his scales."

"You still can't have him unless he signs up with the military of his own free will," Patrick said.

"Oh, fuck no. I wouldn't be caught dead in a uniform," Wade retorted, coming toward Patrick.

"Shut up. You should've stayed in New York so you'd be *safe.*"

Wade ignored him, coming close enough to wrap his arms around Patrick and hug him so hard his spine cracked. "You were in trouble, and I wasn't going to stay behind. Not this time."

Patrick awkwardly patted Wade on the back, knowing that was guilt speaking, but he didn't have the mental capacity at the moment to offer any meaningful comfort.

"The FBI wants your statement," Reed said after Wade finally let Patrick go.

Because of course that agency had been called in to oversee an attack on a federal director. Patrick clenched his jaw and shook his head. "I can't leave yet."

"They're on-site—"

"I mean I'm not talking to anyone who isn't a doctor. Not until I know—" Patrick broke off, glaring at Reed, the world watery at the edges. "Whoever was out there tonight was aiming for *me*."

"Setsuna is the director of the SOA and has a history with you. She is as much a target as you are in this fight. You can't know for sure who they were aiming for, Collins. You can't blame yourself for this."

But he could, and he was, because he knew where that bullet should've gone.

"If that's true, then the lot of you on that fancy joint task force are all targets," Jono said, giving Patrick time to get himself under control when all he wanted to do was rage.

Reed slanted Jono an indecipherable look, blowing smoke out of his nose, no cigarette in sight. "Precautions are being taken as we speak. The various parties and agencies who needed to be updated on what happened have been informed. I have been told that Priya Kohli is now acting director of the SOA. She will be here shortly. We're staging in an administration area of the hospital to stay out of the way of the staff here."

Patrick nodded. "If—"

He cut himself off as the door to the waiting room was pushed open and a doctor was let inside by a military aide stationed in the hallway. The doctor was in scrubs, no white coat, and not wearing any operating gowns or gloves. Patrick could still see traces of blood splattered at the hem of his green scrub pants.

"Usually we contact family first, but I was directed here by an officer," the doctor said, not appearing put off by that instruction.

"It's a matter of national security that we know the outcome," Reed said, turning to face the man.

Patrick stared at the doctor's face, and he knew by the way the other man hesitated—by the way Setsuna's blood had poured through his own hands without stopping—that there'd been no chance of her survival. He'd only been fooling himself in thinking they'd come through tonight with Setsuna ending up in the ICU and not in the morgue.

"I'm terribly sorry, General Reed. We did everything we could, but the trauma SOA Director Setsuna Abuku sustained was too severe. She died on the table."

It was like a silence ward settled over Patrick, the world going quiet, his head a mess of static. He wasn't aware of anything, not until Jono stepped in front of him, blocking out the world. Warm hands framed his face, wolf-bright blue eyes staring into his as Jono pressed his forehead to Patrick's.

"Breathe, Pat," Jono told him, sounding far away.

Patrick sucked in air through his teeth, letting it out on a rattling, choked-off gasp. "*Fuck.*"

Patrick reached for Jono, gripping the button-down he wore so hard he almost ripped the fabric. He rocked forward, moving his head so he could rest it against Jono's shoulder for a few frantic seconds as he tried to get himself under control. Setsuna was gone, and with her, any answers to the swirl of remaining questions bubbling up inside his mind about his past.

She was *gone*.

And he only had himself to blame.

It was bitter knowledge that, after all these years, he'd finally been able to appreciate what she had done for him. But he wouldn't get the chance to tell her anything else, only say the words over her grave.

Tears burned in his eyes, but Patrick knew he didn't have the time to grieve right now. Samhain was eight days away, and they still had a war to fight. He still had a soul debt to pay.

Setsuna would be pissed if he stopped fighting for himself.

Compartmentalizing had never taken so much effort before, but Patrick had no choice here. He didn't have the luxury to grieve such a complicated loss when the threat that had taken her from him was still out there.

Patrick raised his head, let Jono go to wipe away his tears, and stepped around him to face Reed. "I'll give the FBI my statement."

"*Our* statement," Jono said. "I was there as well."

Jono's hand slipped into his, and Patrick gripped it tightly, a lifeline he never wanted to let go of.

Reed studied them with a clear-eyed gaze before nodding. "Follow me."

Wade stuck close as Reed led them out of the waiting room and through the hallways of the hospital, the general's military escort clearing the way for them. Hospital staff didn't seem concerned about their presence, especially not while the doctor who had operated on Setsuna was still with them, using his key card to scan them through restricted doors.

Eventually, they ended up on a lower level, in a wing that dealt with the hospital's administration. It was overflowing with plain-clothes agents, police officers, and men and women in military combat dress. Patrick's shields were still locked down tight, and he could sense a headache coming on, but recognition still got through. Half the people present were magic users of various ranks, most notably Priya, a non-military mage with a strong affinity for defensive magic.

"General Reed, what's the news?" Priya asked, pushing past a pair of uniformed police officers to get to them.

Reed shook his head, his voice coming out rough. "I'm sorry. Setsuna didn't make it."

Priya rocked to a shaky halt and closed her eyes, face losing a little bit of color at his words. She seemed to age a decade in a few seconds, grief an almost physical thing, before she shook it off with visible effort to do her duty. Patrick knew she and Setsuna had worked together for a number of years. Legally, she was now the acting director of a federal agency, and from here on out, everyone employed by the SOA would be taking their orders from her.

"I'll inform the president," Kohli said, opening her eyes again. "Special Agent Collins?"

"Ma'am?" Patrick replied.

"I understand the FBI is waiting on your statement, as well as Mr. de Vere's."

Patrick nodded. "That's why we came with General Reed."

"Then see that you leave nothing out."

She waved him down the hall, in the direction of a pair of men in suits who were staring right back at him. Knowing how these kinds of interviews went, Patrick grabbed Wade by the arm and tugged him aside.

"Stay with General Reed, and if he gives you a minder, don't run off," Patrick said in a low voice.

Wade scowled, a mulish expression on his face. "I'm not leaving you."

"You can't be present for the talks Jono and I need to have with the FBI. So just sit tight. We'll come find you when we're finished."

Wade glared at him before side-eyeing General Reed, who wasn't paying any attention to them. "Fine."

Patrick hoped Wade listened, but considering he'd shifted mass to fly from New York City to Washington, DC, on the basis of a text sent from Jono about what had happened, he had a feeling they'd find Wade where he shouldn't be later.

Patrick moved past Priya and headed for the FBI agents with Jono by his side. He knew how an investigation like this would be run, having been on the other side of it for several years. He'd just never thought he'd be in the position of the grieving person left behind in the wake of an assassination that cut deeper than he thought it ever could.

Strange how you didn't know what you'd lost until it was gone.

"Special Agent Patrick Collins, if you'll follow me? Jonothon de Vere will be going with my partner," the older man said.

Patrick followed where the agent led and found himself in a patient intake office where they could have some privacy. A hospital really wasn't the best place to spearhead an investigation, but this was where Setsuna had been brought. This was where she had died. He hoped someone from the SOA had secured her body.

"My name is Gregory Miller," the FBI agent said, pulling out his phone and holding it up. "I'll need you to tell me what happened tonight. Are you okay with me recording it?"

"That's fine." Patrick crossed his arms over his chest and stared over the agent's shoulder. "I came to DC to speak with the director of my agency about an ongoing case. We didn't stay long. She was shot as we were leaving."

"Did you see the shooter?"

"No. They used a long gun. Sniper rifle."

"How do you know that?"

Patrick finally looked him in the eye, choking back anger. "I was a combat mage in the Mage Corps, as I'm sure you know if you saw the news over the summer. I know what kind of damage a gun like that can do. Besides, there wasn't anyone on the street at the time but us, so it had to be a ranged shot."

"Us being?"

"My partner, Jonothon de Vere."

"No chance the assailant was hiding with the use of spells?"

"I wouldn't rule it out, but it's doubtful."

"What makes you say that?"

"Because most of the people targeting us are tainted by hell and use black magic, and I'm really fucking good at tracking that. Odds are it was a hunter or someone allied with the Dominion Sect who isn't a magic user or carrying a demon in their soul."

The FBI agent kept asking questions, and Patrick answered them to the best of his knowledge, but it was like someone else had control of his mouth. The feeling made his skin crawl, thinking about Andras, even though he knew it was simply a response to

Setsuna dying. That didn't stop the bitter ache inside from digging itself deeper.

The interview lasted nearly thirty minutes according to the clock on the wall in the office, though it felt longer to Patrick. The agent knew Patrick had to leave due to the problem at hand. He wasn't being held as a murderer this time, only a witness, and with Reed present to vouch for his integrity, he wasn't going to be hauled off in handcuffs.

"We'll be in touch to continue where we left off," Agent Miller said before leaving the room.

Patrick only had a few seconds to try to get himself under control before he had to face everyone outside the office. That timing got longer by virtue of the federal agent who slipped inside the office, bringing with him the crackle of ozone and weighty presence of a god.

"DC is never this exciting when you aren't here," Quetzalcoatl said as he kicked the door shut behind him.

Patrick scowled at the god. "I'm pretty sure the DEA doesn't have jurisdiction over Setsuna's murder."

Quetzalcoatl smiled thinly at him. "The DEA doesn't, but I do."

Dark-haired and dark-eyed, the Aztec god made a living in the mundane world these days as a special agent for the Drug Enforcement Agency. He'd been something of an annoyance, if ultimately grudgingly useful, when it came to taking down Tremaine's Night Court and keeping Tezcatlipoca at bay last year.

The DEA windbreaker he wore didn't seem warm enough for the weather outside, but it helped Quetzalcoatl blend in. Patrick took a step back, though there wasn't much space to move around in the small office.

"What do you want?"

"I'm here to give you a warning since it appears the rest of my cousins are busy." Quetzalcoatl dragged the plastic chair away from the front of the desk and swung it around to sit in it. "The veil is getting thin."

Patrick stared at him. "It's not Samhain yet. I thought we still had time?"

"Did you think the veil would break all at once in a single day? You're forgetting what Ethan perpetuated with the Thirty-Day War and the sacrifices last year during summer. It takes time to break through the veil, time we are losing. The Sluagh are following the storm lines. Áłtsé Hashké tells me he has found marigolds in the subways. The dead are restless in their graves."

"What do you want me to do? Ethan could be anywhere. I don't have time to go from city to city chasing after rumors."

Quetzalcoatl's hand snapped out, grabbing Patrick by the wrist with an implacable grip. Talons pricked his skin, making Patrick freeze. The god's true form wasn't the man sitting before him but a huge, feathered serpent, and the reminder made Patrick wrap his fingers around the hilt of his dagger.

Quetzalcoatl was on their side; Patrick didn't think the god wanted him dead before he paid his soul debt, but one never knew.

"You need to call the gods of heaven to fight, the way Ethan has called the gods of every hell," Quetzalcoatl said.

Patrick scowled. "All of you have been telling me for years this was my fight, not yours."

"Yes, but the end of it belongs to every pantheon tied to the mortal plane. What gets you there at last can be drawn from all of us who came before." Quetzalcoatl showed all his sharp teeth in a smile that left Patrick cold before letting go. "Stories are shared, after all. They are how we exist, how we are remembered."

"They're also how you die."

Quetzalcoatl's eyes flashed molten gold for a split second. "Creation is not the sole purview of one pantheon. Neither is death. Sometimes, for a world to be born, another must die."

Patrick stepped back, trying to get some distance between them, but didn't get far, not with Quetzalcoatl still gripping his wrist. "Say I ask for help? Say I pray for it? Since when have any of you ever listened to me? I asked the Dagda for help with the Sluagh, and he said it wasn't his fucking problem."

"I doubt that."

"So maybe he didn't use those words. The sentiment was still the same."

Quetzalcoatl got to his feet, and the room suddenly felt too small, trapped inside it with a god. "Find Ethan and stop this madness. Some of us won't survive the veil tearing again."

They'd lose the prayers that sustained them, their heavens and hells tied to the mortal plane fading faster than before. The current status quo was survivable, but not if Ethan won. Patrick knew that. He was doing his best to pay his soul debt, but the price was getting steeper and steeper, and he wasn't sure the cost wouldn't outright kill him at this point.

The door banged open just then, and Wade barreled inside, an irritated military aide behind him, who stayed in the hallway. Wade scowled at Quetzalcoatl, sliding between the god and Patrick, knocking the god's arm aside and forcing him to let go of Patrick.

"I remember you, Agent Pretzel," Wade said.

Quetzalcoatl looked visibly pained at the misuse of his name. "You're looking better than the last time I saw you."

"No thanks to you." Wade reached behind him, arm waving around frantically until he snagged Patrick by the front of his jacket, never taking his eyes off the god. "I'm stealing Patrick."

"We weren't finished."

"What part of *stealing* didn't you hear?"

Wade hauled Patrick toward the door with a grip he couldn't break unless he wanted to tear his leather jacket and ruin the charms embedded in it. Since Patrick wasn't keen on that, he let himself be pulled into the relative safety of the hallway.

"Remember what I said," Quetzalcoatl called out.

"Yeah, I know," Patrick muttered, knowing the god could hear him.

"Reed said we could go home. He got us a flight on a private jet because of security or something. Do you think I'll get to pick my snacks again like when we went to Chicago?" Wade asked.

"No, because Marek isn't footing the bill. The government is, and they're cheap."

Patrick was cognizant of the military aide following in their wake as Wade led him unerringly to Jono. He was standing off to the side, eyes locked on them, and Patrick gave him a quick nod as they drew close.

"Found him," Wade announced. "Can we go?"

Jono leaned in to brush a kiss over Patrick's cheek, discreetly breathing in. The displeased sound that left his throat at the lingering scent of ozone made Patrick shake his head in warning.

"Pat," Jono growled.

"Had a second meeting with DEA Special Agent Juan Delgado after the FBI agent finished. You remember him," Patrick said.

Jono's eyes narrowed. "What did he want?"

"Just updated me on the case from last summer. He said it would be good if we got more help." Patrick knew Jono would read between the lines. Judging by his frown, he didn't like the order decorated as a suggestion any better than Patrick did. "We need reinforcements."

"I thought the joint task force was working on that?"

"That's not the kind of reinforcements I'm talking about."

"Whatever you need."

What he needed was for tonight not to have ever happened.

Grief churned beneath the veneer of calm Patrick had dragged over everything, willing it to hold until he was alone with his pack. If Reed said they could go, then he wanted to get the fuck gone.

Escape stayed out of reach just a little longer as Priya slipped between a pair of US Marshals before they could find an exit, waving down Patrick. "Collins, a word."

Patrick shrugged off Wade's hand and went to her. "Ma'am?"

"General Reed tells me you're heading back to New York."

"Those are my marching orders."

"I'll be meeting with the heads of the joint task force tomorrow. Expect a call from me afterward, so keep your phone on you. Setsuna—" Priya broke off before sucking in a deep breath, getting herself under control. Her eyes were dry but reddened. "The SOA is transporting her body to our morgue tonight. I'll be requesting a writ of habeas corpus et animum and recalling our top necromancer. The president wants a record of what happened tonight from Setsuna."

Patrick was very glad she didn't order him to stay for Setsuna's court-ordered resurrection, however brief it would be. He wasn't sure he'd be able to handle that.

"Has her death hit the media yet?" Patrick asked.

Priya's grim expression was answer enough. "SOA standard response to any inquiries you get is no comment."

"Understood."

Not like he had any desire to talk with the media. He'd had enough of feeling like prey around people with cameras over the summer.

Priya knuckled one eye before sighing heavily. "I'll be sending a team from the Rapid Response Division to New York for protection of the nexus. I know you can't tap a ley line any longer, but I'll want you to stay abreast of our defensive plans."

Patrick managed to keep a straight face about his supposed deficiencies with tapping external magic in ley lines. "I'll keep in contact with SAIC Ng. If I'm running point on any joint task force missions, then I may not be available for in-person meetings."

She waved off his concern. "General Reed already let me know what you are spearheading takes precedence, and Setsuna had informed me of the same before she—well. I know you had a direct line to her. Considering everything that is happening right now, I want to keep that same communication open. Here's my work and personal cell phone numbers."

Priya handed him a business card, those two numbers already

scribbled on the back. Patrick put them into his phone right there even as he committed the numbers to memory.

"Get home safely," Priya said before walking off.

Patrick ran his tongue over the back of his teeth as he turned around to face his pack. "Let's find General Reed and figure out the flight."

Jono and Wade fell into step behind Patrick, letting him take the lead when he felt less and less like he knew what the fuck he was doing. He still had Setsuna's blood beneath his fingernails and caked into the knees of his jeans. He was afraid that in the future Ethan was hurtling them all toward, he'd only get more blood on his hands.

## 10

THEY LANDED IN LAGUARDIA AFTER MIDNIGHT IN THE PRIVATE JET terminal. Their flight on the private jet wasn't luxurious in any way beyond the seats, though Wade decimated the snacks and food on board. Patrick had drunk his way through five tiny bottles of whiskey, and Jono hadn't tried to stop him. His shields had loosened on the flight home, and the bitter, sharp scent of grief pouring off him made Jono keep his concerns to himself.

"We're dropping you off at Sage's," Jono told Wade as he unlocked the Mustang in the short-term car park.

"I want to sleep in my own bed though," Wade replied before scrambling into the back seat. The Mustang wasn't the roomiest of cars, but Wade was a decent sort about the lack of space.

"You're going to apologize to her for leaving like you did, and then you're pairing up with her. No one goes anywhere alone."

"I'll text her," Patrick said.

Jono started the engine once everyone was buckled up and backed out of their spot. Leaving the car park at that time of the night meant little traffic, the ranks of taxis and ride shares diminished by the late hour. The drizzle of rain was concerning, if only because of what the clouds hid above.

No one spoke on the drive into Manhattan, crossing over the Queensboro Bridge on the way to the Art Deco building Marek and Sage owned in the Upper East Side. When they arrived, the front door opened and Sage came out in a dressing gown tied around her waist over her pajamas and ballet flats rather than slippers in deference of the sidewalk.

Patrick had to get out of the car in order to move the seat up so Wade could crawl out. Jono watched as Sage wrapped her arms around Patrick in a hug he returned after a couple of seconds.

"I'm sorry," Sage said, smelling like worry and sadness that the strong breeze whipped away in seconds. Patrick's grief was stuck in Jono's lungs. All he wanted to do was wrap Patrick up in his arms and promise to keep him safe, but he couldn't keep Patrick safe from loss.

Patrick didn't say anything to that, merely patted her on the back before letting her go and getting back into the car. Sage waved at Jono before ushering Wade toward the building where Marek waited in the doorway, all the while scolding him about his jaunt to DC.

Jono drove away, taking them home. When they turned down their street in Chelsea sometime later, Jono expected to see the media present in front of their apartment, but no one was there. He was determined to make one circle of the block looking for any open parking spot, and if he couldn't find one, he was going to park in the red zone. Except there was an empty spot right in front of their apartment building as luck would have it.

Or maybe not luck.

Jono was all set to back into the spot when the crackling scent of ozone filled the car, and gold-brown eyes reflected in the rearview mirror, staring at him.

"Bloody hell," Jono growled, slamming his foot on the brake. He'd had enough of ozone stinging his tongue for one night.

"Cousin," Hermes said, suddenly sprawled in the back seat. "Pattycakes."

"Get the fuck out," Patrick snarled.

"No."

Patrick twisted around as much as the seat belt would let him, the scowl on his face an ugly thing that Jono wanted to wipe away. "What the fuck do you want?"

Hermes smirked at them, not at all perturbed about being locked in a car with their anger. "I'm here with a message from Hera. She wants to speak with you."

"She could've rang," Jono growled.

"Where's the fun in that?" Hermes leaned forward, causing Patrick to pull back. "She and Zeus are back from Greece. They're waiting for you at her home and require an audience."

"We're parking, and then we're sleeping," Patrick said.

"The parking spot will still be here when you return. Now drive."

Jono tightened his grip on the steering wheel, hearing the leather creak from the pressure. "Does she know anything about what happened tonight?"

Hermes flopped backward. "Your loss was not our doing."

Jono was certain he could trace every loss experienced by Patrick back to the gods, but he bit his tongue on that observation. He waited for Patrick to decide on what course of action to take because it wasn't Jono's right. Not with this.

Patrick pressed his palms over his eyes and rubbed at them hard. "Drive."

Jono drove, not needing directions from their backseat driver. He remembered where Hera's home was in Manhattan. The seven-story mansion was protected by gargoyles, the numbers seemingly doubled from their last visit. They parked out front where a spot was available, probably due to a little bit of magic.

Jono ignored the grating growls that greeted them from the gargoyles once they exited the Mustang. Hermes led the way to the double-door entrance of the home, opening it without needing a key.

The home was summer-warm inside. Jono couldn't tell if that was central heating or the gods that were present. He could sense more than just Hera and Zeus in the home, and he didn't like being outnumbered.

Fenrir roused once they crossed the threshold, teeth and claws sliding through Jono's thoughts, pricking at his control. Beyond the god's presence was the hint of Ginnungagap, Jono's awareness of the primordial void making the hair on the back of his neck stand up.

*Wait,* Jono told the god in the quiet of his mind.

There was no need to let Fenrir out in the Greek pantheon's territory. Depending on how they treated Patrick, Jono would give over his body without a fight. He and Fenrir had come to a delicate agreement over the god's reach through Jono's physical presence. He wouldn't fight Fenrir, so long as the god listened to his reasons for holding back.

"This way," Hermes said.

Rather than going to the roof with its patio and garden, they were led to the third floor, to a room with a gold-veined white marble floor and wide windows overlooking Central Park. Two chairs that could have doubled as thrones were positioned in front of the windows. An altar took up an entire wall beneath a mural of the Greek countryside, dominated by a vision of Hera granting blessings to devotees kneeling before her. It was blindingly color-ful, and Jono was reminded that the white marble of the Parthenon and its ilk used to be painted like a rainbow.

Time made everything fade though, even the gods they stood before.

Hera and Zeus were dressed in modern clothes that were far more in fashion than Hermes' jeans and faded band T-shirt. They could've passed easily as a Wall Street tycoon and his socialite wife, which was how they had lived before losing their current human aliases and retreating to Greece last year.

Hermes waved his hand at Patrick and Jono as he sauntered across the floor, battered Doc Martens squeaking a little on the marble. He sketched a slight bow in the direction of those who headed his pantheon. "Your guests, as promised."

"We asked for the debtor alone," Zeus said, sounding slightly irritated.

"I go where Patrick goes," Jono shot back.

Hera's smile was a bit mocking, but he expected nothing less from this lot. "Of course you do. That's why we gods gave you to him."

"You can preach about that bollocks all you like, but I know where I stand with Patrick, and none of you dictated my choices."

"You carry our cousin in your soul. Do you honestly think he had no say in how you feel?"

Jono loved Patrick of his own free will, and he'd be damned if the gods took credit for the matters of his heart. "I promised Patrick I'd be his weapon. Fenrir never influenced me the way you think he does."

Hera opened her mouth to speak, but her teeth snapped shut with a clack as Fenrir poured through Jono's soul and mind, control a shared experience rather than a fight.

"*This one is not yours, cousin,*" Fenrir said with Jono's mouth. "*Watch your words.*"

Hera's gaze flicked to Patrick, and Jono wanted badly to put himself between them. Fenrir kept him where he was, and Jono didn't fight the god.

"We all felt when Ginnungagap touched this earth once again," Zeus said, his voice rumbling like a storm through the large room. "The beginning to an end called us back to these shores."

Patrick stiffened a little beside Jono, but he couldn't reach out to comfort him in any way, not with Fenrir clawing beneath his skin.

*"Ginnungagap is not your concern,"* Fenrir said.

"What approaches is all of our concern. Every god who walks this earth on the mortal plane is aware of what comes."

Armageddon. Ragnarök. Judgment Day. The Fifth World. It had many names across many continents and adherents, but the end-times were all the same in the only way that mattered.

An ending.

Jono knew that from Fenrir and Patrick, but it didn't make it any easier to face.

Hera pushed herself to her feet, the diamond-tipped gold pins keeping her riot of loose curls in place glinting in the light from the chandeliers. She strode forward, high heels clicking against the marble. The goddess came to stand in front of Jono, her aura breaking open between one blink and the next, haloing her body like the sun.

"Your teeth found Odin once before, cousin. I wonder what they will find this time?" Hera asked.

*"This is all our fight,"* Fenrir reminded her.

Her attention shifted to Patrick. "Some more than others."

"I know what needs to be done, but we aren't going to be enough even with all our alliances. Quetzalcoatl warned as much. Gods within your pantheon and others are helping Ethan out. If you aren't willing to back us when it matters, then you can't blame me for the fallout," Patrick said.

"Our stories aren't yours."

*"You've tied him to the gods of heaven through a soul debt. It is in all our interests to ensure he sees it through,"* Fenrir said.

Hera's gaze snapped back to them, eyes narrowing. "His blood is at fault."

Jono felt himself smile, the sharpness of his teeth catching on his lips. *"I do not argue that. I argue where you place the blame. One of yours took half of the twins to ensure a way forward. Yet it is also one of your own who perpetuates an alliance with Ethan and the Dominion*

*Sect. Mortals have a saying about glass houses. Be careful of your stones, cousin.*"

Hera stared at them with enough animosity in her gaze that Jono could almost feel the heat of her anger. Behind her, Zeus got to his feet and went over to his wife's altar to pour himself a glass of red wine.

"Do what you promised," Zeus said, attention on Patrick. "Finish what your family started and pay the debt you owe us."

Patrick's expression was stony as Fenrir faded to the background and Jono found himself in control again, capable of looking at his lover. He ignored Hera in favor of taking Patrick's hand in his.

"Let's go home," Jono said.

The gods didn't stop their leaving, and if they had tried, Jono would've gone for their throats, Fenrir's teeth always willing to bite.

———

JONO LOCKED the door to their flat, watching with worried eyes as Patrick made a beeline for the kitchen. The sound of a cupboard opening and a bottle clinking on the counter made him sigh quietly.

"That won't do anything but give you a hangover," Jono said gently when he went into the kitchen.

Patrick hadn't even bothered with a glass, simply drinking straight from the bottle. "That's a tomorrow problem."

"It is tomorrow."

Because it was after midnight, early on a Friday morning, one week from Samhain, and the warnings they'd received in two cities tonight was stress Jono could've done without. When it looked like Patrick would keep drinking until he found the bottom of the whiskey bottle, Jono removed it from his hands with a firm tug.

"Jono—" Patrick snapped.

"No." Jono turned him around, pushing him back against the counter. "I'm not letting you grieve like this. I'm here, and I'm not going anywhere."

Patrick drew in a sharp breath before surging forward, kissing Jono so hard their teeth knocked together. Jono lifted a hand, tangling his fingers in Patrick's hair to tilt his head back, holding on while they kissed with a ferocity that went straight to his cock.

Desire was salt-tinged between them, whiskey on his tongue, Patrick's bitter scent in his nose. Jono breathed it all in, licking deep into Patrick's mouth, swallowing the strangled gasp that tried to escape. He hauled Patrick up into his arms, hands curved over his arse. Patrick wrapped his legs around Jono's waist, still kissing him.

"I want you to fuck me," Patrick got out between biting kisses that tasted like whiskey.

Jono wasn't about to argue because he'd rather Patrick drown in him than a bottle. He carried Patrick out of the kitchen and to their bedroom, dropping him on the bed before turning on the lamp rather than the overhead lights.

Patrick was already divesting himself of his weapons, shoes, and clothes, eyes on Jono. He stripped out of his own clothes, tossing them about the bedroom floor before crawling onto the bed, chasing after Patrick's mouth. He reached for Jono, fingers frantic in their touch, clawing at his skin.

"Fuck me," Patrick said, voice tinged with a desperation Jono hated to hear.

His shields were down, scent a mess of emotion Jono didn't have the time to pick apart, not with the way Patrick moved beneath him. He dipped his head low to lick across the scars on Patrick's chest, teeth scraping over unmarked skin and scar tissue alike. He slid a hand beneath the pillow, searching for the bottle of lube until he found it, pulling it free.

"Whatever you want."

Jono would never deny Patrick anything, especially not tonight. So he kissed his way down Patrick's chest until he reached his cock, taking the half-hard length down to the root. Patrick arched against him, and Jono pinned him down, swallowing hard around his cock. Jono only pulled off when he needed to breathe, sucking at the crown and tonguing the slit as he slicked up his fingers.

When Jono swallowed Patrick back down, he pushed one slick finger into his hole, feeling Patrick's groan as much as hearing it. Fingers grabbed his hair and pulled, but Jono ignored the sting in his scalp as he worked Patrick open until he could slip another finger inside. The weight of the cock on his tongue couldn't distract him from seeking out Patrick's prostate, pressing his fingers against it hard enough to make Patrick cry out.

"*Fuck*, Jono," Patrick ground out. "Stop teasing and just fuck me."

The needy edge to his tone was matched by the hard length in Jono's mouth and the way Patrick lifted a leg over Jono's shoulder to dig his heel into his back. The pressure might have bruised anyone else, but Jono pushed back against it as he pulled his mouth off Patrick's cock. He kept his fingers where they were, still pushing in deep, watching as Patrick tossed his head back, sweat sliding down the line of his throat. He had one hand pressed flat against the headboard, using it as leverage to push back against Jono's touch.

The salt didn't diminish in the air, lingering on Patrick's skin, dampening his lashes. Jono leaned over to kiss him, tasting it on his lips, the bitter flavor washing through Jono's mouth.

The grief in their bed was born of guilt and war, and Jono did his best to kiss it away, to fuck it out of Patrick when he pushed his cock in sooner than he'd have liked but giving in to Patrick's want. The hiss of discomfort that escaped Patrick's mouth was muffled against Jono's throat where he hid his face. His hands dug into Jono's shoulders, legs locked around his waist, touch desperate in a way Jono couldn't soothe.

He still tried.

Jono withdrew from that tight heat partway before pushing back in again, hips flexing with a strength he didn't try to temper. Patrick bit his whimper into Jono's skin, and Jono did it again, reminding him they were both alive, both still there.

"I'm right here," Jono grunted, holding Patrick down as he fucked him with a sureness that left him keening.

Patrick never looked him in the eye, taking what Jono gave him while subsumed in grief and regret, and all Jono could do was love him.

When Patrick came, it was with a full-body shudder, teeth sunk into Jono's shoulder to stifle his cry, one hand wrapped around his own cock. Jono didn't stop until he came as well, spilling into Patrick with a groan. He caught Patrick's mouth in a deep kiss, leaving a wordless apology for the bruises he'd pressed into freckled skin on trembling lips.

"I love you," Jono murmured, still in him, still holding on.

Patrick wrapped his arms around Jono, face pressed against his throat, breathing raggedly. In the quiet of their bedroom, Jono could hear Patrick's heartbeat and the hitch of his breath as he struggled to hold back tears.

Jono closed his eyes, wishing he could promise Patrick that everything would be all right, but he'd never liked lying to the man he loved.

## 11

Jono was checking inventory behind the bar when Emma lifted her head off her arms, perking up. "I think someone's arrived."

She slipped off the stool, hiding a yawn behind one hand. She'd worked late with Leon and some of their project managers at PreterWorld and hadn't got much sleep. Her massive to-go coffee cup was empty, so Jono tossed it in the bin. The meeting with outside packs had been set in the afternoon on Friday to account for the people coming this week from the West Coast.

Patrick couldn't make it because he was working at the SOA field office. Sage was spending all day offloading her case deadlines for the next week onto other desks with Tiarnán's approval so she'd be available without needing to worry about her job. Wade was spending the day in Sage's office after the stunt he'd pulled flying to DC.

Jono hadn't wanted to let Patrick out of his sight that morning, especially not with the media camped outside the apartment building again. Setsuna's death was the top breaking news story of the day, and everyone wanted a comment from Patrick. Running the gamut of reporters and cameras again was not how they'd wanted to start the morning.

At least no one had camped out in front of the bar. Jono hadn't smelled anything out of the ordinary when he and Emma had arrived, and none of the protective wards had been tripped.

Jono watched as Emma unlocked the door and opened it to allow their guests to enter. The woman who came through first gave Jono a polite smile, her amber eyes bright in her face.

"Nice place," Monica Woodard said in greeting.

"Want a drink?" Jono offered.

"Dirty martini if it's not too much trouble."

The Chicago god pack had sent their dire and a decent number of volunteers, as had other god packs scattered across the country. While the alphas wouldn't leave their territory, they'd all sent the next best thing in terms of rank. Jono and Patrick had promised everyone pass-through rights, and they didn't need to stand on ceremony. Jono appreciated the respect shown his god pack by those chosen to come and started taking drink orders.

Emma slipped behind the bar to help him out, her attention on everyone milling about and getting comfortable. The majority of people weren't god pack, and the mix of regional accents came from all corners of the country.

Jono set Monica's dirty martini down in front of her before moving on to the next drink. Between him and Emma, they got the drinks poured and mixed within fifteen minutes, quick introductions happening with the hand-offs.

Monica eyed them over the rim of her delicate glass, gaze lingering on Emma. "Your dire?"

Emma flashed her a tempered smile. "No. I've acted as proxy when Jono needs me to though. I'm Emma Zhang, alpha of the Tempest pack."

Monica nodded thoughtfully. "I've heard of you."

Emma shrugged. "Been a lot of rumors running through the

packs in this country over the last year. Hopefully that doesn't color your opinion."

"I don't see anything wrong with throwing your support behind any alpha who wasn't Estelle and Youssef. Neither do my alphas." Monica looked at Jono. "They say hello, by the way, and want you to know I speak for them in full. We've brought willing fighters from a dozen Chicago packs."

"We appreciate the support," Jono said.

Other dires spoke up, representatives of god packs who'd thrown their lot in with Jono's: San Francisco, Los Angeles, Houston, Miami, and New Orleans to name a few. The bar was teeming with werecreatures who wouldn't have set foot in New York City if Estelle and Youssef had still been in charge.

"Not everyone is here with us. We thought the bar would get too crowded, so most of the people we brought are all back at the hotel. We'll inform them of what our orders are," Ava Jepsen said.

A couple of other dires murmured they'd done the same, which made sense. Jono poured himself a beer, opting to stay behind the bar. Emma remained with him, though she poured herself a cider to sip at.

"I know the request was out of the ordinary, but we appreciate the aid your alphas sent us," Jono said.

"Would've been bad form to say no to a patron animal-god," Calvin Tran said. He was dire to the LA god pack, a man in his late twenties with thick black hair and wolf-bright amber eyes.

Jono shrugged. "I asked, not Fenrir."

Calvin smiled thinly. "You're favored by him. My alphas treated your words as his."

It was still strange to know that Fenrir was a presence other packs were aware of. It lent their tiny god pack standing they wouldn't otherwise have, but Jono had spent years letting no one know Fenrir had teeth and claws sunk into his mind and soul. The god might not have a physical form, but that's what Jono was for, and everyone in the bar seemed aware of that.

In reality, they couldn't have kept the god a secret, not after the fight in Central Park, not with the way packs talked. In the end, the god's favor had enabled Jono to bring in more packs for the fight ahead. The logistics of getting the packs situated would be easier if they knew where the bloody hell Ethan was.

"Any hunter troubles where you're from?" Jono asked.

"Here and there. Your warning about the demons was appreciated. What do we need to know about what's going on here?" Monica asked.

Jono mulled over what he could say without giving away the secrets they still had to keep. "Do you know what happened in Paris?"

Monica arched an eyebrow as she swirled the toothpick with the olives speared on it in her drink. "The zombie attack? Who hasn't?"

"We expect something similar to happen. Odds are it'll start here in New York City on Samhain."

"How sure are you about that?"

Jono leaned his weight against the counter, gaze drifting over the crowd. "This city is an altar more so than others. The government is treating it as ground zero, even if that isn't public knowledge. It's why we needed more support. Paris was nearly overrun, even with the preternatural community coming out in force to push back. We're trying to make sure that doesn't happen here."

"The news has been talking about the Dominion Sect lately, especially after what happened last night. Is that who we'll be facing?"

Jono nodded. "It won't just be the packs. We have alliances with local covens, the fae, and the Night Courts. They'll all be fighting alongside us."

Monica seemed surprised about that, as were others in the crowd. "Vampires?"

"They're annoying but useful sometimes," Emma drawled.

"True," Jono said with a snort. "There will be others, we hope.

Some of the support is run through the SOA, so I can't disclose that information right now, but Patrick has made the agency aware of the werecreature community's support."

Some in the crowd appeared uneasy at that statement. Those werecreatures who weren't god pack members risked their anonymity in the fight ahead, but Jono had to believe they were aware of the risk when they volunteered to come here.

"How do you plan to fight the Dominion Sect?" Monica asked.

Jono shrugged and spread his hands. "Block by block."

He and Patrick had worked out the framework of a defense drawn from their experience in Paris. They'd taken input from their allies, and they had a rough plan. He only hoped it would work when the fighting started.

Monica nodded slowly, gaze thoughtful. "We'll trust your lead."

More like they'd trust Fenrir. Jono was willing to leverage the god's presence as much as he needed to if it would gain them more people for their side of the fight. They couldn't trust that the gods of heaven would come when called. They needed to act like they had no cavalry waiting in the wings, because they didn't.

"Anyone need another drink?" Jono asked.

A few people piped up with their requests, and he went about making them some.

***

"Hey," Marek said from the sofa, not looking up from his laptop.

Jono shut the door to Marek and Sage's flat, Emma having stopped off on the floor below where she and Leon lived. The Art Deco building was quite large, the center of a mix of Tempest pack territory and god pack territory.

Hamilton Heights was the traditional territory Jono had no desire to live in right now. He wondered if they could offer it up to any of the packs joining the fight who needed a place to stay. He'd need to take it up with Sage.

"Is Sage still at work?" Jono asked.

Marek nodded. "She's planning to stay late. She has a lot on her desk to offload, and it doesn't even include pack issues. Deadlines can't wait, no matter what gods want."

Jono grimaced, hoping they weren't stretching Sage too thin. Tiarnán was a name partner at Gentry & Thyme, a *duine sídhe*, and one of their fae allies. Jono doubted Tiarnán would fire her, but it was a balance they'd have to work on in the future.

Jono went to the kitchen and rummaged in the refrigerator for any leftovers that could make up a very late lunch. He went through the Chinese takeout cartons he found and carried the plate of food back to the living area once it was heated up.

Only when half the food was gone did he speak. "Have you seen anything?"

Marek's fingers stilled on his laptop, hazel eyes meeting Jono's. "If I had, you and Patrick would be the first to know. Right now, everything is just black. Empty."

"Empty?"

Marek set his laptop on the coffee table and slouched on the sofa, rubbing his eyes. Being a seer might be financially lucrative and come with federal security support when needed, but the cost was brutal. Jono still felt guilty for Marek's loss of color when it came to everything surrounding Patrick.

"Ever since Patrick came to New York, it's been difficult to see anything, but I could always feel the Norns looking at the future when I searched for a vision. Lately it's as if nothing is there, not even a wall. It's a void."

Jono thought about Ginnungagap and the beginning it represented, and the end Fenrir had embodied once before, laid down in a story become myth, lost to history. He didn't know which way they were careening toward, but he hoped it was where they were all alive when it was all over.

"Don't look," Jono said.

Marek dropped his hands to his lap, giving Jono a wan smile. "I already promised Sage I wouldn't."

"Good."

"How did the meeting go with the outside packs?"

"As expected. I don't know if they'll be enough in the end, or even if we had them come to the right city, but they're here."

"More is always better when fighting the hells."

Jono could only agree.

They sat in silence for a couple of minutes before Marek got to his feet with a heavy sigh, heading to the kitchen. When he came back, he had two beers in hand, one of which he offered to Jono. Despite the amount of alcohol he'd had at the bar, Jono didn't turn it down.

"You're worried," Marek said, retaking his seat on the sofa.

"I'd be a bloody fool not to be." Jono picked at the label stuck to the bottle, staring blankly at the opaque glass. "Patrick thinks whoever killed Setsuna was aiming for him."

"Are you surprised?"

Jono grimaced, taking a swallow of beer. "No. They've been after him since before I met him. This was different."

"How so?"

"If they weren't aiming for him and were aiming for Setsuna, then Ethan's going after the people close to him."

Marek frowned, the spike of worry in his scent making Jono's nose itch. "Do you think your pack is in danger?"

"That's our general status right now."

"You know what I mean."

Jono slouched in the armchair and stretched out his legs. "Ethan was after Patrick's blood for that fertility rite Cernunnos most likely did. If he got what he wanted, then he has no need to keep Patrick around."

"So you *do* think the shooter was targeting him."

Jono closed his eyes and dredged up the old, violent memory of when he was Ethan's prisoner last year, how the mage had reveled in torture. How pleased he'd looked in the face of Jono's agony.

"I think Ethan wants to hurt Patrick before killing him. Patrick doesn't care about his own skin, but he's proven he cares about us," Jono said slowly.

"That makes you a target."

"*Us*. I'm sure Ethan knows the lot of you are allies, and he's the sort of bloke to salt and burn."

Marek brought his beer to his mouth and chugged it. When he finished, he let out a burp. "Well, we have a week until we're either all dead or all alive. I'll tell Emma to have our pack double up how we did when the hunters were in town and implement some check-in requirements."

"That's what I was going to suggest to Pat and Sage for all the packs to do. We're a week out until Samhain. Hunters are probably already in town."

"If they are, they're lying low like the Sluagh, unless they've all fucked off to some other city."

Jono grunted agreement before finishing off his beer and leftovers. "I'd wager the bar that the whole bloody mess happens here."

Marek smiled wanly at him. "Don't tell me you're a seer now."

"Not in the least."

The future might not be knowable beyond the upcoming fight, but Jono was determined to make sure it wouldn't end how Marek had seen it before—with a graveyard.

Patrick was lying on the couch, sprawled against Jono as they watched the Saturday night news, when his phone rang. He reached for where it sat on the coffee table, fingers scrabbling at it. He finally got a grip and lifted it to eye level. He didn't recognize the number on the screen, but he answered anyway. He knew too many people who used burner numbers these days to send it to voicemail.

"Special Agent Patrick Collins. Line and—"

"Get to Ginnungagap," Lucien snarled, his voice difficult to hear over the music on his side of the line.

Patrick shoved himself to a sitting position, swinging his legs around so he could plant his feet on the floor. "What happened?"

"Constructs just tried to enter the club. Ashanti is keeping them at bay, but they're still outside and don't seem in any hurry to leave."

"Constructs?"

"Jaguars."

The scent-memory of marigolds was suddenly in Patrick's

nose, and he had to swallow against the rise of bile in the back of his throat. "Tezcatlipoca?"

"Just fucking get here."

Lucien ended the call. Patrick stood and shoved the phone into his back pocket on his way to the bedroom to retrieve his dagger and pistol, Jono half a step behind.

"Do you want Sage and Wade to meet us there?" Jono asked, shoving his feet into his shoes.

"Wade doesn't have to come if he doesn't want to. I'd rather he didn't, to be honest," Patrick said as he yanked on his leather jacket.

"I'll let them know."

Patrick didn't want Wade to have to face off against the god who had held him captive and forced him to fight to the death in order to survive. Patrick knew a thing or two about facing off against nightmares, and if he could spare Wade that, he would. Besides, it wasn't like Wade would have room to shift mass. Most of Manhattan's streets were pretty narrow for a dragon.

He and Jono left the safety of their apartment and took the stairs down to the ground floor two steps at a time. Patrick slammed open the building's front door, making one of the gargoyles on the stoop railing hiss in that rough voice they all had. A handful had come off the front of the building to guard the entrance. The reason for their territorial attitude were a couple of reporters lurking on the sidewalk, the last stubborn holdouts of the media wanting Patrick's opinion on Setsuna's death.

He fucking hated them.

"Do you have a statement you'd like to give the American people on who you think is behind the death of SOA Director Setsuna Abuku?" one woman asked, spitting the words out so fast they ran together.

Her phone was thrust in their direction as they reached the sidewalk. Patrick could see the recording app running on the screen of her phone. He bit his tongue to hold back how badly he wanted to tell the media to fuck off.

"No comment," Patrick gritted out as they headed for the Mustang parked at the corner of the block.

"It's being reported you were present when she died. How does her death affect your standing with the SOA after everything that happened over the summer?"

"Fuck off," Jono snarled, clearly as annoyed as Patrick was.

The woman was persistent, as were the other two vying for a comment. Patrick bit his tongue, knowing that to do anything but look straight ahead and ignore them would only feed their desire for answers.

Setsuna had always taught him *no comment* was the greatest defense against the media. He was all set to respond that way when recognition cut through his magic so hard he nearly doubled over. The presence of hell exploded in the street, searing through him.

Jono's hand caught him by the shoulder even as Patrick ripped his shields outward to cover where they stood. The reporters startled hard at the manifestation of his magic, eyes going wide when he conjured up half a dozen mageglobes right as a hellfire bomb crashed against his layered shields.

Defensive magic wasn't his affinity, but he'd been in fights like this often enough to know how to dig in and hold on. He sank his awareness into the soulbond, reaching through Jono's soul for the ley line snaking below the earth because he'd long since lost the ability to channel it through his own soul. He tapped the wild magic and poured external power into his mageglobes, setting them with strike spells.

The reporters screamed, running past where Jono and Patrick stood, looking for a way out, only to crash into his shields. They had nowhere to go, and their panic would be a problem.

Then the gas tanks on two nearby cars exploded, and their screams got louder.

The fierce heat melded with the hellfire, creating a fireball that blew toward the sky. Patrick extended his shields with a snarl, the pale blue glint of his magic reflecting the flames as he struggled to encase the explosion before spot fires took hold on the surrounding buildings.

Hellfire was like magical napalm, and the horrendous stuff burned through anything, even magic given enough time. If some of the hellfire made it onto the buildings, they'd have an even worse problem.

Not like they weren't already in the midst of one.

Hellfire meant Hades, and Patrick wouldn't mind shoving his dagger into that god's back if the bastard showed up.

Concentrating on the explosion meant he didn't see the mage-globe with the strike spell cutting through the smoke until it exploded against his shields, tearing into them. The world went strangely quiet beyond the ringing in his ears. Luckily, his eardrums didn't rupture, even if the top layer of his shields did. Patrick threw up another layer to shore up his defenses, squinting through the smoke at the shadows coming their way, ignoring the ache blooming in the back of his head.

Sickly red-orange magic that Patrick thought was fire at first flickered in the air. Then the mageglobe became more prominent as Zachary Myers stepped through the veil, guided by an emaciated woman that made Patrick freeze where he stood.

Santa Muerte hadn't changed much since the last time she'd stepped foot in New York City. She was like a walking skeleton, skin stretched tight over bone, the black dress she wore with its heavily embroidered skirt overwhelming her desiccated form. Her hair was braided into a crown, marigolds tucked amongst the sections like a flowery halo, the color starkly bright.

Her face was painted like a sugar skull, the black-and-red detailing around her eyes and mouth coming across like bruises in the light from the still-roiling explosion of hellfire and gasoline behind Patrick's shaky shields. Her pitch-black eyes reminded him of Ashanti's and Lucien's, but that's where any similarities ended.

Behind them came a dozen other men and women, some dressed like hunters, others obvious Dominion Sect magic users, spells sparking at their fingertips. The veil they'd slipped through with Santa Muerte's help seemed ragged at the edges, threadbare and worn. The Dagda's warning about how the veil was eroding from the other side day by day rang like a warning siren through Patrick's mind.

Jono shifted with a crunch of bones and the wet sound of tearing flesh. The shift was quicker than any other werecreature could ever do, urged on by Fenrir. Patrick spared a glance at the massive werewolf now standing beside him, eyes burning white when they'd normally be bright blue.

"We have an audience," Patrick hissed.

"*I've summoned ones who can fix that,*" Fenrir said, the words scraped out of a throat not meant to speak.

He hoped that meant backup. They could really use some.

Patrick yanked his dagger free and realigned his mageglobes. The matte-black blade burned with white heavenly fire, silvery prayers floating across the metal. "Zachary."

Ethan's favored acolyte spread his tattooed hands, summoning up more mageglobes. The spells didn't contain any more hellfire bombs, but the magic users with Zachary might have some in reserve.

"I heard you went home. You'll never be wanted by that blood," Zachary sneered.

"I'm not wanted by Ethan."

"You've always been wanted in some form or another."

"Dead isn't a good look on me."

Zachary smiled, teeth flashing red in the light of his magic. "How was that visit with your grandmother? I'm sure she was far more polite to you than she was to me."

Despite the heat coming off the hellfire, Patrick felt as if he'd been doused in ice water. "What?"

"Thresholds are meaningless when it comes to blood. I hear she welcomed you with open arms."

It hurt to breathe, cold sweat breaking out down his spine at the implications of Zachary's words. Somehow, Patrick didn't think Zachary was talking about the visit he and Jono had done.

There was no time to process the threat, not when they were so clearly outnumbered with civilians to protect. Patrick gestured sharply with his left hand, and his mageglobes streaked forward through his shields, twisting through the air toward the enemy.

Zachary countered the ones aiming for him easily enough. Patrick's strike spells broke on the other mage's shield, the pale blue shine of his magic tearing itself apart. The other mageglobes were thrown back at him by Santa Muerte's power, never finding their target.

Patrick rocked back on his heels as his mageglobes slammed into his shields. He absorbed the magic, bones aching as he sent the excess down into the earth through the soulbond to ground it. A ripple ran through the shield, and Patrick swore, tightening his grip around his dagger.

Fenrir snarled, the noise drowning out the screams of the reporters behind them. Then he threw back his head and howled, the sound echoing in the night air with enough magic in the call to make Patrick's teeth ache.

The soulbond pulled tight between him and Jono. Patrick could sense the power in Fenrir's cry for support from surrounding packs. What good they'd do against a goddess, Patrick didn't know, but he'd take what help they could get right now.

*Your children will not be enough, cousin,* Santa Muerte said.

The goddess extended her arms, and a black scythe materialized in her hands. She curled her bony fingers around the long snaith, not looking as if she had the strength to wield such a large weapon, but wield it she did.

Santa Muerte lunged forward, bringing the scythe down in a

slashing motion that could cleave a man in two. The hunters with guns opened fire around her, aiming for Patrick's shields. His shields wouldn't last long against spelled bullets and an immortal's weapon.

Fenrir lunged forward, pushing through Patrick's shields with enough force that his head throbbed. Patrick shifted the radius of his shields, shrinking it so Fenrir didn't break them.

"A little warning would be nice!" Patrick snapped as he conjured up a couple more mageglobes.

Fenrir ignored him, intent on getting his teeth into Santa Muerte. Space was limited on the sidewalk, the burning hellfire nearby heating the air to the point Patrick's cooling charms on his leather jacket were activated automatically.

The bullets stopped flying, but the spells replacing them hit like a freight train. Patrick stepped back from the physical blows against his shields, his focus wavering. He patched over the cracks and let his own mageglobes fly. His attack was hampered by Fenrir in Jono's body fighting Santa Muerte directly in front of him.

Needing space to maneuver better, Patrick spun around and peeled his shields open on the back end. The reporters were frozen in place from fear, but they got moving when Patrick grabbed two by the arm and yanked them forward. He needed them out of the line of fire if he was going to survive this fight.

"*Move*," he snapped, slamming the edge of his shield against the nearest building. "Up the stairs!"

He didn't have a key to the apartment building, but he had a mageglobe, and it shattered the glass pane on the door easily enough. Thresholds existed around individual apartments, not the building's very public entrance, which was why his magic wasn't stopped. One of the reporters shoved her arm through the open space, frantically reaching for the lock to get the door open. The small group hurried inside the questionable safety of the building, but anything was better than the street right now.

Patrick took his eyes off them once they were inside, but that brief moment of distraction was all it took for one of Zachary's mageglobes to slam *through* his shield with enough force his vision went black at the edges.

He dived out of the way of the attack on instinct, head spinning, and ended up between the bumpers of two parked cars. Patrick coughed air out of his lungs, feeling as if he'd been punched in the gut hard enough to bruise. The mageglobe exploded some distance away, shattering windows.

Patrick struggled to his feet, reeling from the realization that Zachary's magic had slipped past his defenses because it wasn't just the fucker's magic. Zachary was adept at blood magic, and what had been threaded through his spell was drops of Ethan's blood.

*"Fuck,"* Patrick spat out, throwing himself into the street, heart practically in his throat. "Jono!"

He needed Jono with him, to know the other man was *safe*. He couldn't lose Jono the way he'd already lost Setsuna and possibly Eloise.

Patrick's magic was caught between keeping up his multitude of shields and needing to cast spells to keep Zachary and the others at bay. His ability to defend was shit if Zachary could bypass his magic using Ethan's blood.

Because blood would always call to blood, even if Ethan wasn't standing right in front of him.

Hunters veered around the burning mass of hellfire still contained in Patrick's increasingly shaky shields, weapons in hand and demons staring out of their eyes. He turned to face them, drawing more power from the ley line and channeling it into three mageglobes. The shockwave spells took shape, the command trigger resting on the tip of his tongue. He released the mageglobes at the same time the hunters opened fire.

The glittering wave of magic ripped through the air. The concussive force it carried rocked nearby cars on their wheels, blew out windows, and sent the bullets flying in all directions. The hunters were thrown back, landing hard on the asphalt. Patrick doubted any of them were truly incapacitated, but it bought him a few seconds' reprieve.

Not that it was worth much.

Not having permanent shield anchors burned into his bones meant he had to consciously funnel some of his magic and concentration at all times to his shields. Patrick was stretched thin even with tapping a ley line, and Zachary had a way through his defenses that Patrick couldn't wholly defend against.

The attack from the sidewalk shattered his personal shields, and Patrick went down on one knee to make a smaller target. Blinding pain from backlash cut through his skull, but he forced it aside because to give in was a good way to die.

Zachary strode toward him, hands shaping a mageglobe between them, tattooed palms dripping blood. "Your father wants you back."

"Fuck you and fuck Ethan," Patrick snarled, trying desperately to raise his personal shields again. His magic was brittle and barely holding shape. It was all he could do to keep the shields up around the hellfire still burning in the street.

Zachary hurtled the mageglobe at Patrick, malice in his eyes. Patrick raised his dagger as a last defense against magic designed to break through his own. Jono let out a howl, or maybe Fenrir did, the sound echoed by other werecreatures in the distance and racing closer. None of them would reach Patrick in time, but it didn't matter.

PIA Special Agent Nadine Mulroney always had his six when he was trapped in a corner.

A violet-tinged shield slammed down between Patrick and Zachary's attack, the mageglobe exploding harmlessly against a defense that would take more power than Zachary had at his disposal to break through. Patrick blinked at the shield before wrenching his head around, eyes going wide.

Nadine, flanked by Shiva and Áłtsé Hashké in his coyote form, raced down the street toward them, the shimmer of the veil sealing up weakly behind them.

"Collins!" Nadine shouted, flinging a mageglobe forward in advance of her rush.

"Mulroney!" he called back.

Another violet-tinged shield wrapped around the hellfire burning in the street, and Patrick gratefully withdrew his own battered shield. Concentration no longer split, he rose to his feet to square off against Zachary. The other mage had come to a stop at Nadine's arrival, mageglobes in hand but spells not yet cast. The frustrated snarl on his face told Patrick that Zachary hadn't anticipated the surprise backup.

Nadine skidded to a stop next to Patrick, wearing leggings and a loose T-shirt beneath a stylish trench coat. She had sneakers on her feet rather than heels. It wasn't the sort of outfit one wore to a fight but to travel.

"Glad to see you, but what the hell are you doing here?" Patrick asked.

"My director is recalling field agents. I was getting off a flight in DC earlier when I got picked up by those two," Nadine said, jerking her thumb at Shiva and Áłtsé Hashké.

The pair of immortals had bypassed Zachary altogether in favor of backing up Fenrir against Santa Muerte. It had been a stalemate before their arrival, and now it was three against one, odds which didn't favor the goddess or the Dominion Sect supporters she'd dragged through the veil.

Patrick knew when that realization hit Zachary. He saw the moment the other mage tried to retreat, but his avenues of escape were supremely limited. Patrick raised his dagger and stepped forward.

"Let me through. I'm going to kill that fucker," he said.

Nadine grabbed him by the elbow, fingers digging in. "We need to get you out of here."

"Fuck that. He—"

Patrick broke off as inky black shadows erupted from the street to curl around Zachary. Santa Muerte's shroud was like a living thing that pulled the mage into her skeletal arms and through the veil.

Patrick slammed the hilt of his dagger against Nadine's shield in frustration. "Gods fucking damn it!"

The hunters and other Dominion Sect magic users had been left behind, much to the demons' fury. They no longer only faced Patrick, Nadine, and a couple of immortals. Rounding the corners at both ends of the street came numerous werecreatures, followed by a couple of NYPD squad cars and the first FDNY fire engine to make it to the scene.

Amidst the new arrivals, movement from above caught Patrick's eyes. Muninn and Huginn dived down to perch on a stoop railing. Their targets were the reporters from before who'd snuck out of the apartment building to record the fight. Odin's ravens wasted no time at pecking at the reporters' skulls, their beaks passing through flesh and bone to steal their thoughts and memories, their targets none the wiser.

The immortals had done the same thing in Chicago before Yggdrasil burst through the veil, leaving the guests at the fundraiser dinner remembering nothing of that night. The memory loss left holes in people's lives, moments lost forever they would never get back. Patrick was reminded of what Maat had mentioned back in August when they'd strolled the National Mall. His stomach twisted as he realized the Egyptian goddess had been right after all.

"Killing Ethan won't be enough," Patrick said.

Nadine pressed her hand against her shield, glancing back at him. "What do you mean?"

Patrick watched Muninn and Huginn launch themselves back into the air. "It's like the Hydra. Cut off one head, two more take its place."

Ethan's death would be meaningless if what supported his

efforts wasn't cut down with him. Killing the memory of what Ethan had built was the only way to win, but Patrick didn't have the power to do that.

Only the gods did.

"We'll figure out a game plan later. I'm not the only one the joint task force is sending out here." Nadine pointed at the hunters and Dominion Sect magic users currently contained under one of her shields and surrounded by snarling werecreatures. "I'll handle those bastards. Go check on Jono."

Nadine lowered the shield surrounding them and started down the street. Mageglobes flickered into existence around her before streaking away toward the handful of conscious Dominion Sect magic users who needed to be contained.

Patrick left her to handle that problem. He kept his dagger and a mageglobe at the ready as he returned to the sidewalk, letting out a quick, heavy sigh of relief when he got eyes on Jono. Santa Muerte had thankfully not doubled back, though Shiva hadn't disappeared how Patrick thought the god would in the face of mortal attention.

"This was not the only incursion," Shiva said as Patrick approached.

"I know. Lucien said Ashanti was holding off jaguar constructs over at Ginnungagap. I'm guessing Tezcatlipoca hit that location while Santa Muerte came here for a two-pronged attack," Patrick replied.

The god stroked the snake coiled about his shoulders, third eye barely open as he looked at Patrick. "I will check on our cousin."

Shiva stepped backward through the veil and disappeared as only a god could. Jono shifted back to human in a churning motion of breaking bone and blood-spattered skin. His clothes were a lost cause, having been ripped to bits during the initial shift. At least they were close to their apartment and he'd be able to easily replace them.

"Are you all right?" Jono asked, stepping close to settle his hands on Patrick's shoulders.

Patrick swallowed, shields down, not knowing what Jono was getting off his scent but not really caring either. "Zachary used Ethan's blood to get through my magic. I think that means they still want me alive."

Jono's mouth twisted with worry. "They can't have you."

Patrick wasn't sure how long he'd be able to stay one step ahead of Ethan when they kept circling each other like sharks in the lead up to Samhain. "We need to go back to Salem."

"Why?"

Patrick flexed his fingers around the hilt of his dagger, Zachary's words leaving him a little nauseous. "I think something's happened to Eloise."

Jono's grip tightened hard enough to bruise before he pressed a dry kiss to Patrick's forehead. "We'll drive up as soon as we can."

Patrick gazed out over the ruined street, hellfire still burning behind Nadine's shields, wondering if New York City would end up like Cairo during the Thirty-Day War after all.

13

"THIS ISN'T GOING TO PLAY WELL IN THE PRESS, NOT AFTER THE summer we've had," Casale said as he squinted down the street at the hellfire that wasn't yet completely put out.

Jono scowled, attention on where Patrick stood as he coordinated the cleanup with Nadine and a handful of other SOA agents. Their street was teeming with police officers, federal agents, and firefighters despite the hour turning past midnight from Saturday night to Sunday morning. Several of the buildings had been evacuated while the hellfire bomb was taken care of, with the Red Cross handling their displacement for the night.

Packs that had come to their aid earlier had been sent home by Jono once their statements were taken by the police and SOA under strict anonymity. Before all of that, Jono had dodged back inside their flat after the scene was initially secured in order to grab a change of clothes. Chatting with police while naked was never something he liked doing.

"This isn't our fault," Jono said.

Casale pursed his lips. "I'm not saying it is. The pair of you were targets. I have multiple eyewitnesses who will attest to that, including several reporters. But a street turning into a warzone is never going to shine a positive light on anyone."

It was only going to get worse, whether Casale knew it or not. Their pack's professional relationship with the PCB was strained, and the nascent one Jono had with Casale had been torn up back in August. But he didn't have it in him to risk innocent people if a warning could help. Angelina and the covens might have been warned, but hard specifics hadn't been shared because of government restrictions.

"Has the SOA kept you updated on what's been going on with the Dominion Sect?" Jono asked.

"The NYPD as a whole received a level orange threat warning from that agency."

Jono eyed what remained of the hellfire before turning his back on that mess. "Bit more than a threat now, if you ask me."

"You and Collins have been at the dead center of every major preternatural or supernatural event or attack this city has dealt with since last summer, not to mention some other cities. Angelina said the covens are preparing as if they're expecting a war. Tell me straight, Jono. What is coming at us?"

Jono scratched at an itch on his jaw as he turned away. "Your wife is right. We're looking at war. Talk to the mayor. Tell him to set a curfew again. Things are going to get messy."

He walked away from Casale because this mess wasn't the only attack they needed to deal with. According to Patrick, the SOA was covering the attack here and the one at Ginnungagap. They didn't have any information yet on what had occurred over there, and Jono knew they still needed to find out. Lucien was bound to be in a temper, which would put Patrick in a mood, and Jono wasn't looking forward to that headache.

Patrick saw his approach and extricated himself from the other SOA agents to meet Jono halfway. Nadine came with him, casting a discreet silence ward that made Jono's ears pop from the sudden quiet.

"Nadine said General Reed has recalled the Hellraisers and Spencer," Patrick said.

"When do they arrive?" Jono asked.

"Hopefully soon. They're all outside the country right now. My guess is transport is being arranged."

"Paperwork is being pushed through," Nadine confirmed. "They're not the only ones coming back."

Jono crossed his arms over his chest. "Is the government focusing the bulk of their support here or elsewhere now?"

Patrick looked down the street at the first responders doing their best to contain the damage, and Jono followed his gaze. "I think if Ethan isn't going to use Manhattan and the surrounding boroughs as a sacrificial altar, it's a damn good distraction from wherever he actually will."

"Odds are high the fight happens here," Nadine said, crossing her arms over her chest.

Jono glanced over his shoulder at the Mustang, having miraculously survived the fight unscathed by virtue of where it had been parked. "We should stop by Ginnungagap before heading to Salem."

"Nadine?" Patrick asked.

"I'll come with you. I'm of more use to you while dealing with Lucien than if I stay behind. This isn't my purview," she said.

She worked for the Preternatural Intelligence Agency and was stationed out of Paris. The PIA handled international problems, while the SOA laid claim to domestic ones. Jono wasn't sure which agency had the best claim to whatever came from past the veil right now, but she'd retracted all her magic from the street once other magic users had arrived.

"We can drop you off wherever you need to be afterward," Patrick said on the walk to the car.

"My luggage is probably sitting on a carousel in JFK. It had my service weapon in it."

"It'll hopefully still be there."

"The lockbox is spelled to my fingerprints, so it's as safe as it can be for right now. I just hate leaving things behind right now."

"You're a nice surprise though," Jono said.

Nadine smiled tightly. "Getting picked up by a couple of gods and traveling through the veil was unexpected, but definitely quicker than sitting in traffic."

"What was it like past the veil?" Patrick asked.

Nadine didn't answer until they were in the car and on their way, her silence ward long since broken. "The veil is thin. Ragged. Like it's being ripped apart from the other side layer by layer. I know it's always thinner around this time of year and we get more incursions from other planes, but this seemed different. It *felt* different."

Jono grimaced as he maneuvered the Mustang past the last police line a block and a half away from their home. "That's what the gods warned us about."

Everyone was quiet for a few more minutes as Jono kept to the speed limit on the drive away from their flat. The number of police cars in their general area was way more than usual, and he didn't fancy getting pulled over for going a tad over the speed limit because the police were jumpy. He'd get out of any ticket with two federal agents in the car with him, but they didn't need any further delay.

They were waiting at a red light when Nadine broke the silence. "I'm sorry about Setsuna."

Out of the corner of his eye, Jono saw Patrick stiffen in the front passenger seat. His hands curled into fists over his thighs, but Jono couldn't get any scent off Patrick. His personal shields were locked down tighter than ever.

"They were aiming for me," Patrick said.

"They are always aiming for you."

"She shouldn't have been collateral."

"Everyone is collateral in some way to Ethan's ego and greed.

Even you. Don't blame yourself for her death. You didn't pull that trigger."

Her voice was quiet, a kindness to her tone that didn't make Patrick look as if he wanted to hit something. Patrick and Nadine had a past with shared experiences Jono would never live through. He only hoped she could give Patrick a sort of comfort that Jono didn't have the background to give. Patrick could use all the support he could get right now.

"I know," Patrick finally said as the light turned green.

Believing it would be another story. Jono had spent months trying to get Patrick to unlearn bad habits and recognize he wasn't alone. What forward momentum they'd made in that area was quickly losing ground after the last couple of weeks.

Jono pressed down on the gas pedal. "Where are we meeting Lucien?"

Patrick slouched a little in his seat. "We aren't. Carmen is the only one who remained on scene. The rest of the vampires scattered."

"I bet that's going to piss off the police."

"She's acting under her guise as the human owner of the club."

"Is it the same alias as the one in London?"

"No. It's a different one."

Jono snorted. "She has more names than a bloody titled Catholic."

"She is originally from Venice, remember?"

Whatever her mysterious background, he knew Carmen wouldn't be pleased to see them. When they arrived, it took both Patrick's SOA badge and Nadine's PIA one to get Jono past the police manning the cordoned-off area. His eyes apparently made everyone jumpy tonight.

Jono winced at the acrid scent of hell still lingering on the air, despite the wind. It had been over a year since they'd fought Tezcatlipoca, but he still remembered what that god smelled like, the same way he'd known Santa Muerte. It wasn't a coincidence those two immortals had attacked at the same time.

Patrick led the way down the cordoned-off street with Nadine by his side, and Jono stayed close to the pair. As they approached Ginnungagap, Jono could see the front door had been completely ripped off its frame and tossed into the street in pieces. A hole had been punched through the front-facing wall, the damage bigger than a human could pass through.

He didn't miss the bodies covered in yellow tarp or the blood splatters all over the pavement.

"Fuck," Patrick said under his breath.

"Mayor needs to set a bloody curfew," Jono said.

"No shit."

They flagged down the officer in charge of the scene, not a bloke any of them were familiar with. The officer was out of the PCB and seemed aware of who they were, at least.

"Is the SOA taking over?" the officer asked.

"It's a possibility. Right now I want to make sure the Dominion Sect didn't leave any surprises after the hit at my place," Patrick said easily.

"Our magic users cleared the area."

"Great. Any witnesses?"

"Plenty. We've taken statements and let most go home who weren't wounded. The injured were sent off to various hospitals. The owner is still inside with a couple of workers."

"Wonderful."

It really wasn't, in Jono's opinion.

They headed through the damaged front entrance into Ginnungagap, bypassing the abandoned security checkpoint. The overhead lights were disturbingly bright compared to the last time they'd stopped by.

Chairs and tables had been overturned during the panic, but he didn't see any bodies. The scent of fear was tacky in the back of his throat as he breathed. Police officers milled about, but the blokes weren't interested in Jono's little group. Patrick made a beeline to where Carmen sat, wrapped in her human glamour, at the ground-floor bar, legs crossed at the knee, manicured nails tapping hard against the counter while Naheed tidied up behind it.

Jono didn't think he'd ever seen someone sip so murderously at a cocktail before.

"You're late," Carmen snapped once they were in earshot.

"We were busy getting *attacked*, just like you," Patrick said, though he kept his voice low.

Carmen smiled thinly at him, eyes strangely blue in her face, while her hair was a dark brown, sleekly straight as opposed to her normal black curls. "We held off the attack, but not before attendees got taken out in the crossfire. What is it with humans panicking like fools?"

"We've always run from the monsters in the world."

Carmen knocked back half her drink in one swallow before putting the delicate-looking glass on the counter with more care than Jono thought she'd give it. "Ward us."

It was Nadine, not Patrick, who cast the silence ward, mage-globe tiny against her palm, fingers curled around it. Quiet settled over their area, and Jono half turned to keep an eye on everyone else around them so they wouldn't be surprised if others approached. They'd had enough bad optics with keeping secrets over the summer. They didn't need to give the police an excuse to be suspicious in a situation like this.

"We thought Tezcatlipoca was banished, along with Santa Muerte," Carmen said.

"He was, as far as I know. But it's almost Samhain, and Ethan is carving out the veil from the inside out. The gods and other immortals are coming out of the woodwork," Patrick replied.

"We had some other Night Courts present tonight who didn't believe gods were real."

"Don't they pray to Ashanti?" Jono asked.

Carmen shot him a vicious look. "They have always prayed, but belief in her is not the same as belief in others."

"I bet they believe now," Nadine drawled.

Carmen smiled, though it lacked humor. "Tezcatlipoca wasn't expecting Ashanti to have returned. It would've been a different fight otherwise."

Jono would've said that was a shame, but it wasn't the political thing to voice. Sage would've been proud of him for holding his tongue.

"I wanted to make sure no one was dead," Patrick said after a moment.

Carmen studied him for a handful of seconds. "Ashanti heard about Setsuna. She wants to see you."

"Is she here?" Jono asked.

"No. She went chasing after Tezcatlipoca before losing him in the veil. She's home now, but she'll come out to neutral territory to speak with you."

Surprisingly, Patrick shook his head. "It'll have to be tomorrow."

Carmen's eyes narrowed. "This isn't up for discussion."

"Zachary knows I went to see Eloise. He says he *saw* her. I have to go and make sure she's okay."

Nadine looked at him in surprise. "I didn't know you'd gone to visit her."

Patrick grimaced, his jaw clenched tight. "I couldn't keep ignoring her forever."

"Might've been for the best," Jono murmured.

Nadine shot him a sharp look, the question in her gaze easy enough to read. "Not friendly?"

"Friendly enough on the surface."

"They worship Persephone," Patrick said in a flat, emotionless voice.

Nadine jerked as if she'd been hit, brown eyes going wide. "They *what?*"

Carmen reached for her drink again. "Setsuna always did warn you about them."

"Don't talk about her," Patrick ground out.

"Human lives are fleeting. Her death was always going to happen."

The callousness of her words had Jono stepping between the two so that Patrick didn't do anything he'd regret. If he laid a hand on her in plain view of the police, that would turn into an ordeal they didn't have time for.

Carmen tipped her head back to look Jono in the eye and smirked at him. She looked and smelled human, probably wearing an artifact to help hide hints of her true self the way Sage used to.

"Watch your words," Jono said in a low, harsh voice.

"I speak the truth. Ashanti would say the same thing, for all that she and Setsuna guided him when he was younger."

Jono reached out and covered the top of her drink with his hand. Rather than take it from her, he curled his fingers in toward his palm, shattering the delicate glass and causing the rest of her drink to spill all over her expensive-looking clothes. Carmen hissed at him, the sound nowhere close to human, but she didn't move.

"You don't get to play word games with Pat using Setsuna's name."

Carmen snapped her teeth at him but didn't seem cowed in the least as she brushed shattered glass off her lap. He supposed that's what came from living so long—a sense of inevitable life. But she wasn't immortal and could still be killed. Fenrir rumbled a question through his mind, but Jono mentally shrugged off the offer of murder.

He wondered if some bit of the god had come through somehow—his aura or his eyes maybe, if not his voice—because Carmen's demeanor changed just enough that Jono could see Naheed reach beneath the bar counter out of the corner of his eye, most likely going for a weapon.

"We're on the same side until after Samhain," Jono reminded her, moving so that he could once again see everyone in the club.

"And after, we will no longer be bound by alliances," Carmen said in a low, sweetly dangerous voice as she waved off Naheed's protectiveness. "None of this changes the fact Ashanti wants to see Patrick."

"Tomorrow night. We'll make the time."

"Now."

"Jono's right. We'll meet with Ashanti tomorrow night at a place of her choosing. We're going to Salem tonight, and I need to deal with the SOA tomorrow at some point regarding the attacks," Patrick countered.

"You are not going to Salem tonight," Nadine said with a frown.

"We have to. A phone call isn't going to cut it."

He didn't know Eloise well enough to ask over a phone call, which was why he had no plans to reach out to her. There was no truth to be found in a call, not right now. Setsuna had always warned him about his mother's family, and while they worshipped Persephone, Patrick didn't think they were aligned with any other god. Besides, he knew better than to telegraph their intent right now.

He swallowed hard, the knot lodged in the back of his throat something difficult to undo. Compartmentalizing Setsuna's death didn't mean he forgot her; it merely meant the grief would keep trying to break through at the most inopportune times despite him trying to wall it off.

"You're talking about a four-hour drive. You've been up for almost twenty-four hours already and had to fight off Zachary. You don't know what's waiting for you in Salem."

"Nadine—"

"You know better than to go on a mission blind while fucked out of your head from possible backlash. Get some rack time, a couple of hours at least, and then get on the road. Tired makes you slow. You can't afford to be slow."

"Considering that you don't know what you'll find in Salem, it's even more imperative you meet with Ashanti tonight." Carmen slid off the barstool, her eyes cold.

Nadine hummed softly before nodding at Patrick. "We'll go with Carmen, then back to Sage's to get some sleep. I'll go with both of you to Salem tomorrow. You could use the backup."

Patrick scowled, looking ready to argue, but Jono shook his head. "Unfortunately, I think she's right. And Pat, I love you, but you're *not* thinking straight right now."

Though his tone was kind, Patrick still shut down, expression going absolutely blank. Jono sighed tiredly and stepped closer to wrap his arm around Patrick's shoulders. Patrick didn't lean into him, not right away, but Jono was nothing if not persistent. He wasn't going anywhere, and Patrick eventually folded into his touch.

"You aren't in this alone. If the Fates are to be believed, you were never going to be," Jono murmured.

"Fine," Patrick said after a moment. "We'll see Ashanti tonight."

Carmen gestured at Naheed without looking at her. "Let's go."

Jono lifted his free hand to rub at his eyes. They'd feel like sandpaper right now if he didn't have enhanced healing. He was tired, and the night wasn't over yet.

"Right, let's be off," Jono said, steering Patrick toward the entrance, refusing to let him go.

---

As FAR AS neutral territory went, the New York City Public Library next to Bryant Park was one that offered up a better escape route than most. After how their night had gone so far, Jono much preferred the open-air meeting to one indoors.

Ashanti and Lucien weren't the only ones waiting for them at the park after hours. Several of the vampires Jono remembered seeing at the other meeting were present as well. They stood well away from the nearest streetlamp, Jono's eyes easily picking out the vampires in the dark. Patrick fixed that problem for them by casting a small number of witchlights to illuminate the area enough so he and Nadine didn't trip and fall.

Carmen sauntered her way into Lucien's arms, shedding her glamour like a coat. Lucien pulled her close in a proprietary way.

"You're all right?" Patrick asked Ashanti before anything else.

Ashanti waved aside his words. "Tezcatlipoca was always a fool to think he could ever find me unawares."

"Was anyone else with him? Santa Muerte brought Zachary along with some magic users and hunters when she came after us."

"No one but Tezcatlipoca." Ashanti tipped her head to the side, studying Patrick intently. "It appears we were kept busy while Ethan went after you."

"Yeah, looks like it."

"Samhain is less than a week away at this point. We need to find Ethan. We will use your blood to do it."

"No," Jono got out before Patrick could agree to something so bloody idiotic.

Ashanti's searing attention settled on Jono, but he wasn't one to cave in the face of her desires. "You seek an end to this war, do you not? A means to an end still provides us with an end."

"You aren't using Patrick. Find another fucking way."

"Watch how you talk to her," Takoma snapped.

Jono ignored the out-of-state vampire in favor of the goddess looking for a favor. "We'll talk to her however we like."

Takoma stepped forward before Lucien could, and Fenrir reared up through Jono's soul, stealing control of his voice and body between one breath and the next.

*"There are other tricks in play, cousin. They must be seen to first,"* Fenrir said through Jono.

Takoma was brought up short, while Lucien merely looked bored as he hooked his chin over Carmen's shoulder.

"Enlighten us," Lucien bit out.

"I need to go to Salem. I think Zachary did something to Eloise," Patrick said, looking at Ashanti and not the other vampires.

"*As we said. Tricks,*" Fenrir said.

Lucien flashed his fangs at them. "But no treats. You go to Salem, wolf. When you come back, Patrick bleeds."

Jono railed against that order, but Fenrir didn't let him speak. Patrick was the one to agree, and Jono would've thrown a fit if he could.

"Fine," Patrick said flatly.

Ashanti smiled, iron teeth dark between her lips in the faint glow of witchlights. "I will use the spell book you brought me from DC. You just need to bring yourself."

Fenrir gave Jono back his voice, and he turned his head to scowl at Patrick. "You don't need to bleed for her."

Patrick wouldn't look at him. "This isn't your choice. It's mine."

Jono would've flinched if they were alone, but he refused to give their audience the satisfaction of watching their disagreement. Choice was important, especially considering Patrick's past. Clenching his teeth, Jono kept silent for the rest of the meeting, which was mercifully brief.

With the promise dragged out of Patrick, Ashanti saw no need to stay and fled into the night with all of her children except Lucien. The master vampire stayed behind with Carmen, his black-eyed gaze not friendly in the least.

"You brought Nadine," Lucien said.

"The gods brought her, but she's been recalled by the PIA. So have others," Patrick said.

"What passes as reinforcement from your government has never been very impressive."

"We did all right during the Thirty-Day War."

"Aim to do better than you did back then. Ashanti isn't dying for you again."

"I've never wanted anyone to die for me."

Patrick's voice was quiet, flat in a way that spoke of buried trauma, and Jono wanted badly to hold him. He wouldn't appreciate the outreach in full view of Lucien, so instead, Jono reached for his hand, sliding his fingers between Patrick's.

"Let's head to Sage's," Jono said.

They had a long day ahead of them, and it started with getting a few hours of sleep before they faced whatever—or whoever—waited for them in Salem.

## 14

THEY WERE ON THE ROAD BY DAWN, HAVING ONLY SLEPT A HANDFUL of hours. Patrick's eyes felt as if they had glass in them, the dryness irritating. Not even the coffee Sage had prepared for them all in massive travel mugs was enough to make him stop rubbing his eyes.

They'd stopped at JFK International first so Nadine could retrieve her luggage. It had required her badge, but what she'd packed in Paris was currently tucked away in the Mustang's trunk, sans an outfit that, while not super fashionable, would be durable in a fight.

"Who do you think will be there when we get to Salem?" Nadine asked, the familiar sounds of her cleaning her service weapon coming from the backseat.

Patrick stretched out his legs and rolled his left ankle, feeling it pop. "I don't know. Maybe members of Eloise's family. I think they do brunch every Sunday or something, but I'm not sure if we'll get there when that happens."

"We'll get there during brunch," Jono said.

Nadine sighed. "That wasn't what I meant."

Patrick let his head *thunk* back against the headrest, staring blankly at the road lit by headlights. "I don't know what we'll find when we get there."

"We haven't had a call from Georgelle, so if anything has happened to Eloise, it was out of sight of the packs up there, and quite possibly any SOA agent," Jono said.

He was driving because Patrick was apparently not allowed behind the wheel, and Wade had stolen his keys and wouldn't give them back. Patrick was fairly certain Jono had them tucked away in his pocket, but he hadn't had a chance to check.

Wade had wanted to come, but with everyone pairing up, he'd had no choice but to stay with Sage since she was holding their territory for them as proxy with her dire rank. Patrick knew he'd be fielding more phone calls than he already had from Priya and General Reed after last night. Nadine had already taken a nearly hour-long one with PIA Director Franklin.

With five days now left until Samhain, the veil thinning from the other side, there was only so much time they had to get everyone in place. Federal agents were all well and good, but Patrick hoped General Reed could get boots on the ground through the National Guard with the governor's support. If not, getting anyone from the Department of the Preternatural would be even more difficult.

But soldiers on the streets of an American city wasn't typical, and Patrick couldn't be sure that support would come in time. It was a numbers game, and he knew they were coming up short.

"We should've asked Lucien for a carbine," Nadine muttered.

"I wasn't going to ask Marek to front that kind of money like last time. We have too many eyes on us right now, and I'm still not sure our finances aren't being watched," Jono said.

Patrick's murder charge had brought a lot of scrutiny. While he and Jono were operating as any other god pack when it came to tithes and money handling, he wasn't stupid enough to think the federal government wasn't monitoring their activities.

"As much as I'd like a carbine, showing up for brunch with a rifle would probably get their threshold to block us," Patrick said.

"How powerful is it?" Nadine asked.

Patrick sighed. "Strong. It's had generations to build in that one spot. It might toss you out if you try something."

"Duly noted."

It was going to be tricky, showing up how they were. No one had announced Eloise was missing, but that wasn't to say the Patterson family was hiding that information. The Dominion Sect had clearly been making exploratory forays into Salem. While Patrick was more and more certain New York City was where Ethan would cast whatever sacrificial spell he had in his repertoire to turn himself into a god, they couldn't rule out Salem.

They had too much ground to cover and not enough people to guard it.

Halfway to Salem it started raining, a downpour that turned the windshield into a waterfall no matter how fast the wipers moved. Jono never let go of the steering wheel, keeping his eyes on the road, while the drenched scenery passed them by.

"This doesn't feel normal," Nadine said.

Patrick nodded in agreement. "I think it's safe to say the reactionary storms are growing in strength."

It was a problem no number of magic users with an affinity for weather magic could fix. This was the natural world responding in a slow rise to an imbalance of magic. An action would always cause a reaction, and one couldn't mess with magic on a large scale and think everything would be all right.

If the storms held, as Patrick was pretty damn certain they would, they'd be fighting in what amounted to a landed hurricane. It wasn't anyone's idea of fun.

"So what's the plan?" Jono asked when they finally drove into Salem, the sun struggling to get light through dark rainclouds. It was midmorning but could've easily passed as early evening.

"We knock and hope we get asked inside," Patrick asked.

"And Eloise?"

"Best-case scenario? She's there and fine, and we just make a fool of ourselves. Worst case?" Patrick shook his head, curling his fingers between the straps holding his dagger in place to his thigh. "At this point, I don't know what the worst-case scenario is."

Because death wasn't the comfort people tried to make it out to be at times. He didn't want his grandmother to be dead, but he also knew the nightmares that came with every other option his mind dredged up.

Tension left Patrick hyperaware as Jono parked some ways down the street from Eloise's house. Nadine cast a discreet shield to hold off the driving rain as they headed for the home.

"It has defensive wards around it," Nadine said as they turned up the walkway.

"SOA agents should've set them after our visit the other week," Patrick said, taking the lead.

He climbed the porch and rang the doorbell, hearing muffled voices from inside. The curtains shifted slightly over the window to his right, wide eyes peering out. Then the door opened, Madelyn standing there to greet them in surprise.

"Patrick! What are you doing here in a storm like this?" she asked, gesturing them all inside with a hurried wave of her hand.

"Sorry to drop in unannounced," Patrick said.

"We saw the news this morning about what happened to you last night. We wanted to call you, but Mother said to leave you be, that you were probably busy. Are you all right?"

"We're fine."

Behind him, Jono and Nadine crossed the threshold. Patrick saw Madelyn's gaze linger on his and Nadine's sidearms, a faint frown settling on her face. "Are you here on SOA business?"

Patrick ignored the question. "Is Eloise here?"

"Of course. We're having brunch. We can make up a spot for you three if you like."

"That won't be necessary."

Madelyn eschewed asking them for hospitality and led them to the back of the house, which was packed with family. It was a whole coven affair, presided over by the woman sitting at the head of the long dining table, who only had eyes for them.

"Pat," Jono said in a low, warning voice. "It's not her."

No hint of ozone stained the air; no cut of recognition burned through his soul and magic from hell or something else. Patrick might not be able to sense the imposter—the more powerful a god, the harder it was to find them when they were playing at being human sometimes—but he trusted Jono and whatever ability Fenrir gave him to sniff out a problem.

"Demon?" Patrick asked.

"No."

Patrick unsheathed his dagger, the matte-black blade erupting in bright white heavenly fire, and stared at the person wearing his grandmother's face. "Where is she?"

"Patrick?" Madelyn asked, staring at him. "What are you talking about?"

She wasn't the only one starting to look concerned at their arrival. Finley and Grant stood from the table. Brittany and the other cousins twisted around in their seats at the table and in the living area to stare at them.

Patrick pushed past Madelyn, eyes on his target. "I won't ask again. What the *fuck* did you do with Eloise?"

"What the hell are you talking about?" Finley demanded.

Patrick ignored him. Grant tried to step in Patrick's way but came up short against Nadine's shield. His expression of shock lasted only a moment before he conjured up a mageglobe, the spell in it not tactical in any way. For all that he was a mage, Grant wasn't trained in combat, and his magic's affinity was for weather.

"Get out of our family's ancestral house," Grant ordered.

Nadine made a punched-out sound behind him as the threshold rose up to defend against a perceived threat, the power of it sliding right over Patrick. He spared a single glance back to see Jono with his arms wrapped around Nadine, keeping her in place, the blue in his eyes replaced by the shining white fire of Fenrir's presence, the god more than enough to stand up against a threshold. Nadine's shields held, cutting around his mother's family in a desperate bid to keep them safe against the threat in their midst.

The imposter masquerading as Eloise put down her fork, expression never changing. "Is this any way to behave, Patrick?"

Grant's mageglobe exploded harmless against Nadine's combat-ready shield as Patrick skirted past the man, holding his dagger tight.

"Answer my fucking question. Where the hell is Eloise?" Patrick ground out.

"I'm right here."

The condescension in her tone went well with the frown on her face. Whoever was masquerading as his grandmother pulled off genteel annoyance frighteningly well.

Patrick got closer, dagger raised, heavenly fire burning along its edges. The imposter's blue eyes flicked to the dagger for a single second, all the answer Patrick needed to know it was a god of hell standing before him, one with a penchant for shapeshifting.

He'd only had to deal with two of those in recent memory.

Patrick lunged around the corner of the table, ignoring the way Grant yelled and beat his fist against Nadine's shield. The imposter flung themselves out of their seat with a fluidity no eighty-something-year-old woman would ever have. Patrick grabbed the chair and tossed it aside, clearing his way forward. He never took his eyes off Eloise's figure as the imposter darted around the other end of table, so quick they were only a blur.

Nadine had segmented her shields to cover the Patterson family, and the imposter cut between them. Patrick moved so he stood opposite the enemy, shifting his weight to be ready to move in any direction.

"I see Zachary finally sent along our message," the imposter said in a male voice laced through with amused mockery. The juxtaposition of it coming out of the shape of his grandmother's mouth was jarring.

"Mother?" Finley asked, head snapping around to stare at the imposter with wide eyes.

"I won't ask again," Patrick warned through clenched teeth.

The imposter smiled, the visage of his grandmother's face melting away. Patrick never blinked, watching as the god shed Eloise's figure for his own—tall and leanly muscled, wearing casual clothing more appropriate for a summer day than a stormy one. Eyes the color of rich earth stared at him from a sharply featured face, the smile on the god's face more a sneer than anything else.

Patrick kept the dagger between them, ignoring the fearful shouts from the people around him. "Loki."

The trickster god lifted a hand and lazily gestured with it. When Loki folded his fingers down toward his palm, they settled around the pole of Gungnir, Odin's spear he'd stolen back in Chicago.

"I suppose I should thank you. You've saved me from having to spend another day in this stupid little town, pretending to worship my cousin," Loki said.

Patrick tapped into a ley line through the soulbond and conjured up a mageglobe, filling it with a strike spell. It wouldn't be enough against a god, but it might give him a second or two reprieve to dodge whatever came his way.

"What did you do with Eloise?" Patrick snarled.

Loki never stopped smiling. "That's you asking again."

He swung Odin's spear down in an arc, magic crackling at the sharp tip. Patrick braced himself for the blow, the dagger taking the brunt of it in an explosion of heavenly fire, but he was still thrown backward by the force of Gungnir's magic slamming into the combined prayers of hundreds of gods.

"Patrick!" Jono shouted.

The rest of Jono's voice was drowned out by the storm Patrick was tossed into as he crashed through the pair of french glass doors that led to the first-level porch. He landed on his back, sliding over glass, head slamming against the wooden floorboards. Colored spots flashed over his eyes as the air was driven out of his lungs, ribs aching from the landing.

Patrick sucked in a breath through the pain and rolled to his feet, barely quick enough to get his dagger up to catch Odin's spear on the small cross guards. He grunted at the blow, shoulders burning as he pressed his other forearm beneath his wrist to brace his position. He guided the mageglobe from the house and aimed it at Loki, but the god sent it flying over his shoulder and away from the building to explode harmlessly in the backyard.

Loki bore his impressive strength down, wielding a weapon that wasn't his, eyes practically glowing. "Your grandmother has been our guest since you walked through these doors the other week. Blood calls to blood, and we still have yours. She never knew I wasn't you."

"*Fuck* you," Patrick snarled, the fear coursing through him icier than the rain that beat down on them, blown sideways by the wind.

A snarling howl rent the air like thunder as Fenrir in Jono's wolf form lunged through the opening Patrick had made in the house. Loki's head snapped up, expression twisting, before he yanked the spear up and vaulted over the porch railing for the ground below. Fenrir followed, passing right over Patrick in an impressive leap.

Patrick scrambled to his feet, his attention snagging on movement across the water that lapped at the property lines of Eloise's home. The roiling mass breaking free of low-hanging clouds was a familiar sight he'd hoped to never meet again.

"Mulroney!" he shouted, throwing himself at the stairs leading to the ground. "Sluagh! I need shields around the house!"

He felt the snap of her shields reforming and expanding outward in his gut, her magic passing through him harmlessly as it encased the home in a military-grade defense. The rain cut off, leaving behind a cold that wasn't all to do with the weather.

Patrick clamored down the stairs to the backyard, hearing Nadine's pounding feet seconds behind him. He conjured up more mageglobes, pouring magic into their shape, laying down attack spells.

The vicious howling screams of the Sluagh echoed across the sky. Normally they'd only hunt at night, but the veil was thin, and the cloud coverage was so thick now that daylight was an afterthought.

Lightning flashed above from cloud to cloud before cutting through the air to stab at the water raging just beyond the shore. More and more bolts of lightning zapped the waves in front of the Sluagh. Thunder was a foundation-shaking noise around them, rivaling Fenrir's snarl coming from Jono's throat as the pair dodged Odin's spear wielded by Loki on the muddy ground.

"Should've asked for a fucking carbine," Nadine said, eyes on the sky, a mageglobe forming against one palm.

Too late to regret not having a long gun in hand. Despite the spelled bullets in their pistols, the weapons would be useless against a god and wouldn't do much damage against a horde of the unforgiven dead. Patrick opened his mouth to speak but snapped it shut when half a dozen bolts of lightning touched Nadine's shield, lighting up the backyard with an eerie electric glow. The smell of burning ozone drove out every other scent in the air.

Nadine swore. "Those fuckers are calling lightning to our location."

"How long can you hold them off?" Patrick asked, attention caught between the fight on the ground and the oncoming threat.

Nadine flexed her fingers around her mageglobe, the shine in her eyes not a reflection of lightning but her magic when Patrick glanced at her. "With a god inside my defenses with us? I don't know."

Fenrir didn't have Loki cornered, but he had the god distracted.

Patrick could work on keeping the Sluagh at bay. "Just keep your shields up."

A wave of lightning crackled over the shield in a wave of eye-watering electricity, the sound of thunder that followed like shells exploding in a battlefield. Patrick fought the urge to cover his ears as he lined up his mageglobes in front of him, pale blue spheres burning with attack spells.

"This fucking storm," Nadine muttered through clenched teeth.

"It's reactionary," Grant said from behind them on the stairs.

Patrick didn't bother looking over his shoulder, gaze locked on the Sluagh, who had halved the distance between them. "No shit."

"I can try to move the lightning away. I can't do much about the rest of the storm though, not on my own."

That did make Patrick finally look over his shoulder, surprised to see his uncle wasn't the only one outside. Nearly everyone from inside was now lined up on the porch and stairs, magic at their fingertips. As much as Patrick appreciated their willingness to fight, none of them had combat training, and he couldn't risk a multitude of spells going off all at once.

"Collins," Nadine snapped.

Patrick pointed at Grant. "Weather magic *only*. If you can't push the lightning away, then don't drain yourself trying. The rest of you? Keep your shields up, and *don't* cast a single fucking spell."

"But—" Brittany protested.

Patrick cut her off. "None of you are trained for this, so stand the fuck down and don't get in the way."

Nadine never took her eyes off the threats in front of them. "*Collins.*"

Patrick faced forward again, command triggers tumbling through his mind as he cast his multitude of mageglobes toward the water. "Make me a hole, Mulroney."

They'd done this many times before when they'd been on the same front lines, the same base, or when she was requisitioned for a mission with the Hellraisers. Twelve mageglobes streaked through her shields, followed by twelve more, filled with strike spells and shockwave spells.

The shrieking mass of the unforgiven dead that filled the ranks of the Sluagh scattered around his attack, but mageglobes weren't bullets bound by a single trajectory. Patrick changed their course, chasing after clusters within the Sluagh before exploding in close proximity.

His magic erupted like fireworks, tearing through the air. Patrick couldn't kill the dead; he could only hold them back. Right now, holding the line was all they could do while Fenrir and Jono kept Loki occupied so the trickster god didn't damage Nadine's shields.

Patrick and Nadine worked in concert, striving to keep the Sluagh at bay while the storm churned above them. No more lightning rained down on them, the lack attributed to his uncle's magic. The change in air pressure and buzz of elemental magic scraped against his personal shields, but not in a bad way.

They could've maybe held the line against the Sluagh if Loki hadn't landed a lucky strike along Jono's right flank. The snarling howl that Fenrir let loose was drowned out by the explosion of magic that erupted from Gungnir's spear tip. Loki spun the spear in a vicious arc that sent ancient magic crashing into Nadine's shield.

Nadine could hold her shields against most human-made weapons—magical or otherwise—but a god's weapon was something else entirely. Nadine crashed to her knees with a ragged scream, mageglobe splitting down the center and fading to nothing, the same way her shield did around them. The howling wind grew louder, bringing with it stinging cold rain that crashed against Patrick's personal shield that he raised over himself and Nadine.

"Mulroney!" Patrick shouted, leveling a multitude of shockwave spells at the Sluagh to buy them some time.

She didn't respond in words but in actions. Another mageglobe flared to life in front of her face—jagged and misshapen, but whole enough to do the job. Nadine was a combat mage like he'd been, and she knew she couldn't quit unless she was buried six feet under.

Her shield started to piece itself back together, but some of the Sluagh got past her defenses. Patrick threw bursts of raw magic at them, drawing from the ley line to sustain the attack.

On the ground, Fenrir threw himself at Loki, who dodged easily enough, holding Gungnir between them in a threatening manner. The god pushed Fenrir back with another complicated spin of the spear before shifting his attention.

"You want your grandmother back?" Loki called out, voice nearly drowned out by the rumble of thunder and the shrieks of the Sluagh vying for prey. "Bring us the missing piece of the Morrígan's staff. That is our price."

It was a bitter payment because one life couldn't be worth the world, but Patrick knew he had no choice but to make it. That was a truth Patrick had run from for years, mistakenly believing he could save his twin sister when there was no saving someone who was already dead in most people's memory and where it mattered most—her soul.

Patrick conjured up a fusillade spell, ready to deploy it, when the ear-piercing war cries of a thousand voices rang through the air. Patrick held his spell while Nadine retracted her shield to shrink around them in a closer radius, leaving Fenrir in Jono's body outside the defensive perimeter.

"*Jono!*" Patrick shouted.

The Sluagh were regrouping in the lull of no magical bombs going off, but instead of diving after Jono, they flew *up*.

Up to meet the Wild Hunt, led by Gwyn ap Nudd.

They came through the veil, an unearthly force that would not be denied their prey. The Sluagh screamed a challenge, one the Wild Hunt refused to let pass as the new arrivals approached with weapons held aloft and a war cry on their ghostly lips. When they crashed together in the sky, the air itself vibrated, lighting up the clouds with fae magic.

Patrick held on to his fusillade spell, command trigger at the ready, but didn't let it loose now that the Sluagh were targeting someone else. Loki seemed to think the odds of two gods against one weren't in his favor, and the trickster slipped through the veil before Fenrir could sink his teeth in the bastard.

Patrick spared Nadine a glance, who gave him a grim nod, blood trickling out of her nose, a sure physical sign of magical backlash.

"I'll keep them safe. Go to Jono," she said.

Nadine created a hole in her shield just wide enough for him to cross through, her magic sealing shut behind him once he passed. The wind and rain slammed into him again, the gale force nearly driving him back a step. Patrick ducked his head and ran to where Jono crouched near the shore at the far end of the unfenced yard.

Jono was in the midst of shifting to heal the wound Gungnir had inflicted on him, blood washing away beneath the pouring rain when Patrick reached him. The wound was still raw-looking in human form, bleeding sluggishly along his thigh.

"Need to shift again," Jono got out through gritted teeth.

Patrick knelt beside him, keeping an eye on the fight above. "Do it. I'm not going anywhere."

Jono was halfway through the shift back to wolf, more a mass of fur and skin twisting over breaking bone, when a handful of screaming Sluagh came rushing over the water toward them. Patrick stood, threw his mageglobe at the unforgiven dead, and released the fusillade spell.

The mageglobe acted as an anchor for the spell, the sustained attack forcing the Sluagh back. They scattered with inhuman shrieks, the ugly, ghostly creatures all teeth and claws as they tried to come back around. Patrick fed the spell magic, the soulbond pulled tight between him and Jono, the never-ending flashes from his mageglobe like a mini supernova burning over the water.

The Sluagh screamed their aggravation, circling around them like vultures, with more dropping from above to join the fight. The Wild Hunt shifted positions to hold the stragglers back, but one spirit got through, screeching as it targeted Patrick and Jono.

Not willing to let anyone be carried off and killed, Patrick raised his dagger, the heavenly white fire burning like a beacon around it. The Sluagh never changed trajectory, and Patrick layered his shield around them both even as he thrust his dagger through his defenses. The blade found a home in the incorporeal form of the Sluagh.

The spirit couldn't die, but the prayers in the dagger could harm anything, no matter their state. It howled in agony as the magic in the dagger ripped it apart, burning the spirit down to nothing. Unlike with a soultaker, not even ash remained at the end, just the afterimage of its shape floating across Patrick's vision.

When his vision cleared, Patrick saw the Wild Hunt chasing the Sluagh into the storm clouds, lightning leading the way.

# 15

Patrick turned his back on the horizon, drawing down his magic. The fusillade spell cut off, the roar in the air that of the wind and not a battle. He let go of the soulbond, even if he didn't lower his shields. Jono was back to human, Fenrir having helped speed up the shifts. The wound on his thigh was closed, but the bruised line marring his skin showed he wasn't completely healed.

"Are you all right?" Patrick asked, offering him a hand up, ignoring the mud they were both caked in.

"I'll be fine. Healing is happening, just slow because of that sodding spear."

Jono staggered to his feet, and Patrick checked him over for any other wounds. "You need clothes."

"I have some in the Mustang's boot."

Patrick nodded. "We'll—"

A shadow drifted over them, growing larger by the second. Patrick's head snapped up, squinting against the rain pounding against his shield and blurring out the world. He didn't loosen his grip on his dagger, even when he figured out who it was coming their way. The ghostly horse and its rider descending weren't the enemy, but Patrick would never consider the god a friend.

The specter's hooves touched the ground nearby, half the horse's head more bone than rotten flesh in appearance. The empty eye sockets made for a strange gaze, but it paled in comparison to Gwyn ap Nudd's attention.

The Welsh god urged his steed closer, his black eyes shot through with molten gold staring at them through the metal-and-leather helmet he wore. He carried a spear in his right hand, the metal at the point burning red orange, as if newly made.

"We've been chasing the Sluagh since they fled the Otherworld and made it past the veil," Gwyn ap Nudd said.

"Did Medb send them?" Patrick asked.

"There is no whip that drives them this time, merely opportunity."

"That's just fucking great."

Gwyn ap Nudd frowned, never blinking. "I was not aware you held a piece of the Morrígan's staff."

"No one ever asked." Patrick turned his back on the god to check on everyone behind them, seeing Nadine was back on her feet. "I'm not giving it to you."

"You cannot give it to Ethan or the gods of hell. It belongs to the Morrígan."

Patrick clenched his teeth, not in the mood to listen to what gods had to say. "I'm well fucking aware of what's at stake if I give the damn thing away."

"As are we all. That is why I am here."

Patrick looked back at the god, blinking against the bright shine of his cracked-open aura. Everything smelled too sharp in his nose right now after all the lightning strikes. "Not just to save our asses, I take it?"

"I promised you that I and mine would fight when called to war. You have yet to ask."

"It isn't Samhain yet."

"The veil still tears, and I would see my promise fulfilled."

"Brilliant," Jono muttered. "We'll keep in touch."

He grabbed Patrick by the shoulder, hauling him toward the house. The mud was slippery underfoot, and Patrick could either get dragged along willingly or dig in his heels, and he'd never not go where Jono led.

When he looked back over his shoulder again, Gwyn ap Nudd was gone.

Probably for the best, considering the police sirens ringing through the air, coming ever closer. Nadine lowered her shields as they approached, then bent over to brace herself on her knees, breathing hard. Patrick hurried to her side, kneeling to get a look at her pale face, curling one hand over the back of her neck.

"You with me?" he asked.

"Fucking migraine," she muttered, eyes squeezed shut as blood dripped from her nose. She reached up to pinch her nostrils shut, trying to stem the flow.

"Let's get inside." Patrick looked up at everyone on the porch, skin crawling from their attention. "They should have some potions you can take."

Nadine's mouth screwed up in a grimace. "I'll eat a bottle of Tylenol if you let me."

She straightened up, and Patrick moved his hand to her hip as he guided her through the mud back to the house. No one had gone back inside yet, and Patrick pointed at the shattered glass doors he'd been knocked through.

"Get inside," he ordered as Nadine got a foot on the first step.

For a wonder, everyone obeyed without arguing. Madelyn paused just past the shattered glass doors inside the home, one hand outstretched toward them. Magic sparkled at her fingertips before she made a fist.

"Be welcome once again," she said with a formality that was recognized by the threshold.

Nadine gave a jerky nod before steeling herself to step inside.

The threshold didn't push her out, which was good because Patrick didn't really want to have the upcoming conversation in the rain.

Patrick and Jono were the last to make it inside, with Patrick kicking aside the broken glass so Jono didn't tear open his bare feet and need to shift again.

"I'll get towels," Madelyn said, pale-faced and already moving.

Some of Patrick's cousins huddled together around the table, staring at them as he guided Nadine to the couch. He kept a hand on her shoulder in a steadying gesture as she sat, catching Finley's eye.

"Do you have potions in the house? Anything for backlash by chance?" Patrick asked.

"Yes, but what just happened?" Finley replied.

"Potions, or I'll go ransack the nearest medicine cabinet."

"I'll get it. Gran keeps plenty in her workroom," Easton said, hurrying out of the living area.

He bypassed Madelyn as she came back from somewhere with clean towels in hand, which she passed to Jono, politely keeping her eyes above his waist. She offered one to Patrick, who took it and wrapped it around Nadine's shoulders. Neither of them was too soaked due to her shield, but Nadine dried off the dampness anyway.

"Cheers," Jono said as he wrapped the towel around his waist. "I'll go get my clothes."

"Stay put. The police are on their way, and I'm betting the SOA agents that were on guard duty are going to show up soon. You walk out like that and you're liable to be held at gunpoint," Patrick said.

Jono rolled his eyes. "I'm not getting interrogated in a bloody towel."

Patrick dug out his cell phone from his back pocket, glad to see it had survived the fight mostly intact. The top right corner was cracked, but it still worked. "You're not getting interrogated at all."

Jono huffed in irritation before digging his fingers into Patrick's front pocket to snag the car keys. Then he tossed them to Brittany, who managed to catch them after a brief fumble. "There's a duffel bag in the boot of the Mustang outside. Please go get it."

"It's not safe for her to go outside," Madelyn protested.

"I'll be fine, Mom," Brittany said, already hurrying for the front door before anyone could hold her back.

Patrick ignored everyone as he automatically started dialing Setsuna's number and then swore when he realized what he was doing, grief sticking in the back of his throat so suddenly he could practically taste it. Canceling the call with a stab of his thumb, he called General Reed instead.

"Collins? What's going on?" Reed grunted.

"I'm in Salem. The Dominion Sect has Eloise Patterson. Loki was impersonating her for who the fuck knows how long. We got attacked by the Sluagh, but the Wild Hunt ran them off," Patrick said, sparing no detail because there wasn't any point in mincing words, and Reed believed in gods. The Patterson family had borne witness to the messy truth, and there was no hiding it anymore. "No casualties, but there's no goddamn way you can hide the fight that just happened, sir."

The heavy silence that settled on the line lasted long enough that Patrick pulled the phone away from his ear to make sure he still had signal in the reactionary storm howling outside. It was long enough that Brittany returned, soaking wet, with the duffel bag in hand. Jono took it from her with a nod of thanks before ducking into the hall bathroom to get dressed.

"I'll inform the joint task force. Do you think Salem is Ethan's focus and not New York City because of this?" Reed finally said.

Patrick chewed the inside of his bottom lip for a couple of seconds before answering. "No. I think New York City is still where his spellcasting will happen, but they focused here because of the Pattersons."

"You're sure they have Eloise? That she's alive?"

"I don't know if she's still alive. Ethan's never been one to take hostages. He tends to murder everyone instead."

Someone made a choked-off sound, and Nadine huffed out an irritated sigh as she straightened up from her hunched-over position. "You're still shit when it comes to dealing with people, Collins."

Patrick made a face at her, still talking to Reed. "I need to call Director Kohli."

"Keep me updated," Reed ordered.

"Yes, sir."

Patrick ended the call right as someone pounded on the front door. "SOA! Open up!"

Nadine stood, letting the towel drop from her shoulders as she fumbled her badge out of her back pocket. "I'll handle your fellow agents. Call your acting director."

Patrick watched as she headed down the hall, only pausing long enough to take the potion vial from Easton when he came down the stairs and down it in one swallow. Patrick dialed Priya's personal cell phone rather than an office line since it was still the weekend. He knew she was probably working like all the rest of them, but there was no guarantee she'd be at her desk.

"SOA Acting Director Kohli," Priya said when she answered.

"Ma'am, we have a problem," Patrick said, pulling his badge from his pocket in preparation to prove his identity.

He updated her as succinctly as possible, watching as SOA agents entered the home, weapons drawn and magic at their fingertips, to take stock of the situation. Patrick raised his badge for them to see, most of his attention on the conversation at hand. Police arrived minutes after Jono left the bathroom, fully dressed save for shoes, and the home was quickly becoming crowded.

The only time Patrick broke away from the conversation with Priya was when one of the police officers tried to get Jono to leave to take his statement. He tilted the phone away from his mouth and said, "He's not going with you."

The officer frowned at him. "We need—"

"The SOA is taking lead. You don't need to do anything except what we tell you."

The officer bristled, and Priya sighed in his ear. "That isn't going to endear us to the local law enforcement, Collins."

"Ask me if I care." Patrick glared at the officer. "Jono's giving his report to the SOA, not you. So back off."

The officer turned his back on Patrick, irritation clear in the line of his shoulders, but Patrick put the man out of his mind and continued his conversation with Priya. By the end of the call, longer than the one with Reed, Patrick had his marching orders.

"Are we staying or going?" Nadine asked.

"The SOA is sending a team from the Rapid Response Division out of Boston. They'll get here in less than an hour and take over. We need to stay and hold the scene until they arrive for the hand-off, and then we're free to go back to New York," Patrick said as he put his phone away.

"What about us? What about our mother?" Grant demanded from where he stood behind the couch, hands gripping the top of it so tightly his knuckles were white.

"You knew that person wasn't her. How did you know that?" Madelyn asked.

Patrick glanced at the Salem police officers and other SOA agents that were still within earshot. For all that he'd spilled his family's secrets over the past few months, the public didn't need to be privy to this conversation.

"Want me to shield?" Nadine asked from her sprawled position on the couch, looking a little better.

"I got this," Patrick said.

She'd done enough. Having magical defenses broken by a god's weapon would take a lot out of anyone. He wanted her to rest up, so Patrick waved his aunt and uncles closer so he could cast a silence ward without anyone else getting caught up in it. The furniture in the living area acted as a decent barrier to keep everyone else at bay.

"The SOA knows Eloise is missing. They're putting out a BOLO that's hitting every agency," Patrick said.

"You just said Ethan had her," Finley said.

"Yes, but we don't know where Ethan is."

"What about the man who took her place? You called him Loki."

"He wasn't a man. He was a god."

Grant didn't look as if he believed Patrick. "Gods are just stories."

"You worship Persephone, unless your prayers are just lip service," Jono retorted.

Grant scowled, a flush coloring his cheeks. "My belief in our coven's chosen deity isn't at issue here."

"Pretty fucking sure it is." Jono jerked his head in the direction of the backyard. "Loki's been impersonating your mum since after our visit. That's why we came back, because we got a warning and we needed to see if it was true."

Uncertainty flickered in Grant's eyes, but the irritated anger didn't leave his expression. Patrick wasn't in the mood for it.

"Do you want to know why I never let any of you know I was still alive?" Patrick asked, staring at his aunt and uncles and trying not to let the bitterness in the back of his throat turn into bile. "It wasn't just because Setsuna wanted to keep me hidden and safe from Ethan. I'd be dead if it weren't for Persephone, but the cost of her saving me from Ethan after he murdered my mom was a soul debt I still haven't paid. Your chosen deity dictates my life, and there's no way I'd ever join a coven that puts her on a pedestal like you do."

Madelyn went white in the face, while Finley and Grant appeared just as stunned. Patrick drew in a breath, antsy with the need to leave but knowing he couldn't until the job here was finished.

"Ethan's planning to turn himself into a god. He already stole a godhead, but it got trapped in Hannah's soul. That's why he didn't kill her," Patrick continued.

Not back then he hadn't, but she'd crept toward death for so long that she was just flesh these days—breathing but no longer alive. Patrick shoved that thought aside, staring at what remained of his family.

"That's…" Finley's voice trailed off, the horror in his tone recognizable.

"Can you save her?" Madelyn asked, choking on the words.

Patrick didn't answer.

"Ethan wants a trade, and it's not a trade the government can make," Nadine said into the tense quiet.

Patrick grimaced. "The government doesn't negotiate with terrorists. Ethan's side gave their demand through Loki. There's not going to be a ransom call for something like this, but I'll do what I can to bring Eloise back to you."

He couldn't promise alive because he knew what Ethan was capable of. Patrick had borne the scars of that truth since he was eight years old. Neither could he pass on the demand because the government didn't know the Morrígan's staff had been broken and he had kept a piece of it. If Setsuna had still been alive—

Patrick cut that thought off, ignoring the stab of grief.

"If there was a ransom request, is it something the government would even pay?" Finley asked.

"No."

"Then our coven will," Grant said.

"Ethan doesn't want money. You don't have what he wants."

"It seems he thinks you do. Or that god did, at least."

Grant's disbelief about Loki had faded some, but Patrick could still hear shades of it in his voice, as if his uncle didn't think the gods his coven and others prayed to were actually real.

Patrick sighed. "Technically, that's classified."

"She's our *mother*, and we love her, but that's not the only reason why we need her back," Madelyn said.

"Maddie," Grant warned.

She turned her head and gave him such a cold stare that he wilted beneath it. "I am head of this coven until our mother returns. I am well within my right to speak our secrets."

Oh, Patrick did not like the sound of that.

"What the fuck are you talking about?" he asked.

Madelyn sighed heavily. "If Ethan has your grandmother, then he has access to the nexus under Salem."

Patrick stared at her. "Why would Ethan have access to a nexus just because he has Eloise?"

"The nexus under Salem is small. It's an offshoot of the one beneath Boston. Our family has retained control of it since our ancestors arrived in this country."

Which was a polite way of saying they'd stolen it from the indigenous people who'd lived in the area first, but Patrick let that thought slide away. Any nexus and the ley lines leading to them were always monitored for activity. Only mages could access those rivers and lakes of power, but governments were usually the ones to oversee their protection.

"Are you saying our family is the only one with the right to tap that nexus?" Patrick asked.

Grant shook his head. "No. We've always allowed other mages access to it. But our family, our coven, is responsible for the protective wards that contain it, not the government. That was agreed to during the Salem Witch Trials."

"Who controls the anchor points of the protective wards?" Their silence was answer enough, and Patrick's stomach twisted. "*Fuck.*"

"The SOA, and all the agencies that came before it, have been aware of our claim on the nexus for generations," Finley said.

Patrick wondered if Priya even knew or if she was still so busy trying to get a handle on filling Setsuna's spot that she hadn't absorbed everything yet.

"*I* didn't know."

"You aren't in charge of a federal agency."

"Setsuna was."

Grant snorted derisively. "Forgive us if we still don't view her in a positive light for her actions in keeping you from us."

"Your mother was supposed to be the next high priestess of the Salem Coven. Clara would've excelled in that role. Ethan knew what she was going to have access to with that rank. I've always believed he loved power first and our sister second," Madelyn said quietly.

Patrick squeezed his eyes shut for a few seconds before opening them again, trying not to think of a bloody basement. "You wouldn't be wrong."

He'd known Ethan had taken Hannah to keep Macaria's godhead alive and always thought his father had used Hannah's magic the same way a parasite drained energy from a host. It seemed Patrick hadn't been far off the mark with that comparison, if what they were saying was true, if their family had the ability to tap the nexus beneath Salem with no one the wiser.

The Pattersons had generational claim to a nexus, one the government hadn't been able to pry out of their hands. No wonder his grandmother was always listened to whenever she went to Capitol Hill to chastise Congress about the Dominion Sect.

No wonder Hannah had been able to support a godhead in her soul for as long as she had, if Ethan could draw from a nexus through her without anyone tracking his access, because blood would always let blood through. Patrick wondered how many times Ethan had taken Hannah back to Salem to support her soul until it no longer worked, until it took godly interference to keep her alive.

He wondered if the breaking point was when she became pregnant.

"This is information my superiors need to know. Most likely they'll send mages out of the Boston field office to barricade the Salem and Boston nexuses like we did during the Thirty-Day War," Patrick said.

Barricading the ley lines and nexuses in the Northeast would take a level of coordination and power the government could probably deploy in time, but there was no guarantee. Bureaucracy was the government's lifeblood at all levels, and not even war could make that move quickly. He hoped General Reed would be able to make something happen though.

"Please find your grandmother. She never stopped looking for you and Hannah after we buried Clara," Madelyn said in a quiet voice that broke a little on her sister's name.

"You all thought we were dead for years."

"We held out hope we'd get to bury you in our family's cemetery. We wanted that closure."

"I'll do what I can."

Madelyn wiped the tears from her eyes before stepping around the coffee table. Patrick tensed, not sure what she wanted and unprepared for what it ended up being.

A hug.

Madelyn wrapped her arms around him, hugging him as tight as she could. Patrick didn't know what to do with his arms for a few seconds before he very carefully hugged her back, holding himself stiffly.

"Thank you for protecting our family today," Madelyn murmured. "And thank you for coming back to us, Patrick. You might go by Collins these days, but you're still a Patterson to us, and always will be."

He swallowed tightly, nodding jerkily before pulling away. Madelyn let him go, giving him a watery smile. When Patrick searched her face, he didn't see any anger in her eyes.

"Will you let us know what happens?" Grant asked, sounding more tired than fearfully angry now.

"If it's about Eloise and within my ability to safely do so, then yes," Patrick promised.

It was the least he owed them for putting the family at risk.

"You'll need our phone numbers," Madelyn said.

They exchanged numbers before he broke the silence ward. Sound rushed back in, the murmur of voices and crash of thunder overhead filling Patrick's ears. It wasn't much longer after that when Rapid Response Division's team deployed out of Boston arrived, having probably driven with lights and sirens the entire way. Patrick handed over the scene to them upon their arrival, ready to get back on the road.

The storm was still raging when they left the Patterson home and hurried to the car. Patrick was the one who got behind the steering wheel this time, fully focused on getting back to New York City while Jono seemed more focused on him. Nadine sprawled out in the back seat and went immediately to sleep, having nodded off in worse places over the years.

"Promise me you won't give Ethan anything he wants," Jono said an hour into the drive.

Patrick gripped the steering wheel tighter, eyes on the horizon, and bit his tongue so he wouldn't lie.

"Patrick. Please."

"I can't promise that," Patrick got out, practically choking on the words. "You know why."

"If Ethan has a remade Morrígan's staff, we won't be able to stop him before he turns himself into a god."

"And I'd like everyone I'm related to or who I care about to stop *dying*."

Jono reached over the console to settle his hand on Patrick's thigh, his touch warm even through Patrick's damp jeans. "Setsuna's death wasn't your fault, and neither was losing Eloise."

"Yeah? What about when I went and blew off half your arm?"

"You couldn't stop that from happening either, because it

wasn't *you*. It wasn't your fault. I'll keep saying that until you believe it, but I need you alive to do that."

"The Pattersons welcomed me recently, and their threshold knows me. Ethan wouldn't have been able to get past it and grab her if he didn't have my blood. If I hadn't gone back."

"That still doesn't make it your fault. You were kidnapped by Andras and Hades. You were in no position to stop them from taking your blood. For all you know he used Hannah's."

"There's no way to know for sure."

"Exactly, so stop taking all the blame."

Patrick eased up a bit on the gas pedal as traffic started to slow. "Just once I want to do what *I* want, not what the gods require me to do."

He'd been at their beck and call for over two decades, and other people had paid the price of his position when it should've been him every time. He was tired of standing at gravesites, staring at the names of people who should still be alive.

Jono's fingers dug into his thigh, and his touch grounded Patrick in a way nothing else ever had. "Tell me if you plan to hand over the piece of the Morrígan's staff. Can you promise me that?"

Patrick chewed on his bottom lip before finally nodding. "Yeah."

If there was a way he could save Eloise and keep the piece of the Morrígan's staff out of Ethan's hand, he'd do it, but it seemed like such an impossible task.

# 16

THEY ATE DINNER SUNDAY EVENING CLOSER TO MIDNIGHT, HOURS past their usual mealtime. Halfway home the drive had been interrupted by a conference call from the directors of the SOA and PIA that neither Patrick nor Nadine could ignore. Jono had kept his eyes on the road while listening in on a conversation he technically shouldn't have been privy to.

The meetings hadn't stopped, not even after they dropped Nadine off at Sage's. Patrick had been stuck on video conferences for hours at home while Jono fielded calls and texts from outside packs who were still arriving. By the time Jono managed to get dinner going, Patrick was in danger of sliding out of his seat at the dining room table.

When Jono was ready to dish up their plates, Patrick had finally reached the end of his calls and was closing his laptop. Jono set an open beer bottle down next to him on the table. Patrick snatched it up and gulped down half the beer before he even said thank you.

Jono reached out and framed Patrick's face with his hand, one thumb swiping over the dark circles that had come up beneath those green eyes. "You need some rest."

Patrick hooked a finger through Jono's belt loop. "So do you."

"Dinner first, then bed."

"I'm not going to fight you on that." Patrick sighed heavily, leaning into Jono's touch. "At least we have the National Guard being deployed, though I guess it was too much to hope they'd move in the Army."

"You always say it would be terrible optics, having troops deployed on home soil like that."

"Yeah, well, I'm not opposed to having a tank or twelve on hand, especially if we'll be facing soultakers."

Jono pulled his hands away and snorted. "I'm betting everyone else was opposed."

"Everyone who wasn't Reed."

Jono laughed tiredly. "Of course. Come on, let's eat."

He'd made steak and roasted vegetables, their fridge having been restocked by Sage while they were in Salem. It'd been a nice surprise to not have to go to the shops for a grocery run or order delivery when they couldn't be sure whoever buzzed the call box wouldn't be out to murder them.

They ate in silence, Patrick's shields down now that they were home. Jono kicked out a leg underneath the table so he could tap his bare foot against Patrick's. The touch was comforting, and dinner was hearty, but sleep was still a long way off when they were interrupted by a call.

"You'd think the government never bloody sleeps at this rate," Jono muttered.

"It doesn't," Patrick said, picking up his mobile. "But it's not Priya. It's Casale."

Jono waved his fork at Patrick. "Let's see what he wants."

Patrick accepted the call and put it on speakerphone, then went back to cutting up the last of his steak. "Collins. Line and location are secure."

"I saw the news out of Salem. Are you back in the city?" Casale said, not even bothering with a hello.

"We're home now."

"Good. I'm on my way over with Angelina. We need to talk."

Jono watched as Patrick rubbed tiredly at his face. As much as he wanted to wait until morning, they both knew time was in short supply. "All right. We'll buzz you in when you arrive."

Patrick ended the call and stabbed at his steak.

"If he's bringing Angelina, I wonder if it's coven related," Jono said.

Patrick shrugged. "We'll find out soon enough."

They managed to finish their meal, and Jono was placing the dirty dishes in the sink when Patrick's mobile went off again. Jono dialed up his hearing to listen in.

"Are you downstairs?" Patrick asked.

"Yes. Your gargoyles are making a mess," Casale said.

"Can't be worse than the one the Dominion Sect left behind. I'll buzz you up."

Jono remembered the last time Casale had entered their home and how it had ended with Patrick in handcuffs. "Hospitality?"

Patrick raised an eyebrow. "What makes you think Casale needs to enter by way of hospitality?"

"Because it's safer."

"He's not here to arrest me."

Patrick didn't go for the bread and water when Casale and Angelina entered the flat, despite Jono's preference. Casale wasn't in uniform, and Angelina wore casual clothes and rain boots. They left their umbrellas in the small bucket on the landing, bringing the scent of the storm into the flat.

"It's late," Jono said. "What do you want?"

Patrick shot him an exasperated look before turning back to Casale. "Despite his attitude, Jono isn't wrong. What brought you over here at this hour that couldn't be asked over a phone call?"

"The mayor finally agreed to enact a curfew. It starts tomorrow. Can't happen soon enough, according to Angelina." Casale nodded at his wife. "We won't keep you long, but she was told to speak with you in person."

Jono eyed Angelina. She had been helpful when demons were stealing werecreature souls, but she was still one of Hera's priestesses. "What's wrong?"

Angelina frowned, tucking a lock of hair behind one ear. "I've been contacted by representatives of other covens in the five boroughs. Everyone is aware that the nexus has been barricaded by the SOA. The reactionary storm is a pretty strong signal that something is going on here. The mayor's office has been cagey about answers, and the news coming out of DC is cryptic at best. The covens want to know if your plans have changed any."

Jono stayed quiet, letting Patrick take the lead on this. He'd answer for the packs and their alliances, but he had no authority where the government was concerned. The covens had been willing to lend their help to the fight when contacted over the last couple of weeks, but many had done so reluctantly.

"What has the mayor or your police brass told you?" Patrick asked Casale.

"Time off has been canceled. Every available officer is scheduled to report to work starting tomorrow. The orders are similar to when we have to police a large event like parades, but this isn't a parade," Casale said.

"It's a parade to hell."

Jono sighed. "Pat."

Patrick rolled his eyes. "I can't tell you anything different than what you already know. I don't have the authority to disclose anything further. What I *can* tell you is it's going to be worse than all the attacks that have happened here before. Tell your covens to strengthen their thresholds and stay within their designated areas to protect people when shit goes down like we discussed. If you have anyone you want to keep safe still in the city, you should maybe think about telling them to leave."

Casale's expression darkened, but it wasn't anger Jono smelled wafting off him; it was fear. "You think it's going to be that bad?"

Patrick tipped his head back and stared at the ceiling, his heartbeat strong and even in Jono's ears. "I think the Thirty-Day War is going to seem like a picnic if things go how I think they will."

"Is that the federal government's official stance?"

Patrick looked Casale in the eye. "It's mine."

"Ours," Jono corrected. "We've brought in other packs from outside the city to bolster our numbers. Our alliances with the fae and the Night Courts means they'll aid us. They'll work with the covens."

Casale raised an eyebrow. "The vampires are playing nice?"

"More like they're playing to win."

"We don't want civilians running around and getting caught in the crossfire. But if you could spread the word to bolster thresholds and lay down some protective wards for anyone who doesn't leave, that would be helpful. It'll be a block-by-block fight whenever the Dominion Sect finally attacks. That hasn't changed," Patrick said.

"And if people ask where we got this information?" Angelina asked.

"There are enough rumors running around at the moment. People are primed to believe anything right now, so let them believe the rumors."

Casale studied them for a long moment before finally nodding sharply, mouth set in a grim line. "We told our son to leave the city. He took a train out this morning."

"He won't be the only one after we put the word out," Angelina said, reaching for Casale's hand. "Those who stay will aid you, as promised. My high priestess commanded it for our coven, which is why I'm not going with our son."

"Maybe you should find someone else to pray to," Patrick said.

Jono thought it was cruel of the goddess to not disclose to her followers that they were basically being conscripted into a fight they weren't prepared for. He and Patrick had done all they could over the months to shore up their position, and Jono knew they couldn't possibly have accounted for every threat clawing its way through the veil.

"It would've been helpful if we had more than a couple weeks' notice for this fight," Angelina said pointedly.

"I couldn't be sure any of you would agree to help when it wasn't your fight."

"It is now."

Patrick crossed his arms over his chest and sighed tiredly. "You aren't trained for what's coming, so whoever doesn't leave the city needs to stick to defense."

"Best offense is a good defense," Casale said.

"Yeah. Get your people to stretch your protective wards to cover as many buildings as you can. Working alone won't help anyone survive. It needs to be a team effort if we want to keep the casualty count down."

Casale's expression became troubled as he shared a look with Angelina. "We'll pass on the warning."

"Just don't say you heard it from me."

Casale and Angelina didn't stay much longer after that, though Jono escorted them to the door only so he could lock it behind them. When he turned back around, Patrick had linked his hands together behind his neck, staring down at the floor with a grimace.

"It's going to be a bloodbath," Patrick said.

Jono went to him, wrapping his arms around Patrick and leading him over to the sofa. He sat down, pulling Patrick into his lap, knees on either side of his hips. Jono settled his hands on Patrick's hips, anchoring him there.

"The gods will be fighting with us. That has to be enough of a difference to matter," Jono murmured.

Patrick framed Jono's face with cool hands, leaning down to kiss him with a fierceness that Jono would never turn away from. "I have you this time."

Jono dragged his lips over the edge of Patrick's jaw, down his throat, and scraped his teeth over the pulse there. "You'll always have me, love."

The bitter scent of him was thick with a multitude of emotions that resonated through the soulbond. Having Patrick in his arms was comforting, even if the next words out of his lover's mouth made Jono freeze.

"I'm taking the piece of the Morrígan's staff with me tomorrow," Patrick said.

Jono raised his head, staring Patrick in the eye. "Why?"

Patrick lifted a hand to stroke back some of Jono's hair, his touch gentle, before he pressed their foreheads together. "Because I can't leave it behind anymore."

"Patrick."

"I don't have a choice. I never did. But I can't drag you down with me."

"You have to know I'll follow wherever you go."

Jono meant it with every last fiber of his being, the soulbond humming between them with a truth that might not be enough to see them through this whole nightmare.

When Patrick spoke again, his voice was tight, the words bitten off. "I can't let Ethan win."

Jono tightened his grip on Patrick. "Then don't give him what he wants."

Unspoken went Jono's fear that Patrick would give *himself* up, and Jono would lose him, maybe for good. It was a recurring nightmare that had woken him up too many times to count lately.

Patrick pulled back just enough so he could gently brush his lips over Jono's, the touch electric. "I'll come back."

The promise in his words was one Jono desperately wanted to believe, but he knew, deep down, it might get broken through no fault of their own.

Because there were always sacrifices needed to win a war, and

Jono knew Patrick was all too willing to give himself up to the gods if it kept everyone he cared about safe.

Jono chased after his mouth with a single-mindedness that had Patrick dragging both hands through Jono's hair and yanking on it to keep him in place. Jono let Patrick ravage his mouth, sliding his fingers beneath soft cotton to find warm skin. He gripped Patrick's hips with a strength that could bruise or break, a strength Patrick had never flinched from, only leaned into.

With a groan, Jono lifted Patrick off his lap and pushed him flat on the sofa. Patrick's hands stayed in his hair as Jono rucked up his shirt to press a hot, openmouthed kiss against taut muscle. Patrick hissed out a breath when Jono licked his way lower, hands undoing his trousers.

"Jono," Patrick got out.

The desire in his scent, the need in his voice, had Jono working his half-hard cock free in seconds. He licked at the tip, pinning Patrick down with one firm hand when he arched into the touch. Fingernails scraped over Jono's scalp as he ducked his head, swallowing Patrick down in a slow glide that drew a keening whine out of his lover's mouth.

The weight and taste of Patrick's cock on his tongue had Jono swallowing around the length. He worked Patrick over with a relentlessness that had Patrick yanking at Jono's hair, heels pressed hard against his back, holding on for all he was worth even as he spilled down Jono's throat.

Jono pulled off and licked his lips, listening to Patrick's heavy breathing. The insistent tugging on his hair drew him upward and into a messy kiss that Patrick didn't shy away from.

"Come on me," he muttered against Jono's mouth, keeping him close with a firm grip.

Jono fumbled at his own trousers, cock straining against the zipper. He kissed at Patrick's mouth, his jaw, his throat, breathing him in. When he got his cock free, it only took a couple of strokes before he was spilling across Patrick's stomach. Patrick didn't move, keeping him close, as they breathed each other in.

They were both a mess, but the comfort in their closeness had Jono pressing his ear over Patrick's heart, the sound a soothing tempo that matched his own.

## 17

Jono shook his head as he pushed his way through the revolving door of the downtown building where Gentry & Thyme was located. Even just those few seconds from the taxi to the entrance had been enough to soak his trousers from the knees down and wet his hair. An umbrella was useless in the gale force winds howling between Manhattan's skyscrapers.

"You look like you got no sleep," Sage said as Jono approached her in the lobby.

Wade was practically glued to her side, eating Dunkin' Donuts hash browns out of a paper bag three at a time. Jono didn't know how many orders he'd bought to make the bag bulge like that.

Sage held two travel mugs of coffee in her hands, one of which she handed to Jono. He took it from her with a tired nod of thanks. "You'd be right."

Wade tilted his paper bag toward Jono. "Want some?"

"I ate," Jono said, though the offer was appreciated.

"More for me, then. Where's Patrick?"

"At the office. I took a taxi over."

Sage shook her head. "You really need to get another car. Buy it with tithes. It's technically a pack expense."

"Maybe when this whole bloody mess is over."

"Speaking of that mess, let's get upstairs for the meeting with Tiarnán."

At half past eight on a Monday morning, the lobby was bustling with people arriving for work despite the ugly weather outside. The weather in Salem had followed them home yesterday, and a reactionary storm was slowly building over New York City. The radar maps on the morning news had looked absolutely horrendous, with warnings of gale force winds and possible flooding in the lower areas around Manhattan.

Jono knew it was only going to get worse.

They took a lift up to the floor Gentry & Thyme was on. Sage waved at the receptionist as they passed, leading them to the large conference room where all their alliance meetings with the fae were held. Tiarnán was already seated at the table, the fae lord flanked by Deirdre. Their heritage was impossible to miss, from Deirdre's dark green hair and pale pink eyes to Tiarnán's violet-eyed gaze and sheer otherworldly presence.

Tiarnán's gold-tipped cane was set across the table in front of him. Jono's gaze caught on the silver filigree plates and links that wrapped around Tiarnán's right hand, anchored by a thin silver cuff and adorned with gemstones. He could practically taste that metal, and it made the back of his throat itch.

"I understand you had some trouble in Salem," Tiarnán said in greeting.

Jono took a seat in between Sage and Wade. "It would've been worse if Gwyn ap Nudd hadn't shown up."

"Yes, we are aware of his aid. Brigid sent out a warning that the hawthorn paths are unstable. She's sending support to guard them."

"That can't be good. There's one smack in the middle of

Central Park. What's going to come out?" Wade asked, sounding a little alarmed.

"It's difficult to say."

"We know the veil is thin. Samhain is on Friday, but every warning from the gods makes it seem as if the veil will rip open before then," Jono said.

Tiarnán nodded. "That's a strong possibility."

"Yeah, well, you lot aren't the only ones who believe that. It hasn't hit the news yet, but the government is sending in the National Guard after everything that happened with Setsuna and the mess in Salem yesterday."

Tiarnán shared a look with Deirdre. "That is unexpected."

"In a bad way?"

"The demonic incursion in Cairo that jump-started the Thirty-Day War already had demons and soultakers in the street before soldiers showed up. Other than a few attacks centered around your pack, there's been no other signs here of a demonic incursion."

"The government knows Ethan's side has the Morrígan's staff and several million zombies at their disposal. I think they're just being prudent," Sage said.

"They also murdered a government official. I mean, people are pissed about that," Wade pointed out.

Jono was glad Patrick wasn't present. Setsuna's death was still a gaping wound for him, despite how he kept working through the grief. It manifested itself in nightmares and the occasional tears in the shower where it was impossible to distinguish them from water, but Jono always recognized the scent of salt beneath soap.

"The deployment is apparently being announced later today. They'll arrive within a day or so, according to Patrick," Jono said.

Tiarnán looked out the windows lining the length of the conference room, the outside world distorted from all the rain. "Are you sure they'll make it in time?"

Jono froze at that statement. "What do you mean?"

Deirdre tapped a perfectly manicured fingernail against the table, staring at them with unblinking eyes. "If the veil tears open similar to how it did in Cairo, New York City is going to be caught between this world and the ones beyond. It won't be easy to send in reinforcements. It's why we've gathered our side and have been bringing them through the hawthorn path in advance to get them situated how we agreed on. Block by block."

"Though in a city of iron, our power won't be as it is past the veil," Tiarnán warned.

"You can still fight," Jono said before taking a sip of his coffee. If the fae tried to find some way to wriggle out of the alliance, he'd let Fenrir tear into them.

"That was never in doubt, but do you have more of a battle plan than the one we're working with?"

Jono shrugged. "My country's military tried to recruit me, and I gave the bloke knocking on doors in the block a two-fingered salute. Your best bet is to talk with Patrick on something like that. We have packs from here and out of state ready to fight, as well as Night Courts moving into Manhattan proper. We're organized to a point, but nothing on par with the military."

"What about covens?" Deirdre asked. "Do they remain committed?"

Jono had had enough of covens in recent days, but he knew they couldn't afford to be picky, especially after last night. "Casale and Angelina stopped by last night. The covens are gathered, though they're sending some of their adherents outside the city in anticipation of what's to come."

"They aren't the only ones fleeing," Tiarnán said.

"I don't want anyone here who isn't willing to fight. That's a weakness we can't afford."

"Then what about every citizen who isn't aware of what waits beyond the veil, who your government has not adequately warned?"

"We fight for them and try to keep them safe."

"It's why we'll move block by block and leave allies in strategic areas. The covens may not have the sort of fighting experience those in the military have, but they're still an asset. We'll work with them, and they with us, despite any reservations either side might have," Sage said.

Tiarnán hummed thoughtfully. "You mortals do all right when it comes to war."

"Yeah, but you guys have actual gods of war," Wade said.

Tiarnán gave him a droll look. "You are a dragon."

Wade flapped his hand in Tiarnán's direction. "I'm not a *god*."

"Small blessings," Sage muttered under her breath.

"Hey!" Wade exclaimed. "I'd make a great god!"

"Oh? And what would you be a god of?"

"Snacks."

Sage chuckled. "That won't help us win this war."

"It'd keep us fed. Aren't supply lines important in something like this?"

"If it gets to the point of us needing supply lines, we'd be in a shit position. Between our combined alliances, the government, and whatever help the gods give us, we'll need to be enough," Jono said.

They had to be, because there was no way Jono was letting Patrick lose this fight.

There was no way Jono was losing the man he loved.

Tiarnán met his gaze and nodded grimly. "If this world falls to hell, we all do."

It echoed what Ashanti had said when speaking about her children starving if hell were to win. Letting Ethan turn himself into a god of hell would create a new myth none of them would survive.

"Just have your people ready, and we'll have ours."

Tiarnán inclined his head. "We *daoine sídhe* will not shirk our duty."

That was as close to a promise as they would get out of the fae.

Deep in his soul, Fenrir seemed satisfied, so Jono would have to be as well.

The meeting didn't last much longer after the confirmation of support was obtained. That was one more group of fighters they could count on when everything went to shit.

"I'll walk down with you," Deirdre said as she stood. "My Starbucks order should be ready."

Jono didn't know where the Starbucks was, but he figured it had to be close by, if not in the building somewhere, because venturing out in this weather wasn't worth it, even for coffee. Patrick would probably say otherwise, but he wasn't there.

Sage and Deirdre made small talk about things that weren't related to the alliance as they left the office and waited for a lift. Jono pulled out his mobile, switching it out of silent mode now that the meeting was over. Patrick hadn't texted him an update, but he had a couple from several pack leaders he'd need to respond to.

The lift arrived, and they took it down to the lobby, picking up a couple of other riders on the way down. Jono ignored the double takes he received, while Wade scowled pointedly at the people who began stinking up the elevator with their fear-tinged anxiousness.

Jono was glad to leave the small space behind in favor of the lobby—right up until he realized who waited for them. The group of men and women in business attire wouldn't be out of the ordinary if it weren't for how they smelled bitter and acrid from demons riding their souls.

"Take cover!" Jono snarled, grabbing Wade by the shoulder and shoving him back into a lift, forcing everyone else back as well.

Sage threw herself against a pair of closed lift doors, the gold-and-white marble edges of the lift frame protruding outward to provide mediocre safety from the bullets aimed their way. Jono did the same while Deirdre raised a shield between herself and the Krossed Knights taking aim at them from the lobby. Whatever spells they'd used to get their weapons past the security desk, they'd dropped them now.

The handful of people who were in the lobby screamed and ran for the entrance, including the pair of people manning the security desk. Considering they weren't armed, Jono didn't blame them.

"Jono!" Wade shouted as he popped back out of the elevator before the doors could shut and take him to safety.

Deirdre's shields were a glittering, effervescent pink and slightly opaque. They stopped the bullets well enough but couldn't hold up against the cross-bolt one of the hunters fired. It ripped through her shield like it was nothing but tissue paper—spelled, Jono guessed—and Deirdre wasn't quick enough to dodge it completely. It cut across her arm, the wool of her sweater tearing along with her skin. The cry she let out was one of shock more than pain, and her shield cracked like pressure applied to a frozen-over lake.

She staggered, reaching out with one hand to brace herself against a lift door. She'd gone white in the face, holding her wounded arm close to her body, struggling to keep up her shields.

"Deirdre!" Sage cried out.

The fae blinked rapidly. "Iron-tipped."

Jono swore, knowing how badly iron affected the fae. They couldn't count on her shield, and when it finally shattered, Jono stood on four legs instead of two, the shift to his wolf form having taken less than a minute with Fenrir's help.

Wade belched fire at the hunters before they could get off any more bullets, forcing some of them to scatter out of range. Jono used those few seconds to get clear of the lift bank and sink his teeth and claws into the hunters carrying guns. The acrid scent of hell hung heavy in the air, hints of the demons riding their souls. They tasted even worse once Jono bit into them.

Blood filled his mouth as his fangs bit through an arm like it was nothing, the pressure in his jaws tearing through clothes and flesh and bone. He jerked his head, and the hunter's arm came with him, tearing clean out of its socket. Flesh split, the wet sound buried under the hunter's scream as Jono spat the limb out, blood pumping from the man's brachial artery. A dull roar filled his ears as a flash of negative light exploded around the hunter. The demon left its host to die, and Jono moved on to the next target.

Deirdre struggled to get her shields back up, but she was pinned down in front of a lift. The flicker of opaque pink around her body hinted at her troubled state. The magic in the iron was sharp in Jono's nose, as was the silver he could practically taste in the other half of the hunters' arsenal.

Aconite made his eyes water, but Jono refused to let it bother him as he took down another hunter, claws tearing open a rib cage with a single swipe. He pivoted, just missing getting a bite out of another hunter, when a vicious roar echoed through the lobby. Sage barreled out of the lift bank and slammed into a hunter taking aim at Jono.

They went down, Sage's teeth in the man's face before he could curl his finger around the trigger. When she lifted her head, there was blood on her teeth and lips that she didn't bother licking away. Jono's attention was on her for only a second, but that was more than enough time for a demon to cause trouble.

"*Jono!*" Wade screamed.

Jono heard the whistle of something cutting through the air behind him. He tried to dodge the attack, but demons could move fast, even when taking up residence in human bodies.

Sage was faster.

A blur of orange and black slammed into Jono with enough force one of his ribs cracked. Jono skidded across the gold-and-white marble floor, claws raking furrows in the stone. Sage took the blow meant for him, the hunter's aconite-laced and spelled silver machete sinking into her lower body instead of his.

The sound she made as the hunter gutted her would haunt him for years.

Jono howled, his wordless protest drowned out by Sage's

agonized roar as she collapsed to the ground. The hunter wrenched the machete out of Sage's body with a vicious twist of his hand, raising it again for a killing blow. Jono was on him before the blade could descend, mouth clamped over the man's head and biting down with enough force he chipped several fangs.

The hunter's skull popped in his mouth like an over-ripened berry, brain matter and fluid slipping past his lips. The demon fled, leaving behind the bitter taste of hell that washed away every other taste in his mouth. Jono spat out blood and bits of bone, globs of brain stuck between his teeth, but he didn't care.

All he cared about was Sage.

"Sage!" Wade yelled, his voice breaking on her name. "*Sage!*"

The remaining hunters weren't going to survive Jono's rage as he crouched over Sage's writhing body.

Neither would they survive Tiarnán's.

The fae lord stepped out of a lift, cane clenched in his hand like a sword, violet eyes shining with magic. The very air vibrated with his arrival, but Jono barely felt it as he shifted back to human now that Tiarnán had arrived. Even with the twisted, melting colors that assaulted his changing vision, Jono could see how all the gold veins in the marble that made up the floors and walls of the lobby burst into light and broke free of the expensive stone.

The floor undulated like in an earthquake while the precisely cut slabs of marble on the wall cracked and shook, some falling off their mountings. Every bit of brilliant metal called forth by the Lord of Ivy and Gold wrapped around the remaining hunters—cut *through* them—tearing them apart in a burst of shining gold and bright red blood.

They ended up in so many pieces that Jono knew identifying them would be practically impossible.

But he couldn't care about that, not with the gaping, bleeding wound in Sage's side taking up all his attention once he was human again. Aconite glistened against the ragged edges of her flesh and over the organs sliding out of the wound. Worse than that was the smell of black magic that had settled all around her.

Jono placed his hands against her heaving chest, Fenrir clawing at his soul, and poured everything he was into the order that came out of his mouth. *"Change."*

He forced Sage to obey him despite the agony it put her through, her pain all he could smell, all he could taste. When she was finally human beneath his hands, Jono choked on her name, the syllables lodging in his throat.

She looked at him with tears in her wide, shocked eyes, blood trickling out of her mouth, the wound in her gut still gaping open, not even close to being healed.

Tiarnán knelt on her other side, taking off his suit jacket to drape it over Sage's naked body to help stave off shock.

"I'll call for an ambulance," Tiarnán said.

Jono nodded tightly, his hand finding Sage's beneath the suit jacket as Wade hurried over with a frantic look on his face.

"Stay with me," Jono said, trying desperately to make it an order she had to obey.

BELLEVUE HOSPITAL WAS a Level 1 trauma center that had specialists on hand to handle anything that came through the emergency doors.

They were not exactly prepared for being inundated by a group consisting of werecreatures and the fae, every single one of them waiting for an update on Sage's and Deirdre's condition. Legally speaking, the only one allowed to receive a report on her status was her husband, but Marek had Jono's wrist in a viselike grip, ensuring he'd know she was out of surgery the second Marek did.

Because she was coming out of surgery. Jono refused to believe otherwise.

He closed his eyes and tipped his head back until it hit the wall.

The lunch hour had come and gone, but he wasn't hungry. They'd all given their statements to the PCB who'd followed them to the hospital, because Jono hadn't been willing to stay at the scene. He and Wade had been driven to Bellevue in Tiarnán's private car, the driver skirting speeding laws to get them there mere minutes after the ambulance arrived.

Patrick always complained about how the hurry up and wait aspect of missions was his least favorite part back when he'd been in the Mage Corps. Sitting there, not knowing Sage's status, Jono could understand why.

He opened his eyes and moved his head to crack his neck. Emma and Leon were curled up together on a chair in the private waiting room they'd been escorted to. Wade hadn't moved from his seat beside Jono, too worried to even fidget. Tiarnán and several other fae from his law firm took up other seats in the waiting room, the lot of them waiting on word from Deirdre.

Whatever aconite mixture the blade had been coated in, it had been deadly enough that Sage couldn't shift without Jono's command, and shifting wasn't healing her. Deirdre had been transported in a second ambulance, iron-sick in a way the fae rarely were when the wound wasn't deep. No one was taking any chances right now, not with demons in the mix.

It had been five hours since Sage was first rushed into surgery, and Patrick still hadn't answered his mobile.

Jono stared at Patrick's number in his call log, having tried calling him every ten minutes since Sage had been loaded into the ambulance, but every attempt went straight to voicemail. The slew of texts in the group chat and the private one between them had all gone unread. He wanted to leave to find Patrick but couldn't until he knew Sage had made it through her surgery.

Handling all the incoming texts from the pack alphas only distracted him so much before his thoughts started circling again. Looking for a distraction, he tried calling Patrick again but had no luck getting through.

"Why isn't he answering?" Wade asked after Jono ended the call.

"I don't know," Jono said, thinking about what Patrick had said last night.

"What if he was attacked like we were?"

"I'd know."

Jono knew Patrick was alive and on this side of the veil because the soulbond thrummed between them. It wasn't like when they were separated by cities or the veil, or even when Andras had taken over Patrick and blocked it, but Patrick wasn't paying any attention to it.

"But—"

"He went to work this morning. The government is planning the defense of New York City. He's probably still neck-deep in that meeting."

Wade lapsed back into silence, worry etched into his face. Jono sighed and flexed his fingers around his mobile, wondering if he should send another text or try calling again. The only other direct number at the SOA he had was Patrick's office line, but if he was in a meeting, he wouldn't be there to pick up. Calling was all Jono could do while they continued to wait, but it didn't feel like enough.

Another hour passed by before they received any news of Sage's condition. The doctor who entered the waiting room was in clean scrubs, but she still smelled like Sage's blood to Jono's nose.

"Family of Sage Taylor?" she asked, gaze tracking around the room.

"Here," Marek croaked out, shoving himself to his feet and dragging Jono with him. "I'm her husband. Jono's her alpha."

The surgeon nodded, taking the information in stride as she stared at them. "We'll start with the good news first. Your wife made it through surgery and is currently being transported to ICU. The severe allergic reaction she sustained to the aconite poisoning is something we need to monitor since she's not healing."

Jono's eyes burned, and he had to take a moment to wipe away the tears of utter relief those words caused.

Marek opened his mouth, but it took a second for him to speak. "*Will* she heal?"

"The aconite needs to be flushed completely out of her system first. We cleaned the wound and sent samples of the poison to the labs to get the results of what sort of structure it has. Aconite is known to impede werecreature healing, but I expected to see some movement toward biological repair already, except nothing has started. That usually indicates some level of magic in the mix. We had to stitch her up since she's not healing."

Jono drew in a sharp breath. "What about healing potions?"

The surgeon shook her head. "Until we know what sort of spell was in that poison, we can't give her healing potions just yet. I won't risk a bad interaction when she's barely stable."

Marek finally let Jono go to wipe the tears from his eyes. "Can I see her?"

"Once we have her established in an ICU room, then yes, but only one person at a time will be permitted to see her."

"Go," Jono said, nudging Marek in the side.

"Can I see her after?" Wade asked.

"The ICU wing has its own waiting room. A nurse can escort you all there," the surgeon said.

As badly as Jono wanted to stay, he knew he had to leave. Sage might still be critical, but she was alive, and he needed to believe she'd remain that way. "I need to find Patrick."

Marek nodded, not smelling angry at all. "I'll keep you updated on Sage."

"Yeah." Jono half turned, gesturing at Wade. "Stay with Marek and keep an eye on the ICU entrance."

Wade nodded jerkily, mouth set in a hard line, no hint of scales pushing through his skin despite his fury. "None of those fuckers are getting past me if they show up. I promise."

"Where are you going?" Emma asked, finally disentangling herself from Leon to get to her feet.

"Home first. I need to get something from there," Jono said, worry making his skin itch.

"I'll drive you. Leon will stay with Wade."

Emma walked over to give Marek a hug before slipping past the surgeon. Wade took Jono's place by Marek's side, looking grimly determined in his promise to watch over Sage.

"Let me know when you find Patrick," Wade said.

Jono nodded. "You'll be the first person I ring."

Because Wade was pack, and he needed to know before anyone else.

Jono turned to face Tiarnán, meeting the fae lord's gaze. "Can one of yours remain with Marek and Wade? We need someone with magic to help guard Sage."

"The firm is closed today after what happened. One of our partners will remain with your pack," Tiarnán said.

The fae had been enough that morning; he had to believe they'd be enough now. That's what their alliance was for, after all.

Jono met Emma out in the hallway, and they headed silently for the exit, receiving a couple of double takes as they went. Jono didn't know if it was because of his eyes or the bloodstains on his trousers from kneeling beside Sage in the lobby. He needed a shower, just not one from the storm outside.

They ran through the rain for the car park two blocks away, preternatural speed helping them get there in less than a minute, but they were still soaked when they arrived. Emma didn't seem to care Jono was ruining the leather seat of her Maserati.

Emma started the engine, and Jono tried calling Patrick one more time once they were on the street. It went to voicemail, and he ended the call, trying not to break his mobile.

"Do you want me to send out word for the packs to keep an eye out for Patrick? Or start a search?" Emma asked as she pointed her car Uptown.

"You're driving," Jono told her.

"I can call Leon and tell him what to do and drive at the same time."

Jono gritted his teeth together and shook his head. "Let's just get to the flat."

Emma never took her eyes off the road, the wipers set to their highest speed against the downpour. "Are we going to wait for Patrick there?"

"No."

"Jono."

He rested his elbow against the car door and rubbed at his eyes until colored spots burst across his vision. "I know he won't be at the flat, but I need to retrieve something from there just in case."

"Where do you think he is?"

"Hopefully still at work. I'd like to believe Patrick hasn't fucked off to do something stupid."

"This is Patrick we're talking about."

"I know. That's why we're going home. We'll need every weapon we can possibly get."

"And then what?"

"I keep trying to reach Patrick."

His continued silence was worrisome, though it wasn't anything Jono could fix right then. Despite the promise last night, Jono knew what Patrick was capable of when he got it in his head to do something. Jono needed to know that Patrick wasn't paying the price Ethan demanded in exchange for Eloise without telling him first, because they both knew it was a shit deal.

"Maybe it's like what you told Wade. Maybe he's in a meeting and he can't answer his phone," Emma said at the next red light.

Jono licked his lips. "Maybe."

The flat was empty, like he knew it would be, when they finally arrived. Jono went straight to the bedroom and pulled open the nightstand drawer on Patrick's side of the bed. Resting beside the empty space where the iron box had been was an old Greek coin, the only one remaining from the multitudes that Hermes had given Patrick last year before the whole mess with summer solstice.

"Jono?" Emma said from the doorway.

"When we were in Paris, Patrick stopped Ilya by using Srecha's blessing to break the Morrígan's staff. We came home with a piece of it. Ethan knows we have it. Loki told us in Salem that if Patrick wanted Eloise back, he had to bring them the piece of the Morrígan's staff. Patrick promised me he'd tell me if he was going to trade it for his grandmother. He told me he was taking the piece of it with him to work today," Jono said.

Emma stared at him for a long few seconds, all the blood draining out of her face. "Do you think that's why we can't get ahold of him? Because he's trading himself for his grandmother?"

"I don't know."

Jono pressed a hand to his chest, wishing he was wrong, knowing he wasn't because Patrick's self-sacrificing tendencies were well-known within their pack. It would have been infuriating if it weren't an essential part of Patrick's makeup and part of the reason Jono had fallen in love with the man in the first place.

Sighing, he picked up the Greek coin with his other hand, finding it cool to the touch, the edges not perfectly circular, and it smelled ever so faintly of magic.

"The gods have only ever given him weapons. I don't want him to be without a single one," Jono murmured, staring at the coin.

An unexpected knock on the front door had his head snapping around. Jono clenched his fingers around the coin, staring at Emma as he dialed up his hearing, listening to the dozen or so heartbeats on the landing. Jono shoved the Greek coin into his pocket and left the bedroom, Emma on his heels. He yanked open the front door, staring at the group before him.

Captain Gerard Breckinridge smiled grimly, dripping water on the landing. He wore a black uniform that wouldn't be out of place on a battlefield and carried a duffel bag large enough to hold a long gun and other gear. "Jono."

"Going to let us in?" Sergeant Keith Pearson asked, looking as soaked as Gerard and kitted out just as similarly.

Jono's gaze jumped from Keith to the man standing on his other side. Ranged down the stairs and to the lower landing, and probably lower than that, was the entirety of the Hellraisers who'd fought with them in Ireland to save Órlaith.

"Patrick said the joint task force was recalling people," Jono said, gaze flicking back to Gerard.

"We aren't the only team the Department of the Preternatural is deploying to New York City, but we were the one specifically told to meet up with you and Patrick," Gerard said.

"So it's not just the National Guard, then?"

"The Department of the Preternatural is bolstering the National Guard's forces, even if the general population isn't aware of that. Our teams are better prepared for something like this over the regular Army, even if it's not an official deployment of the Army inside our borders."

"Because you've fought Ethan before."

"Him and his allies." Gerard rubbed at his jaw with a gloved hand. "General Reed has boots on the ground in Manhattan. He's in charge, whether anyone will like to admit it on the civilian front or not."

Jono had only met the dragon masquerading as a man twice, but he wasn't impressed by the bloke. "He'll need to take orders from us."

Gerard arched an eyebrow. "It's your fight, I won't deny that, but you don't have military training."

Jono tapped two fingers against the center of his chest, a silent reference to the god he carried in his soul. "I don't need any."

Thunder erupted overhead, loud enough it made Gerard look

up at the ceiling. "The reactionary storm outside is getting worse because the veil is tearing."

Jono tightened his grip on the doorknob, denting the metal. "I know."

"You don't understand. It's like Cairo all over again, except it's tearing open from the other side rather than this one."

Jono swallowed back bile. He knew what waited past the veil. They all did. "I take it that's worse."

"Ethan doesn't need sacrifices here on Earth to keep the veil open if the gods are the ones doing the tearing from their worlds. They won't stop until everything on the other side of the veil pushes through here. It's going to be hell. Literally." Gerard's gaze moved past Jono, landing on Emma, and he frowned. "Where's Patrick?"

Jono tried to breathe but found his chest didn't want to expand all the way, the soulbond unresponsive to his desperate pull. "I don't know."

Gerard's silver eyes went flat and hard. "Tell me everything."

## 18

THE MORNING DRIVE INTO WORK WAS AN EXERCISE IN WHITE-knuckled driving. Terrible weather made for terrible drivers, and Patrick probably could've written a symphony with his horn by the time he parked in the garage adjacent to the SOA field office.

Patrick was prepared for the weather. He wasn't prepared for who he found waiting for him in his office, sitting behind his desk as if he owned it.

Patrick rocked to a halt just inside the door, eyes going wide. "Sir. What are you doing here?"

General Noah Reed blew a smoke ring up at the ceiling, the cigarette held between his fingers nothing but the filter, and stared at Patrick. His gaze went unerringly to the small iron box tucked under Patrick's arm, and he narrowed his eyes.

"Close the door, Collins," Reed ordered.

Patrick obeyed automatically, casting a silence ward while he was at it. Static flowed through the room, making his ears pop. "What's going on?"

"I think that's my question." Reed pointed at what he carried. "*That* was never in any of your after-action reports from Paris."

Patrick reached up to grab the box from under his arm, holding it tightly in one hand. "It didn't need to be."

"I gave you a mission, Collins."

"And the gods gave me a soul debt. Sorry, sir, but you're dead last where they're concerned. The Morrígan's staff was never coming back to you or the government."

Reed stared at him with eyes that never blinked, the steadiness of his stare almost otherworldly. "Eloise Patterson is missing, you fought a god in Salem, and now you're carrying a broken piece of the Morrígan's staff. What are you planning on doing, Collins?"

"Nothing but fight. That's why we're all here, isn't it?" Patrick eyed the general. "Did the president send you?"

"We're trying to stave off an incursion from every hell in existence without panicking the masses. Of course the president sent me."

Patrick had never met the president, but considering how many immortals held government jobs, part of him wondered if the person sitting behind the Resolute desk was a god. He wasn't sure he ever wanted to find out.

"Bad optics if the media sees you and whoever came with you," Patrick said quietly.

Reed smiled, teeth far too sharp for a human mouth. "Optics won't matter if everyone is dead and this world has gone to hell. I have my people to think about, same as you."

Patrick swallowed tightly. "The packs who have come for the fight have their orders, as do the Night Courts. Jono's confirming with the fae today about their support. The covens stand ready."

"And the gods?"

Patrick shrugged stiffly. "If the fight is here—"

"It will be."

Patrick stared at him, tapping a finger against the iron box. "It's been confirmed? New York City is ground zero?"

Reed blew out a puff of smoke that didn't come from the

cigarette, the gray plume drifting between them. Patrick hoped it wouldn't trigger the building's sprinklers. "Close enough."

"So what now?"

"Priya's writ for habeas corpus et animum was granted. Setsuna's soul will be called back from the afterlife today during the joint task force meeting." Patrick froze, choking on air. Reed's gaze didn't waver. "I can't excuse you."

"Why the fuck not?" Patrick demanded hoarsely.

"Because the rest of the people on the joint task force who don't trust you need to see you there. They need to know you had nothing to do with her death."

Patrick bit out a harsh laugh. "That bullet was meant for *me*."

"Maybe. But you still have a job to do, Collins. She would want you to finish it."

He closed his eyes, tears burning against his lashes. "They should let her rest."

"There is no rest in war."

Not even if you were dead, it seemed.

The sound of the chair creaking made Patrick open his eyes, watching as Reed got to his feet. The general came around the desk, settling his hand on Patrick's shoulder for a couple of seconds.

"Meeting starts in ten minutes," Reed said before leaving.

The door shut quietly behind him. Patrick drew in a shaky breath and scrubbed at his eyes before yanking out his phone from his back pocket. He set the iron box on his desk and thumbed it open, staring at the carved raven sitting innocuously inside. He knew better than to touch it, Srecha's blessing all that had saved him last time.

Samhain was four days away. Patrick knew what he risked by giving it up, but he also knew what he would lose if he didn't.

He closed the box and called Ashanti, because Setsuna might be dead, but she hadn't been the only one to keep an eye on him over the years. It took a few rings before the mother of all vampires picked up.

"What is it now?" Ashanti asked, not bothering with pleasantries.

"Did you know my mother's family had ownership of the Salem nexus?" Patrick asked.

"No one owns a nexus."

"The Pattersons say they do."

"They guard it. They do not own it."

The dismissive tone to her voice reminded Patrick of Lucien's opinions about any contract or treaty. "You still knew."

"Does it matter? It was never going to change your situation."

"It matters if Ethan has Eloise."

She made a soft, thoughtful noise. "Ah. The blood kin. It would be unwise to give him whatever he wants in exchange for her."

Patrick closed his eyes. The idea churning in the back of his mind was bound to piss off Jono, but Patrick didn't see a way through this mess without trying the impossible.

"I have a meeting to get to. They're calling back Setsuna's soul."

"She is dead. She cannot help you."

Patrick bit at the inside of his cheek. "You can. I need to talk to you after my meeting."

"I am in Brooklyn ensuring my children's territory is well guarded for the fight ahead."

Patrick mentally calculated how long he thought the meeting might take, then doubled it. "I can meet you there around 1600."

"Very well. If it's that important to you, then we will meet. Call me when you get to Brooklyn, and I will direct you to a neutral location."

Ashanti ended the call, and Patrick pulled the phone away from his ear. He glanced at the clock on the screen before turning it off and shoving it into his back pocket.

"Fuck," he said tiredly, running a hand over his face.

He wished this wasn't happening, but wishes had never

changed anything in his life, and neither had praying, so Patrick left his office and went to do his job.

<hr>

HOURS LATER, sheet lightning illuminated the reactionary storm churning over New York City, sometimes forking down to crackle on the rods erected on top of every skyscraper and bridge. The wind was a cold, howling thing that drove the rain sideways with gale force speed. The black clouds moved in a way that reminded Patrick of the start of a tornadic supercell storm in the Midwest. Few people walked the streets, and if they did, umbrellas were useless.

Worse than the storm was the frightening pressure in the air that wasn't just a barometric issue. Patrick remembered the weight of wild magic in Cairo, how it had hung over their heads like a guillotine during the fighting. All the sacrifices Ethan's side had done back then to keep the tear between worlds open had caused that reactionary storm to be brutal. It'd taken close to a year for weather patterns to settle after the Thirty-Day War.

Patrick hoped that wouldn't happen here.

He drove through the pouring rain, windshield wipers working frantically. He kept his eyes on the road as he oriented himself for the drive to Brooklyn. At the next red light, he finally turned on his cell phone.

He'd turned it off before the start of the long virtual meeting with Henry, the governor of the State of New York, the heads of the joint task force, the Dagda in his guise as the mayor, and the NYPD commissioner.

Their first order of business had been calling Setsuna's soul back into her body, and Patrick hadn't been able to make himself look at the television screen during that time. Hearing the echo of her voice, long after she was gone, had been difficult. His palms still throbbed with the cuts his fingernails had dug into his own flesh.

That hour had crawled by, and he'd asked no questions to the dead while everyone else had. When the necromancer finally put Setsuna back to rest, Patrick didn't feel relieved, only hollowed out. The rest of the meeting was spent discussing the rapid deployment of the National Guard—who couldn't arrive soon enough in Patrick's opinion—and what magical defenses could be erected around Manhattan and the other boroughs, as well as the nexus in Salem.

It made him wish the barrier they'd set last year with the Greek coins and cliff roses had survived. But Cernunnos had destroyed it after sucking out all the life in every park to keep Hannah and her unborn child alive. Patrick didn't trust the gods, but at this point, he'd take any help his side could get.

As soon as his phone was fully booted, the notifications started rolling in. Patrick's heart skipped a beat at the number of missed calls, voice messages, and texts showing up on the screen. He didn't bother reading any of the texts or listening to his voicemail. Instead, he called Jono, who picked up before the first ring even finished going off.

"What happened?" Patrick asked tightly, gripping the steering wheel with both hands.

"We were attacked by hunters at Gentry & Thyme this morning. I've been trying to reach you all day. Sage took a blow meant for me and got gutted by a fucking poisoned blade," Jono said, sounding tired and angry.

A ringing noise filled Patrick's ears, drowning out the rain. The rattle in his chest was him trying to breathe. "Is she—"

"She's alive but in the ICU at Bellevue. Whatever was on the blade is making it difficult for her to shift right now."

Patrick opened his mouth to speak but couldn't find the words, heart pounding as if he were running a race. The light turned green, and he pressed on the gas pedal. "Will she be okay?"

"She's stable. Marek and Wade are with her. Where are you?"

His stomach twisted, and he swallowed hard. "I just finished a meeting with the joint task force. I'm on my way to meet with Ashanti."

"Why?"

Patrick wanted to lie to protect Jono, but he couldn't find the will to do so. "I need her to do something for me."

"You couldn't ring her and ask?" At Patrick's silence, Jono let out an angry laugh. "You promised me you wouldn't fuck off without telling me first."

"And I told you before I don't have a choice."

"Right, then. I'm putting you on speaker."

The fury in Jono's voice made Patrick flinch, but it didn't stop him from driving toward the Brooklyn Bridge rather than Bellevue, despite everything in him that was demanding he turn around and go check on Sage.

"What the fuck is going on, Collins?" Gerard asked.

Patrick jerked at the sound of his old captain's voice coming over the line but kept the steering wheel steady in his hands. "Gerard? When did you get here?"

"Today. I have the whole team with me, and we need a sitrep."

Patrick clenched his teeth until his jaw ached before finally speaking. "Did Jono tell you Ethan has my grandmother?"

"We've been filled in."

"Then you know the Salem Coven and my mother's family are responsible for the protective wards around the Salem nexus. If we give up the piece of the Morrígan's staff, I can get Eloise back and block Ethan's power source."

"We both know that's a fucking lie. Don't do it, Collins. Don't trade yourself for her. The veil is tearing as we speak, and we need you here."

"And what happens when Ethan drains that nexus dry? The SOA is going to send mages to barricade it, but the protective wards are generational. The SOA can't just tear them down. Ethan will still be able to get through the defenses because of Eloise. She's a back door to the damn thing like my sister is. She's the only one that has the command trigger for those wards and can take them down."

"He's not related to her."

"That doesn't matter when Hannah *is* and he has my blood as well. But getting Eloise back means she can take down her family's wards, and the SOA can block Ethan. It's two fucked choices, but taking away a power source might buy us time to figure out where the hell Ethan is, because I guarantee you he isn't in Salem."

"There are millions of zombies and demons and who knows what else waiting to break through the veil. Whatever time you think you'll buy us isn't going to mean shit if we spend days fighting that army. It'll mean even less if Ethan has a working weapon."

"Ashanti can help us track Hannah with my blood. We wouldn't be fighting blind."

"You'd have to be *here* for that spell to be useful."

"Patrick," Jono bit out, cutting into their argument. "Listen to Gerard. Don't hand it over. You know Ethan won't accept just the broken piece. He'll want you as well, and you can't give yourself over to him."

The fear and anger in Jono's voice made Patrick flinch. "I don't plan on negotiating with him."

"Yeah? Then who are you going to negotiate with?"

Patrick hesitated before steeling himself for his lover's fury. "Hades."

"Are you fucking *mad*?" Jono snarled.

"Patrick, that's the stupidest idea you've had in years. Don't give me another goddamn heart attack," Gerard said.

"Hades has only stayed with Ethan because of Macaria. He's said before he's not leaving his daughter. If I have a way to get her back, then he might go along with it," Patrick argued.

"No he fucking *won't*."

"He will if Persephone can persuade him." Patrick blew out a harsh breath. "I know none of you like this idea, and fuck knows neither do I, but this was never your debt to pay. I'm paying it the only way I know how."

"Bollocks. Fucking *bollocks*. We're a *pack*. You aren't doing this alone," Jono protested.

"I won't be, because you'll find me. You always do, and I need you to do that here." Jono's silence settled heavily over the line. Patrick kept driving. "Jono. You'll find me."

"I can't leave New York City. I can't leave Sage and everyone else to what's coming through the veil. I have to hold the line for you here."

The anguish in Jono's voice cut right through Patrick, but he'd spent years flaying himself down to the bone for other people in order to keep moving forward. He couldn't stop now. "Then stay. I'll come back to you. I always do."

"Patrick—"

A hideous electronic whine drowned out Jono's voice before the call went dead, along with the car. Patrick braked hard and kept control of the wheel as all around him, other vehicles jolted to a stop. Lights in the buildings and streetlights all down the street went out. With the blanket of storm clouds overhead, the world was plunged into an eerie, almost twilight gloom.

"*Fuck*," Patrick snarled, lifting his hips so he could shove his bricked phone into his back pocket.

He didn't bother trying to start the engine again. He grabbed the iron box from the glove compartment, gripped it tight, and got out of the car. He ducked his head against the vicious wind and rain that slammed into his personal shields and started running.

The rain came down like a waterfall on his mad dash to the Brooklyn Bridge. More people were out in the storm now that the electrical grid was dead and Manhattan had gone dark. Cars clogged the streets, and those that weren't tied to computers in order to function were boxed in and going nowhere fast. Patrick stuck to the sidewalks, shoving his way through throngs of people who didn't know what was going on.

Patrick knew, and it kept him running.

When he finally turned onto the pedestrian pathway leading across the Brooklyn Bridge, heaving for air, the storm had gotten worse. As Patrick gained elevation, he paused for a moment to catch his breath and turned to look back at Manhattan.

The spinning heart of the reactionary storm spanned the length of the island now and was rapidly moving toward the outer boroughs. The weight of it pressed down on the air, blocking up his inner ear. The wind howled over the Brooklyn Bridge so loud Patrick could barely hear himself think.

It was a wonder, then, that he heard Ashanti at all or that she'd managed to find him in the midst of the burgeoning chaos. But gods were known to do the impossible, so he shouldn't have been surprised.

*"Look up."*

The words echoed in his ears, or maybe his mind, causing Patrick to turn and stare up at the first tower of the Brooklyn Bridge and the suspension wires that created a spiderweb effect around him. He squinted through the pouring rain, catching sight of a shadow drifting along the top of the tower against the glare of lightning.

Patrick headed up the path for the tower, the only one on the pedestrian portion of the bridge. He could see countless people in the lanes below hurrying between stalled cars, having left the safety of their vehicles.

The shadow became a blur that slid down one of the suspension wires before dropping to the ground in front of him. Ashanti's clothes were waterlogged, her skirt clinging to her legs and bunching up around the ironshod curved bone hooks she stood on. Her bloodred hair was done up in Bantu knots this time around in deference to the weather.

Ashanti flashed her iron fangs at him, black eyes reflecting the lightning from above. "The veil is tearing."

"I know," Patrick said, raising his voice to be heard over the wind. "That's why I'm here."

Ashanti's gaze flicked from his face to the iron box clenched in his hand and back again. "You come bearing a gift."

Patrick tightened his grip around the iron box. "Not for you."

"It wouldn't be for anyone if you were smart."

"I've been known to have stupid ideas before."

"Patrick."

"They have my grandmother, Ashanti. She has a generational access to the nexus under Salem. I can't let Ethan do to her what he did to my mom and sister. We can't let him have that power. He won't need sacrifices and souls to turn himself into a god if he can mainline a fucking nexus to power his spell."

"Some sacrifices must be made to win a war."

Patrick swallowed against the dryness in his throat. "Not on his terms."

"You give Ethan a path to everything he wants if you give him that bit of the Morrígan's staff, because you will be handing yourself over to him as well. This isn't how I taught you to weigh costs."

The Morrígan's staff was made to raise the dead but the almost-sentient power that lived inside that horrific weapon wasn't one Ethan could channel, not without godly sacrifices. He had no gods save those from the hells who'd made whatever bargains they could to fight with him instead of die for him. Removing the nexus beneath Salem from Ethan's control would deny him power for the altar he was building up New York City to be.

"No, but you taught me to be a weapon. This is me wielding myself. If I take Eloise's place, I have a better chance at keeping Ethan from the nexus."

"We need you here to find him, not out of reach in Salem."

Patrick blinked rain out of his eyes, licking it off his lips. "I promised to bleed for you, and I will. But I need to do this first."

"You are blood kin to both Eloise and Ethan. His magic will walk right through yours."

"Maybe. But I have a soulbond. Jono might be enough to help me keep Ethan at bay."

"If your wolf is to come after you, he best leave soon. Manhattan will soon be impassable."

Patrick hesitated, wishing his phone worked to pass on that warning. "Jono needs to stay here. Sage is hurt, and the rest of the packs and our allies need guidance. Gerard's in town. If Jono can't leave New York to come after me, Gerard will."

"Cú Chulainn is needed on the front lines where he belongs."

Patrick narrowed his eyes at her. "Did you always know who he was?"

"What do you think?"

He should've been angry about that, but he'd already lost Setsuna, and regret was still a bitter taste in his mouth even these many days later. Being angry at Ashanti wasn't worth it now, not with what they were facing down.

"I think the gods all hate what you taught me."

To question; to fight; to survive. Patrick had lost a lot in his life, but he was still standing, and his foundation wasn't laid at Persephone's feet, but Ashanti's and Setsuna's in ways he was only recently beginning to recognize.

Ashanti stepped closer, tilting her head back a little so she could look him in the eye. The incline on the pedestrian pathway wasn't so steep that she stood above him, but Patrick hadn't felt so small beneath a person's gaze in a long, long while.

Then Ashanti smiled, a hard curve of her mouth, and the laugh she let out was stolen by the wind. "The end has always started with a sacrifice. Let it be yours then, and let us win this war."

Patrick swallowed, throat dry, and hoped he wasn't making a

mistake. "I need to find Hades. If you know where he is, can you take me to him?"

"She can't, but I can, Pattycakes," Hermes said from behind him.

Patrick jerked around, coming face-to-face with the Greek messenger god. The immortal's aura was cracked open and burned Patrick's vision, causing him to squint. Hermes was unbothered by the storm, dry beneath the rain due to magic. His dyed blue curls were faded, dark roots showing when he raked a hand through them, grinning at Patrick with a light in his gold-brown eyes that made him look manic.

"Where's Hades?" Patrick asked.

"Not in the Underworld, so lucky you, there's no payment involved for this trip," Hermes said.

"Shows what you know. I'll need you to take me to him after our first stop."

"And why should I do that?" Hermes pointed at the iron box, smile disappearing from his face. "This doesn't belong to him, to any of them. Giving it up is not how you pay what you owe us."

"It buys us time."

Hermes gestured at the city behind him. "Time is irrelevant now."

Patrick's gaze was drawn to the fog creeping through the skyscrapers of Manhattan, a familiar darkness he remembered from Cairo all those years ago building deep inside the city.

"Bullshit. It's not Samhain. Ethan can't break the world until then."

"Are you willing to bet the world on that?"

"I'll bet it on my pack." Patrick stepped closer until he stood toe-to-toe with Hermes. "Ethan has mercenaries in Salem. He hasn't removed them from the field. Whatever he's planning, he needs power from that nexus, which means Eloise is probably still in Salem somewhere. Wherever she's being kept, Hades can take us to her if he isn't with her already."

"What makes you think he'd parley with you instead of outright kill you?"

"Because Persephone is coming with us."

Hermes threw back his head and laughed. "Oh, is she now?"

Patrick smiled, teeth cutting into his lips. "Hades owes his wife too much to piss her off more than he already has. This is how I pay my debt, so yeah, she'll come. All of you will in the end."

It was a wild request Patrick wasn't sure would be granted, but he had to try. The veil was tearing, and they were out of time to stop the end of this whole fucking mess from happening, but they could hold the line on two fronts for long enough to get their people in place. They had to.

"What say you, Ashanti?" Hermes asked, never taking his eyes off Patrick.

"What better weapon to use for the kill than the one you never see sliding between your ribs?" Ashanti asked as she stepped up beside Patrick. "You and yours gave him this task. Let Patrick pay his soul debt how he sees fit."

"As all heroes ought, yes?" Hermes lifted a hand and dragged his fingers through the air, peeling it apart, wisps of the veil falling away from his touch. He did it with an ease Patrick knew wasn't normal, because crossing the veil was always difficult, even for gods. It just proved how thin it had been reduced to. "Shall we, Pattycakes?"

Patrick tucked the iron box under one arm before bending over to undo the straps of the dagger and sheath strapped to his thigh and hooked to his belt. Once it was free, he held it up for Ashanti to take.

"Bring this to Jono for me," he said.

She looked at him with those black eyes of hers, rain falling around her diminutive figure. They were miles and miles away from the desert they'd been in last time when they stood like this, holding a gods-given weapon between them, but some echoes of his past would always find him.

This time, Ashanti wasn't carrying the naked blade in her hands, passing it to him as she crumbled to dust amidst a sacrificial spell. No heat, no fire, no ash floating on the wind and ground down beneath his fingernails. Only a raging reactionary storm and the end of everything unfolding along the Manhattan skyline bore witness this time to the exchange.

Ashanti wrapped her fingers around the leather sheath, protected from the prayers that could burn even one such as herself. "Good hunting."

Patrick nodded at Hermes and followed the god through the ripped-open veil and into cold gray fog that washed the world away.

19

THE WIND FOLLOWED THEM FROM EARTH TO THE SHORES OF THE River Styx, the gray wasteland of the Underworld cast in shadows. Patrick blinked rapidly to try to get his vision to settle, cold even with the heat charms running hot in his leather jacket. He wondered if it was a reflection of the reactionary storm on Earth, but he rather thought this version of a hell was always as cold as a grave.

"Patrick."

Persephone's voice came from behind him, a warmth blooming around where he and Hermes stood. He turned to face the queen of the Underworld, steeling himself to meet the goddess' gold-brown gaze. "Persephone."

She was dressed for winter despite being a goddess of spring-time. The fitted wool coat she wore fell to her knees, and her flat-heeled knee-high boots were covered in the muck of the river-bank, though she seemed not to care. Her golden-brown skin and curly, dark brown hair stood out against the grayness of the world around them.

Persephone had the same-colored eyes as Hermes, and they

never looked away from Patrick's face, her aura burning like a halo around her. "What brings you across the veil when the fight is in the mortal world?"

"I've come about a bargain."

Persephone's eyes narrowed. "Your soul debt is not up for negotiation."

"I know. I'm not talking about what I owe you. I'm talking about what Ethan wants. He has Eloise."

"Yes, I've heard her prayers."

Patrick had to stuff his rage down deep, but some anger still came out in his voice. "Nice of you not to answer her."

Persephone arched an eyebrow. "You're here, are you not?"

Patrick scowled. "If this is some fucked-up game the Fates are playing—"

"The future is unknown to them all right now."

"There will be a new future after Samhain," Hermes said, sounding almost cheerful as he tucked his hands into his back pockets. "Even odds on which side wins."

"Hermes."

"Come now, dearest. We both know that to walk upon the earth and be seen again is to be remembered."

Hermes smiled at her, but Persephone didn't return one of her own.

Patrick cleared his throat, tapping a finger against the iron box. "I have an idea, but I need your help, Persephone."

"It is not my place to aid you," she said.

"Maybe not, but the whole reason you indebted me was to get Macaria back. In order to do that, we need to halve Ethan's power. I'm betting Eloise is being held in Salem somewhere, and Hades would know where. He'll talk to you if you ask him to. Hermes can pass on the message for us."

Persephone's formidable attention shifted from Patrick to Hermes. The messenger god removed his hands from his pockets and shrugged expansively. "Pattycakes has never had the best ideas."

"Indeed," Persephone said, glancing back at Patrick. "I have nothing to say to my husband."

"Pretty sure he's got plenty to say to you," Patrick replied.

"That is irrelevant."

"War says otherwise." Patrick lifted the iron box for her to see. "Loki said they'd swap Eloise for this, but we all know they'd soon as kill her than hand her over alive."

"My high priestess is not worth the Morrígan's staff."

"Yeah, well, the Morrígan likes war, and we're going to give her one. Look, just come with me to talk to Hades. Think of this trade like your own personal Trojan horse."

"Dying won't pay your soul debt."

Patrick gritted his teeth in an ugly smile. "I don't plan on dying."

His plan wouldn't work without her though. Hades would murder him on sight if he went alone and handed his body over to Ethan. In a situation like this, Patrick wasn't above playing dirty. Hades and Persephone had spent over twenty years on opposite sides of this fight, trying to save their daughter in their own way—Hades by never leaving Macaria while she was effectively held hostage and Persephone aiming at the heart of Ethan's power through Patrick.

Divorce wasn't an option for them, but he'd settle for an argument because at least the two immortals would maybe be on speaking terms that way.

"You told me to win this war, and this is how I'm doing it," Patrick said. "Don't you want your daughter back?"

Hope wasn't just a mortal thing; he could see the spark of it in Persephone's gold-brown eyes. "You would not be here if I didn't."

"Then let me pay my soul debt. You want Ethan dead? This is how I kill him. All you have to do is have a conversation with Hades."

None of them spoke, the only sound between them that of the wind blowing across the Underworld and the waves lapping at the shore of the River Styx. What felt like an age passed before Persephone stepped closer, lifting her hands to frame Patrick's face. Her touch was warm, bringing with it the scent of spring, but her words reminded him of winter ice.

"Play your part to the end and bring my daughter back to me. I'll allow no flowers to bloom on your grave if you fail," Persephone said.

Patrick didn't blink. "No daisies. Got it. Now let's go have a talk with your husband."

She withdrew her hands and gestured imperiously at Hermes. "We will speak to Hades alone. Tell him to bring my high priestess. Carry my request with great speed."

Hermes placed a hand over his heart and bowed. "I shall be but a moment."

He turned and walked away, disappearing into the veil. Patrick hoped that moment didn't last long. Time ran quicker in the mortal realm than past the veil. Every second he remained in the Underworld was hours back on Earth. Patrick couldn't afford to lose that much time, not this close to Samhain.

Hurry up and wait was never so nerve-racking as it was right then. Patrick didn't let out a sigh of relief when Hermes finally returned, but it was close. The god stepped through the veil some minutes later, the fog of its edges clinging to him.

"He awaits your arrival," Hermes said to Persephone.

Persephone said nothing as she led them to the shoreline. Patrick was unsurprised to see a faint, hazy glow bobbing closer on the horizon. When Charon finally made it close to shore, the ferryman bowed his cowled head in deference to his queen.

Persephone led the way to his boat, brackish water splashing against the bones that made up the hull. The skulls that acted as lanterns at the prow of the boat and on top of Charon's ancient wooden pole provided just enough light to see by. Patrick clambered into the boat, the vessel rocking ominously. When they were all three sitting on the cold wooden benches, Charon used the pole to shove the boat away from the shore.

No coin was needed for passage this time, not with Persephone and Hermes seated with him in the boat. Patrick settled the iron box on his lap and held it with both hands, staring into the fog around them and trying not to think about what existed below in the waters of the River Styx.

When the fog finally parted and the boat came to ground on another shore, Persephone rose smoothly to her feet. "Thank you, Charon."

The ferryman waited until they all made it to shore before pushing away again, drifting back into the currents, ready to ferry whatever souls came his way to the Underworld. Hermes led them away from the River Styx and through the fog of the veil back to the mortal realm.

Patrick's feet sank into wet grass as the veil finally faded away, replaced with Salem Common. The reactionary storm here wasn't as bad as the one in New York, but it was still proof of an excessive amount of magic at play. He didn't know what day it was, only that it was night, and he doubted it was the Monday he'd left behind on the Brooklyn Bridge. If he was lucky, it was very early Tuesday morning.

The gazebo that took up prominence in Salem Common was guarded by Cerberus, but Patrick barely paid the three-headed hellhound any attention. All of his focus was on the god standing inside the gazebo with his grandmother. Despite all the times they'd faced each other before, Patrick appeared to be an afterthought to the god compared to Persephone.

Lightning flashed above, illuminating the park. Persephone walked forward without worry, holding out both hands to Cerberus. The immortal bent all three heads to her hands, shoving against each other to get the first pet.

"Oh, my darlings, I've missed you so," she crooned.

Cerberus wagged his tail, looking for all the world like an overgrown puppy.

"Seph," Hades said after a moment, the diminutive endearment of her name practically ground out between his teeth.

She stared up at her husband, the rain pouring down around her but missing her entirely by way of magic. "I must admit, I did not expect you to come."

"You haven't reached out to me in over twenty years."

"You know why." Something like grief passed over Hades' face before it was replaced with a hardness that made Persephone firm her jaw. "You've enabled our demise."

"I've worked to keep our daughter safe," Hades countered.

"You've let that bastard prey on her godhead for over two decades. How is that keeping her safe?"

"He hasn't laid claim to it since he ensnared her. All his attempts have failed."

"You've stood by his side and watched him *try*. That doesn't absolve you."

Hades walked down the steps of the gazebo, dragging Eloise with him. Hellfire preceded every step, burning outward to surround where they stood.

Eloise was gray-faced in the lingering flash of lightning and the glow of hellfire that rose up to encircle where they stood. Her gaze was vacant, as if she weren't present in her body. Patrick tightened his grip on the iron box, wanting desperately to get her out of Hades' reach.

"I came because Hermes said you wished to talk. So *talk*," Hades ground out.

"I am not who you need to talk to." Persephone turned her head to look at Patrick. "He is."

Patrick held up the iron box. "Loki said something about a trade. So here I am."

Hades' eyes narrowed, but he didn't let go of Eloise. "It was unwise of you to come, even with my wife."

"It seemed an acceptable risk."

"You think highly of your survival."

"I'm here to ensure Eloise's."

Hades' lips curled upward in cold amusement. "You would've done better not to come at all."

"But I came, and you're going to listen to my bargain."

"And if I don't?"

"Then you're never getting Macaria back, and I'd bet good money dead or alive Persephone will divorce your ass."

The hellfire surrounding them flared up higher, chasing away the cold. Sweat trickled down the back of Patrick's neck from the heat.

"You know nothing of what I have done to protect my daughter," Hades hissed.

"I don't care," Patrick shot back. "You let her languish in my sister's body and soul. You let Hannah essentially die beneath the weight of carrying a godhead she shouldn't have because you didn't have the fucking balls to confront Ethan."

"He tied himself to your sister. Killing him would have killed them both."

"So instead you let them suffer all these years while Ethan worked to become a god and did nothing to stop him. That's a negative number on the parenting scale. But you're in luck—I'm here to save your marriage. You get this—" Patrick held up the iron box. "—and me, and Eloise goes free."

"And if I keep you both?"

Patrick jerked his thumb in Persephone's direction. "She won't let you because I'm in her debt. This exchange is the only way you get the piece of the Morrígan's staff. This is the only way you get *me*. Take it or leave it."

There was still a chance Hades wouldn't give up Eloise, that he'd stick to whatever plan Ethan had drawn up. But he'd pulled Eloise from wherever she had been and come alone. Ethan's control of Hades began and ended with Macaria. Patrick was banking on Hades' desire to see his daughter alive winning out over seeing Patrick dead.

When Hades' gaze flicked briefly to Persephone, longing in his eyes not even a war could kill, Patrick knew he'd get his way.

And it just might kill him in the end.

"Your presence and the Morrígan's staff made whole for a woman who you barely know. Some bargain," Hades said before he flung Eloise forward.

Patrick dived for her, feet slipping in the wet grass, but he managed to get his arms around Eloise's frail body and keep her upright. She didn't seem coherent, magic thick around her, and he only hoped whatever lingering spellwork she was tied to would be severed when she went through the veil.

"I'll take her," Hermes said, suddenly there and drawing Eloise out of his arms.

"Take her to Jono," Patrick said. "Tell him—"

A hand came down on his shoulder—heavy and cold, freezing him down to his bones. He flinched with his entire body, remembering the feel of Hades' magic when the god had burned out the anchor wards on his bones back in August.

"You'd throw away your last chance to win this fight with him, Seph?" Hades asked as he tightened his hold on Patrick.

Persephone looked at her husband with as much hate in her eyes as love, the rawness of both in her voice. "I'm doing it to save us, my love. If you can't see that, then perhaps we were never meant to be in this world, the same way we would never be in the one you're helping Ethan build."

Hades' fingers bit into Patrick's shoulder hard enough to bruise. "What would you have me do?"

She closed the distance between them, bringing with her the scent of spring that replaced the acrid stench of hellfire in Patrick's nose. He held his breath as Persephone set her hands on Hades' chest and rose up on her tiptoes to brush her lips over his in an anguished kiss that made the god shake so hard even Patrick could feel it.

"Let Patrick pay his soul debt," Persephone murmured before pulling away. "Prove your love and do this one thing for me."

Persephone turned her back on them, following Hermes and Eloise through the veil, leaving Patrick behind. And even though that had been the plan, Patrick couldn't help the fear that curled up and made a home in the center of his chest.

A suicidal idea indeed.

Hades pried the iron box out of Patrick's hand and thumbed it open. The carved raven nestled inside seemed to glimmer beneath the lightning that flashed above them.

"You made a mistake coming here, no matter what my wife believes," Hades said after a moment.

Patrick thought of Jono and his pack, of everyone he'd left behind in New York to face the horror clawing its way through the veil. "I'd sell my soul over and over again for the people I care about, but you wouldn't know anything about that."

"I did everything for my daughter."

Patrick turned to look at the god, lips pulled back in a mocking smile. "You never fought for her."

Truth was a blessing or a curse, and no one ever truly liked to hear it, least of all a god. Hades let go of Patrick's shoulder to backhand him across the face so hard the world went slippery and sideways, the burn of foreign magic chasing him into blackness.

## 20

No one saw the sun rise over New York City on what might have been Tuesday morning.

Cold gray fog covered the world in a layer so thick Jono could barely even see Central Park out of the window of Sage's and Marek's home. The sun was impossible to make out through storm clouds that still churned somewhere above the fog, casting Manhattan in a darkness more reminiscent of twilight. Cars remained abandoned in the street, and a strange, eerie quiet had settled over the city, broken only by the howls of things that were definitely not werecreatures.

Jono turned away from the rain-streaked windows, taking in the mess that had become of the living area. Crates of weapons hauled over last night by Lucien's Night Court were scattered on the floor, the tops peeled back, and their inventory laid out on any available flat surface. Gerard's Hellraisers had brought their own gear, but it paled in comparison to what Lucien could provide.

After the Hellraisers' arrival at the flat in Chelsea yesterday, they'd left for the Upper East Side. They hadn't gone far when the veil started tearing and all electronics died. It had been a mad dash crosstown through crowds of panicked people who would've been safer home and behind a threshold. It reminded Jono a lot of Paris, and he wondered if that had been a dry run for this.

Probably, knowing their luck, but at least he knew what fighting in the streets would be like. The only difference was Patrick and how he wasn't there. Thinking about his lover made Jono's heart speed up with worry.

He still hadn't heard from Patrick since their call cut off yesterday. The soulbond had gone tight and cold the way it always did when Patrick was beyond the veil. It hadn't snapped back into place until sometime before dawn, the tightness of the connection hinting at the distance. They were city and states apart, but the distance wasn't as bad as when Patrick had been in Chicago. The general direction was northeast, and Jono knew Patrick had to be in Salem, but there was no bloody way he could leave the city now.

Every bridge and tunnel leading into Manhattan had been closed off and barricaded by the military in the outer boroughs as the torn edges of the veil settled over the city. His pack was even more scattered than before because there was no easy route downtown to Bellevue, and Jono had no way to contact anyone. At least Gerard seemed to know what needed to be done in a situation like this.

"The National Guard and active-duty soldiers out of the Department of the Preternatural have made it to New Jersey across the Hudson. General Reed couldn't tell me if they're able to get across since we don't know if the scrying crystals are compromised," Gerard said from his spot on the sofa.

"I bet the public isn't keen about that."

Gerard shrugged. "I'm not questioning the support."

"The soldiers might question what they see when things go to shit."

"They'll obey orders."

"Let's hope so." Jono eyed the flat, beveled crystal sitting propped up on the coffee table that was far larger than the one he remembered looking at in Tiarnán's car last year. "Pity there's not more of these things. They'd come in handy right now."

"This one belongs to Brigid. The one at the Pentagon had to be taken out of the Repository. There aren't many available outside Tír na nÓg, and my queen is still a bit pissed about the ones in mortal hands."

"Her loss, our gain."

Gerard smiled thinly. "Don't ever say that where Brigid can hear."

"Pissing off the gods is more Pat's wheelhouse than mine."

Gerard's smile faded away. "Still no news?"

Jono grimaced and shook his head, resisting the urge to press a hand over his heart where the ache of the soulbond had centered. "We can't talk through it. We get emotions sometimes, and a general direction of where the other is, but nothing that would help us right now."

"Do you still think he's in Salem?"

"It's the likeliest possibility."

But it wasn't a solid *yes*, and Jono couldn't send people on a wild goose chase when he wasn't sure they'd even make it out of Manhattan alive in the first place. He had enough problems right now worrying about the rest of his pack and those under his protection.

When Patrick had described how the fighting had gone down during the Thirty-Day War, they'd agreed to have the packs work together with the fae, covens, and Night Courts in designated areas. Everyone would keep clear of Central Park and the subways. They'd concentrate on city blocks, much how they had done in Paris. The SOA and the military would get folded into their defenses along the way under Reed's orders.

A distant, heavy pounding caught Jono's attention, and he dialed up his hearing. The sound came from the building's front door floors below. Gerard appeared to hear it as well, but none of the other Hellraisers did.

"Expecting anyone?" Gerard asked as he stood, grabbing his long gun where it rested on the coffee table.

"The packs know this is where we're staging the fight in the beginning and should remain together where they are. It could honestly be anyone."

Groups of police officers had been out during their trek crosstown yesterday, trying to corral crowds. It had been a losing endeavor in the storm, but that didn't mean they weren't out there again patrolling. Electronics might not work, but guns and magic certainly did.

Gerard headed for the flat's front door and the set of emergency stairs in the small foyer beyond that led to the ground floor. Jono stayed on his heels and wasn't at all surprised to find that Emma and Nadine had beaten them to the building's entrance on the street level.

"Smells like vampires and ozone," Emma said, not taking her eyes off the door but not moving to open it either.

There was only one person who smelled like that, and Jono stepped past Gerard to open the front door. Standing on the porch, drenched from the rain and barred from entering by the home's threshold, was Ashanti. The mother of all vampires smiled, baring her iron fangs, and held up a familiar sheath and dagger.

"I come bearing news. Going to let me in?" Ashanti said.

Jono's attention remained riveted on Patrick's dagger. "What did you do with him?"

"I did nothing. Patrick took it upon himself to leave this behind."

"When?"

"Yesterday afternoon. You've already let my child past your doors, wolf. Show some respect and grant me the same courtesy."

Emma ducked under Jono's arm to glare at Ashanti. "Be welcome, but the second you go for anyone's throat, the threshold will toss you out on your ass."

She lived here too and was capable of inviting Ashanti inside.

Jono, for all his status as their god pack alpha, didn't call this building home. The threshold here knew that, and it recognized Emma's words in a way it would never recognize his. They had no bread or water to offer in terms of hospitality, but Jono wasn't sure mortal magic would stand against a goddess anyway.

Jono and Emma moved out of the doorway, allowing Ashanti to step inside, her ironshod bone hooks clicking against the floor. Nadine shut the door behind her and locked it, her wards flaring up around the doorframe once again. She'd erected a barrier ward around the building last night, and the weight of it had settled into the foundation itself.

Ashanti offered up the sheath and dagger, holding them out to Jono. He snatched them out of her hand, nostrils flaring as a hint of Patrick's scent reached his nose. "Where is he?"

"Patrick asked to be taken to Hades to trade a weapon for his grandmother's life. His request was granted," Ashanti said.

Jono clenched his fingers around the sheath, fingernails biting into the leather, before shoving it into the waistband of his trousers. "By you?"

"By Hermes. Traveling through the veil is easier now, as you can see from outside, but beyond it was never a place I called home. It has broken through to the mortal plane. Everything else will soon follow."

"We need to know where Ethan is before it's too late," Gerard said.

"I could find him with Patrick, but he's busy cutting off Ethan's power source. We will make do until you retrieve him."

"We don't know where he is."

"I do," an annoyingly familiar voice drawled from the stairwell.

Jono jerked around, staring at where Hermes lounged against the wall, smiling down at them all in an unkind way. Jono didn't process moving until he had his other hand wrapped around Hermes' throat, pinning the god to the wall.

"Is this any way to greet an old friend?" Hermes wheezed, not fighting his grip.

"You aren't a friend to anyone here," Jono growled.

Hermes grabbed Jono's wrist with bruising force and wrenched himself free. His heels hit the step below, and he caught himself against the wall. The smile never left his face. "Eloise is upstairs. You'll want to hear what she has to say."

Jono took the steps two at a time back up to Sage's and Marek's flat, the others scrambling after him. When he came back inside, he saw Eloise sitting on the sofa, so pale it was as if she had no blood running through her veins. But her blue eyes were clear enough when she looked at him, though the lingering scent of terror spoke of a horror Jono knew well when one was held hostage by Ethan.

"Eloise," he said, closing the distance between them.

"Jonothon," she said in a voice empty of the vibrancy it had carried during their first and only meeting.

Jono sat down on the sofa beside her, careful not to crowd her. When she reached for him with a shaking hand, he took it. "It's all right to call me Jono. How are you?"

As badly as he wanted to ask about Patrick, Jono knew steamrolling an old woman who'd gone through a trauma wasn't the way to get answers.

She blinked rapidly at him, heart beating faster than was probably healthy for someone of her age. "I don't want to talk about me. I want to talk about Patrick."

Jono could barely hide his wince at the way she glossed over the probable torture she'd been put through. "Then talk. I'm listening."

Eloise drew in a breath, the sound a rasp in her throat. "Patrick traded himself for me. They'll put him in the spellwork I was tied to because it needs someone from our family to make it work."

"Where is the spellwork located?"

"The Burying Point Cemetery."

Jono froze, Marek's vision coming back to haunt him in that

moment.

*I saw a graveyard, which means there's some kind of ending we're now running toward.*

"That's in Salem," Nadine said. "You were right about the location, Jono."

"I can take the Hellraisers through the veil. Whatever gods are in Salem, I'll handle them," Gerard said.

Eloise's eyes were wide in her face, wet with unshed tears. "I need to tell you about the spellwork and the Salem nexus."

"We know about your family's ties to it. Patrick told us," Jono said.

Eloise frowned, lips trembling. "How did he know?"

"One of your children told him."

"Oh."

"Jono," Emma said. "She can't stay here. It'll be too dangerous."

Jono grimaced, knowing she was right. "Gerard? Can you take her with you through the veil to Salem?"

Gerard frowned before nodding. "Can do. We'll drop her off somewhere safe before extracting Patrick."

"The Salem god pack will help you. Georgelle is their alpha."

Jono had the number memorized, and he rattled it off to Gerard, who gave him a thumbs-up. "I'll make that call once we have boots on the ground in Salem."

Jono gently squeezed Eloise's hand. "We'll—"

He was interrupted by one of Gerard's Hellraisers thundering down the stairs, weapon in hand and trailing water behind him. "Got movement in Central Park, sir."

Gerard hurried over to the windows facing Fifth Avenue. Jono left Eloise on the sofa to go see what was happening. The fog obscured most of the area, even with the storm winds, and it took a long minute for Jono to see what Gerard's soldier had spotted.

Through the swirling fog, he could just make out the thick black brambles growing over the wall surrounding Central Park. Gangly figures with the look of the Unseelie fae to them were using the brambles to climb over the wall, falling to the sidewalk below.

"*Fuck,*" Gerard snarled. "If they're coming from Central Park, then Medb has control of the hawthorn path. We'll most likely run into her forces past the veil."

"You need to go," Jono said, already turning around. "Take your team and Eloise and get to Salem."

Hellraisers were already snapping on their hard helmets, while the werecreatures present were kicking off their shoes, getting prepared to shift. Nadine, geared up and ready for the fight ahead, gave Jono a grim nod.

"If it's anything like Cairo, that's going to be the first wave. We had less powerful demons at first, so stands to reason Medb is sending her least powerful fae. They'll try to wear us down with an escalation of forces," Nadine said.

"Then let's get moving south like we planned."

"The veil will be difficult to navigate where it's torn, and Cú Chulainn is right. It will be overrun with the enemy, and there are too many worlds to slip through if you aren't careful," Hermes said from where he stood by the door. "If you want to ensure Cú Chulainn can return with Pattycakes without getting lost, then you need to stay put."

"Fuck you," Gerard retorted.

Hermes wiggled his finger at Gerard, but his gaze never left Jono. "You'll be a moving target on the streets, and you'll be directionless. Ethan's side wants you dead after Patrick."

Deep in his soul, Fenrir let out an amused huff.

"And if we stay here, we'll be a sitting target," Jono argued.

"You'll be alive."

"I need Patrick to perform the blood rite in order to locate Ethan. If staying in one place ensures his arrival through the veil, then we will hold the ground here until Cú Chulainn returns with him." Ashanti gave Hermes a contemplative look that spoke of murder. "You will guide Cú Chulainn through the veil."

Hermes let out a put-upon sigh. "If I must."

Gerard scowled. "I know my way through the veil."

"Hermes knows it better. He's traveled its breadth more than you over the centuries. Take the help," Ashanti ordered.

After a fraught few seconds, Gerard inclined his head in her direction. "Very well."

"Brilliant, but Sage is at Bellevue with Wade and Marek. I'm not leaving them there to face this alone," Jono said.

Ashanti arched an eyebrow. "Then you should have brought them here when the veil first started tearing over this island. You need more than who you have with you here to make it that far south. Nearby packs will not be enough. You, however, are a target because of your connection to Patrick. Stay here and act like bait so Cú Chulainn has an easier time through the veil. Defending a location you know is easier than one you do not."

Jono clenched his jaw, the need to shift making his skin itch. He glared at Hermes, the god not fazed at all by the intensity of his anger. "You're a messenger god, yeah? Send a message to all the bloody gods in your heavens and tell them to get their arses here after you take Gerard to Salem."

"What makes you think they aren't on their way?" Hermes asked.

Jono would believe it when he saw it.

"We're wasting time arguing. My team and I are leaving," Gerard said, cutting through their raised voices.

Jono looked over at the assembled Hellraisers, hating that he had to stay behind. He wanted badly to find Patrick, but if he left New York City, something told him he'd never find his way back. They'd gone through too much to give up their territory now.

He gave Gerard a sharp nod. "Bring Patrick back."

"You bet your English ass we will."

The Hellraisers queued up, each person grabbing the shoulder strap of the person in front of them. Their sorcerer took up the rear, magic gathered in his free hand, while Hermes went to stand in front of Gerard. Keith checked over his shoulder that everyone was ready before grabbing Gerard's vest and giving it a hard yank.

"Ready to move out," Keith said.

Jono went to the sofa where Eloise still sat and offered her his hand. "Time to go."

She took it after a small hesitation, getting to her feet with his help. "I'll make sure my family's wards are taken down when we get to Salem. Ethan won't be able to get to the nexus if they're gone and the SOA has theirs up."

"Good luck," Jono said as he escorted her over to Gerard.

"Ma'am," Gerard said, offering her his elbow. "Let's get you home."

Eloise slipped her arm around his and held on so tight her knuckles went white. For all the fear that Jono could smell coming off her, she put on a decently determined face.

Jono looked at Gerard, hesitating only a moment before he thrust Patrick's dagger in the god's direction. "Bring this back to him."

Gerard took the dagger with gloved fingers. "I'll make sure he gets it."

"Ready?" Hermes asked with a smile on his face.

The messenger god didn't wait for an answer, reaching out for the air in front of him with both hands. He ripped it open, the gray fog of the veil spilling into the living room. He pushed it wider with an ease Jono knew wasn't normal.

"Stay close and don't let go," Gerard ordered.

Hermes went through first, Gerard right on his heels with Eloise held protectively against his side. The Hellraisers followed him into the veil and whatever waited for them beyond. The tear sealed shut behind the last man, but the coldness remained, along with the threat waiting for them on the street.

"We take this fight block by block when Patrick gets here like we planned," Nadine said as she turned toward the door. "Until then, we hold this one."

"Wait," Jono called out.

Nadine paused in the doorway, looking back over her shoulder. Jono approached her and dug out the last Greek coin he'd left the flat with, the weight of it eerily heavy in his hand. He held it out to her, and the recognition in her eyes was tinged with surprise.

"I thought we used them all up last year?" she asked.

"Hermes left one with Patrick when he was in hospital. I didn't want to leave it behind in case we could use it, but I can't carry it with me when I shift."

Nadine took the coin and placed it in a secured pouch on her belt. "I'll keep it safe."

Jono nodded. "I know you will."

She was Patrick's best friend, and he'd seen the shields she could hold back in Paris. Jono looked over his shoulder at everyone who remained. "Let's go hold our territory."

Nadine took the lead downstairs, mageglobes forming around her as she went. Members of Emma's Tempest pack who hadn't been upstairs joined them on the way down or were already waiting for them on the ground floor.

Ashanti peered through the side window by the door and let out a pleased hum. "It seems your request has already been granted, wolf."

Jono came up behind her, squinting through the glass at the fog drifting through the street, the rain unable to dissipate it. His eyes widened at the sight that met him. "Nadine."

"I see her," she said, opening up the front door.

They stepped outside into the roar of a reactionary storm not even the veil could swallow whole. The wind and rain drenched Jono in seconds as they exited the building. Nadine hadn't bothered with a personal shield to keep the rain out, conserving her energy. She didn't immediately raise a larger one.

On the street, unbothered by the pouring rain, the Cailleach Bheur offered them a toothy smile, her single stormy eye unblinking in her forehead. "Medb has opened the hawthorn paths and the crossroads they cradle to all and sundry. Tír na nÓg is falling into Earth. The rest of Underhill will soon follow."

"It won't be the only world to do so," Ashanti said from behind Jono.

Jono scowled. "Then we push it back. It had its time here. All your heavens and hells did. This world is ours now."

The Cailleach Bheur rapped her staff against the pavement, ice expanding around where she stood. "Ethan would make it his."

"It doesn't belong to that bastard either."

Shadows skittered through the fog along Fifth Avenue off to their left. Jono kept walking until he made it to the street where the Cailleach Bheur stood in a blanket of winter cold, attention on the threat coming their way. Emma and her pack spread out around him, some of them already shifting.

"We need to keep them here so they don't go after Gerard in the veil. Let's give them a fight," Jono said.

The Cailleach Bheur turned to face the darkness of Central Park, the gray cloak she wore shifting around her naked body. She raised her staff high above her head before slamming it onto the ground. The *crack* that echoed in the air from the impact set Jono's teeth on edge, but it drew the attention of the creatures creeping through the fog.

The spine-chilling cries that cut through the air weren't human at all.

The Cailleach Bheur pointed her staff in the direction of Central Park, letting winter loose. Ice exploded forward to cover the cars parked on the street and those left by the wayside after the electrical grid had died. It flowed like a tsunami from the Cailleach Bheur's staff, crashing into the first group of spider-looking fae crawling toward them, freezing them where they stood. Their brethren not immediately affected crashed right through the ice statues, shattering them to pieces.

"Resetting my barrier ward to expand. I'll be your rearguard," Nadine called out.

Glittering violet-colored magic peeled away from Sage's and Marek's home, expanding outward. It burned brighter than usual against the grayness that had taken over the world, like a beacon the enemy couldn't resist being drawn to.

Jono narrowed his eyes at the sound that reached his ears—the movement of hundreds of bodies in a tight space coming up behind the fae. Beneath the scent of winter, Jono could smell the dead.

The fog shifted, twisting around shadows that became an ugly mass of bones. The remnants of those who once resided beneath Paris slipped free of the veil, backed by fae from the Unseelie Court climbing out of the hawthorn path in Central Park.

"Keep them off our streets," Jono called out before he started to shift.

The breaking of his body came easily to him, nerves switching off his ability to feel pain as the world shifted around him. Skin split, muscle tore, and bones twisted into new positions. The shift from human to wolf took less than a minute, but that was more than enough time for the zombies to halve the distance between them.

Ashanti landed in a crouch beside him when he finally stood on four feet instead of two. She smiled at him, the excitement in her scent that of a predator ready for the kill.

"It has been an age since we have hunted like this. Shall we, wolf?" Ashanti asked.

Fenrir flowed through Jono's soul and mind, sinking into every last crevice of who he was. Jono let him, not minding the god's presence in the face of hell.

"*Let us shake the world*," Fenrir said, the god's voice coming out harsh around teeth and tongue not meant to speak in the form they were in.

When Fenrir charged forward with a challenging howl that echoed eerily in the air, two goddesses joined him, and the Tempest pack followed in their wake. Nadine kept growing the radius of her shields in meters, the edge of it nipping at their heels as they dove fangs and claws first into the horde.

Fenrir rode Jono's consciousness but didn't fight him for control. The god was ever present as Jono ripped his way through the zombies, shattering bones between his teeth as he clawed at the fae moving between the dead. Those were more irritating than the zombies, with gangly limbs and claws that could find their way deep into his fur if he didn't shake them off quick enough.

The werewolves around him were a snarling mass of support that spanned the width of the street amidst parked and abandoned cars. They needed to push the fae back so Nadine could set her shield's boundaries over the block. But like in Paris, the dead kept coming, and even with the Cailleach Bheur and Ashanti lending their power to the fight, the sheer number of the dead and the Unseelie Court fae coming at them would overwhelm their position soon.

Jono kicked out with his hind paws, slamming them into an abandoned car and sending it crashing through a group of zombies. It created space for himself and Emma to maneuver in as they fought the next wave of fae. They were about to charge when the glow from Nadine's magic disappeared in the area they stood in, and Jono tensed.

The crackle of her magic was replaced by the thunder of hooves.

Jono wrenched his head around in time to catch a glimpse of a familiar streak of gold and black darting forward through the legs of werewolves, bits of the veil trailing from between her small teeth as Fatima yowled a vicious challenge.

A group of Seelie fae warriors on horses galloped their way from the intersection behind them, Órlaith leading the charge, a sword clutched in one hand, her armor gleaming. Perched behind her, one hand outstretched around her, sat PIA Agent Spencer Bailey dressed for a fight, a dark green mageglobe burning against his palm.

The dead around them fell in waves, Fatima drawing their souls into her mouth and guiding them to where they belonged at the behest of Spencer's uncanny magic. Órlaith's steed galloped past Nadine, and Spencer flung himself off it at her position. He stumbled on the landing, but Nadine grabbed his shoulder, steadying him.

"Sorry I'm late!" Spencer shouted. "I needed a ride in."

Jono faced forward again with a snarl as Órlaith's steed clambered onto a frozen car with inhuman sure-footedness. It might look like a horse, but it had fae blood running through its veins. The rain beat down on them both, flattening Jono's fur and weighing down her thick braid.

Órlaith looked down at him with a fierceness to her gaze. "What do you need?"

Fenrir took control of Jono's voice, words tearing through his teeth. *"A barrier they can't get through."*

Órlaith nodded tightly before she pointed her sword at the brambles still pushing over and through the wall surrounding Central Park. "Pull your people back."

Jono threw his head up and howled, putting power into the wordless command. Emma's pack retreated over the bones of the dead and iced-over cars, weaving past the fae soldiers who had come up to form ranks around Órlaith and Jono.

The Cailleach Bheur and Ashanti slipped past the horses to stand by Jono. Ashanti's lips were covered in black blood, her clawed fingers wet with it. She seemed unconcerned about the horde of zombies and Unseelie Court fae still coming their way.

Órlaith sheathed her sword, freeing both hands. She extended her arms outward and clenched her hands into fists. For a second, nothing happened. Then the earth began to shake in such a way that Jono worried about the integrity of the buildings around them and the subway below.

The color of the brambles went from black to a dark green as Órlaith's magic called forth the life of summer. The fae screeched a challenge, but Órlaith was the Summer Lady of the Seelie Court and Brigid's heir. Even in the in-between plane of existence that New York City had fallen into, there was still life, and Órlaith called it forth.

The brambles exploded, growing twice as fast and doubling in size in seconds. The tangled maze of thorns and branches cut through the enemy on Fifth Avenue, blood spraying through the air. As the bramble barricade grew, wintery ice filled every space between the thorns, until an icy wall the width of Fifth Avenue, two blocks in length, and three stories high settled into place.

Nadine's barrier ward passed over them to anchor itself to the base Órlaith and the Cailleach Bheur had created. The dome of her shield encompassed their block and the one beside it, supporting what the pair of immortals had created.

"This will not stop them forever," Ashanti warned.

"It only needs to stop them until we plan our next move," Órlaith said coolly.

Jono worked his way backward, bone crunching beneath his paws, until he could leap over a car and make it to the sidewalk. Crouched low, he shifted back to human with a speed that almost made him dizzy, Fenrir helping him back to human shape. Without fur, he shivered in the biting cold that had settled over their street, feeling it in a way he normally never did.

"Who did you bring with you other than Spencer?" Jono asked over his shoulder.

Órlaith maneuvered her steed off the car. "A strike team of warriors. We came through before the hawthorn path fell. Brigid is fighting for control of it on the other side. When she gets here, she will aid you, cousin."

Jono glanced back at the ice and bramble wall filling the street beneath Nadine's shield. Hermes' warning to stay in one place rang through his head, but it would be meaningless if they died under siege.

"How long can you both keep up the barriers?" Jono asked.

Nadine squinted up at the mix of magic and ice walling them off from Central Park. "Under normal circumstances, I can hold a shield up for days. We're within the veil's boundaries now. If it's going to be like Cairo, I'll want to conserve my strength."

"I was on the other side in New Jersey with a group of PIA agents when Órlaith showed up with her riders. Scared the shit out of the soldiers with us," Spencer said.

"Didn't take you long to get here."

Spencer shook his head. "Órlaith came on Monday. We traveled through the veil to get here, and we lost time. What I'm trying to say is the fight this time is going to be worse than Cairo. The damage to the veil is worse. More threats are coming across. I don't know if defending one location would be better or worse than staying on the move."

"A sitting target is still a dead target eventually," Jono said.

"You risk Cú Chulainn being unable to return with Patrick," Ashanti warned from her crouched position on a damaged car roof.

Jono scowled at her. "You lot soulbound Patrick and I together. He'll be able to find me, or I'll find him, when he gets back to New York."

"Are you certain of that when we stand within the veil's boundaries?"

He wasn't, but Jono was sure of Patrick's promise to come back to him. Whether guided by Gerard or the soulbond, Patrick would find his way to them.

"Have a little faith in the bloke who's cleaning up your messes." Jono looked back at the werecreatures ranged around him, staring at him with steady gazes, at the fae warriors on steeds who hadn't set foot on this earth in countless generations. "We'll leave your barrier up for as long as possible as a distraction while we head downtown."

"The fae are already gathering for an attack. I can sense their presence beyond the barrier," Órlaith said.

"They are not the only things coming this way," the Cailleach Bheur said.

"We won't be here when they arrive. We'll take Park Avenue south for as long as possible," Jono said.

He turned around and started down the street, intent on putting distance between his group and what clawed at the other side of the barrier behind him. Emma's pack followed him, walking between vehicles and shoving them aside to provide room for Órlaith and her group's steeds to walk through.

Nadine and Spencer dodged around iced-over cars to join him on the sidewalk, Fatima trotting at Spencer's heels. She let out a trill, causing Spencer to glance down at her.

"She wants to know where Wade is," Spencer said.

Jono's shoulders tightened. "With Sage at Bellevue. Hopefully safe."

"Bellevue?"

"She was gutted by a hunter's poisoned blade. She couldn't shift. She was in hospital when the veil tore."

Spencer looked stricken, pausing long enough to pick up Fatima and cradle the psychopomp in his arms. "Fuck. What about Patrick?"

"Being his usual self-sacrificing, idiotic self," Nadine muttered.

Spencer winced, giving Jono a sympathetic look. "Oh, that's never good."

"He's coming back," Jono said, lengthening his stride.

Spencer nodded absent agreement, half his attention on Fatima as they walked. "She says there are more dead in this direction than at Central Park."

Jono nodded and stopped long enough to shift back to wolf, body breaking and ripping to a different form. When he stood on four legs once again, Jono shook his head to settle his vision before leading the way to their next fight.

The grave was filling with water.

Patrick blinked slowly up at the stormy sky he could see far above where he lay at the bottom of the six-foot-deep grave, mind disconnected from a body he couldn't move. There was no coffin beneath him, just cold mud soaking all the warmth out of him. He blinked again, lips pressed stubbornly shut against the rain, wondering if he'd burn up from the spell first or drown.

Zachary's spellwork was extensive, the pentagram folded down into the grave with Patrick lying on its center. The ugly shade of his magic burned brighter than the lightning that Patrick could occasionally see flash across the sky. It wrapped around his body, cut through his skin to settle like poison in the burned remnants of the shield anchors carved into his bones.

He could feel the flow of magic draining out of the nexus below, flowing through a carved-out hole in the defenses his soul was helping to keep open. The tiny, lingering thread that tied him to his twin sister—what he'd felt back in Chicago and subsequently buried—had been forced wide open like an old broken dam.

He could sense through it the overload in Hannah's soul, the way it flowed into her and through her to Ethan, the way it always must have. Patrick thought the burned-out channels in his damaged soul ached, but his pain was nothing compared to the raw agony that existed in the remnants of Hannah's soul.

Being the center of the spellwork holding open a back door to the nexus meant his own soul was overloaded by Zachary's magic, forcing his heart out of rhythm from time to time with every spike of power. If this was what Eloise had been put through since being captured, it was a wonder she was even alive. She wasn't a mage, just blood kin recognized by the generational wards around the nexus, and really, that was all Ethan had ever needed for Zachary to work with.

His blood.

Zachary came into view, standing at the edge of the grave. The red-black mageglobe hovering at his shoulder burned like a miniature sun, providing enough light to see his face by.

"The spellwork is holding," Zachary called over his shoulder. "I don't know why Ethan sent you. You're needed in Manhattan."

"The spellwork was disrupted when Hades removed the woman from it. I am here to ensure it remains intact and report back on my findings," a familiar demonic voice said, sending fear snaking down Patrick's spine.

"That disruption was not my fault."

"Hades is lucky the trade was worthwhile. Ethan wasn't pleased about the backlash that happened with the body swap."

A second figure came to stand on the other side of the grave, Ilya Nazarov's face illuminated by Zachary's magic, though it was Andras, Grand Marquis of Hell, that spoke through the necromancer. They held in one iron-gauntleted hand the Morrígan's staff, whole once more.

Patrick stared up at the demon through the rain, panic eating away at the edges of his thoughts. He'd been woken up by too many nightmares over the past weeks about being a prisoner in his own body, screaming into a void, lost in his own skin. Facing the cause of his nightmares again made him want to scream, but he couldn't.

Patrick wondered if Ilya had willingly accepted the demon into his soul or if Ethan hadn't given him a choice. The Morrígan's staff couldn't be wielded by mortals, not without a price. It stood to reason Andras' presence in Ilya would help the necromancer command it.

What sentience existed in that weapon could really only be controlled by a god.

Patrick hoped Andras wasn't up to the task.

Andras stared down at him, face cast in shadow, before he suddenly flung Ilya's body off the edge of the gravesite. His feet sank into the mud on either side of Patrick's hips, the malevolent presence of the Morrígan's staff biting at Patrick's soul, as if it remembered him.

If Patrick could've moved, he'd have run away from the damned thing.

Ilya's body settled over his stomach, the weight of the man with a demon riding his soul forcing Patrick deeper into the mud. It slithered into his ears, muffling the roar of the reactionary storm above, even if it couldn't drown out Andras' voice.

Fingers wrapped in cold metal gripped his chin, tilting his head back, and Patrick moved where the demon wanted him to go. Mud squelched in his hair as rainwater trickled down his nose. He could barely get his throat to swallow it, the sensation like he was drowning.

"It's a pity you won't see the hell we're building. We'll bury you here, and no one will find your body," Andras said.

His grip tightened past the point of bruising, the pressure against Patrick's jaw so hard he thought Andras would dislocate it, when the sound of automatic fire rent the air. Andras wrenched Ilya's hand free, the gauntlet scraping Patrick's skin open. The demon jumped back up to solid ground with supernatural ease.

Patrick remained in the position he'd been left in, sinking into mud and drowning beneath rainwater.

The spellwork lines flickered ominously, his heartbeat stuttering in response. His chest felt bruised already from the connection, and Patrick tried to breathe through the panic, but he could barely get any air in past the water running down his nose into his throat.

He heard voices shouting as if from a distance, the jagged sound of automatic fire cutting through words he couldn't make out. All Patrick could see was the reactionary storm, rain falling like daggers into his eyes, lightning flashing in tandem to every pulse of magic that shook the ground.

Except it wasn't just magic.

Skeletal hands pushed through the side of the grave, brittle, yellow bones grasping at open air. Thick globs of dirt slid down the side of the grave as the dead sought their freedom from their burial spot. Patrick couldn't move, bound by the spellwork that was threatening him with a heart attack.

If he died by way of zombies, he was going to have words with whatever god met him in the afterlife.

A zombie dragged itself free of the side of the grave, its muddy skull tilting downward. Half its jaw was missing, and the glow in its eye sockets was all magical control from the Morrígan's staff. It clacked its rotten teeth together, reaching toward Patrick with one arm. Its finger bones scraped against his chest, pulling at his T-shirt.

It reminded him too much of the soultaker when he was a child, and the rapid beat of his heart came from him this time, not someone else's magic. Fear was difficult to tamp down, but he tried, even as the zombie crawled free of its grave and into Patrick's.

The stink of death was foul in his nose, making him gag, but he couldn't throw up because then he might choke on it. Patrick tried to move, but no part of his body obeyed him as the zombie crawled on top of him, skeletal hands reaching for his throat.

The bone was cold where it touched his skin, sliding through the mud he was sinking into. Its fingers scraped over the back of his neck as thumb bones settled against the front of his throat over his trachea, pressing down with a strength the dead should never have.

Patrick struggled to breathe, caught between the force of the spellwork and the brutal grip of the dead who held his life in its hands. Dark spots ate away at the edge of his vision, creeping inward as the pressure forced his tongue out between his lips, air a necessity not granted to him. The burn in his lungs was an ache he choked on and would've succumbed to if the body that dropped down into the grave hadn't gotten in the way.

White-hot, heavenly fire burned through the skeleton, breaking through the control Andras had over it. The skeleton shuddered, its grip going lax around Patrick's throat as it collapsed into pieces on top of him. Patrick blinked his eyes, trying to breathe but finding he couldn't get his throat to work.

Then a warm hand gripped the collar of his jacket and hauled him free of the sucking mud, giving him a firm shake as Gerard's face swam into focus. "Come on, Collins. I need you to fucking *breathe.*"

Patrick's lungs unlocked, air wheezing past his teeth. It wasn't enough, not when he was still tied up in the spellwork. The lines of the pentagram folded around him, keeping him anchored to the hideous magic that threatened to burn him up until nothing was left.

Gerard cupped the back of Patrick's head, keeping him upright and stable, as he wielded the dagger given by the gods with brutal ease, cutting him loose of the spellwork. With every line he sliced through, agony shot through Patrick's body, as if his entire nervous system was doused in acid. Control came back in pieces, and by the time Gerard had cut him free, backlash had him screaming into Gerard's chest at the bottom of the grave.

"Oh, good, he's alive!" Keith shouted from somewhere above them on solid ground.

Patrick's thoughts were too scattered for him to understand what it meant that Keith was there. Fighting for focus was excruciating, almost as difficult as getting enough air into his lungs.

He forced himself to stop screaming, breathing raggedly, mud sliding down his body beneath the torrential downpour. Gerard tensed against him, and Patrick lifted his head, blinking hard as the world swam around him. Several more skulls and bony arms had pushed free of the rapidly destabilizing grave walls, driven by magic.

"Let's get the fuck out of here," Gerard grunted, hauling Patrick to his feet.

His knees nearly buckled once he was vertical, feet sliding in watery mud. Gerard stabbed the zombies reaching for them with the dagger, heavenly fire flashing in the dark, brighter than lightning.

"Raise your arm over your head," Gerard said.

Patrick did as he was told, flinching when warm fingers wrapped around his wrist with bruising strength. He looked up, right into Hermes' eyes, and blinked rain out of his vision.

"Ready to pay your soul debt?" Hermes asked.

Patrick unstuck his tongue from the roof of his mouth. "Fuck you. Let's go fight a war."

Hermes laughed, and between him and Gerard, they got Patrick out of the grave he was supposed to die in.

Up on the surface, the graveyard tucked away between buildings in the middle of historical Salem was overrun with zombies called forth by Andras and the Morrígan's staff. The Hellraisers were holding their own against the horde, aided by over two dozen werecreatures picking off Dominion Sect magic users and hunters. Supporting the werecreatures were SOA agents in lettered windbreakers, magic at their fingertips and focus circles burning beneath their feet.

Andras in Ilya's body stood behind the Dominion Sect forces, the Morrígan's staff held aloft. The quartz crystal trapped within the knotwork glowed like a lighthouse beacon. In the swath of illumination it provided, Patrick could see more of the dead clawing free of the ground.

Zachary stood to Andras' right, sending mageglobes in the direction of the SOA agents. Neither of them had fled yet, and Patrick half wondered if they even had a way out. Their job was to provide access to the Salem nexus. Eloise had been traded away from Patrick, and now the spellwork no longer held him.

Hades, Patrick realized, was nowhere to be found.

Another one of Zachary's mageglobes slammed against the shields Patrick's fellow SOA agents were holding up. The crackle of magic that fluctuated through the defense spoke of damage.

"Collins."

Patrick jerked his head around, blinking in Gerard's direction. Gerard grabbed Patrick's right wrist and pushed the dagger against his hand. Patrick reflexively curled his fingers around the hilt, breathing harshly as he stared at the heavenly white fire dancing across the matte-black blade.

The screaming, metal-breaking sound of soultakers arriving echoed through the storm just then, catching everyone's attention. Patrick knew they'd need the prayers in the blade now more than ever.

"Oh, fuck me, I didn't sign up for those fuckers again!" Keith yelled from his position by a shattered gravestone.

"Yes, you did!" Gerard yelled back.

"You brought your team," Patrick managed to get out, breathing coming easier the longer he was free of the spellwork.

"They go where I go, and I promised Jono I'd bring you back."

Patrick flinched at Jono's name. "How pissed is he?"

"Eh, if there's a couch left in your apartment after all of this, I don't think you'll be sleeping on it. Are you ready to fight?"

Patrick could do with about forty-eight hours of sleep and several good meals, but that was wishful thinking. "Yeah."

Gerard smiled tightly, the look shared between them that of soldiers who knew there was no standing down in a situation like this. Gerard unclipped his rifle and passed it over to Patrick, who took it with his left hand. Patrick watched dazedly as his former captain made a fist, fingers wrapping around the pole of the *Gáe Bulg* as it was called forth. The spear crackled with power, Gerard's eyes glittering with an inner light, his true aura leaking through. The smell of ozone cut through the air, so strong not even the rain could dampen it.

"They'll eat the magic in your spear," Patrick said, mouth dry and throat scratchy despite all the water he'd swallowed.

Gerard spun the spear in one hand, the deadly blade at the tip flashing with every rotation completed. "They can't feast on all of it. I'll draw the soultakers in so you have a chance to stab them."

He had mud in places it should never be, his nerves were shot, and his chest ached in a way that made it difficult to catch his breath. Patrick still nodded agreement to the plan, blurry gaze trained on the handful of soultakers staggering their way through centuries-old headstones. He blinked hard several times until his vision cleared.

"Wonder how different Cairo would've been if I'd had the dagger at the beginning," Patrick croaked out.

Gerard gripped his shoulder in a brief gesture of support. "It doesn't matter. You have it now, so do some damage."

Patrick nodded, getting a better hold on his dagger.

"I'll take this," Hermes said, taking the rifle out of Patrick's hand. He braced it against his shoulder, comfortable with the weapon and the damage it could do.

"Bullets can't kill soultakers," Patrick warned.

Hermes' smile was cutting with its ferocity. "Who said anything about demons?"

The messenger god slipped away through the storm, and Patrick couldn't watch where he went, attention drawn to Gerard's advance. Patrick followed on shaky feet, grabbing at any bit of concentration he could get in the aftermath of being cut from the spellwork. His body felt weird, but it obeyed him, and at least this time he was coming out of paralysis brought upon by magic, not demonic possession.

Patrick stayed on Gerard's six, keeping some distance between them for maneuverability. Other Hellraisers shifted position, and Keith came up on Patrick's left to flank him.

"Doing all right, Razzle Dazzle?" Keith asked.

Patrick nodded. "Getting there."

"Good. Let's get you close to fuck shit up."

Gerard's aura spilled out around him, godly in its brightness, and the soultakers zeroed in on him like he was their next meal. The monstrous screams coming out of their wide mouths would have been a warning for anyone else to run, but they just set Gerard into motion.

He surged forward, a blur to Patrick's eyes. The *Gáe Bulg* was like an extension of Gerard, flashing through the air as he fought soultakers. He used his magic to draw them in between the headstones before attacking, using his position to drive them to Patrick. Gerard's otherworldly speed was all that saved him from the soultakers' tongues that whipped through the air and their wide maws ready to bite.

Patrick went a little light-headed, thinking of how tonight so eerily mirrored the one all those years ago in a Salem basement. But he couldn't dwell on it for long, because the first soultaker was forced past Gerard, and the demon had caught his scent.

Its bulbous head turned their way, the dark maw of its mouth parting on a scream. Patrick conjured up a mageglobe and filled the pale blue sphere with raw magic, baiting the soultaker ever closer.

"I hope you know what you're doing," Keith said.

"You and everyone else," Patrick muttered.

He took a steadying breath before lunging forward, sending the mageglobe left while he dodged right. The soultaker's hunger meant it followed the path of Patrick's mageglobe through the air for a second, tongue lashing out at the magic.

It was enough time for Patrick to fall to his knees, miss getting his neck snapped by the slashing of the demon's tongue when it whipped back around, and slam his dagger into its chest.

Light sparked along the blackened bone and muscle where the blade cut through with an ease like nothing else. Even air strikes couldn't guarantee a soultaker's eradication, but prayers from the heavens burned the demon to ash that turned to mud beneath Patrick's feet. He went to his knees, sliding in the grass.

Then Keith was there, grabbing his arm and hauling Patrick upright. "No lying down on the job, Razzle Dazzle."

Patrick sank his heels into the mud, steadied himself, and took aim at the next soultaker Gerard herded his way. "Keep the others off me if you can."

"Distraction by wasting bullets. You got it."

Armor-piercing rounds could rip through a soultaker's skin. The Hellraisers were equipped with spelled bullets, and while the demons would brush off any other projectile, the hint of magic caught their attention. It wouldn't be enough to hold it, so Patrick reached deep for his magic. His soul felt scraped raw, but Patrick formed a mageglobe despite the pain.

The magic in it called to the soultakers' hunger, and two of the demons left Gerard to target Patrick. Two-on-one odds weren't great, but the odds got worse when three of Zachary's mageglobes cut through the air toward them with lethal intent.

Patrick didn't have the focus for a good counterattack, still shaking off the lingering effects of the spellwork. Jono wasn't there to help him tap a ley line, and he had two soultakers nearly within dagger reach. There wasn't time for him to defend against both attacks.

Zachary's magic was malevolent and capable of killing, but so was the god that slipped free of the veil, his arrival announced by the haunting, echoing sound of a conch shell.

Kū swung his wooden spear lined with shark teeth into the trajectory of the oncoming mageglobes with a furious war cry. The sound of it was taken up by the Night Marchers that poured into the graveyard, war drums a counterpoint to the thunder booming through the night sky above.

The feathers on Kū's cloak and helmet didn't wilt beneath the rain. When his spear made contact with Zachary's mageglobes, the explosion was brutal, but the god stood like a mountain in the face of the concussive force.

The soultakers lost their footing from the shock wave of the explosion that rolled over the graveyard. Patrick braced himself against a headstone, squinting against the wind-driven rain at the demons. The godly support to the fight was prayers answered, but demons still walked the earth, and Patrick needed to do something about that.

Gritting his teeth, he lunged for the closest soultaker, sending his mageglobe at the other one. He dredged up his personal shield to block the whiplike tongue of the one closest to him from landing a blow. When the other soultaker ate his mageglobe, he felt the loss of magic like a skipped heartbeat in his chest.

Then his dagger found its target, burying itself in the black muscle of the soultaker's malformed thigh. The crackle of heavenly fire incinerated the demon in seconds, and Patrick gasped for breath, twisting around and sliding his shield with him. He missed getting a soultaker's teeth sinking into his skin by half a second, though his magic took the brunt of the demon's hunger.

"I have one more for you!" Gerard yelled.

"Great," Patrick muttered as he watched the soultaker on the other side of his shield bite its way through.

The drain of magic wasn't something he could afford right then, but he was the only one with a weapon that could kill a soultaker. The exhaustion settling in his body had to be ignored for a little longer, but it made him slower than he liked.

As his shield went down, the soultaker pitched forward with a scream. Patrick jerked backward, never taking his eyes off the demon as it advanced. His hip slammed into a headstone, and Keith shouted a warning.

"Duck!" Keith yelled.

Patrick ducked, missing getting his head bitten off by a single second. His soul was a bruised mess, and the recognition of hell and black magic was everywhere in the graveyard, making it impossible to pinpoint the enemy's position.

Facing off against a soultaker was a good way to die, and maybe Patrick's luck would've run out. Except the veil was thin, and gods walked the earth once more, and Gerard never cared for letting the men under his command die.

The *Gáe Bulg* pierced the closest soultaker's bulbous head, the weapon an incandescent line of light. The spearpoint protruded from the demon's maw, its teeth trying desperately to bite it in half. It wasn't dead, despite being on the receiving end of an attack that would kill anything else. Hell's shock troops really were a pain in the ass to kill.

"Hurry up," Gerard got out through clenched teeth. "Fucker is strong."

Patrick stabbed the soultaker in the neck, wincing at the scream it let out before being abruptly cut off as its body disintegrated. The ringing in his ears didn't go away even after its ashes got mixed into the muddy ground.

Patrick levered himself upright and tried to get eyes on the last soultaker—and went down beneath its weight. The metal-tearing screech of its voice nearly deafened him, and Patrick felt his personal shield give way beneath the demon's teeth and never-dying hunger.

"Patrick!" Gerard yelled.

He couldn't get leverage to twist around and stab the fucker, but Gerard solved that problem by using the *Gáe Bulg* to batter the soultaker off Patrick. The spear was enough of a magical distraction that the soultaker followed it rather than trying to bite Patrick's head off.

Getting an elbow underneath him, Patrick twisted onto his side and slammed the dagger into the demon's hip. He flinched as the demon's tongue dragged over the personal shield wrapped around his arm, its teeth snapping down around his elbow. Patrick's shield wavered beneath its bite, but it only took seconds for the soultaker to burn to ash.

He didn't have time to stop and breathe, not with a fight still happening around them. Gerard offered Patrick a hand up, and he took it. Staggering to his feet, Patrick turned to face where the Dominion Sect mages and hunters appeared to be on the defensive.

Walking their way came Kū, the Hawaiian god beheading a zombie with his shark-teeth-encrusted spear as he passed by a gravesite. "My Night Marchers tell me the demon summoned all the dead in Salem."

"Of course he did," Patrick muttered before coughing.

He scanned the cemetery turned battlefield, and his eyes widened when he saw who was running their way between a pair of Hellraisers.

"Patrick!" Madelyn called out, face white as a sheet, but the magic at her fingertips felt steady to his senses. Keeping pace beside her was Brittany.

"What the fuck are you doing here?" he exclaimed.

"Making sure the generational wards are down," Brittany said.

Patrick conjured up a mageglobe, fighting to keep its shape intact before filling it with magic. He cast a shaky shield around their little group once his aunt and cousin made it over. "This isn't a fight for civilians."

"Salem is our home, and the nexus is our responsibility."

"We brought Eloise home before coming to get you, Collins. Some of your family insisted on coming with us," Gerard said.

Patrick glared at him. "You should've said *no*."

"They made a compelling argument about the spellwork."

"Brittany and I are the next ones in line for control of the Salem Coven, and that includes the wards around the nexus. Eloise handed over the command triggers to us. Now that you're clear of Ethan's spellwork, we can take our family's wards down. We had to make sure you were free first," Madelyn said.

Gerard jerked his head in her direction. "See? Compelling argument."

Patrick flipped him off but kept his attention on his aunt. "Andras summoned all the dead in Salem to fight for him. You need to get behind a threshold."

He didn't want them to die—*couldn't* let them die—but this wasn't where the fight was going to end. New York City and Jono were calling, and Patrick couldn't stay.

Madelyn nodded jerkily. "Whatever is best."

"Let's get them back with the SOA agents for cover. Then we'll go," Gerard said.

Madelyn pulled out a small plastic bottle from her jacket pocket and offered it to Patrick. "Here. Drink this. It's a restorative potion. It can't heal you, but it'll keep you moving for now."

"I need a fucking vacation, not a potion," Patrick said, but he took the bottle anyway, unscrewed the cap, and downed a drink that tasted sickeningly sweet.

The effects were immediate. The fog in his brain washed away, leaving him more clearheaded than he'd been in hours. It helped him focus, and while it didn't cure the exhaustion, it enabled him to ignore it more easily.

He tossed the empty bottle over his shoulder and nodded at Gerard. "Ready when you are, sir."

"Need to get you actual gear when we make it back to New York," Gerard said, already moving toward where the fighting was still going on.

"I had a rifle."

"You don't have it now."

"Blame Hermes."

Patrick grabbed Brittany by the elbow and turned her around. Madelyn followed suit, sticking close to her daughter. Keith came up to flank them, and the other two Hellraisers took up the rearguard. Gerard had point, and Patrick kept his shield up as they ran across gravesites, taking shots at zombies as they went.

Several werecreatures came up from behind, helping to guard them. Patrick didn't know if any of them were Georgelle, but he needed to remember to thank her at some point.

The Night Marchers helped clear a way forward, with Kū focusing on the Dominion Sect magic users. The number of witches, warlocks, and sorcerers supporting Zachary had been halved. Zachary was still standing, though Patrick didn't have eyes on Andras. It left him feeling chilled in a way he couldn't blame on the storm.

The second he got within arm's reach of Hermes, he was taking back that rifle.

Werecreatures tore through zombies on either side of them, their ferocity enough to keep their area clear of danger. The Dominion Sect magic users were being whittled down in numbers, but several had come back as zombies. The Night Marchers were dealing with those particular walking dead.

Gerard led them behind the front line the SOA magic users had set up, handing Madelyn and Brittany back over to federal protection. They weren't dressed for a fight, and Patrick hated the thought of leaving them there, but he couldn't put their lives over everyone else's, even if they were related.

"Undo the generational wards around the nexus, then let the SOA know when they're down. The agents here will look after you. Keep your shields up, and do what they say," Patrick said, raising his voice to be heard over the thunder crashing overhead.

"What about you?" Brittany asked, eyes wide in her pale face.

"Pattycakes here has a soul debt to pay," Hermes said, slipping between two Hellraisers to come stand beside Patrick.

He was empty-handed.

"Where's my rifle?" Patrick demanded.

"It wasn't yours, and besides, I ran out of bullets."

Lightning flashed above, reflecting in Hermes' eyes. The hissing crackle in the air didn't come from the storm but the mageglobes careening their way.

"Someone get shields up!" Gerard yelled.

An SOA sorceress managed to cobble together a defense just in time, and the strike spells crashed against a shield that wavered in a threatening way. The color of the dissipating magic was all Zachary's signature, and Patrick knew they couldn't leave here until the asshole was taken care of.

Patrick grabbed Gerard by the arm, getting his attention. "Is Andras on the field?"

Gerard shook his head. "The demon left once the zombies were raised."

"He didn't take Zachary with him?"

"Maybe he thinks the fucker has a chance at keeping the spell-work going with some other person in your mother's family."

Patrick scowled. "We aren't leaving until Zachary is dead."

"You want that kill?"

Patrick gestured with his dagger, dragging heavenly fire through the rain. "You're the one with the long-range weapon."

Gerard grunted wordlessly before shaking off Patrick's hand. "Stay here."

Patrick didn't want to obey the order, but he'd spent years following Gerard in and out of battlefields. With his aunt and cousin behind him, Patrick watched as Gerard signaled whoever was holding up the shield to let him pass through.

Keith sidled up to Patrick, knocking him on the shoulder with a gentle fist. "Give him a minute. He's been wanting to murder someone for days now."

The Night Marchers swarmed the space between where the two sides fought, and Patrick lost sight of Gerard in the midst of those ghostly warriors. The SOA agents kept their focus on the fight with Dominion Sect magic users while the Hellraisers and werecreatures handled the zombies.

Beyond the graveyard, the little area of Salem's historical center should've been empty, but Patrick could see figures racing through the dark in the aftermath of every lightning strike. He couldn't tell if they were friendlies or not.

"Anyone call for reinforcements?" Patrick asked.

"We got backup coming from Boston," one SOA agent said without looking away from the spell she was casting.

Patrick's attention turned from the people coming toward them to the man Gerard tossed with ease into their midst as they broke free of the Night Marchers.

"Now you're close range," Gerard said, wiping someone else's blood off his face.

Zachary was missing both hands, blood pouring from the stumps of his wrists, pale in a way that spoke of bad blood loss. The *Gáe Bulg*'s spearpoint was smeared with red along the edge, and Gerard's face was etched in fury in the glow of magic.

Out of the corner of his eye, Patrick saw Brittany turn her face into her mother's shoulder, but Madelyn never looked away.

"I didn't think you were allowed to interfere in the payment of my soul debt," Patrick said.

Gerard looked at Patrick, his aura a crackling thing to Patrick's senses. "I told you once before that you are part of my story. The same can be said of me in yours. There is no point in adhering to the restrictions set upon myself and those like me that prevent interference during the creation of something new when what may result is our own eradication."

Patrick knelt, keeping one knee on Zachary's chest as he settled all his weight onto the wounded mage. No hands meant the tattoos Zachary had used as permanent anchors for his magic were gone, and command triggers were difficult to hold in one's mind when you were in the amount of pain he had to be in at the moment. The sputtering flicker of magic that never formed into a mageglobe proved Zachary's concentration was gone.

Patrick settled his dagger against Zachary's throat, the glow of heavenly white fire washing the other man out, or maybe it was the blood loss.

"Where is Ethan performing the spellwork to turn himself into a god?" Patrick asked.

Zachary's lips peeled back from his teeth, eyes almost too bright in his face but losing focus. "He will rise and be remembered."

"Not if I have anything to say about it."

There wasn't any point in saving Zachary for further questioning. He was too much of a zealot, held too much adherence to Ethan's dreams of godhood. Patrick didn't wait for Zachary to bleed out on the ground beneath him. He slit Zachary's throat with his dagger in a single movement, the matte-black blade cutting deep. Zachary heaved beneath him, the stumps of his arms pushing at Patrick's body, but it didn't matter.

He was never getting up again.

"That's for Hannah," Patrick said, his words quiet beneath the roar of the storm, but he knew Zachary heard him before death stole the mage away.

When Patrick looked up, Madelyn was staring right at him, but there was no judgment in his aunt's face, no disgust or horror. She looked at him with a fierce sort of grief in her eyes as she held Brittany close, keeping her daughter's face tucked close to her shoulder to keep from seeing what Patrick had done.

"Thank you," Madelyn said in a raw voice.

Patrick might have lost his mother, but Madelyn and everyone else had lost a sister and daughter and, later, an aunt. Nothing would bring her back, but closure was still something the Patterson family could get.

That Patrick could get.

Gerard helped Patrick to his feet. The Dominion Sect magic users were faltering beneath the attack now that Andras was gone and Zachary was dead.

"We need to go back to New York," Patrick said.

"I'll get us there," Gerard promised.

Hermes spread his hands and nodded at Madelyn and Brittany. "I'll see these two behind a threshold. Persephone won't speak to me for decades if I let her high priestess die. I'll join you in New York once they are safe."

It was probably the kindest thing Hermes had ever done for Patrick, but really, it was to the god's benefit more than anyone else's. Persephone could hold a grudge if the way she'd frosted out Hades over the years as if she was a goddess of winter and not spring was anything to go by. Patrick didn't doubt she'd blame Hermes for any grievance she took on behalf of her followers, and the messenger god still had to work with her in the Underworld.

"Kū!" Gerard called out. "Gather your warriors and let's go!"

The Hawaiian war god lifted his spear in silent acknowledgment, letting out a fierce cry that served to draw the Night Marchers to his position. Gerard hefted the *Gáe Bulg* with both hands and used it to carve open the veil.

The rush of cold air that followed the fog spilling into the cemetery made Patrick's teeth ache. It looked as if it didn't take any effort at all to open the veil, and that didn't bode well for what they'd find on the other side.

"Is it Samhain?" Patrick asked.

"It's Tuesday night. Samhain is three days away," Madelyn said.

Gerard rotated his spear around, gripping it with just one

hand. "It took us almost a day to reach you. It could be longer than that this time when we go through."

There was only one way to find out.

Patrick stepped up to grab Gerard's shoulder strap on his Kevlar vest, still holding his dagger. "Let's go."

Keith grabbed Patrick by the jacket collar as the rest of the Hellraisers lined up to pass through the veil, Kū and his Night Marchers taking up the rear. Gerard spared a glance over his shoulder to see that everyone was accounted for before plunging into the tear between worlds, and Patrick could only follow.

# 22

A PERPETUAL TWILIGHT HAD FALLEN OVER MANHATTAN, MAKING IT impossible to figure out what day it was or even the time. The drifting fog, the unceasing rain, and the stormy sky above that never changed left them fighting in a strange stretch of timelessness. The one silver lining of that dodginess meant the vampires weren't bound by a sun because it didn't rise and didn't set and didn't seem to exist at all in the new world Ethan was trying to build in increments.

It had been a hard fight downtown to get to where they were after they'd left Tempest pack territory by Central Park. A couple of hours' respite in some apartment buildings across two blocks that were being shielded by covens and the Cailleach Bheur hadn't been enough time to drive the exhaustion out of Jono. He could only run on adrenaline for so long, could only ask the same of those fighting beside him, before it became too much.

It didn't matter that he carried Fenrir in his soul. The god could do nothing with a body incapable of going on.

A streak of shadows up ahead in the fog caught Jono's eyes, but he kept walking. He could smell who it was. Ashanti had ordered some of the vampires with them to scout ahead and around their constantly moving position. Not all of them had returned over the hours, something Jono knew Lucien would hold against their pack if any of them turned out to belong to his Night Court.

Takoma landed on the road some meters ahead with a fellow vampire. The Native American vampire straightened from his crouched position, eyeing Jono before giving a respectful nod to his mother.

"The military is set up on the Park Avenue Viaduct up ahead. Their concern seems to be Grand Central Station," Takoma said.

"Why?" Ashanti asked.

Takoma flexed his hands, his nails more like claws. "It smells dead."

"Zombies," Spencer said grimly.

"The subway's protective wards are broken. It would be easier to move the dead through the tunnels than the streets, even with trains in the way," Nadine said.

"This is not where we stand our ground. We must keep moving," Órlaith said from astride her steed.

"I could use a restock on our way through Midtown," Spencer said, glancing down at his rifle.

Nadine nodded. "Me too."

Jono huffed and started forward again, not blinking at the glittering violet shield Nadine raised in front of his nose. Despite knowing that whoever waited up ahead had to be on their side, Jono couldn't stop wondering about the safety of his pack. The soulbond was quiet, and Jono didn't know where Sage or Wade were, if any of them were safe and alive. But Jono couldn't let himself dwell on the terrible *what-ifs* plaguing him. That helped no one, least of all the people he was fighting with or for.

They trudged through the rain, weaving around abandoned vehicles, shoving some aside to create space for the fae's steeds to more easily move through. The fog shifted around them, wind peeling it away from the road ahead.

They'd reached the Park Avenue Viaduct between Grand Central Station and a hotel. As Takoma had reported, the road teemed with soldiers and police officers. Thunder rumbled through the air so loudly that Jono could feel the vibrations in his paws as he walked forward with Nadine and Spencer to his left, while Ashanti kept pace on his right. He'd yet to shift back to human since they'd left the Upper East Side, letting Fenrir speak for him when he needed to give orders.

The malevolent power brewing inside Grand Central Terminal didn't bode well to the people stationed outside it. The soldiers manning a hastily built barricade consisting of abandoned cars kept their weapons trained on them as they approached. No one was shooting—yet—but Nadine hadn't lowered her defensive shield.

"I'm PIA Special Agent Nadine Mulroney," Nadine said loudly. "I'm with allies."

"Looks like you're with werecreatures and vampires," someone shouted.

"Like I said. Allies."

"If they don't let us pass, we'll go through them," Lucien said as he sauntered up to stand by Ashanti.

Jono turned his wolf's head to keep the master vampire in his sights. Lucien's pale face was splattered with blood from the demons and hunters he'd killed on their push downtown. He cradled a rifle with the casual expertise of someone who rarely went anywhere without a weapon.

"We're with the joint task force," Spencer called out.

The murmur of voices spiked, and Jono dialed up his hearing to catch what he could beneath the roar of the reactionary storm. Fenrir's presence settled on the surface of Jono's mind, a thought away from taking control if things went south. Finally, someone with some sort of rank waved them forward with a commanding gesture.

"Mulroney, was it?" the woman in uniform asked. "General Reed said to provide your group support if we crossed paths."

"Is General Reed within the vicinity?" Nadine asked.

"The brass are coordinating the defense of Grand Central Station on Park Avenue down the way."

"What's going on with Grand Central?"

The woman's expression was grim beneath her hard helmet. "We don't know."

Jono growled his displeasure before moving forward, and everyone else followed. He could hear the noise from what had to be at least hundreds of fighters both on the viaduct and below on the street level, scattered in groups for blocks by the sound of it.

Jono knew the streets of Manhattan well, and fighting in this area would happen in tight quarters. With the Morrígan's staff in play, anyone who died would just be resurrected to fight again like in Paris. The loss of life was going to be staggering if those in charge didn't have a decent plan of attack.

Jono's group merged into a single column consisting of werecreatures, vampires, gods, and Órlaith's fae. They must have made an interesting spectacle judging by the stares and the spike of anxiousness that hit Jono's nose.

The military had set up some sort of command center on the viaduct where it curved at the corner. Jono's group came upon the section covered by a small domed shield that glittered gold in the fog. It was heavily guarded by soldiers and police in black riot gear. Jono didn't miss the way a few people's hands strayed closer to the triggers on their rifles and handguns as they approached.

"We're here for General Reed," Nadine called out.

A darker gold line cut perpendicular down the shield, parting it so the people on the inside could pass through it. Jono sat on his haunches and watched as General Reed and Casale came out, joined by several other people in uniform.

"Sir," Nadine said, her greeting echoed by Spencer.

"I wasn't sure you'd make it," Reed said, his gaze raking over their group. Jono knew when the dragon came up short by the frown that settled harshly on his face. "Where's Collins? And Captain Breckenridge?"

At those questions, Jono started to shift, quickly tearing his body back to human shape. He ignored the way someone in police riot gear gagged, the rain washing blood and viscera off his skin as he stood. The cold rain made his skin prickle, but he wasn't going to be human long enough for it to matter.

"Jonothon," Reed said, crossing his arms. The smoke curling out of his nose couldn't be explained away by a cigarette, not in this downpour. "Where's your pack?"

"Patrick went to Salem to trade himself for Eloise on some spellwork there. He said something about cutting off Ethan's power source," Jono said.

"We got word through scrying crystals the Salem nexus was barricaded by SOA mages out of Boston Tuesday night," Reed said.

Relief practically gutted him, but the news was only a silver lining because Patrick wasn't with him. "When did you scry?"

"Whatever passed for morning. Time isn't running normally here. It's difficult to gauge."

"Samhain is happening now," Órlaith said, urging her steed forward. She towered over them all, practically glowing the way only immortals did. Quite a few people behind Reed and Casale eyed her with not a little worshipfulness in their eyes.

"The veil tears," Ashanti agreed.

"We could use Collins, but Bailey will do for now," Reed said.

"No," Jono shot back. "He stays with us."

Reed stared at him with narrowed eyes. "You don't give the orders here, and we need his magic to hold off what's coming up from below."

"You sent him to my pack."

"And now I'm reassigning him."

"*I think not,*" Fenrir said, taking control of Jono's mouth.

People jerked on their feet, weapons moving to train Jono's way, but he couldn't focus on them, not when Fenrir ran the show. Nadine hadn't yet dropped her shield, so if anyone took a shot, he'd still be standing when they stopped shooting.

"Uh, guys?" Spencer said.

"Do you even know where Ethan is?" Reed demanded.

"No, but we will," Ashanti said with all the derision of someone who was ancient compared to a dragon.

"*We're passing through. Our business is elsewhere,*" Fenrir said.

"Guys," Spencer said, sounding agitated.

His tone of voice made Jono want to tense, but Fenrir still had control. *Let me go.*

Fenrir's answer was all teeth in his mind. *Not yet.*

"Spencer?" Nadine asked sharply.

Fenrir deigned to glance at Spencer, and the look on his face was a sort of carefully bitten-back horror that came out in his eyes.

"Those aren't just any zombies." A multitude of screams that Jono remembered from London tore through the air, followed by the desperate shouts of men and women trying not to panic. "They're drekavacs."

"Hold the line!" Reed roared in a voice that rumbled with a depth to it no human would have. Then he stabbed a finger at Jono. "If you don't help us blockade Grand Central Station, they'll have a clear shot into the streets."

"They already do with the subway's other stations," Lucien sneered.

"Massing here enables them to cut off the lower half of Manhattan from the rest of the island. They'll spread out along the parallel streets and create a wall of the dead like the Dominion Sect did in Cairo when they split our forces with demons."

Lucien scowled, fangs gnashing together. "I remember. It still won't stop them from spreading out across the lower half of Manhattan, if they aren't already doing so."

Reed bared his teeth, the points too sharp for any human as smoke trailed out of his nose. "Get your people into the field, Lucien."

Jono wondered if those two had known each other at all before the Thirty-Day War or if Lucien was just that skilled at cultivating animosity with everyone he came in contact with.

Fenrir gave him back control, and Jono unclenched his teeth to speak. "Drekavacs move fast."

"I know." Reed's attention shifted from Jono to Spencer. "Bailey, I want you up front. Buy us some time to get a foothold in this fight."

Jono was gratified to see Spencer look at him for approval first. "Do what Reed says, but when I leave, you leave."

Spencer nodded. "Understood."

Jono stared at Reed. "You can give him orders for this fight, but some of those with me will help guard him."

Emma planted herself by Spencer's side without needing to be asked, her wolf ears flattening against her skull at the next wave of eerie screams that echoed through the stormy air. Takoma and two other vampires joined her on guard duty. Fatima tilted her small head back to look up at them all before letting out a yowl that was deeper than her tiny body should've been capable of producing.

"Yeah, I know," Spencer muttered as he conjured up a dozen mageglobes. "Let's go break some souls."

Blackened streaks of magic crawled up the façade of Grand Central Station, a warning that had everyone rushing to their assigned position if they weren't there already. Jono knew the zombies would come up on the street level first, which meant everyone who'd come with him up here had to get down there.

"Bailey," Reed called out.

Spencer looked over at him. "Sir?"

"The nexus is barricaded, but the ley lines can still be tapped. Use caution, and don't burn yourself out."

Spencer nodded. "I'll try my best."

"Then get your feet on the ground and put the dead to rest."

The only way down for a human would result in broken bones. Takoma fixed that problem by grabbing Spencer around his waist and hauling the mage over the side of the viaduct they were on with preternatural speed, Emma a mere second behind.

To his credit, Spencer only let out a startled yelp before disappearing out of sight in the arms of a vampire.

"What makes it through his magic will be our problem," Reed said.

"We'll aid you, but this isn't where we stand our ground," Jono warned.

"Noted. Now shift and get your ass into the fight. We're going to try to funnel the damn things into a kill box."

Jono rolled his eyes, already kneeling for the shift. "I'm not one of your soldiers."

"Now you sound like the fledgling. Where is he?"

Jono was already shifting when the question was asked, jaw breaking in half as his human bones changed into something else. Fenrir pushed the shift faster than ever, and the world was a sickening twist of smeared color as his vision changed with it. When he was fully wolf and all his senses had settled, Jono tossed back his head and howled a challenge the drekavacs answered in kind.

*Let us fight*, Fenrir said.

Fenrir's presence seeped into Jono's thoughts and bones. It wasn't stolen control but a gifted partnership that gave him speed like nothing before when he flung himself off the viaduct for the pavement below right in front of a barricade. The soldiers manning it thankfully didn't shoot him or the other werecreatures that followed him down to the ground.

Grand Central Station loomed above them, magic still crawling over its façade and seeping out of the windows. The wind blew harshly through the street, whipping rain over everyone. No one wasted power on personal shields, though he could see the glitter of a powerful layer of shields up ahead over the entrances. As Jono ran forward, he saw the familiar violet of Nadine's defensive magic join what was already there to try to keep their fighters safe.

If it was anything like Paris, he knew it wouldn't be enough.

The screaming coming from within Grand Central Station didn't stop. Jono watched as up ahead Takoma hauled Spencer back behind a barricade while Fatima stayed on the other side. Ashanti landed beside Jono as he loped forward to take position by a barricade manned by soldiers instead of police. He didn't know where the Cailleach Bheur had gone, but hopefully someone was watching over them up on the viaduct.

"I told the dragon to let the zombies through. No sense in tiring out the magic users completely when we still have fighting ahead," Ashanti said.

"*Will he listen?*" Fenrir asked for the both of them.

Ashanti shrugged one thin shoulder, blinking those black eyes of hers. "If he wishes for eradication of the walking dead, then he will give the order to draw down the shields. Be ready."

Jono kept his attention focused on the entrance located beneath the bridge that crossed East Forty-Second Street. The street in their immediate area was empty of vehicles save for the ones used to create barricades. Jono could see the maze Reed had created to try to funnel whatever came out of Grand Central Station farther away to be killed. He just hoped no one on their side got caught in the crossfire.

"Lower the door shield!" Reed yelled from above, his voice echoing through the air with a reach no one human could attain without magical help.

The magic users manning the shield in that area peeled their layers free, and what poured out of the broken doors through the rain and fog was a mass of bones and rotten flesh, their bodies lined with the light of the magic that sustained them.

Cutting through the initial mass were creatures that moved with deadly swiftness. Elongated limbs and torsos gave the drekavacs' human-shaped bodies an almost nightmarish look. Their heads were larger in proportion to their bodies, and they carried the scent of a grave with them as they surged forward, screaming all the while.

Fatima met their charge with a yowl of her own, the wind picking up as Spencer's particular kind of magic rose around her. The psychopomp acted like a beacon for the dead as his magic spread through the first wave, cutting through the control Morrígan's staff had over them and breaking souls free. Fatima swallowed the souls like a tiny vortex, sending them on to rest wherever possible.

Ashanti hissed out a laugh and flung herself into the pathway of a drekavac that Spencer's magic had missed. She tore its head off with shocking ease, tossing the body one way and the head another before scouting out her next target. Jono stayed where he was as more zombies walked over the bodies and bones lying on the street.

Spencer's magic wasn't hitting all of the dead, and some escaped his reach. They reached the first barricade where Jono and the soldiers waited. He turned his head to the side to eye the men and women in uniform standing ready behind the half circle of abandoned cars.

"*Watch your aim,*" Fenrir said.

A couple of soldiers swore, but Jono didn't wait to see if any would respond to the warning. He lunged at the zombies coming their way, intent on tearing them to pieces. Paris had taught him that exhaustion was inevitable when it came to fighting millions of dead. They'd do what they could to help Reed, but short of turning Grand Central Station into a pile of rubble, Jono knew nothing they did would stop the dead from coming through the veil.

Automatic fire rained from above onto the zombies coming out of the entrance. The area was quickly becoming a bottleneck, and the zombies were creeping ever closer. Jono spat out a foul-tasting limb and kept fighting. Down the street, Órlaith and some of her fae were regrouping, having somehow made it off from the viaduct without killing their steeds.

Even with the bottleneck in play and Spencer's magic breaking souls free and leaving bodies behind, the sheer number of zombies coming out of Grand Central Station was a problem. The soldiers in the forward barricades abandoned them for the next one closer to Órlaith's position, a calculated retreat that Jono covered with a violence that left pieces of the dead scattered all around him.

It wasn't a sustainable approach. Even Jono, with his lack of military expertise, could've told Reed that. But then Reed's full plan came into play when shouted orders had shields going up around the barricades and anyone on their side in the field, including Jono. The incineration spell that hit the street nearly melted the pavement in areas.

The zombies stood no chance.

Fire broke all sorts of magic, and Jono remembered how Patrick had used it in London to kill the drekavacs in Tottenham. It burned through the zombies like an inferno, licking at the stone and viaduct near the entrance. But even as the fire faded, the zombies kept coming.

The fire stopped, and the shields were lowered to conserve magical strength. Lucien landed beside Jono, the vampire joined by Carmen without her glamour.

"If Reed wants his kill box, he can have it, but we can't stay here," Lucien said.

"We've secured extra ammunition from him that will get us to the next cache," Carmen said.

Lucien had dipped into his Night Court's inventory of weapons and set up locations all around downtown they could feasibly reach to reload in an ongoing and moving fight. The cartel he owned had moved the weapons through the southern border at the beginning of October, and Jono knew the inventory was large.

"*Clear us a way south past Pershing Square*," Fenrir said, repeating Jono's thoughts.

Lucien and Carmen left in a blur. Jono swung his head around, ready to face off against the next wave of zombies, when the ground bucked beneath his paws.

"Earthquake!" someone yelled.

Jono planted himself firmly, rolling with the motion as the ground seemed to shake itself apart. A crack appeared in East Forty-Second Street, splitting wide. What lifted free of the shadowy hole had Jono howling a warning with Fenrir's help.

"*Do not shoot!*"

Fenrir's voice roared through the air louder than Reed's, and whatever power he'd poured into the words stilled fingers on triggers of those around them as Baba Yaga rose up on her floating mortar made of bones, pestle in hand.

She whacked her pestle on the mortar, her keen hunter eyes fixated on the second wave of zombies clawing over the bodies building up near the bridge. Her mortar floated away from the hole, and what came up after her would've made Jono gag if he'd still been in human form.

The man was little more than a corpse, intestines hanging out of a wound that was only half-closed, skin rotten around it. The rest of his skin was chalk white, as if he'd lost all the blood in his veins, but the manic brightness in his eyes and the crackle of ozone on the air hinted at a god hell-bent on ignoring death, even when it knocked on his bones.

"*Peklabog*," Fenrir growled, to Jono's surprise. "*So you are not dead.*"

The god of the Slavic Underworld smiled, revealing blackened teeth. "My Patriarch of Souls betrayed me, but he could not keep me dead after the staff broke. My godhead was set free and came home."

To a walking corpse, it seemed.

Baba Yaga pointed her pestle at the zombies coming their way. "Is time to feast."

Jono was reminded of what Baba Yaga ate, and if she wanted to gorge on the dead, he wasn't going to stop her.

The god and immortal rushed forward, Baba Yaga letting out a gleeful cackle that people would remember in their nightmares.

**23**

Leaving Pershing Square was brutal, even with Peklabog and Baba Yaga on the street to aid them. Because of their presence, Reed had made the decision to remove the shields on the corner entrances of Grand Central Station. That meant drawing the soldiers and officers farther down into the foggy streets so they weren't overrun.

The immortals bought everyone time, and Spencer helped. Piles of bodies and bones remained on the street, none yet resurrected by whatever magic had given them temporary life. The flash of dark green magic erupted through groups of zombies like spot fires, leaving the dead in its wake. Jono didn't know where Spencer was, but he knew Emma and hopefully Takoma would keep him safe.

Órlaith's steed used its hind legs to kick a drekavac in the face, sending the fast-moving zombie flying. That gave her space to ram her spear into the drekavac's chest when it threw itself back at her, half its head caved in. When she jerked the spear upward, it split the body in half, and it fell to the ground. Seconds later, it rose again, stumbling their way.

Órlaith snapped her fingers and set the drekavac on fire. "We are losing ground."

"*Manhattan was already lost when the veil tore,*" Fenrir replied before biting down on a zombie and shaking his head so rapidly the bones flew apart.

Jono hated the taste of zombies. No wonder Wade complained so much about eating them and demons. Thinking of Wade made worry rise to the forefront of his mind again. Jono didn't know where they were or how they were doing, and the uncertainty ate at him.

"Your pessimism is, as always, unwanted, cousin."

"*Watch your left.*"

Órlaith twisted in her saddle and slammed the spearpoint through the rotting head of a zombie about to claw her steed. She shifted position, putting space between them to better cover the area they'd been pushed to.

Around them, werecreatures savaged zombies before darting out of the way so soldiers could fire spelled bullets at the walking dead. The sheer number of zombies pouring out of Grand Central Station was enough to overwhelm an army, and they weren't even that. What they did have was gods walking the earth once more, and Jono wondered how many survivors of this mess would vow to worship them. The cynical part of him wondered if maybe that was the whole point of this fight.

Despite Peklabog's stomach-churning appearance, the god could put down more zombies than Spencer. Between him and Baba Yaga, they rerouted zombies into areas where magic users other than Spencer could take them down. Stragglers got pushed down the street into kill box areas, but those stragglers were turning into a wave at this point.

Jono's people had pushed south, keeping on the street that ran parallel to the Park Avenue Viaduct. They fought to hold their ground with soldiers and police officers. Jono knew he couldn't leave until Reed had the situation under control, but that might be wishful thinking at this point.

Especially when the hunters showed up.

Hidden by the fog and the noise of the battle already happening, Jono didn't realize hunters had arrived until shots rang out from behind where they stood facing Grand Central. A couple of soldiers went down, and their fellow fighters had to hurriedly pitch their bodies outside the barriers.

Jono was saved from taking a bullet by virtue of being surrounded by zombies. He snarled and spun to face the new threat walking out of the fog. Jono tossed back his head and howled a warning that was taken up by other werecreatures. Soldiers and police officers shouted to each other as they worked to split their forces to deal with the heavily armed hunters.

Jono barreled his way forward through zombies, shaking off their grasping hands, to take cover near a barricade of cars. The police hunkered down in that questionable safety barely gave him a second glance, all their focus on the hunters taking indiscriminate aim at the battlefield.

Carmen landed lightly beside him, having dropped down from the viaduct to his right. She knelt beside him, shouldering an RPG with deft hands. Jono cocked his wolf head at her and eyed her weapon, noticing the lack of a reload.

"Reed is attempting to seal the entrances to Grand Central Station with something more permanent. Nadine is with him, so there is no defensive magic to spare this way," Carmen said.

Then she stood in one swift motion, aimed, and fired the RPG in the direction of the hunters. The burn of explosives and magic stung Jono's nose as the large grenade flew toward its target. The hunters had brought magic users with them, and he expected their shield to hold up against the attack.

It didn't.

The grenade slammed right through the magical barrier, whatever spell adhered to the grenade forcing its way through to the other side. The crackling magic of the broken shield couldn't be reset fast enough to block the attack. When it exploded, pieces of bodies went flying far enough they got lost in the zombies. Jono hoped they wouldn't get resurrected.

Carmen ducked back down and tossed the now empty RPG over the barricade of abandoned cars. "Military-grade spell. Messy, but useful."

Jono wasn't about to complain, but a quick glance down the road showed the one explosion had merely dented the hunters' forces. He growled, not sure how they were going to get out from where they were cornered between zombies and hunters. Peklabog and Baba Yaga had their hands full closer to Grand Central Station, and Jono wasn't sure they'd leave their feast of the dead if he called for help.

Ashanti landed on a nearby car, crunching the hood before vaulting off it to reach Jono's side. The mother of all vampires had bits of blood and rotten flesh sticking to her clothes, her hands messy from tearing through bodies alive and dead alike.

"This is unsustainable, cousin. We must leave," Ashanti said flatly.

*No,* Jono thought, forcing Fenrir to listen.

*"We cannot give up ground,"* Fenrir said for Jono.

Ashanti's lips curled over her iron fangs. "We lose it if we stay."

As if to prove a point, bullets ripped through the air, forcing everyone to take cover. Jono breathed in a lungful of rot tinged with ozone, the dead coming closer despite the hail of bullets tearing through the advancing horde. Cutting through the slower-moving bones and decaying bodies were the elongated forms of drekavacs, their inhuman eyes locked on prey.

The soldiers and police were forced to split their focus between the zombies and the hunters, creating more crossfire that Jono's people couldn't fight through. Werecreatures were forced to the edge of the street, at risk of being boxed in. Fenrir clawed at his mind and soul, searching for complete control, expecting Jono to give it.

He would have if the world didn't erupt in dragon fire.

The thunderous roar made his ears ring badly enough Jono had to dial down his hearing. The searing heat of dragon fire coming from above was hot enough to melt asphalt. The negative flashes of light that signaled demons fleeing dying hosts were almost impossible to see in the flame that burned through the magic to bodies behind shields. Jono looked up at the sky, expecting to see Reed, but the fire dragon whose beating wings forced the fog aside was a welcome, unexpected sight.

Wade landed on the Park Avenue Viaduct with a building-shaking arrival, his long, sinuous neck extending farther out as he belched more flame at the enemy. Magic couldn't hold against dragon fire, and what spells the hunters had cast broke beneath the fire. Those who could flee down side streets did so, most likely running into the arms of Reed's people to hopefully be cut down.

Jono howled a welcome as Wade folded his wings against his back, long tail lashing out behind him as he turned his focus to burning up the dead once the hunters on the street were eradicated. As Wade shifted position on the viaduct, Jono caught a glimpse of three people scrambling off his back. Jono's heart skipped a beat, the relief flooding through him like a balm on his frayed nerves.

Jono wasted no time in using his preternatural strength to claw his way up the Park Avenue Viaduct, momentarily safe from bullets with Wade the bigger distraction. When he made it to the street level, Leon had already shifted to his wolf form, guarding Marek and Sage.

Marek had his arm wrapped protectively around Sage's waist, hand low on her hip in deference of the gut wound she still suffered from. Sage was pale to the point of looking as if she would pass out, but the tight set to her mouth was a stubbornness

Jono knew well. Both were soaked to the bone from flying through the reactionary storm.

He took a risk and shifted back to human, Fenrir forcing the change so quick he nearly vomited once he stood on two feet. Shaking his head, Jono hurried to where Sage and Marek stood, Wade having yet to move from his crouched position. The rancid smell of burning bodies was too much for even the wind and the rain to push aside, and it drifted up to them with a foulness that made Jono's throat itch.

"How did you find us?" Jono asked once he was in earshot.

"The explosions were kind of hard to miss," Marek said, teeth chattering a bit.

"Wade and Leon got us out of Bellevue once the veil tore," Sage said.

Jono wrapped his arm around Sage's shoulders, providing her support to lean on, breathing in her scent. "You should've stayed in the ICU."

Sage shook her head, wavering on her feet a little. The hospital gown she wore clung to her skin wetly, and she felt cool to the touch in a way that was worrisome. Werecreatures had higher core temperatures, and she wasn't anywhere close to that heat at the moment.

She looked him in the eye, blinking slowly. "I wasn't leaving you to fight alone."

"You can barely stand."

"I tried that argument with her already. It didn't work," Marek said.

Jono grimaced. "Clearly."

Sage nudged him in the side with her elbow. "Wade got us out from downtown. We didn't have much trouble flying up here. He seemed to know where to go."

"Reed's here. Maybe that's why."

Marek lifted one shoulder, drawing attention to the rucksack he carried. "I have Wade's clothes in here. I wasn't sure if you wanted him to shift back to human or not, but he was adamant about not running around naked in the streets."

Another burst of fire from Wade aimed below on the street sent a wave of heat their way. Jono eyed Wade critically. Manhattan streets were too narrow and hemmed in on all sides by tall buildings for Wade to safely traverse even on a clear day, much less the strange twilight they were currently fighting in amidst the veil.

"Wade," Jono yelled. "Shift back to human."

Wade twisted his long neck back around, one large golden eye blinking down at him from his wedge head. He spat another burst of fire at the street in a different direction, though the force of it was lessened some. Then he shifted mass with a rapidness that left his body a blur until he appeared as human, crouched between two cars he'd crunched flat upon landing.

"Am I glad to see you!" Wade yelled before sprinting their way.

Marek shrugged off the rucksack and tossed it to Wade, who hurriedly got dressed in clothes that got immediately wet from the rain. Red scales shined along his neck and face, pushing through skin. His eyes remained gold, and the smoke coming out of his nose was torn away by the wind.

"Are you all right?" Jono asked.

Wade shoved his feet into a pair of sneakers, staying low to the ground as gunfire sounded through the air from the street below. "I'm fine. Where's Patrick?"

Jono shook his head. "Not here."

A stricken expression crossed Wade's face. "Still missing?"

"Gerard and the Hellraisers went to get him back with Hermes' help. I'm hoping they arrive soon."

"You can't feel him?" Sage asked.

Jono's mouth twisted. "We're past the veil, or it passed us. Until he's back with us, I can't feel him through the soulbond."

Even then, he wasn't sure he'd be able to. He'd been trying, but whatever distance stretched between them was too far for him to know where Patrick was. Jono could only hope he was alive and unharmed.

An explosion had them all ducking low, Sage nearly falling over. Between Jono and Marek, they kept her upright.

"What was that?" Wade asked.

Jono craned his head around, looking at the smoke rising up from Grand Central Station. "I think they blew the entrances to keep the zombies from getting out."

"That won't stop them," Sage said, one arm tucked around her middle. She held herself stiffly, breathing tightly through her clenched teeth. The scent of pain rolled off her, making Jono feel helpless about being unable to help her. "We learned that in Paris."

The zombies had come up from the Paris Metro at every stop they'd pushed past in that city. Jono figured Manhattan would be the same. Reed's plan to bury the dead wasn't going to stop them from clawing their way up another subway stop farther down the line.

"We need to keep heading downtown. Whatever altar Ethan will use, it won't be built on houses but skyscrapers."

Fenrir growled agreement on that through his mind, the god's surety like ice in Jono's veins. The chill came from within, not the rain beating down on his bare shoulders.

Leon snarled a warning, and Jono's head jerked up, attention focusing on the threat coming their way out of the broken windows of Grand Central Station. Drekavacs flung themselves onto the road of the viaduct, having found a way out like Jono knew they would've. The barricade that Reed had set up at the viaduct's intersection had either been abandoned or fallen, because there was no one in that area to stand their ground.

"Fuck," he said.

"Oh, I hate those things," Wade groaned. "You sure you don't want me to shift and eat them?"

"We can't risk you bringing a building down on top of us. Guard Sage and Marek. Leon and I will handle them."

"You got it."

Jono sucked in a breath and exhaled harshly before shifting again. The ache in his bones faded as his nerves were turned off, leaving behind no pain as his body broke itself down into wolf form. When he stood on all four legs, the drekavacs were halfway to their position.

Leon planted himself beside Jono, lips curled up over his fangs as he snarled a challenge at the oncoming, fast-moving zombies. Jono was absolutely *done* with fucking zombies. Too bad no one told the drekavacs that.

The horde coming their way was ten strong, quick and vicious. Two werewolves might not be enough to hold them off, even with Fenrir riding his soul, so it was probably a good thing Wade was incandescently angry and willing to spit fire at any who got close to his position. Dodging the fire while dodging teeth and claws as Jono went in for the kill time and time again meant he and Leon had to spread out along the road between abandoned cars.

Space was tight, and while they didn't have to contend with bullets on the viaduct, the drekavacs weren't easy adversaries. They were worse than the slower-moving bodies taken from Paris or graves. But the zombies weren't the only problem they had to contend with though.

Wade's panicked warning shout caught Jono's ear. He spat out a broken arm before looking behind him at where Wade now stood with his back to them. Coming through the fog up the viaduct from the street level was a group of all-too-familiar jaguar constructs.

*Sodding hell. More gods.*

"We need to get off the viaduct," Sage said from where she stood wrapped up in Marek's arms.

Both easy routes were blocked. Their only option was to jump, but Jono wasn't sure Sage had strength enough to hold on to him. Jono howled, calling for help from the packs and any vampires or fae who could be spared.

The help that arrived was unexpected.

Lightning flashed directly overhead, and the thunder that boomed through the air sounded like a continuous drum. The jaguars paused in their advance up the viaduct, and their hesitation cost them. Spears thrown from above lodged themselves in the constructs, shattering the jaguars into so many pieces of obsidian.

Jono looked up at the sky over Grand Central Station and howled a welcome to the valkyries on their pegasi flying toward them. Joining them was Hinon, the Haudenosaunee thunder god's huge, storm-colored wings flapping powerfully in the air. Lightning crackled around the god, and he aimed several bolts to strike the enemy on the ground.

Over a dozen valkyries dived to their position, picking off the remaining drekavacs as they flew over the viaduct. Several landed lightly on the road amidst the rubble and shattered bits of the jaguars. Brynhildr was in the lead, with Thor seated behind her astride her pegasus.

She leaned over and gripped a spear embedded in the road, yanking it free with inhuman strength. She straightened up in the saddle, eyes blazing in her face. "We heard the call and came as quickly as we could through the veil."

Thor slid off the pegasus behind her, Mjölnir clenched tightly in one fist. Lightning crackled around the hammer, crawling up his arms, but he didn't appear bothered by it. "Well met, cousin."

"*You made decent time,*" Fenrir said.

"Would've been faster if the veil wasn't spreading where it shouldn't. Containment will be difficult, if it's not already too late," Thor said.

Fenrir snapped Jono's teeth together. "*This is a god's beginning we shall end.*"

Thor's smile was cold and vicious, eyes dark with memory Jono could feel was shared with Fenrir. "May your hunger be all-consuming."

"Eir," Brynhildr called out. "Tend to the wounded."

The young-looking valkyrie slid off her saddle with ease, clutching a spear in one hand. Jono watched as she ran toward Sage, who watched her come with wide eyes. Jono didn't know what the immortal was going to do, but he wasn't going to stop her if it meant Sage could stand upright for longer than ten seconds without support.

Another explosion echoed through the air, smoke drifting on the wind from around the corner behind them. Jono blinked rainwater out of his eyes, seeing more zombies climbing out of the ruined windows of Grand Central. Sparks of Spencer's magic flashed over zombies, but he couldn't see where Peklabog or Baba Yaga had got to.

Hinon streaked toward them in a tight dive, his massive wings folded behind him. When he landed, the road shook with his impact, but he appeared unaffected. "Where is Patrick?"

"Not here," Ashanti rasped as she vaulted over the side of the viaduct, landing lightly on her bone hooks amidst scattered skeletons.

"His absence is not a way to win a war."

"It is being handled."

"By who?"

"Cú Chulainn."

Hinon pursed his lips before shrugging, the arch of his wings moving with the motion. "We can only hope he is successful."

Whatever else anyone was going to say, it was drowned out by the screaming cries of the Sluagh breaking free of the clouds above. The valkyries still in the air let out a challenging war cry as they reformed ranks between the skyscrapers.

"Eir!" Brynhildr called out.

"I'm almost done!" Eir shouted back, not taking her hands off Sage. She and Marek knelt on the road with Wade hovering protectively beside them while Eir used her power to heal what modern medicine couldn't.

Brynhildr spun her spear to get a better grip and tipped her head in Thor's and Hinon's direction. "We will hold off the Sluagh."

She pressed her heels against her pegasus' ribs, urging him into the sky. He vaulted into the air, wings flapping, and they flew through the rain to lead the charge against the Sluagh. Thor didn't watch her go, hefting Mjölnir around to call forth lightning and send a bolt into the horde of zombies coming their way on the viaduct from Grand Central Station.

"What is the plan?" Thor asked.

"We walk amongst Ethan's altar. We must find his sacrificial circle and destroy it," Ashanti said.

"Don't destroy the city. We live here," Wade protested.

"It won't matter if we do not win."

Fenrir growled agreement while Jono stared at where Sage was getting to her feet with an ease she hadn't had before. The sickly paleness of her face was receding, and the pain that had saturated her scent was rapidly fading.

Eir stood, glancing over her shoulder at Jono, the cat-eye makeup she wore staying put despite the storm. "I removed the spell prohibiting your dire from shifting."

"Thank you," Marek said fervently, relief thick in his voice.

Sage kept a hand on Marek, meeting Jono's gaze. "He's coming with us."

Jono wasn't going to fight her on that request. There wasn't anywhere safe in Manhattan right now. Marek's status as a seer was something they couldn't afford the other side to claim.

An explosion sounded so close Jono's ears rang like a bell had been struck right beside him. The Park Avenue Viaduct shook in a dangerous way, all the warning they got before it started to collapse underneath them. The shattering of asphalt, cement, and rebar rolled like a wave through where they stood.

"Get clear!" Thor yelled, his voice booming like thunder through the air.

Eir vaulted onto her pegasus, and Wade scrambled up behind

her. Sage shoved Marek into Hinon's arms before racing with preternatural speed toward the teetering edge of the viaduct. Fenrir reacted before Jono could, vaulting onto a car and using it to propel himself off the viaduct for the ground below.

Leon landed a mere second after he did. Jono forced Fenrir to stay still long enough for Sage to get a good hold of his scruff before they ran from the collapsing viaduct. The ground shuddered beneath them from the impact, dust rising into the air despite the rain. He didn't know if the cause of the collapse was their side or the Dominion Sect's.

They ended up by an abandoned barricade. It provided enough momentary shelter for Sage to shift without risk of getting shot at. Jono and Leon guarded her position while Hinon and Eir flew toward them with their charges.

A mageglobe streaked through the air, causing Eir to veer sharply upward, the pegasus' wings flapping hard to escape the attack. Wade's startled yell was met with Sage's weretiger roar, different from the howls of wolves.

"War arrives," Thor said, staring south down the street.

Jono stared at the shifting fog and the figures marching through it—more hunters, along with Dominion Sect magic users led by a god carrying a short sword and round shield, a golden helm on his head. The rest of his clothes were modern tactical gear, though he carried no guns.

"Cousins," the new god said.

"Ares," Hinon said as he deposited Marek behind the barricade. "I'd heard you'd left your spine in DC."

Ares scraped the edge of his sword against his shield, creating a line of fiery sparks that scattered before him as the Greek god of war marched forward. "Rumors of my death have always been false. I have never been forgotten."

"A pity," Thor rumbled.

Eir swooped low, using her spear to knock aside another mageglobe. They escaped the edge of the magical explosion, and Wade flung himself off the pegasus' back and to the ground beside Jono. Eir rose into the air, leaving for the battle in the sky above.

Sage wedged herself between Jono and Leon, her weretiger form a welcome presence. She snarled a warning, the sound causing Ares to laugh.

"You chose the wrong side in this fight," Ares said.

"You're one to talk, asshole," an achingly familiar voice called out.

Jono's entire body jerked, the soulbond snapping tight in his chest from close proximity after so long being still and quiet. He turned his head, following the tug on the soulbond the way a compass always pointed north.

Stepping through the veil amidst the rubble of the Park Avenue Viaduct came Patrick, backed by Gerard and the Hellraisers, Kū, and the Night Marchers. He was covered in mud, but he was here and *alive*, and Jono howled a welcome that echoed like a warning to the other side on the storm-driven winds.

# 24

WHEN THEY PUSHED THROUGH THE VEIL ONTO A RUBBLE-STREWN Manhattan street, Patrick only had eyes for Jono and his pack. The sight of Sage in her weretiger form standing beside Jono and Wade soothed the quiet terror living in the back of his mind since he'd met Ashanti on the Brooklyn Bridge. In its place was a fierce pride for the people he considered family, tempered by a violent spike of hate for the enemy they faced off against.

"Ares," Gerard cried out as he slammed the butt of the *Gáe Bulg* against the ground. "You want to be gutted again that badly?"

Ares came to a hard halt in the street as Patrick and his group closed the distance between themselves and where Jono and the others stood. Thor raised Mjölnir in a welcoming manner at them, lightning crackling along all sides of the hammer.

"Cú Chulainn," Ares snarled with a hint of wariness in his voice. "Come to die?"

Gerard smiled with a sort of manic, murderous look in his silver eyes. "I think not."

"We fight for our memories, and you will be lost to time," Thor warned Ares before swinging his arm forward. Lightning erupted from Mjölnir, aimed at the enemy.

Patrick sank his awareness into the soulbond, the connection soothing his frayed nerves. He sent his awareness down below to the ley lines, not even trying for the barricaded nexus. The rivers of external power were choppy to the touch, reacting to the battle within the veil. Patrick still drew on one to power his magic as he ran to Jono's side. He conjured a mageglobe as he raised a shield against the spelled bullets aimed their way.

Wade intercepted him long enough to hug Patrick so hard his spine cracked when he was lifted off his feet. "Am I glad to see *you!*"

Patrick hastily patted Wade on the shoulder, eyes still on Jono. "Me too. Feel free to set fire to anything you want."

"I plan on it."

Wade let Patrick go, and it was only two strides more before he could sink both hands into Jono's scruff and press his forehead between Jono's ears, breathing in the scent of him after too long apart. Jono leaned hard against him, causing Patrick's feet to skid over the cracked ground.

"I came back," Patrick said, the words drowned out by gunfire.

Jono shoved his nose against Patrick's throat, licking at him. Patrick patted him on the head before straightening up and taking in the situation on the ground. The Dominion Sect and hunters had scattered for cover, while Ares held his ground against the advancing gods. Patrick hoped the god's hubris left him bleeding out on the street badly enough not even prayers could save him.

"I am pleased to see you've returned," Ashanti said from behind him.

Patrick looked over his shoulder at where the mother of all vampires crouched on a wrecked car, Marek's head peeking over the roof from behind it. She looked monstrous in the dim twilight, but Patrick was incredibly glad to see her.

"We cut Ethan off from the Salem nexus. He won't be able to power his spell with external magic," Patrick said.

"He is still casting it. You must bleed so we can find him through your twin."

"Not here in the middle of the street," Keith said as he planted himself beside Patrick to watch his six.

Ashanti blinked slowly, her eyes difficult to make out in the shadows. "The Morgan Library. We will do the blood rite there. We can no longer afford to keep running blind."

Jono growled his displeasure, but Patrick merely gave his fur a firm tug. They'd already argued over this, and Patrick had won. "Then let's get everyone and move out. Where's Mulroney?"

"With the soulbreaker."

Keith let out a distracted, happy sound as he took potshots at zombies. "Dead Boy is in the field? I'd say great, but why are there so many zombies?"

"They're leftover from Paris," Patrick said, pouring more magic into his shields that covered them.

"That's—" Keith broke off with a curse as his rifle clicked empty and he had to reload. "—a lot of zombies."

"We need to take back the Morrígan's staff to get rid of them, but Andras has taken over Ilya."

Wade's eyes got huge in his face. "Oh, that rat bastard. I'm going to eat him."

Patrick opened his mouth to tell Wade *no* but then thought better of it. "Go for it. Just don't complain about the taste afterward."

Thunder crashed so loudly Patrick instinctively ducked his head. He stared at where Thor and Gerard had Ares pinned between them. The three gods fought each other amidst the rubble of the Park Avenue Viaduct with a viciousness that would've been deadly for a mortal.

"Radios don't work, so I don't know how you want to spread

the word to move out," Keith said, weapon locked and loaded once more.

"My children will gather those who need to come with us," Ashanti said before flinging herself back into the fray.

"That's great, but where the fuck is this library?"

"About five blocks away," Wade said with the sureness of someone who'd been there before.

Patrick shot him a look. "Wade."

"What? You can't prove anything is missing from their collections."

"I'm sure we could if we checked your apartment."

Wade belched out a stream of fire at a drekavac crawling across the façade of the building they were backed up against, burning it to crispy bits of bone and ash. "Not if I clean it first."

Patrick decided the best way to win that argument was to fight zombies.

It was easier.

He conjured up some more mageglobes, filling them with strike spells, and sent them careening at the Dominion Sect magic users hunkered down behind concrete rubble and cars. Some of them had shields up, but a couple were in the midst of moving and got caught in the blast radius of Patrick's combat spells.

Even coming late to the fight, Patrick knew the area around Grand Central Station was a lost cause at this point. The soldiers and police he'd spotted upon arrival were pulling back, giving up ground. The mess of rubble they'd come out on top of and the pile behind them now surrounding Grand Central Station indicated a salt-and-burn type of approach he remembered from Cairo.

Leave the enemy nothing.

Ethan already wanted to rip the world apart, and here inside the veil, this was where Patrick's side tore it up first. It was a lesson learned late during the Thirty-Day War, but they'd learned it.

"Let's go," Patrick said, calling up more of his magic, powering it through the soulbond. "We have a wannabe god to kill."

They pushed forward with the help of the Night Marchers, the ghostly warriors going after the hunters and the demons riding their souls. Kū let out a furious war cry as he took aim at a particular group of Dominion Sect magic users working together on what Patrick thought was an earth-based spell. The last thing they needed was an earthquake.

Jono never left his side, and Patrick was grateful for that down to his bones. Not knowing the status of his pack while he'd been trapped on the sacrificial spell in Salem had been a horror he never wanted to go through again.

Sage and Leon guarded Marek while the Hellraisers ranged around them, picking off targets with spelled bullets. The screaming cries of the Sluagh and the crackling snap of lightning above was a continuous sound that became background noise as they fought their way down Park Avenue.

Nadine arrived at some point, watched over by Einar and Irena as Lucien and Carmen gave orders to what remained of their Night Court. She took over shielding their group from Patrick, who was more than happy to hand off that task. She knocked a fist against his shoulder as she came up to his position, attention on the street ahead.

"Glad to have you back," Nadine said.

Patrick aimed another mageglobe at an embedded group of hunters behind a cluster of abandoned cars at the intersection ahead. "Could've done without the world ending."

"You and me both."

Staggering through the fog behind the hunters came a horde of zombies. Patrick conjured up a couple of mageglobes and filled them with a strike spell. Before he could throw them at the hunters and zombies, a black-and-tawny blur streaked past them, slipping through Nadine's shields as if they didn't exist.

Fatima let out a yowl that made Patrick wince, though it only served to make Wade twist around to face her direction with a quick smile. "Fatima!"

The sound of someone landing heavily from a great height came from behind them. Patrick looked over his shoulder in time to see Spencer scramble out of Takoma's hold to get both feet on the ground. Past Spencer, Patrick could see Emma skidding to a stop beside Leon, bumping noses in a quick greeting.

"Oh, good. Gerard managed to save your ass," Spencer said, a mageglobe already in hand.

"Did you doubt him?" Patrick asked.

"Never."

"What happened back there?"

"Reed blew a bunch of bombs to bring down the Park Avenue Viaduct. The zombies will have to scatter now. Peklabog and Baba Yaga are feeding on the rest to give Reed's forces time to get clear and make it to new positions." Spencer blinked rapidly beneath his hard helmet, his gaze a little distant. "Maybe we should ask them to come up here and take point."

Patrick faced forward again, watching as Spencer's magic rolled through the zombies, Fatima dancing through bones as she swallowed souls whole. "Break as many souls as you can for now. We're heading for the Morgan Library."

The fight down to East Thirty-Seventh Street was a hard push through a line of demon-backed hunters, zombies, and dive-bombing Sluagh. Nadine's shield held against spelled bullets while the Night Marchers targeted hunters. The valkyries and Hinon did their best to force the Sluagh back, and Patrick kept having to talk Wade down from shifting mass and joining the aerial battle.

"You'll bring a skyscraper down on us, and that's the last thing we need," Patrick shouted as they finally turned the corner on East Thirty-Seventh Street, breaking through a barricade held by hunters.

"Ugh, fine," Wade complained right before he spat dragon fire at a hunter's face.

The agonized scream was drowned out by Jono's snarl as he nearly bit a hunter in half, the hole left behind in the body's trunk bloody and spilling out organs. The negative light of a demon fleeing left Patrick blinking to clear his vision. When the hunter's body started to rise off the street, called to fight by the Morrígan's staff, Spencer put the soul to rest.

The vampires covering Spencer were a mix of Lucien's and Takoma's Night Courts. With Peklabog and Baba Yaga having fucked off to wherever, Spencer was their heavy-hitter against the dead. If he went down, they'd be backed into a corner.

The narrow street was lined on either side by apartment buildings, none with lights on, but all surrounded by enough magic it made the hair on the back of Patrick's neck stand on end. The reason became apparent when several doors opened up down the length of the street and nearly two dozen magic users stepped out past their thresholds. Patrick mentally placed where they were and realized they'd reached a block where covens had promised defensive support.

Lucien ejected the empty magazine from his carbine and reloaded in a swift motion. "Get to the library. Ashanti is waiting for you there."

She'd gone on ahead some time ago, and Patrick had lost sight of her in the fight. Jono stepped close, ducking his massive wolf head low to shove at Patrick's hip. The burning white of his eyes was a sure sign it wasn't Jono urging him on but Fenrir.

"I'm going," Patrick snapped.

The violet glow of Nadine's magic created a dome over the two blocks. At either end of the street, thick brambles broke through the asphalt, shoving abandoned cars aside. The living wall was courtesy of Órlaith, still astride her steed and following in Gerard's wake.

Those were the only two immortals Patrick could see. He didn't know where the others had gone off to; he only hoped they were still fighting.

Wade threw himself over the hood of a car and landed next to Patrick. "The library's entrance is on Madison Avenue."

Patrick really needed to check Wade's apartment hoard when this was all over.

It wasn't a retreat so much as a hard-fought-for break in the battle. The coven magic users on this block were focused on defending both ends of the street. The Hellraisers, werecreatures, and most of the vampires and fae took time to deal with any wounded, reload their weapons, and rest.

Patrick and his pack, Nadine, Spencer, Marek, Lucien, and Carmen double-timed it to the Morgan Library and Museum on Madison Avenue. The contemporary front of the building was situated between two buildings with older-style architecture. The floor-to-ceiling windows lining the ground floor had been shattered in one area. Patrick could see Ashanti standing amidst the broken glass inside.

"I thought vampires couldn't enter without permission?" Wade muttered.

"It's a public building," Patrick said.

Screams from the Sluagh made Patrick glance up, staring past Nadine's shield. The spirits clawed at the magic only to be driven off by a trio of valkyries.

"Let's get this over with. I don't want to hold this shield up forever if we have the rest of Manhattan to fight through," Nadine said, striding inside the library.

Glass crunched underfoot as they entered the building, the quiet hush of the place interrupted by the shrieks of the battle outside. Patrick cast witchlights into the air, and Nadine and Spencer did the same to help light the space. The lobby was done up in pale hardwood floors and darker wooden paneling for the walls interspaced in the entrance. Patrick could see a set of stairs just past the empty security desk.

"Are we doing the blood rite here?" Wade asked.

"It's not defensible," Spencer said.

Jono and Sage shifted back to human, the sound of breaking bone and tearing skin loud in the confines of the lobby. The pair had no clothes to change into, but their nudity didn't bother anyone. Jono didn't care about the glass underfoot as he strode over to Patrick.

Despite the mud still caked into his clothes and ground into his skin, despite the lingering foulness in his mouth from the spell he'd been subjected to, Patrick didn't hesitate to drag Jono into a kiss. Patrick bit at his mouth, drawing him in with a desperate fervor that loosened every single muscle in his body.

"You're all right?" Jono asked once they parted, his grip like iron on Patrick's shoulder and waist.

His soul was a bruised mess from the Salem spell, he couldn't shake off the ghostly reminder of bruises, and exhaustion pulled at him in a way he hadn't felt since the Mage Corps. None of that mattered now that he was holding Jono in his arms.

"I can fight," Patrick said.

Jono stroked the knuckles of one hand over Patrick's cheek before cupping the back of his neck and tugging him forward to press a kiss to his forehead. "Don't pull that shit again."

Patrick let out a ragged little laugh. "It worked."

"I don't care."

He could hear the tired hints of anger from their last phone call in Jono's voice, but it was nearly subsumed by relief. Patrick pressed his hand over Jono's chest, feeling his heart beat steadily.

"You know why I had to do it."

Jono's expression twisted, his wolf-bright blue eyes never looking away from Patrick's face. "That doesn't mean I have to like it. You've given up enough for this world."

Patrick curled his fingers against warm skin, as if he could hold on and never let go. "You *are* my world, and I'd make that same choice every time if it could keep us safe and bring me back to you."

It wasn't what he wanted to say, but it was what he could say, and Patrick let the words go rather than keep them behind his teeth. Offering himself up to take away one avenue of Ethan's power to keep his pack safe would be worth it every time.

Jono kissed him, hard and quick, holding him tight enough to bruise, before stepping back. "You're mine as well. Don't ever doubt it."

Patrick nodded before he looked to where Sage stood off to the side, her long wet hair draped over her bare breasts. He couldn't see the wound in her gut that had sent her to the ICU, but her unmarked skin didn't quite assuage his guilt.

"I'm sorry I wasn't there," Patrick said, voice cracking a little.

Sage stepped closer to hug him tightly, and Patrick hugged her back just as hard. "You weren't the one gutted by a spelled and poisoned blade."

"I could've gone back. I *should* have."

Sage ruffled his hair with gentle fingers before loosening her hold. "You did what you had to do, like any good alpha would. I won't ever blame you for that, so don't blame yourself."

Patrick swallowed hard and nodded, because there was no use in telling her he'd feel guilty about that choice for years. Sage knew him well enough to know the guilt would stick with him.

"Wade got us out of Bellevue, and we went looking for Jono. Eir healed me after she and the other valkyries arrived," Sage explained.

"If you are finished," Ashanti called out, "come this way."

She curled her fingers at them in a command gesture before moving farther into the lobby, flanked by Lucien and Carmen.

They walked through a glass-encased court filled with empty tables and chairs, the reactionary storm raging beyond the wall of windows. Glass rattled with a soft hum as thunder boomed above the library. They left it behind for a set of stairs and a hallway that led into a marble rotunda decorated with murals and plasterwork. The witchlights reflected off hints of gold before it all fell into shadow again as they entered the library itself.

The walls were three levels high and packed with bookshelves behind metal wire barriers. Narrow catwalks circled the large room on the second and third levels, metal sliding ladders tucked into corners. The arched and painted ceiling reflected the light along gold-leaf edges. Books inside sealed glass display cases sat on either side of the entrance they'd come through. A pair of low-built, leather-covered benches sat near the unused fireplace.

The smell of old paper filled the air, and the scratchy sensation of activated protective wards brushed against Patrick's personal shields. Whatever preservation magic was in the room wasn't tied to a threshold, but that didn't mean it was welcoming.

"What now?" Marek asked, taking a seat on one of the benches.

Lucien unstrapped his Kevlar vest enough to reach beneath it and pull out the small, human-skin-bound book Patrick had taken from the Library of Congress. He passed it to his mother, and Ashanti took it with a nod.

"Now Patrick bleeds," Ashanti said.

"How much?" he asked warily. "I've been drained enough lately."

Even with access to a ley line through the soulbond, Patrick's magic was less than what it had been before lying on that spell-work in Salem. He really didn't need to lose more than a pint of blood to whatever spell Ashanti was going to cast.

"As much as the spell needs."

Patrick sighed and shrugged out of his leather jacket. It took some doing, with Jono needing to help on the final tug. Patrick's shirt felt heavy from mud being ground into it after lying at the bottom of a grave.

"What happened to you?" Wade asked.

"They had me in a grave," Patrick said, trying to wipe off streaks of mud on his bare arms, but it was a lost cause.

Jono's gaze became flinty. "They *what*?"

Patrick shrugged. "Gerard found me in time, and I killed Zachary. So, you know, revenge was had."

"That fucker's finally dead? Good riddance," Nadine said.

She let her assault rifle hang from the strap connected to her Kevlar vest and pried open a pocket on the front. She pulled out a gold coin and tossed it through the air to him. Patrick caught it with one hand, the ancient Greek obal shining beneath the witchlights.

"I thought this was back home?" Patrick said, staring at the coin.

"I brought it with me and had Nadine carry it while I was shifted. I thought you might need it," Jono said.

Patrick pocketed it. "I don't think laying down a barrier using the cardinal points will work this time. We don't have enough coins or time for that."

"It would be a useless endeavor. There is nothing that will stop the veil from carving out a new plane if Ethan wins," Ashanti said.

The spell book in her hand was opened near to the end, the spider-scrawl of the words and symbols written in faded blood. Patrick couldn't read the language, nor did he recognize it. The lines flickered with magic, his soul recognizing the feel of it as dark and wrong. Blood magic wasn't inherently evil, but the spells it powered usually were.

He'd just gotten off one spellwork only to willingly put himself in the middle of another. If it was anyone else other than the people in this room asking, he'd probably think twice about it.

Patrick sighed tiredly. "How do you want me?"

Ashanti blinked, a strange glint to her black eyes that couldn't be explained by the witchlights. "Here is fine. Give me your arm."

Patrick extended his left arm, fingers curled in a fist. Ashanti reached for him, sharp nails more like claws pricking the soft skin at the bend of his elbow. She stared at him, the godhead that sustained her crackling through her aura in a way no other vampire could ever duplicate. Her children were soulless beings, carrying a hole where their soul should have been, powered by blood magic that stemmed from Ashanti's making.

They were starved things craving the blood that sustained

them, and Ashanti was their god as much as their mother. She was his teacher, and if this was how he was to wield himself, then Patrick would do so with eyes wide open.

"Do you give of yourself freely?" Ashanti asked, voice low and edged in power.

"Yes," Patrick said, tasting the truth of it on his tongue.

He winced when Ashanti's nails pierced his skin, slicing downward the same way Cernunnos' had. Blood dripped down his arm and fell to the hardwood floor below with soft little splats. He could feel—*something*—in the air around them before Ashanti began speaking.

It was a language he couldn't understand, ancient in a way that called to the hindbrain terror of humanity's ancestors, that gut instinct that warned of the horrors hidden in the dark. It pulled at his blood, at the tangled essence of who he was, gliding through every cell until it subsumed him down to his soul.

His heart beat, and then it didn't.

Someone else's beat in his chest instead.

The tie to Hannah's soul, buried beneath the soulbond and walled off by damage, was peeled open through the blood that tied them together. Patrick wanted to scream, but all the air in his lungs was locked up tight as his consciousness plunged into magical chaos.

*Focus*, Ashanti told him somewhere in the roar of his mind.

She guided him with a strength he couldn't break free of. It took effort to ground himself, to find his center, and the only way he could was by leaning into the soulbond. It pulled tight between him and Jono, an anchor in the inferno that was eating through his veins.

*Find her for me.*

Ashanti's voice in his mind was a command he couldn't ignore, the whole of who he was tuned to the threadbare connection tying Patrick to his twin sister. Ashanti's magic burned through him, the heat of it driving out the chill from fighting in the reactionary storm.

Blood was iron, it was earth, it was life, and it was death. It could not be denied, and neither could Ashanti's demands. Patrick let himself be used by her spell like a compass that would always point true north, only instead of finding Jono through his soul-bond, he found Hannah through his blood and soul.

Scattered flashes of buildings exploded across his vision as his consciousness was dragged through a blurred cityscape, the library disappearing to sight, replaced by empty streets and flashes of lightning. He could sense how Ethan's spellwork gripped every skyscraper in Manhattan like the roots of the world tree anchored continents. It gripped him just the same, wrapped around every limb as rain fell onto his face, the ground cold beneath him, the wind white noise in his ears.

In Hannah's ears.

The echo of where thoughts used to be in his sister's mind was a cavernous void to his questing soul, the connection there ragged on her end with nothing left to anchor it. Their blood tie was all that was really left to bind them.

For this, it was enough.

*Show me.*

Ashanti's voice rolled through his thoughts with the power of a command trigger. Patrick could feel the distance between where he stood and where Hannah lay mapped out in his bones, the way it had always been so long ago when they were children.

He remembered, now, how they'd always been able to find each other until that fateful night in Salem.

When Patrick spoke, blood coated his teeth, was slick on his tongue, but the answer came easy, as sure as the iron holding up the altar of the city they stood in. "The Battery."

Ashanti pried her magic free of his skin, withdrew her nails from his arm, and licked his blood off her fingers. Jono pulled him back from that insidious edge in his mind, the soulbond anchoring him in his body rather than Hannah's.

Patrick wavered on his feet, light-headed from the spellwork unraveling from his body, blood still dripping down his arm. Jono held him close and allowed Patrick to lean on him.

"I've got you," Jono murmured into his ear.

Patrick blinked spots out of his eyes, the witchlights burning his vision. He spat blood out of his mouth, breathing through the copper-penny taste of it. When he could see again, he met everyone's gaze with dry eyes. "Let's finish this."

If Ethan wanted a fight at the end of the world, Patrick would give it to him.

## 25

"Incoming!" someone yelled.

Patrick threw his mageglobes at the onslaught of spells cutting through the air toward their front lines. The strike spells collided in midair and exploded with enough force to rip off some of the bare branches from the trees still standing in Union Square Park. It did nothing to stop some of the Sluagh from attempting another dive at where their side was dug in around the historic intersection.

Nadine expanded her shields upward, the violet-colored barrier forcing the Sluagh back. It prevented the collected soldiers, police officers, and agents' ability to shoot at the enemy. Patrick conjured up another set of mageglobes, powering them through the soulbond. Jono wasn't within eyesight, but he was close by, waiting for Nadine's shields to drop so he and Fenrir could rip apart more zombies.

"We need to break through their line, but we're losing ground," Casale said from behind Patrick.

"Half your people are running out of ammunition. You should send them to hole up with the covens," Patrick said.

Casale hefted a riot baton wrapped in barbed wire that had bits of rotten flesh stuck on the spikes. "They're equipped enough to provide support for the forces fighting in the street."

A bright bolt of lightning slammed into the massed group ahead of them, sending bodies flying. Patrick squinted up at the sky, seeing Hinon's winged outline against the clouds. He was flying low, but soon the Haudenosaunee thunder god was forced into the clouds by a screaming group of the Sluagh. Sheet lightning lit up the sky soon after, followed by thunder so loud it momentarily drowned out the sounds of the battlefield.

War was chaos on the ground, and that was proven true once again amidst the latest battle. Patrick's group had fought their way south after leaving the Morgan Library. Reed's people had fallen back to join them, and they'd collected others along the way. Mixed in between all the uniforms were civilian magic users, werecreatures, fae, and other members of the supernatural community. Immortals and gods walked amongst them all, and Patrick hadn't missed the wonderous looks cast at Thor and Hinon and the others. He had no doubt they'd come away with new worshippers when this was all over.

Spencer elbowed his way between two soldiers, carrying Fatima in one arm. Takoma and a couple of other vampires were right behind, still playing bodyguard for him. "Collins! We have a problem."

"We have a lot of problems right now. You need to be more specific," Patrick grunted as he flung another mageglobe through a hole Nadine made for him in her shield.

"This one is coming up from behind. Zombies, and a lot of them. Vampires brought word, but Fatima can feel them as well. I'll need some support to take them down."

"Anyone seen Peklabog or Baba Yaga?"

"Not recently, but we haven't been ranging out to the side streets."

"Subways?"

Spencer scowled and let Fatima jump out of his arms. "Do I look like I have a death wish? That's not all though. There were sightings of soultakers in the horde."

Patrick closed his eyes for a brief second. "Fuck. Okay, grab who you need to help you keep the zombies off our six."

"And the soultakers?"

"I'll get Wade."

Patrick turned away and ran down the line of fighters. Not having radios or cell phones to communicate made coordinating their attack difficult but not impossible. Wade was easy enough to find if only because the teen hadn't gone far. He was crouched on the nearby pavilion's roof, breathing fire at the Sluagh who kept targeting their allies on the ground. Nadine's shield had retracted low enough that Wade was outside its safety radius now, and he hadn't seemed to notice.

"Wade! Get down here," Patrick yelled.

Wade snapped his mouth shut, smoke streaming out of his nose and from between his lips. He threw himself off the roof and landed on the ground behind a group of soldiers keeping hunters pinned down near the barricades by the fountain. Red scales lined his jaw and throat, creeping outward from his hairline. His eyes were a molten gold, pupils slitted like a reptile's.

"What?" Wade asked.

"We have zombies and soultakers coming from the direction of Uptown. I need you to shift mass and get ready to burn or eat them."

"I thought you didn't want me to shift mass?"

"There's enough space in this area that you won't risk damaging any buildings."

Union Square was wide open in terms of space, the intersection ringed by buildings, but Wade's wingspan couldn't touch them. In dragon form, he'd do a lot of damage against the enemy.

If their group could break through here and stay on course, they could take Broadway down to the tip of Manhattan where the

Battery was. Just thinking about how far they still had to go made Patrick's head throb.

Wade stripped out of his shirt and tossed it to Patrick. "Give my clothes to Marek. I'm not running around naked like everyone else."

Patrick peeled the shirt off his head. "No one cares."

"*I* care."

"Just shift."

"Yeah, yeah. Shift mass, don't shift mass. Eat demons, don't eat demons. You're carrying my mouthwash next time we fight like this."

Wade got rid of the rest of his clothes, and Patrick backed up, yelling for everyone nearby to give Wade space. The pockets of fighters shifted position where they could, a few looking back curiously at them to get a sense of what was going on.

Red scales pushed through the rest of Wade's skin, the illusion of a human body disintegrating in the outward shift of mass. It wasn't like how a werecreature changed shape, with a twisted body becoming something else. Wade's dragon form expanded into the space around them in the blink of an eye, towering over their side of the fight.

Wade stretched out his long neck and roared, spitting fire at the Dominion Sect magic users and hunters blocking their way down Broadway.

"I said zombies and soultakers!" Patrick yelled up at him, pointing in the direction of Park Avenue.

Wade blew smoke at him before flapping his wings hard to get airborne. The wind stole most of the smoke, but some of it filtered down to where Patrick stood. He coughed, ducking his head against the downdraft, and headed back to the front line that had apparently gained ground with Thor's help.

Thor was using Mjölnir to throw lightning at hunters while the Night Marchers wreaked havoc through the enemy ranks. It was a two-pronged attack, because the Night Marchers weren't bothered by the lightning bolts and were hell-bent on going after the demons riding souls.

"Where did you send the fledgling?" Thor asked when Patrick made it to the god's side.

"We got zombies and soultakers coming up on our six. He's got orders to go to town on them," Patrick said.

"Where is Peklabog? He and Baba Yaga would be the best to handle the dead and those particular demons."

"Last time anyone saw them was at Grand Central Station."

"I'll find them," Hermes said.

Patrick wheeled around to find the Greek messenger god slipping out of the veil, startling more than one nearby federal agent. Luckily, no friendly fire occurred.

"Is Salem still standing?" Patrick asked.

Hermes shrugged. "Mostly."

"Great. We need Peklabog and Baba Yaga to help us with our walking dead problem. I don't care what they're doing, just bring them here."

Hermes' gaze flicked past Patrick, focusing on something behind him. "You need more help than that."

Patrick really didn't want to look, but he couldn't afford not to. Facing south again, he caught sight of what was causing almost everyone around him to look afraid.

Marching up Broadway and University Place came ranks of fae belonging to the Unseelie Court. Goblins and trolls, spiderlike beings, winged and not, the vast array of fae were hideous in appearance, well armored and well armed.

Riding astride a Ceffyl Dŵr at the front of the group on the left was Medb. The Queen of Air and Darkness was dressed for war, as was the fae riding to her right. Cairbre Nia Fer raised his sword aloft and made a slashing gesture with it, causing the fae to split ranks and spread out in a maneuver that Patrick recognized.

"They're going to box us in," Patrick said.

Hermes let out a derisive snort. "They're going to bury you."

"Had enough of that lately, thanks."

The Sluagh broke away from their aerial battle with the valkyries and flew through the air to gather in the sky above their queen. Hinon and the valkyries regrouped above Patrick's side of the fight as the ground shook from the marching of the new arrivals.

Weaving through the ranks of the fae on the right-hand side of the square were packs of black jaguars that Patrick was pretty sure outnumbered the werecreatures on their side. Leading them was Tezcatlipoca, the Aztec god's feathered headdress unencumbered by the rain. He was joined by Santa Muerte, the goddess' shroud creeping outward like a river of darkness ready to swallow them all whole.

"I," Patrick announced to anyone who might be listening, "seriously don't get paid enough for this shit."

"To me, my *daoine sídhe*!" Órlaith shouted from further down the line, her voice ringing like a bell over the panicked shouts from their side.

Thor smacked the side of Mjölnir against his palm, expression grim. "Where is the Dagda?"

"Oh, you know politicians. They talk a good game but are shit at the actual grind," Patrick said.

"I will handle Medb," the Cailleach Bheur said, seemingly arriving out of nowhere. The blue-skinned goddess wrapped both hands around her staff, the tip where it rested on the ground spreading ice beneath her feet. "Who else comes, Hermes?"

Patrick turned around in time to see the lazy salute Hermes gave her, unperturbed by the icy glare sent his way.

"Everyone has been called, but few can be spared. Shiva is helping Osiris hold back Náströnd along the shoreline. Hart Island has been emptied of its dead, and Hel has command of the bodies. Montu stands guard at the Brooklyn Bridge against Seth. Those of his pantheon on the side of the heavens have taken up watch at all the crossings over the Hudson River and the East River," Hermes said.

"Does anyone have an army they can spare? One that isn't dead?" Patrick asked.

"You have gods. We will be enough."

Hermes stepped back through the veil, leaving coldness in his wake. Jono took his place, eyes burning white with the presence of Fenrir. More than one nearby soldier took a few steps away from him.

"*We must break their line,*" Fenrir said.

"Easier said than done," Patrick replied.

They were outnumbered in terms of bodies and firepower. The dead just kept coming, aided by immortals and gods who'd chosen Ethan's side of the war. At some point, the creeping exhaustion Patrick and others were doing their best to ignore would overwhelm their side. Their people needed rest, but it was out of reach right now.

"Yield and your deaths will be quick," Medb called out, her voice carrying through the air to be heard by everyone.

"Fuck no!" Gerard angrily shouted back.

His defiance was echoed by dozens of voices and howls. The only thing louder was Wade's roar as he spat dragon fire at the zombies coming up behind them. Spencer's magic danced over the horde Wade was fighting, and Patrick hoped the other mage could keep them at bay.

Medb didn't bother with a response to Gerard's answer. She gestured with her sword, and the fae of her Unseelie Court surged forward with preternatural speed. Tezcatlipoca's jaguars slid between the fae like liquid shadows, wrapped up in Santa Muerte's shroud.

Patrick's heart rate ratcheted up as he yanked free his dagger from its sheath and conjured up some mageglobes. He tapped the soulbond, glancing over at Jono and the god who'd taken over his wolf form.

"Stay close," he said.

Fenrir gape-grinned at him. *"I go where the battle leads me."*

"If you get Jono killed, I'm shoving this dagger through your throat."

Violet shields cut through the oncoming fae in an unpredictable pattern as Nadine used her magic to funnel the enemy into numbers their side could hopefully handle. Reed shouted orders that had soldiers moving position and bringing everyone else with them who were used to military commands.

The result was groups scattered around the plaza and intersection facing the monument and park, with magic users up front and those with guns standing behind. The setup hopefully reduced friendly fire hits.

"Here they come," Patrick said.

The Seelie fae with Órlaith followed her and Gerard into battle, leading the charge as Medb's fae finally broke free of the maze of shields Nadine had created. Patrick didn't know how long she'd be able to hold them up with so many gods in the mix. He only hoped someone was in place to watch her six.

Thor charged forward with a thunderous war cry, swinging Mjölnir in an arc that sent lightning stabbing outward. The leading push of fae and jaguars coming their way couldn't dodge the hit. The fae were thrown off their feet, bodies smoking, while the jaguars shattered into millions of pieces of obsidian. When the airborne fae finally landed, they were trampled by their own side.

Off to the left, Kū led the Night Marchers at a cluster of hunters that broke free of Nadine's shields. The gods acted as individual breakwaters against the enemy, capable of handling more than the mortals behind them.

The Sluagh outnumbered Hinon and the valkyries in the sky. Hinon's great wings crackled with lightning that danced against the clouds above as the Haudenosaunee thunder god led the valkyries into aerial battle once more.

Nadine's shields flickered before suddenly shattering, falling victim to Santa Muerte's shroud and the shadowy spears of darkness that slammed through her magic. The maze of defensive magic keeping Medb's forces in a manageable group disappeared. Patrick only hoped whatever backlash she was hit with wasn't terrible enough to put her out of commission. But a god's attack was different than mortal magic or weaponry.

Unencumbered, the Unseelie fae ranks surged forward, a wave of death they couldn't possibly escape from. Patrick threw his mageglobes high into the air, aiming for the deeper ranks rather than the front line so as not to hit anyone on their side. Fenrir charged forward with an ear-splitting howl, and Patrick could only follow, dagger held in his right hand, the matte-black blade burning bright.

Jaguars peeled free of the crowd and headed their way, but Fenrir intercepted most of them, tearing the constructs to pieces. One got through, and Patrick aimed a mageglobe down its throat. The construct exploded from the inside out, and obsidian shards flew through the air like shrapnel. He spun on his feet, managing to sidestep a jaguar and catch it in the side with his dagger.

The construct's roar was like breaking glass that faded when it shattered. Patrick's combat boots crunched over obsidian shards as he sent a strike spell at the troll staggering toward them, holding what looked like an entire uprooted tree in its hand. The troll swung the tree in an overhead strike, but before it could hit the ground and anyone standing there, a rocket-propelled grenade slammed into his chest.

The explosion of body parts sent bone and blood and meaty flesh flying through the air. The rest of the troll collapsed, tipping over backward as the tree fell to the ground. The earth vibrated from its landing. Patrick ducked his head against the bloody rain and slammed a mageglobe into a group of spider fae clacking their way over a dead hunter to his position.

Nadine's shields reformed in quick snakelike bursts, creating room for them to fight in. The battle lines had blurred, which meant when Patrick finished clearing his immediate area of Unseelie fae and turned to look for Jono, he shouldn't have been surprised at coming face-to-face with Tezcatlipoca, but he was.

"Oh, shit," Patrick breathed out, taking a step back.

The Aztec god wore traditional clothing and a gold headdress decorated with obsidian and jade. The colored heron feathers a meter in length that were attached to the headdress had yet to be torn out by the wind. His right foot was carved from polished obsidian, shiny like a mirror and all the pieces of his constructs they'd destroyed so far.

"You took what belongs to me," Tezcatlipoca said, his godhead shining through his aura.

Patrick held his dagger between them. "Wade? Yeah, you can't have him, so fuck off."

Tezcatlipoca lunged at him, mouth open wide around teeth that would've looked more at home in a jaguar. Patrick stood his ground because there was nowhere to run, but he didn't have to go toe-to-toe with the god because Jono handled it for him by ramming Tezcatlipoca to the ground. Jono's teeth flashed in the scrum, and Patrick thought he'd get the upper hand, but that was before Tezcatlipoca started shifting.

"Fall back!" Patrick yelled, scrambling to get out of range. "Everyone, fall back!"

He remembered how large Tezcatlipoca was in his jaguar form, how the god had destroyed the Crimson Diamond. Jono seemed to remember as well, sticking with Patrick over continuing the fight. The form that Tezcatlipoca took was larger than any earthly jaguar could ever hope to become and deadly enough to turn the tide of the fight before they even made it to the Battery.

The spider fae hurtling itself toward them from the right was cut in half by Kū's shark-teeth-lined spear. The Hawaiian war god stepped up beside Patrick and pointed his weapon at Tezcatlipoca in a warning manner.

"Get out of our way, cousin," Kū ordered.

"I think not," Tezcatlipoca snarled.

He opened his mouth and roared, the nightmarish sound louder than the thunder from gods and the reactionary storm.

It was not, however, louder than Quetzalcoatl's answering roar that shook every building surrounding Union Square.

Patrick's head snapped around, gaze locking on the new arrival. The feathered serpent god flew over the buildings north of them, wings dipping low in greeting to Wade. Breaking free of the clouds behind him came the entirety of the Wild Hunt led by Gwyn ap Nudd.

Jono's teeth snagged the hem of Patrick's leather jacket, and he found himself being swung around and dragged from the line of fire. He got the hint. Let the gods fight each other; he had no desire to be caught up in that crossfire.

The shadows of twilight grew darker as Quetzalcoatl dived low. Patrick spared a glance over his shoulder in time to see Tezcatlipoca launch himself at his brother, and the two rose into the air, grappling and fighting each other. Around the pair, the Wild Hunt and the Sluagh clashed together, the screams and battle cries of spirits mixing with thunder.

That was one portion of the battle Patrick didn't have to worry so much about now that Gwyn ap Nudd was leading the charge. They were still hemmed in on the ground though, and he had no idea how they were going to break free.

Jono and Patrick fought their way toward the center of the fight in the plaza, following the blazing light the *Gáe Bulg* let off like a beacon in Gerard's hands. Patrick's former commanding officer fought like a berserker, but he still knew who they were. The handful of Hellraisers watching his six were keeping well clear of the reach of his spear.

"We need to break through Medb's line," Patrick said, ducking beneath the wooden claws of a spriggan. Jono bit the fae in half and spat out wooden chunks.

"She has both streets blocked, and Broadway is the most direct path downtown from here," Gerard said.

"So we go through."

Gerard rammed the butt of his spear into the eye of a fae hard enough it exited out the back of their skull. Gerard pulled the weapon free with a grunt. "We need more manpower than what we have available."

"It's a little late to try for a strike team entry."

A violet shield slammed down around them and expanded outward. The fae beyond the barrier crashed to the ground, rolling over each other as Nadine double-timed it to their position, wiping away blood dripping from her nose.

"Backlash?" Patrick asked her.

"Had worse," Nadine said, sounding out of breath. "Reed wanted me to tell you the zombies are breaking through, but that Wade managed to eat most of the soultakers."

Patrick winced. "Most still means there are some out there. There's nothing on our side that can easily take them out."

Nadine pointed at the sky. "Gods can."

Something exploded at the cloud line like a mini supernova, lighting up Union Square as if it were midday for a couple of seconds.

"They all seem a little busy," Patrick said. "Where the fuck is Hermes? He was supposed—"

Patrick was cut off by the piercing sound of a horn blowing. The pulsing notes sounded like a call to arms, one Gerard knew well judging by the surprised expression that crossed his face. The fae in their immediate area reared back, giving ground and regrouping. Patrick couldn't see anything through the bodies around them, but the ground trembled like an earthquake was rolling through Manhattan and had no intention of stopping any time soon.

Ice spread like a freezing river over the buildings on East and West Seventeenth Street, winter sending a chill through the air that made Patrick's teeth chatter. The Cailleach Bheur's touch was impossible to miss, as was the crossroad that opened up in the middle of Manhattan. It shouldn't have been possible, not through the iron that surrounded them in the form of buildings. Except the veil was as thin as it ever would be on Samhain.

Brigid and her Seelie Court marched out of the crossroad from Tír na nÓg, bringing with them the warmth of spring that refused to fade beneath the reactionary storm and a thirst for battle that would not be denied.

IN THE CHAOS THAT FOLLOWED BRIGID AND THE SEELIE COURT'S arrival, Jono hoped the fighting on the ground would turn in their favor. Fenrir rumbled agreement through his mind as they fought their way back to where Sage stood guard over the command barricade. Reed was barking out orders into a small scrying crystal, smoke drifting out of his nose.

"Brigid is on the field," Patrick shouted as he skidded behind the barrier, Jono on his heels. "We need to break through their line. When that happens, my pack and I will head down Broadway."

"We still have soultakers on the field," Reed warned.

Jono stared at where Wade was crouched, breathing fire at the zombies still shambling their way. Occasionally his long neck snaked down so he could snap at something on the ground and chomp on it.

"I can't stay here."

"*The end begins. Can you not feel it?*" Fenrir asked, causing more than one soldier and police officer surrounding them to stare. Jono could smell their fear but also their wonderment, a mix that stemmed from realizing myths were real and gods walked the earth again. It wasn't the first time he'd smelled it past the veil like this.

Reed scowled, teeth sharp in his mouth. "There's nearly fifty blocks you still need to fight your way through. Your pack won't be enough to get you there in time."

"We're a strike team, the same way the Hellraisers were at the end of the Thirty-Day War. We'll be enough," Patrick protested.

"You'll hit resistance and detours without us."

"Pity the subways are full of the dead, Pattycakes. The trains would've been nice, but I brought you the next best thing," Hermes said.

Jono shifted on four legs, turning to eye Hermes as the messenger god slid free of the veil, one hand tightly gripping the wrist of another god. Fenrir growled a greeting that was met with a smile by the newest arrival.

*"Heimdallr,"* Fenrir said. *"Does the Allfather come?"*

"Odin fights the Fallen south of here," Heimdallr said, gaze steady. The pupils of his pale blue eyes were ringed with a thin rainbow of color, and they seemed to stare right through Jono.

The veil hadn't closed behind the pair, allowing Baba Yaga and Peklabog to step into Union Square. Baba Yaga rapped her mortar against the bone pestle she rode, cackling loudly. Bits of stringy flesh hung from her lips, caught between her teeth.

"Such an end you seek, cousin. Best hurry. Is new beginning clawing at roots of your world tree in this city," Baba Yaga said.

Fenrir growled wordlessly, the sound muffled by the explosion of a mageglobe against Nadine's shield. Fenrir seemed unperturbed by the chaos surrounding them, even if it raised Jono's hackles. Patrick's hand fisted in his fur, the soulbond humming between them. Jono shifted closer until he was pressed against the other man.

"Sir, we're going, with or without you," Patrick said, looking Reed in the eye.

Through Fenrir's power, Jono could see the flicker of Reed's hidden true form around his human shape. The flash image lasted only a second, but the size and age of the dragon meddling with human affairs was startling to witness.

"Then go and take who you must," Reed said, bowing to Fate.

Patrick nodded, attention shifting from the general to Hermes. "What's the plan?"

Hermes only smiled as Heimdallr put the Gjallarhorn to his lips and blew a long, resounding note that rang through the air like a thousand bells. Jono swore his brain rattled in his skull, and he wasn't the only one affected. Many people around them clamped their hands over their ears and looked around for the source of the sound.

A lull settled over the battlefield for a couple of seconds as everyone tried to figure out what was happening. The sound fell away, only to return again when Heimdallr blew a different note. The ground trembled in response, and something exploded in the horizon behind them. In the veiled twilight of Manhattan, what came streaking through the sky was a shimmer of colors that stretched from horizon to horizon.

The Bifröst burned in the air above where they stood, a rainbow bridge of passage for their use.

*At least you lot are good for something,* Jono mused.

Now they just had to get *up* on the bloody thing with the rest of their pack and allies who could be spared from the fight in Union Square.

"Do we really have to run fifty blocks?" Patrick asked no one in particular.

Heimdallr clipped the Gjallarhorn to his belt and withdrew the sword from a sheath on his back. "Bring who you need. The Bifröst will carry you to the edge of the world."

Patrick winced. "The Battery better still be standing."

*Call your pack,* Fenrir said.

Jono threw back his head and *howled,* pouring Fenrir's power into the call, using it to draw who they needed to their current position. Werecreatures weren't the only ones who answered. Jono could see the shift in the battle lines around them as vampires and fae heeded the call as well.

In the distance, Wade flapped his wings and launched himself into the sky, gliding over to them. People scrambled to get out of his way before he landed, even though he was careful of where he put his feet. He shrugged off a couple of spells aimed his way, human magic not bothering him.

"Head downtown when we do," Patrick shouted at Wade.

Wade huffed smoke in their direction before nodding his wedge head. Fenrir tipped their head back and eyed the distance between them and the Bifröst. Before Jono could protest, Fenrir leaped for it, preternatural strength aiding his godly abilities to land them on the rainbow bridge.

The shimmering light was hard beneath his paws, the colors every conceivable shade that existed in this world and others. Jono didn't have much time to appreciate it before Wade picked Patrick up with one claw and unceremoniously dropped him on the Bifröst.

"A little warning would be nice!" Patrick yelled, scrambling to his feet on the rainbow bridge.

Brynhildr and some of her valkyries dived at fast speeds to the battle raging on the ground. They unfurled golden nets and ensnared those who couldn't make it up to the Bifröst on their own, Nadine and Spencer among them. Jono saw a couple of Hell-raisers in the mix as well, along with Gerard. Werecreatures and vampires managed to fling themselves upward on their own, dodging spells and bullets to do so.

Ashanti was the first god after Fenrir to join them on the Bifröst but not the last. Hermes vaulted up with an ease that had him landing lightly on his toes. Fae beholden to Medb tried to climb onto the Bifröst but were summarily driven off by those already standing on it. The sound of assault rifles going off was a drone in Jono's ears.

Jono made his way to Patrick, who was huddled with Nadine and Spencer, all three of them staring south at where the Bifröst followed Broadway through Manhattan. Situated above the fray, Jono could see past the brightness of the rainbow bridge the insidious glow of a creeping spellwork crawling over the skyscrapers.

"Is Samhain over?" Nadine asked.

Patrick shook his head. "No."

"Are you sure? Because that looks like a sacrificial circle to me."

Patrick glanced down at Jono, face pale, jaw clenched tight. Jono shifted on his paws to press against the other man in what comfort he could offer.

"Then you better start running," Hermes said, already racing forward.

"I hate when he's right," Patrick muttered under his breath.

"*Save your breath. You will need it,*" Fenrir said.

*Sod off,* Jono grumbled.

They ran, Jono's long stride eating up ground, though he never left Patrick's side. Time flowed differently past the veil, and it seemed to flow differently on the Bifröst itself. The world bent beyond the edges of the rainbow bridge, blurring and folding the distance between where they were and where they needed to be.

They might have left one ground battle behind them, but the aerial one followed them downtown. The reactionary storm hadn't let up, and neither had Quetzalcoatl and Tezcatlipoca's battle in the clouds. Their battle cries followed them like lightning, though Jono took some comfort in the aerial support of Wade, Hinon, and the valkyries.

The closer they got to the Battery, a heavy sense of foreboding settled in Jono's gut. The acrid scent of hell hung in the air despite the wind and rain, stinging Jono's eyes. Something was burning, or maybe it really was a hell come to earth, and they were too late.

"Do you see that?" Patrick shouted breathlessly, pointing at something in the distance.

The fog ahead was parting, the colors around them bleeding

away to reveal the impossibly large shape of a twisted tree haloed in fiery light. Its highest branches were lost in the fog, but Jono knew from Fenrir's memories how Yggdrasil looked when it held up the world.

The living connection that tied the Nine Realms together had its roots in Manhattan, the same way it'd had its roots in Chicago. He didn't think a spell had called it forth, not with the veil torn all around them. The world tree had slipped through on its own, the same way all the other scattered myths and legends had.

*It grows to carry another world on its branches*, Fenrir warned.

*I don't bloody think so*, Jono retorted.

Yggdrasil became easier to see the closer they got to their destination. Running down the Bifröst meant it should've been a clear shot to the southern tip of Manhattan—and it would've been if Loki didn't blow up the rainbow bridge around them.

The attack hit with a roar, and only Nadine's war-honed reflexes kept them all from getting riddled with solid-light shrapnel. When the Bifröst broke, it wasn't like glass shattering, but like being in the center of a lighthouse with the mirror shining right at them. All Jono could see were smears of light as the solid stretch of color they'd been running on exploded beneath their feet and they fell into thin air.

Jono managed to twist his body so he was close enough for Patrick to grab onto his fur. They were at minimum an entire story off the ground. Jono landed without breaking any bones, Patrick half lying on top of him, cushioned from further harm. Judging by some of the cries around them, others weren't so lucky. Jono's rapid healing cleared his vision in seconds, and he hoped Nadine wasn't injured, because her shields were the only thing keeping the horde of zombies they'd fallen into at bay.

"We got wounded!" Keith cried out.

"Put them behind our front line," Gerard shouted back.

"All our lines are front lines!"

The walking dead clambered on top of each other, clawing at

Nadine's shield. Jono could pick out the elongated forms of drekavacs mixed in, but what was worse were the nightmarish demons that eyed everyone through the shield like prey. The demons looked as if they'd stepped out of someone's twisted nightmare, bodies not of this earth.

"Seems like Andras brought his own army," Patrick coughed out as he slid off Jono. "Where the fuck is Odin?"

As if answering his question, a massive lightning bolt ripped free of the clouds and slammed to the ground in front of Yggdrasil. Fenrir used Jono's mouth to say, *Keeping hell at bay.*

"Hell or, you know, Hel?" When Fenrir didn't answer, Jono and Patrick shared a look. "All right, so we're fucked."

Everyone around them was getting to their feet if they could, assessing the situation past Nadine's shield. As Jono and Patrick moved closer to the front, a handful of spells impacted against the barrier, evidence that Dominion Sect magic users were up ahead somewhere.

The zombies and demons in front of Nadine's shield split apart, opening space in the street. It gave Jono a view of the intersection that curved around the edge of the Battery. Jono growled at the pair of gods who stood before them, their godheads shining through their auras.

Through the shimmer of Nadine's shield, Jono could see that Ares was decked out for war, while Loki looked the same as he had in Salem. Hunters carrying demons in their souls ranged around the pair. Even though Nadine's shield blocked the wind, it couldn't block the overwhelming scent of hell.

Towering over even the skyscrapers was Yggdrasil, the top of the world tree disappearing into the storm clouds. Jono would rather it not be clinging to the edge of Manhattan at all. Nothing good came of another world's foundation digging roots into their own.

Nadine's shield took another hit, but her barrier stood strong against mortal magic. Ahead of them, Loki lowered Gungnir,

Odin's spear glowing in his hands. Jono remembered what damage the god had done to Nadine's magic back in Salem, and he knew they couldn't ask the impossible of her.

Patrick seemed to agree. "Nadine, if the gods attack, drop your shields. We still need you with us."

"Got it," Nadine said, holding her mageglobe tight in one hand.

Loki pointed Gungnir at Jono, but his words were for Fenrir. "Child of mine, it is time you were punished for your actions against us."

*Your father is a fucking wanker,* Jono said.

Fenrir growled, but Jono didn't get any sense of disagreement from the god.

Lightning carved a furrow in the ground right in front of Nadine's shield, charring some of the zombies and demons. Loki and Ares stood their ground as Hinon arrived with the valkyries, Brynhildr leading her shieldmaidens.

Wade dropped down out of the clouds, spitting fire at the horde of zombies surrounding them. He was careful of Nadine's shields, but Jono could still see how close the dragon fire burned against her defenses.

Loki and Ares were lost to sight amidst the fire, along with most of the hunters. Wade dropped down to the street behind them, blocking the damaged Bifröst from view.

The lightning finally let up as Hinon came to earth, his storm-colored wings spread wide over the street, nearly touching the buildings on either side. Lightning edged his feathers and danced at his fingertips as he folded his wings to his back, coming to rest outside Nadine's shield.

As the glare faded from Jono's vision, he could see that Loki and Ares remained where they were behind a glittering golden shield, surrounded by bodies. Wade roared a warning at the gods, smoke and hints of flame escaping from between his teeth as he glared at them.

Some of the charred bones moved, sickly magic flickering

across blackened bodies. Necromancy called the dead to fight still, no matter the body's state so long as it wasn't ash. But even as the corpses rose again, more zombies walked their way, filling the street and the park behind where Loki and Ares stood.

The golden shield disappeared, its magic sucked back into Gungnir. Loki tipped his head back, smirking up at where Wade's long neck snaked protectively over Nadine's domed shield.

"I can see why Tezcatlipoca wanted to keep you," Loki said.

"You don't get to talk to him," Patrick snarled.

Jono bared his teeth in agreement.

"That weapon does not belong to you, Loki," Brynhildr called from above.

The trickster god shrugged carelessly. "It does now."

"Where is the Allfather?"

Loki's smile was sharp and mocking. "He came to meet his end at a new beginning."

"Fuck," Patrick swore softly.

"*This is not our Ragnarök*," Fenrir said.

Loki stepped forward, magic dripping from Gungnir's sharp blade. "Close enough."

Behind the trickster god, sliding between the barren trees of the park, came groups of hunters led by Andras in Ilya's body, holding the Morrígan's staff. Hades walked beside him, the Greek god of the Underworld carrying no weapon in his hand. Surrounding them were the walking dead, puppets to Andras' whims, as well as soultakers.

Past them all, shining against the shape of Yggdrasil, was the sickly glow of magic that smelled of hell. As Andras walked toward them, the intricate lines of the spellwork flared up on the ground with power, lines that Jono had seen on their color-tinted race through downtown, spanning the island.

Patrick rested his left hand on Jono's back. "That's where Hannah is."

And wherever Patrick's twin was, they'd find Ethan.

"If we walk into the heart of that spell, it'll kill us," Nadine said with a sureness that Jono couldn't ignore.

Patrick's grip tightened in Jono's fur, and Jono didn't need a soulbond to know what he was thinking.

*I'm not letting him do this alone, so find us a bloody way through that mess,* Jono snarled at Fenrir.

Fenrir opened Jono's mouth, and what came out wasn't a howl but Ginnungagap, and all the primordial void's limitless possibilities.

This time, it didn't bring forth an angel, only a chance. The yawning abyss sank into the ground and flooded the spellwork, following the far-flung lines of magic through the iron bones of Manhattan and the altar they all now stood on.

Ethan's spell didn't break, only became frozen in time, as every Fate in existence held their breath at the end of the world.

## 27

Ginnungagap was a void in the gloam surrounding them, swallowing up the spellwork Ethan's side had cast. Under any other circumstance, Patrick knew Ginnungagap would be able to undo the magic, but this was a new god's beginning. This was what the yawning abyss existed for—creation.

This was a story that had to be told.

*"It cannot hold back the inevitable forever,"* Fenrir said, eyes burning white in Jono's wolf body.

Ashanti appeared on the other side of Fenrir, a hunger on her face as she looked at Andras in Ilya's body. "Nothing in all the worlds is inevitable."

"The Fates say otherwise," Patrick said.

"I taught you better than to believe in their idea of absolutes."

The crash of magic against Nadine's shield was like grenades going off. The attack spells were aimed from Dominion Sect magic users, but the electric bite to the air spoke of something stronger being prepped for an attack. Nadine couldn't shield them against gods, and he'd never ask her to do that.

"Adjust your main shield for a charge, then drop it when we meet the enemy, Mulroney," Patrick said.

Nadine nodded silently, staring straight ahead. Down the line, Gerard spun the *Gáe Bulg* in both hands, angled for an attack as vampires flung themselves forward to fill in gaps between werecreatures. Sage shouldered her way toward them to plant herself on Patrick's other side.

Outside of the shield, Hinon took the sky to join the valkyries, his flight guarded by Wade, who burned to nothing a couple of spells aimed at the god. Patrick looked up at Wade through the glitter of Nadine's magic.

"Stick to the outer edges of the fight. Don't spit fire on any friendlies," Patrick yelled at him.

Wade huffed out a puff of smoke in acknowledgment. This was as close quarters as things got, and they all had to be aware of that.

Gerard caught Patrick's eye. "Ready?"

Patrick looked down the line on either side of him, letting his attention linger on Spencer, who was wedged protectively between his vampire guards. "Ready, Dead Boy?"

Spencer raised his hands, mageglobes flaring to life against his palms. "I got nothing better to do, Razzle Dazzle."

"Then it's go time."

Nadine's shield shrank down and folded outward, shoving back the zombies and demons that had already surged past Loki and Ares. Everyone on their side followed the push of her magic. Patrick tightened his grip on his dagger and let go of Jono, racing forward with his pack by his side and the gods at his back. Spencer peeled away, Fatima racing ahead, the green of his magic already dancing over zombies as he broke souls free to put the dead to rest.

Nadine's shield was more malleable for a charge, keeping bullets out long enough for both sides to come together in a clash of bodies and magic and not a few blades. Patrick was eye to eye with a demon when Nadine's shield abruptly disappeared, and everything went to hell.

Patrick had his dagger at the ready and slammed it into the demon's chest. Claws sliced against his personal shield as the demon screeched in agony. Heavenly fired danced across the matte-black blade of his dagger, burning the demon to ash. Patrick yanked it out and flipped it around for a different grip, making it easier for him to stab a zombie in the head. Something glinted out of the corner of his eye, and Patrick ducked, missing getting his head taken off by a machete-wielding hunter by millimeters.

He threw a mageglobe filled with raw magic directly at the man's face. The explosion was small in terms of size but still devastating. Patrick's personal shields kept him from feeling the heat, but his magic blew off the man's face nearly to the back of his skull. As the body fell to the ground, black smoke filtered out of the skin instead of a flash of negative light, the demon dying with its host.

Sage put herself between Patrick and a drekavac, savaging the fast-moving zombie with her powerful jaws. The second she brought one down, another took its place. Fenrir had taken Jono off to some other area of the fight, leaving Nadine to watch his six. Close quarters wasn't his specialty, and it'd been years since Patrick had needed to fight like this, but he fell into a natural rhythm with Nadine that had them carving a bloody path forward step by brutal step.

Their side was effectively surrounded, with a never-ending wave of zombies and demons pressing against their front line. Patrick knew they couldn't hold the line for long; it was suicidal to try. Which meant they had to take out the source.

"Anyone got eyes on Andras?" Patrick shouted over the noise of the fight.

He rammed his elbow into a hunter's throat and gutted her with his dagger. She grappled at him until her last breath, black smoke escaping her mouth as the demon burned inside her fading soul.

"No," Nadine grunted as she closed her fist over a mageglobe.

The shield she'd encased three hunters in shrank in seconds, crushing the victims as if an entire building had fallen on them. She withdrew her magic, and when Patrick followed after her, his feet slid through the remains of the hunters. The pieces of their bodies were too small to come together and rise again, but all the rest were fair game save those killed by way of Patrick's dagger.

Wade spat dragon fire on the zombies rising behind them, trying to keep watch on their six. Dominion Sect spells were targeting him more and more though, and Patrick had half a mind to send Wade airborne to get him out of their reach. The teen was too hemmed in by buildings to maneuver easily, and sending flame down on the fight indiscriminately wasn't an option.

But the dead and demons kept coming, and they weren't any closer to crossing the intersection than they had been at the beginning of this fight. The burn in his soul was from overuse of magic, even with having the soulbond channeling most of it from the ley line through Jono. The stretched-out twilight of time had exhausted them all, and it wasn't helping their side.

Which was probably what Ethan had been counting on all along. This was a war of attrition on steroids, but Patrick wasn't willing to die on his knees.

"Someone get eyes on Andras!" Patrick yelled.

He'd give anything for working comms, something to coordinate the battle with. Everyone was too scattered for him to be sure his request was heard. He cast a shockwave spell, throwing the mageglobe ahead of them. When it exploded, magic rippled outward, leveling the demons and zombies in their immediate area. It gave him and Nadine breathing room for all of two seconds before he caught sight of the goddess marching toward them from the shoreline.

Hel was ready for war, walking off the shores of Náströnd and leading an army of the dead onto the streets of Manhattan. Patrick's stomach sank at the realization they were facing numbers his side couldn't stand against, even with the few gods who'd followed them to the Battery in the mix.

"We need to regroup," Nadine said, a thread of panic creeping into her voice.

Easier said than done, but Patrick could at least hopefully buy them some time.

"Wade!" Patrick yelled, hoping the teenager heard him. "Get into the air and aim for Hel!"

Wade immediately launched himself into the air with a roar. He spat fire at the spells aimed his way, gaining altitude. The valkyries on their pegasi flew toward Wade to form ranks around him. Taking Wade off their six was a loss, but they needed to cull the numbers on Ethan's side if at all possible without losing too many of their own people.

An explosion of light had Patrick blinking spots out of his eyes, desperately trying to keep a hunter at bay with limited vision. Jono snarled nearby, and the hunter was dragged to the ground and savaged by him.

When Patrick could see clearly again, his gaze zeroed in on where Gerard was engaged in battle with Loki. Their two legendary spears clashed together again and again with a sound that made Patrick's ears ring, magic flashing searingly bright with every connected hit.

Jono shouldered aside a pair of zombies, snapping at their legs and breaking bone. The dead fell to the ground, and Patrick stabbed them both before they could rise again. Spencer's magic danced around the dead surrounding them, but it didn't appear to be as strong as before. There was less of it, but at least Patrick knew his friend was still alive somewhere in the fight.

Hinon flew overhead, calling down lightning and dodging spells. Thunder was a near-constant rumble through the air, white noise that Patrick barely noticed. The demons ahead of them went down under Sage's teeth and claws. Jono lunged past her at the drekavac preparing to leap onto her back.

What space Patrick had managed to buy them was quickly shrinking. All he could see were the grasping hands of the dead, the nightmarish faces of demons, and black-eyed hunters intent on murder. The dagger in his hand wasn't enough against the sheer numbers battering at their limited defenses.

Then a horn sounded across the battlefield, crystal clear as a bell. Patrick recognized the sound in an instant, and he spared a look back toward the way they'd come, hope a desperate taste in his mouth.

The broken pieces of the Bifröst vibrated off the ground and into the air, rainbow-colored light glowing as bright as the hidden sun. The shards of solid light came together in a wave, the rainbow bridge reforming in seconds, the edge of it curving down to the ground rather than the horizon.

Thundering over it came Odin, the Allfather seated astride the eight-legged horse Sleipnir. Riding in his wake was Órlaith at the head of a contingent of Seelie Court fae and Thor on a borrowed steed, Mjölnir held aloft. Winging above the riders were Muninn and Huginn, Odin's ravens bearing witness to the battle.

"To war!" Thor bellowed.

His battle cry was echoed by the valkyries in the air and the fae. Órlaith and the fae split around Odin and Thor, charging into the fray with murderous intent on their faces.

Thor called down a massive lightning bolt from the reactionary storm. It shook the ground when it hit. The dead in its vicinity exploded from the impact, sending body parts flying through the air to land amidst the fighting. Nadine slammed a shield down around them and shoved the base of it outward, forcing the dead back from their immediate location. She dropped it once they gained a little ground, and some of the charred bits of bodies fell down around them like bloody hail.

"I never want to see another fucking zombie for the rest of my life after this," Patrick said.

Nadine just grunted and kicked a hunter in the balls, tipping him off-balance right into Sage's mouth. Patrick looked behind him at the sound of hooves, coming face-to-face with Sleipnir as the horse clattered to a halt. Patrick looked up at Odin, staring into the Allfather's heterochromatic eyes.

"Heimdallr said you were dealing with the Fallen," Patrick said, trying to catch his breath as Nadine raised another shield between them and the zombies.

"There would have been far more demons to greet you if I had not dealt with many of them," Odin said coolly.

Patrick winced, thinking about that insurmountable number. "They're going to keep coming if we don't get the Morrígan's staff out of Andras' hands."

Odin said nothing, batting aside a cluster of spells that were aimed their way as if they were nothing more than irritating insects. "He stands with Hades at the monument."

Nadine conjured up some mageglobes, staring straight ahead and breathing heavily, both hands clutching at her carbine. "Then let's get the fucker."

"Can you clear us a way?" Patrick asked Odin.

Odin didn't answer in words, but the god urged Sleipnir forward. Nadine hastily lowered her shield, and the demons and zombies surrounding them surged closer. Sage roared and trampled a few zombies and a hunter, who Nadine put out of his misery by carving a line of bullets across his face. The demon fled its host but didn't get far.

Ashanti intercepted the incorporeal demon, drawing it into her mouth similar to how Fatima swallowed souls. Except Patrick knew for a fact that demon was never going anywhere ever again. Ashanti snapped her iron teeth together a few times while tearing through some zombies.

"Odin," Ashanti said, voice raspy.

"Ashanti," Odin replied.

"There are soultakers between us and our prey."

"Leave those to me."

Patrick filled a mageglobe with a shockwave spell and sent it hurtling past Sage. The resulting explosion leveled hunters and demons ahead of them. Sleipnir trampled those already on the ground while Patrick's group did the same, kicking a couple along the way to keep them down.

Nadine blocked a spell from hitting them by raising a shield, but the pair of soultakers that shoved through some zombies were Patrick's immediate problem. Sage roared a challenge the demons screamed right back at her, whiplike tongues snapping through the air.

Odin raised a hand and made a fist. The soultakers were lifted into the air, bodies flailing, held in the grip of a god's power. As Patrick watched, their maws were stretched open, skin and bone breaking as Odin fed the demons their own bodies until all that remained were twisted, broken balls of flesh that fell to the ground.

Patrick let Odin deal with the soultakers massed before them. Some slipped past the god though, hidden in the crush of zombies trying to stop them. Sage veered away from some other demons to guard the area on their right. Ashanti launched herself with brutal intent at one soultaker going after Nadine.

"Behind you," Ashanti warned.

Patrick spun around to deal with the soultaker sneaking up on their six. He wasn't up for losing any more magic than necessary, but baiting the damned thing was the only way he knew to get close enough without dying in order to stab it.

Patrick filled a mageglobe with raw magic and sent it away from him at an angle. The soultaker tracked the magic despite having no eyes, its huge maw splitting wide as its tongue lashed out. The soultaker caught the mageglobe with its tongue before twisting its bulbous head back in Patrick's direction.

He gritted his teeth against the sensation of magic draining away from his soul and did his best to expand his personal shield. The soultaker was fast, snapping at his shoulder in a move that would've bitten his arm off if he wasn't shielded. Patrick lunged around the demon with a grunt. Arm raised, dagger clenched tight in his hand, he rammed the blade into the soultaker's gut, feeling its teeth bite into his shield with vicious pressure.

It screamed, deafening him in one ear, but the heavenly prayers in his dagger incinerated it to ash that didn't blow away because of the rain. Patrick found his footing again, straightening up in time to nearly take a metal bat to the face. Only Nadine's shield saved him from having his skull caved in by a hunter.

The zombies seemed to have multiplied, drawn from the Paris horde or Hel, it was impossible to know. Closing the distance between where they were and where Andras stood seemed almost insurmountable, even with Odin carving a brutal path in that direction. Maybe it would've stayed that way if Spencer wasn't suddenly deposited on their six, swearing at Takoma as the master vampire unceremoniously dumped him to the ground.

Spencer stumbled forward a few steps, working to stay upright, Fatima clinging to his shoulder. "Give me a fucking warning next time!"

"Would you rather die or have me save your ass?" Takoma snapped before going after Ashanti and adding to the mess his mother was creating in the horde.

"Can you drop every zombie between us and Andras?" Patrick asked.

"They'll rise again, so you'll need to move fast," Spencer warned.

"What about Andras? Can you exorcise him?"

Spencer grimaced, a tightness to his jaw that spoke of magical overreach, but there was no time for any of them to stop. "I can try. I'm not at my strongest, and I don't know how much interference the Morrígan's staff will cause."

"I'll take it."

Fatima yowled loudly and launched herself off Spencer to the ground. A chill filled the air, not unlike traveling through the veil, as Spencer focused his magic on the walking dead arrayed before them.

The green of his magic danced over the zombies and drekavacs in a way reminiscent of the Northern Lights. The freed souls were drawn into the psychopomp's mouth, guided to rest, the bones and bodies falling to the ground.

Patrick and Nadine kept Spencer between them as they pushed ahead over the bodies, trying to reach Andras before the dead rose again. Sage and Jono ranged out on either side of them, watching their flanks. Traveling in Odin's wake made it easier, but not by much. Odin was a target that everyone was aiming for, and even a god could come under duress.

Wade managed to clear the sky directly overhead of incoming spells but some of the lower-aimed ones he missed. Patrick took those out with a couple of mageglobes, keeping one eye on the enemy around him. Jono stayed close, having chewed on so many bodies that strings of flesh dangled from his teeth.

Patrick nearly tripped on the edge of the sidewalk, their small group having managed to finally cross the street with Odin's help. That put them closer to Andras, but Patrick knew the Great Marquis of Hell wouldn't go down easy.

"Can you try exorcising the bastard now?" Patrick asked.

Spencer sidestepped Fatima, guiding his magic through a particularly thick group of zombies. "We'll be sitting targets if I do. You'll need to keep moving."

"I'm not leaving you alone for that spell."

Spencer shot him an irritated look, face pale and drawn, dried blood flaking off under his nose. "We're all dead if you don't make it to Ethan."

"We aren't leaving you behind," Nadine shot back.

Patrick craned his head around, getting eyes on Andras and

seeing the demon staring back at them out of Ilya's eyes. The quartz crystal inside the carved wooden knotwork of the Morrígan's staff they held flashed brightly.

Patrick's eyes widened. "Nadine, shield!"

She raised a shield as ordered, barely getting it up in time. The wave of magic Andras called forth through Ilya hit like a punch. Nadine went down on one knee, and Spencer didn't even look when he reached for her, dragging her back upright. Fatima yowled loudly, her small furry head looking up with concern at Spencer.

Around them, souls were fed back into the dead, the Morrígan's staff commanding them to rise again. In the handful of seconds it took for them to reorient themselves, Ares appeared in front of Odin, blocking the Allfather's passage.

"Odin," Ares said, standing tall and proud amidst demons. "You chose the wrong side. When we came to you in Chicago, you should have committed to a hell that would remember you."

"There is no memory of any of us that will survive what is birthed here. You misplaced your faith," Odin said.

"I misplaced nothing."

Odin slid off Sleipnir, no weapon in hand, because Loki still had possession of Gungnir. But the Allfather was head of a pantheon of gods, and Ares might be a god of war, but he wouldn't outlast Odin in a fight. Then Ares looked up at the sky through the branches of Yggdrasil, and Patrick realized why Ares wasn't worried.

Breaking free of the storm clouds came thousands of demons falling to earth, the veil no longer a barrier to keep them out. Wade roared a warning, and Patrick desperately wanted to shout at him to fly away, to not face an army of hell on his own.

None of them could.

Odin looked over his shoulder at Patrick, the steel gray of his left eye shining with power. "Make your stand. I will do the same."

Ashanti blurred to a stop beside Patrick, wrapping her clawed fingers around his arm in a bruising tight grip. "You cannot stop now."

Patrick nodded jerkily, and Ashanti let him go. Ares snarled wordlessly, but the attack the god leveled his way was turned aside by Odin. Spencer and Nadine stayed right by Patrick as they all followed Ashanti into the fray. Sage and Jono stuck closer, snapping at anything that tried to get in their way.

Skeletal fingers and rotten hands grasped at Patrick's legs as he ran, the dead slowing his passage. Jono lunged close, biting off a zombie's head. They kept running, and it reminded him of Paris, only worse, because if they lost here, there would be nothing left to fight for. The torn veil would keep peeling open, breaking over the world as Ethan remade it into a hell.

Hellfire exploded around them as they drew closer to the god and demon holding court over the dead. Nadine barely got another shield up in time, and the heat of the hellfire scorched Patrick's skin for a few seconds. He skidded to a halt, breathing harshly. He tracked the hellfire as it slid down the curve of the shield, thick like napalm and sizzling against her magic. Nadine grunted, shaking her head and wiping at the fresh blood flowing from her nose.

The hellfire slid to the ground, burning there like a sea of flame. Patrick stared across it at where Hades stood. He hadn't seen the Greek god of the Underworld since being put in the grave. He doubted whatever stalemate they'd endured in Salem, brokered by Persephone, would reach here, but a stalemate was no way to win a war.

"Drop your shield, Mulroney," Patrick said.

"Are you fucking crazy?" she hissed.

"Just do it."

Nadine drew her shield in closer rather than drop it, letting it surround herself and Spencer. The heat from the hellfire washed over Patrick like a muggy wave, turning the rain to steam around them. The sulfuric smell made Patrick want to gag, but he didn't.

"If you want your daughter back, then get the fuck out of my way," Patrick said.

Jono's growl of agreement was loud enough to vibrate through Patrick's chest from two feet away, his lover still pissed at what had happened in Salem.

"You know that's not how this works," Hades said.

"It could be. Your wife would want it to be."

Hades' expression twisted, hands curled, calling hellfire to him. "You know nothing."

"Bullshit."

He'd seen the way they'd looked at each other in Salem. For all her fury and demands, Patrick knew Persephone could forgive her husband even if she'd never forgive anyone else the transgressions Hades had let pass.

"I owe Persephone a debt. Let me pay it," Patrick said.

"Your debt is meaningless when hell is already here."

Patrick's gaze snapped unbidden to the demon-infested sky above and the countless dead massed around them on the ground.

Hades raised his hands higher and gestured sharply, fingers spread wide. The hellfire surrounding them spun like a fire tornado, rising into the air. It was enough of a distraction for Patrick to miss Cerberus' arrival, but Jono didn't.

The three-headed beast charged through the circle of hellfire, but Jono met him halfway. Jono, with Fenrir's help, forced Cerberus away from Patrick with vicious bites and swipes of his claws. The momentum of their fight sent them careening past the circle of hellfire, the dead clawing at their fur as demons screamed overhead.

Around them in the street and in the park, zombies rose and fell in a wave as Spencer's magic and that of the Morrígan's staff backed by Ilya's fought for control of the dead. Hades hadn't moved, and Patrick didn't know how he'd get past the god to Andras.

Then Ashanti blurred to a stop beside Patrick, hands dripping blood, mouth red with it. She only had eyes for Hades, and the god's attention shifted from Patrick to her, a stillness settling over his body.

"Still here, I see," Hades said.

Ashanti stood as tall as her diminutive stature would let her, her godhead seeping out of her aura with far more intensity than the hellfire. Ozone hung heavy in the air, mixing with sulfur on Patrick's tongue. When Ashanti stepped forward, her bone hooks snapped the spine of a skeleton, and she kicked it aside.

The mother of all vampires spread her arms, clothes a ruined mess, skin black like the night that hadn't yet fallen. "I have always been here, long before you were ever prayed into existence, cousin. I, who walked this world first, chose my side. The *right* side."

"Kill them," Andras ordered from behind Hades.

Patrick noticed how Andras' attention was no longer on the battle but on Ashanti. The mother of all vampires had a hunger on her face when she looked at Andras that had her focusing like the predator she was. Patrick figured she wouldn't be satiated by anything less than the Great Marquis of Hell.

"Choose. Now. Or be forgotten," Ashanti said, her eyes on Andras, but her words were for Hades.

Hades didn't move, not until Ashanti did, and even then, it wasn't to fight her.

It wasn't even to defend Andras.

The dagger that appeared in Hades' hand and found its way to Ilya's heart was unexpected in its violence as the Greek god found a different target. Patrick could see the way bone caved in, blood flowing from Ilya's mouth like a waterfall. The black of his eyes became rimmed with negative light as Andras turned Ilya's head to stare at Hades with incandescent rage, as all around them, the demons summoned from hell screamed their fury.

"*Traitor*," Andras snarled, spitting blood with the word.

Hades pressed the blade deeper into Ilya's chest, his expression almost serene in its viciousness. "Speaks the Fallen."

Between one blink and the next, Ashanti found her way to Andras, clawed fingers digging into Ilya's throat and peeling back layers of skin and muscle. Hades let go of the dagger while Andras tried to let go of the body the demon had inhabited. But Ashanti had her iron teeth in a vein and in the essence of the demon's soul. That was a fight Patrick didn't want to get in the middle of, but he had no choice.

Patrick threw himself across the hellfire, the heat almost suffocating, even through his shields. Ashanti was tangled up in Ilya's body and Andras' incorporeal presence, but it was the Morrígan's staff that held all of Patrick's attention.

Hades hadn't reached for it, all his focus on watching Ashanti try to devour Andras. Patrick wasn't wearing the sort of iron gauntlet Ilya had on. Neither did he have Srecha's blessing burned into his palm. But he knew better than to touch the staff with his bare hand after what he'd gone through in Paris.

The next best thing was cutting off Ilya's.

Patrick followed Ashanti and her prey down to the ground, dagger already cutting into the limb right above the iron gauntlet. The matte-black blade wasn't a saw, but the prayers in its making made the edge sharper than anything had a right to be. It sliced through Ilya's arm with sickening ease, severing it in seconds.

Blood poured out of the limb, sliding over Patrick's hand and the hilt of the dagger. He grabbed the gauntleted wrist with his left hand and lurched away from the rapidly dying necromancer, getting to his feet. Andras was proving to be a formidable opponent even in an incorporeal form against Ashanti. Despite the way he'd fled from her in Central Park, he had no choice but to fight her now, not when she had her teeth in what passed for his soul.

Lightning exploded overhead—from Thor or Hinon, Patrick couldn't tell. The spots that danced across his vision coalesced into something else. Flying through the ranks of demons, like black spots in an afterimage, were thousands and thousands of ravens and crows, their shrieking *caws* a discordant sound to the cries of demons.

Ilya's fingers were still wrapped around the staff; Patrick curled his own over the iron there to keep the staff in place. He was careful not to touch the notched wood, though he could sense the hunger, the near sentience, that existed in the weapon. It grated against his soul, as if it remembered him and the prayers he'd given it along with a blessing to bring Ashanti back.

But standing there at the edge of the world, Patrick didn't have anything left to give up except the weapon in his hand. Breathing heavily, Patrick raised it over his head, the quartz crystal shining with magic, as all around him, the dead turned to look.

Patrick drew in a breath and let it out on a yell. "*Morrigan*! I call you to war!"

2 8

JONO WAS PREPARED TO RIP OUT ALL THREE OF CERBERUS' THROATS, but he never got the chance.

Patrick's cry reached his ears, and he backed away from the beast, wary when Cerberus didn't immediately charge at him. The hellfire they'd escaped went out, and two of Cerberus' heads turned toward its master. One kept its sinister red eyes locked on Jono, tail still lashing, but the beast stayed put.

Hades stood between Jono and Patrick, but the god wasn't moving. Ashanti had Ilya's body on the ground, her hunger a match even for the Great Marquis of Hell as they battled it out. She seemed impervious to the demons trying to dive at her, though they couldn't seem to get close. Lightning flashed again, followed by thunder, and in that momentary illumination, Jono saw the sky full of thousands of wings that didn't belong to demons.

Jono returned to where Patrick stood, holding the Morrígan's staff aloft by a cut-off gauntleted hand. The weapon hummed with power, making the very air around it vibrate. Fenrir bit at Jono's mind, the warning sharp.

*War comes*, Fenrir said.

With the god's help, his vision sharpened, enabling Jono to see details in the twilight even his preternaturally enhanced sight wouldn't be able to pick out. The ravens and crows that blotted out the sky in between demons swarmed together, coming down like the tip of a tornado seeking the earth. The wind howled all around them, the pitch of it like ghostly screams as it spun the demons away from the center of the fight.

Jono pressed his shoulder to Patrick's side, planting all four feet against the muddy ground. The dead surrounding them lurched ever closer, empty eye sockets or rotten cavities staring at the Morrígan's staff. Jono growled a warning, but Patrick didn't seem to hear him, all his attention on the weapon in his hand and the sky above.

The downdraft that suddenly hit brought Patrick to his knees, his right arm going around Jono's back. Jono stayed upright through sheer stubbornness, though his head was forced lower as the wind burst outward all around them with a continuous pressure. It slammed into the battle, indiscriminate of sides, forcing everyone back and to the ground. The sound of wings flapping all around them was a buzz that turned into a hissing white noise, drowning everything else out.

Patrick's arm shook as he held the Morrígan's staff aloft, lips peeled back in a harsh grimace of pain. He wasn't touching the notched wood of the weapon, but the mere act of holding it was dangerous. Jono wanted to grab it and toss it out of reach, half wondering if Fenrir would be enough protection in that act.

"I can't—" Patrick gasped out, his arm dipping, elbow bending.

Jono twisted his head around, shoving closer so Patrick could rest both arms on his back. Jono held the both of them up as they found themselves inside a vortex of ravens and crows, the shining quartz crystal their only source of light. It was enough to reveal the war goddess descending from the storm clouds, the smell of ozone practically choking Jono.

The Morrígan was pale-skinned and thin in the way starving things hungered. Her hooded cloak was made with a thousand black feathers, and it drifted around her body like wings. Her bare feet were covered in grave dirt, and her splayed hands were stained red with blood along her fingertips. The gown she wore was sleeveless, tangling around her knees. The only bright thing about her was the golden torque she wore, the triple moon carved on the rounded ends that rested against her collarbones shining like sunlight.

"*Cousin,*" Fenrir said in greeting.

The Morrígan's feet touched the earth, and the ground trembled as if welcoming her. "*Vánagandr.*"

Patrick pushed himself upright and offered the Morrígan her staff, his arm shaking with the effort of holding it. "This belongs to you."

The war goddess raised her hands to draw back her hood, revealing inky black hair braided back along her skull and threaded through with feathers. Her eyes, when revealed, were a blue-gray reminiscent of bruised skin on a corpse.

The Morrígan reached for her staff, curling her fingers around the notched wood of the pole. Patrick let it go, and Jono watched as the severed hand in its iron gauntlet fell to the ground. The Morrígan drew the staff close, the light from the quartz crystal shining impossibly brighter. The glow washed her out, illuminating the ravens and crows that still whirled around them, crying out to their mistress.

"*You call for war,*" the Morrígan said.

"War was already happening. We're just here to end it," Patrick said.

The Morrígan raised the staff above her head, fingers tightening around the notched wood of the pole. "*War never ends.*"

"Someone else can fight it, then, after this battle is over."

The goddess of war smiled, her gaze turning to the heavens. "*So be it.*"

When the Morrígan slammed the butt of her staff to the ground, Jono had to dig in his claws to stay upright. The concussive force of her magic rolled through them, knocking Patrick to his knees. Jono angled his body to try to shield Patrick from the pressure, and he felt Patrick turn his head into his fur.

The ravens and crows winged higher into the sky, cutting through the demons like missiles. Bodies fell to the earth, trailing blood and smoke, as the ravens and crows searched for new targets. In their wake, the battlefield was revealed.

In a stunning shift, every single zombie went from fighting against the gods and those allied with Jono's god pack to turning on the demons, hunters, and Dominion Sect magic users. The panicked shouts turned into screams of terror as the walking dead obeyed their rightful mistress once more.

"*Go,*" the Morrígan said to them, already turning to join the fight.

Fenrir wrangled control from Jono, long enough to say, "*May the battle born always pray to you.*"

The war goddess tipped her head in acknowledgment, the gesture fleeting as the ravens and crows called to her from the sky. The Morrígan's feathered cloak rippled in the wind like wings as she strode forward over the bodies of the dead, staff held tight in her hand, exactly where it belonged.

Patrick leaned against Jono for a second before straightening up. "Let's go."

He stumbled toward the park, and Jono could only follow. The grayed-out lines of the spellwork stretched around them, the concentric circles pulsing with power as if they were alive. Jono saw hints of light beginning to crack through, like lava sliding through its hardened top as it flowed. Ginnungagap could no longer keep the sacrificial spell in check.

*This is a beginning,* Fenrir said into Jono's mind.

*I thought it was an end?* Jono asked.

*It is whatever you make it be.*

As riddled warnings went, it wasn't any worse than what the Norns had given them.

Patrick lengthened his stride, picking up the pace. The air vibrated with magic, the taste of hell scratching at the back of Jono's throat. Nothing good waited for them up ahead.

Mageglobes cut through the air, heading their way. Patrick's magic streaked forward to intercept the enemy's attack, but he wasn't able to intercept them all. Jono was all set to knock Patrick down and cover him when one of Nadine's shields slammed down around them. The spells crashed against her defense, ripples flowing through the shield, but it didn't break.

Gunfire erupted from behind them, aiming around Nadine's shield for their targets. People cried out in pain up ahead— whether from bullet wounds or getting ripped apart by zombies, Jono couldn't tell.

"Patrick!" Nadine shouted.

Jono saw Nadine and Spencer before he smelled them, the wind worse now than it was hours ago. Nadine nearly tripped over a pile of bones as she and Spencer closed the distance between them. Lucien ran beside them with Carmen a half step behind. Jono had lost sight of the master vampire at the start of the fight at the Battery, but he should've known even a battle like this wouldn't off the bloke.

Sage let out a roar as she ran toward them, zombies paying her no attention. Jono howled a warning when he caught sight of a hunter taking aim at her, but the man went up in flames courtesy of a blast of dragon fire. Wade's roar was louder than Sage's as he picked off anyone who might be a problem behind them, no longer pinned down by demons. The ravens and crows, backed by the Morrígan's power, were doing an incredible amount of damage alongside the valkyries and Hinon.

"What now?" Spencer asked, panting for breath as the others reached their position.

Patrick's hand settled between Jono's ears, dagger held in his other one. "We go through whoever is left to get to Ethan."

Jono glanced over at Patrick, huffing out a soft growl of agreement. The soulbond was pulled tight between them, heavy with magic drawn from the ley lines below.

"Don't fuck it up," Lucien said.

Jono thought about biting the arsehole, but Fenrir wouldn't let him.

Patrick stepped forward, and Jono stayed right by his side, as did Sage. Jono shared a look with his dire, the pair of them coming to a silent agreement to stay with Patrick from here on out.

Zombies filled the park, but the dead no longer accosted them. They had other targets now, and there was plenty of the enemy for the dead to kill. Dominion Sect magic users had to split their attention between Jono's group and the horde of zombies that never stopped attacking, courtesy of the Morrígan. It made getting past them easier, but not *easy*.

So Wade cleared them a path.

He launched himself into the air, flapping his wings hard to hover overhead. His long neck snaked down, mouth opening wide for the fire that came roaring out. Wade burned everything standing in the way between where they stood and Castle Clinton National Monument. The old sandstone fort was covered in spellwork lines whose magic was breaking through Ginnungagap's hold.

The fort itself was cradled between a tangle of roots at the base of Yggdrasil, the world tree blocking out the sky this deep into the Battery. Jono couldn't see the shoreline behind it, but the dead who had followed Hel were hopefully no longer a problem.

They ran over charred grass and bone, heading for the sandstone and pillared entrance of Castle Clinton. Nadine's shield kept off stray bullets and spells, but no one came after them. The magic saturating the air tasted poisonous to Jono, burning his nose.

Beneath it, he could smell ozone.

They didn't make it to the entrance before the spellwork lines came back to life, glowing malevolently against the walls of the old fort. Ginnungagap had been a pressure between Jono's teeth since Fenrir had released the yawning void, and now that pressure disappeared.

They all skidded to a stop, staring at the magic burning back to life. Then Patrick yanked up the left sleeve of his leather jacket, his intentions clear. Jono immediately clamped his teeth over Patrick's bare wrist, bite gentle, staring at him.

*Don't*, he wanted to say.

Patrick seemed to hear him anyway.

"Blood always calls to blood. I'll walk us through it," Patrick said.

He gently pushed at Jono's nose with the knuckles of his right hand, the shine of the dagger he held growing brighter. Jono reluctantly let him go, licking at his fingers. He watched Patrick drag the blade over his skin, cutting through the scabs of Ashanti's touch given in the Morgan Library. Fresh blood welled up, sliding down his arm, the coppery tang of it filling Jono's nose.

Patrick dragged two fingers across the cut and brushed his bloody fingers over Jono's snout, then Sage's. He gathered more blood, then turned to smear some across Nadine's and Spencer's foreheads like a macabre benediction.

"Will that be enough?" Nadine asked worriedly.

"*I* will be enough," Patrick promised her.

Lucien and Carmen were last, both of them already carrying blood on their faces from the battle. Patrick merely added to it.

Jono had never understood the ins and outs of magic until Patrick came into his life, but he knew what blood ties meant these days. He had faith in Patrick to get them through to the other side. So when Patrick stepped forward, straight-backed and clear-eyed, Jono didn't hesitate to follow him.

The spellwork flared up with the first step Patrick took between the lines. Magic flashed, but Patrick squared his shoulders and kept walking, blood dripping from his fingers to the ground below. It hissed and bubbled when it hit, causing the magic there to grow dimmer. Patrick veered to the right a little, extending his arm so he could drag his dagger across the wall, and Jono followed.

The spellwork cracked and burst where the blade touched, peeling off the sandstone. It wasn't enough to unravel it completely, but between Patrick's blood and dagger, he opened up a path for them. Jono stepped where Patrick did, and the farther they walked over the spellwork, the hotter Patrick's blood smeared over his snout became.

*Steady*, Fenrir said.

The depth of the old fort's walls was suffocating, the glow at the end of the short tunnel ugly and dangerous. Nadine raised a shield in front of them, keeping it moving at their pace as they marched forward. When they finally cleared the tunnel and made it to the courtyard, Jono expected a fight. What they got was an eerie stillness that made his hackles rise.

Witchlights burned like tiny Vesuvius flames along the curved walls of the fort. Hundreds of Dominion Sect magic users stood shoulder to shoulder along the concentric circles of the spellwork, packed together like the Underground during rush hour, all of them blank-eyed and pale-faced, tied to magic that would never give them up. No one moved to attack them, all of the acolytes seemingly frozen in place. When Patrick carefully poked someone in the back with his dagger, they didn't react.

Wade landed on the fort's ramparts above the entrance, shaking the entire historical building with his arrival. His wings were half-folded for balance as he spat fire in the direction of the park, guarding the way in so that no other enemy could follow them inside. They had enough to deal with as it was.

"How many graves must I put you in before you lie down and

die?" a voice Jono sometimes heard in his nightmares asked from up ahead, past the rows of silent, complicit witnesses.

Patrick swallowed loudly, but when he spoke, his voice didn't shake at all. "I'll crawl out of every last one you dig."

Steeling himself, Jono and the others made their way toward the inner circle and a nightmare that was years in the making.

## 29

Patrick sensed Ethan before he saw him. Even through his shields, blood called to blood, and he knew where his father stood amidst the heart of the spellwork.

He knew where Hannah was as well.

Ashanti's blood magic had worn off once he'd reached the Battery. What had faded without him realizing it was the tie connecting him to his twin that he'd first felt in Chicago after years of walling it off. Nothing but a frayed end existed now, peeling out of his soul, and the reason was laid out before him as they pushed past the final circle of frozen-in-place acolytes.

Patrick couldn't unsee what Ethan had done.

In the center circle of the spellwork was a pentagram drawn with blood. Mages with magic burning at their fingertips and demon-backed hunters holding weapons in their hands surrounded the pentagram in a half circle.

Lying on the ground within the star's hexagon, arms outstretched toward two points, was Hannah. Patrick blinked, the sight coming to him in flashes, pieces of a nightmare that would haunt him the same way that basement in Salem had.

Hannah wasn't looking at him this time, her face turned toward the branches of Yggdrasil that obscured the sky. The only thing covering her body was blood, all of it hers, originating from the horrific wound carved into her stomach. What had been taken from her other than her agency and sanity—both long since lost— was the baby cradled in Ethan's arms.

The newborn didn't make a sound, legs and arms drawn tight to their tiny body which was slick with blood and other fluid. They were surrounded by a shining aura that only a godhead could produce. The glow of it flowed from Hannah to the infant and tangled around Ethan, the three of them intrinsically linked.

Patrick clenched his teeth against the bile wanting to crawl up his throat. Maybe it was madness, wanting something no mortal should ever have, but it was calculated cruelty that had driven Ethan to this, and Patrick would never forgive him for that.

Ethan's eyes, once the same shade of green as Patrick's, held no color now, the shape of them bleached to an icy white by magic. Patrick couldn't tell if his niece or nephew was alive or not, but he was determined to get them away from Ethan.

"The gods of heaven wasted their efforts with you," Ethan said, his voice holding echoes of a power that didn't belong to him.

Patrick gripped his dagger tight, trying to ignore how the smell of ozone was only growing stronger. "If that were the case, I wouldn't be here."

"You won't live to see the hell I'll rule over."

"You won't live to see it at all."

While the magic users surrounding them on the concentric circles didn't move, the ones standing guard around the center of the pentagram let loose their spells with lethal intent. Nadine's shield held up against the attack, but the barrier was thinner than Patrick would've liked. Fighting against gods had taken its toll on her magic, and it showed.

"What's the plan?" Spencer shouted, hands raised and holding a mageglobe between them. Fatima crouched low by his feet, ready to charge.

"Carmen and I will handle the hunters," Lucien said, eyeing his prey. "The rest of you deal with Ethan and the mages."

"In case it's slipped your notice, he's a god now," Nadine said.

"Not yet," Patrick said, thinking about the aura shared between the three members of his blood family as the spark of a desperate idea took root. "Spencer, I'll need you with me."

Sage growled before moving to position herself by Nadine in a clear signal of protection. Patrick glanced at Jono, finding Fenrir looking out of his lover's eyes.

"*We shall face Ethan,*" Fenrir said.

"Don't harm the child."

"*Casualties are inevitable in war.*"

"My sister's child won't be one. You harm a hair on that baby's head and I'll find a way to fucking gut you." Fenrir didn't respond to that threat, and Patrick drew in a steadying breath. "Everyone, get ready."

Nadine opened the rear portion of her shield so Lucien and Carmen could slip back behind the first circle of acolytes. Patrick paid the pair no mind once they were out of sight, knowing they could take care of themselves.

"Can you get a shield around Hannah?" Patrick asked. Nadine pressed her lips into a hard line as she nodded, most of her attention on holding off the frontal attack from Dominion Sect mages. "Then do it."

"That won't stop Ethan's spell," she warned.

"I know, but it'll give Spencer some cover."

Spencer glanced at Patrick, understanding dawning on his face. "I don't have the power to do what you're thinking about."

Patrick raised his dagger, a dozen pale blue mageglobes forming in front of him. "I do. I just need you there to help me."

"Ready?" Nadine asked.

Patrick nodded, breath coming faster than he'd like. "Ready."

She pulled back her shield, and Patrick let loose his mage-globes, aiming for the Dominion Sect mages rather than Ethan. Jono and Fenrir had that covered.

Fenrir's aura cracked wide open, his godhead pouring out around Jono's form like incandescent fire. As they raced across the courtyard, the shine of Fenrir's godhead trailed behind them like a comet's tail.

Patrick followed after them, keeping his own personal shields up against the explosions of magic that rent the air in the courtyard. The force of the blasts was pressure against his shields, but he stayed upright.

Spencer and Fatima veered sharply away from Patrick, heading for Hannah. Nadine had clamped a shield around Patrick's twin, and though it was holding up against the pounding the Dominion Sect mages were giving it, he knew it might not last if Ethan set his sights on it.

Which was why Patrick was intent on playing bait.

This wasn't like Cairo, where Patrick's indecision had stayed his hand. It wasn't like last year in Central Park, where the start of the end had begun. They were in the weeds of Ethan's desire come to fruition, and the only way to stop him was to steal back what had never belonged to him in the first place.

Patrick couldn't save his sister, and he'd live with that guilt until the day he died, but he could save Hannah's baby.

He could save Macaria.

The only thing standing in the way of that was Ethan.

He didn't know what kind of god Ethan had tried to become, but the underlying power choking the very air around them was proof enough of a strength Patrick couldn't hope to win against alone. Which was why he let Fenrir and Jono take point, and the rest of his pack and the last straggle of allies with them guarded his six.

Ethan's magic built up like a tsunami, crashing into him with an amount of force that should have driven Patrick to his knees.

He kept his dagger up, left forearm braced against his right, and the point of the gods-given weapon aimed at his father. The explosion of heavenly light at the tip formed a glittering golden barrier that expanded around Patrick, taking the brunt of Ethan's attack in a way his own magic couldn't handle.

Through the glare of Ethan's magic, Patrick watched Fenrir dodge the first blast aimed his way, then a second, intent on his prey in a way Patrick had never seen before. Jono's fur shimmered with the outline of an impossibly larger wolf, the stretched-out shape of the god hidden in the shadow that followed his every step.

Magic cut Patrick's way from his right, and he sent three mageglobes in that direction to intercept them. The shockwave spell he let off knocked a couple of hunters over, but the Dominion Sect magic users standing on the spellwork around them never moved. The lines of the spellwork were a sinister shade of bloodred, crawling up their bodies to anchor them in place.

Thunder rumbled loudly above, the rain and wind from the reactionary storm rising in strength. Patrick gritted his teeth and forced himself to take a step, then another, shoulders aching from the strength it took to hold up the dagger.

Out of the corner of his eye, he caught sight of a hunter running toward him, the demon staring out of her eyes with enough hate to be personal. Then a green mageglobe slammed into her, exploding against her back with enough force that her spine protruded through the front of her rib cage.

With Nadine and Spencer keeping watch, Patrick focused on Ethan. The pressure of magic against his dagger let up only because Fenrir had finally gotten within range to inflict damage with teeth and claws. Ethan could want to murder Patrick all he liked, but not when he had to face off against an actual god.

Ethan's magical attack abruptly dissipated. Patrick stumbled before getting his feet back under him. He conjured up a couple more mageglobes to hold in reserve and kept moving, knowing that to stand still in a fight was a good way to die.

Fenrir had forced Ethan away from the altar, looking larger than life amidst the glow from the spellwork. The god snapped his teeth at Ethan's arm, the snarl he let out reverberating through the air. Ethan stepped back out of reach with a fluid quickness no mundane human would ever possess. He still held Hannah's baby in his other arm, the twisted connection of their souls and the godhead shining in the air around them.

Patrick ran toward them, not sure how to get between the two without coming to harm, when his forward momentum was abruptly reversed. The explosion that erupted right in front of him threw him off his feet and sent him flying across the courtyard.

He expected to hit the ground—was preparing himself for the crash landing—when strong arms caught him around the waist in midair and broke his fall. Patrick twisted with Lucien, the both of them slamming into several of the magic users standing on the concentric circles of the spellwork.

"*Fuck*," Patrick gasped out as they landed on something softer than the ground.

Lucien shoved him off and sat up. "You're a fucking idiot. A head-on rush was never going to work."

Patrick could barely hear Lucien over the ringing in his ears. "I need to get Hannah's baby."

"Dying won't help you with that."

The people they'd crashed into had fallen like dominoes and weren't moving. The spellwork they'd stood on grated against Patrick's shield, the taint in it resonating in his soul. He leaned over and dragged the matte-black blade over the wide line, cutting through the magic there. Heavenly white fire corroded the area, smoke drifting up from the damage. A quick glance at Ethan showed his father hadn't noticed.

Lucien dragged Patrick back to his feet with a bruising grip. "Find another way."

Ethan had gone after gods to use as sacrifices before using this same sort of spell. Trying to drain a nexus through Patrick's mother's family, channeled through Hannah, had been the catalyst to extract Macaria's godhead this time around. Blood called to blood, but Patrick knew souls were different.

"Taking the baby from Ethan is the only way," Patrick said.

Lucien took aim at a hunter coming their way and blew out the man's throat. The snap of negative light around the body indicated the demon opted to flee rather than fight. "You have a death wish."

"I didn't come this far to let Ethan get what he wants."

"He's within grasp of it."

Patrick tracked where Fenrir and Jono faced off against Ethan, having taken down a row of acolytes and trampled their bodies. Ethan still clutched the baby tightly to him, but he had made no move to escape the fort. A twisted bit of magic still tying him to Hannah prevented that. Which meant the spell wasn't finished.

"Quit whining and get the baby for me while I distract him."

Lucien reloaded his weapon without even looking, black eyes locked on Jono, Fenrir, and Ethan. "You better not fuck this up."

"If I do, you can punch me in the afterlife."

Lucien shoved him toward the pentagram. "Don't tempt me."

Patrick ran, casting mageglobes at the ones coming his way. There were fewer of them, courtesy of Spencer and Nadine. Carmen had engaged the remaining hunters with a viciousness that left body parts on the ground, none of them hers.

The split-second assessment allowed Patrick to focus on his target, knowing that most of the other threats were handled. Lucien ran toward Ethan, a shadowy blur that let off bullets Ethan deflected with ease. Fenrir snarled as he and Lucien maneuvered Ethan between them.

Patrick kept his attention locked on his own target. The tangled tie of souls and a godhead that ran from Ethan to Hannah was getting thinner. The shine of it was brighter on Ethan's end, the baby acting as a channel for what had resided in Hannah's soul for so long.

Ethan was half turned away from Patrick, fighting Fenrir and Lucien to a draw with magic that looked similar to Hades' hellfire. But even with a split attention, Ethan still knew when Patrick lunged for that shimmering connection and got his dagger into it. The matte-black blade sliced into the bright shine of a stretched-thin godhead, and the sound Ethan let out was loud enough to shake the branches of the world tree.

A blast of raw power hit Patrick in the side with enough force to send him flying. It drove all the air out of his lungs as he crashed to the ground near the center of the pentagram where Hannah lay. The protective charms on his leather jacket shattered from the blow, taking the brunt of an almost-god's power. The crackle of broken magic seared his skin, and he opened his mouth on a scream that wouldn't come.

Then a fist pounded on his chest with enough strength to almost crack a rib as one of Nadine's shields slammed down around him. Fire exploded around it, but her magic held firm for now. Patrick's chest expanded, air filling his lungs in a painful, heaving breath. He stared up at Lucien, eyes tracking over the raw, burned skin on the left side of the master vampire's face and the ash drifting away from the ever-growing wound.

"Lucien," Patrick croaked out.

"It's not sunlight," Lucien hissed out before dropping something tiny and too-bright onto his chest. "Here. Take your niece."

Patrick's arms automatically came up to cradle the infant, angling the dagger away from the baby's small body. "You're burning up."

Lucien's smile was a twisted thing. "I am my mother's child."

Maybe that heritage would be enough to survive what Ethan had hit him with, maybe not, but Patrick couldn't let Lucien die here the way Ashanti had died in Cairo. There would be no bringing him back if Patrick let whatever Ethan had done to

Lucien continue to burn. As much as he wanted to never see the asshole again some days, Patrick owed him too much for a permanent goodbye.

"The godhead belongs to me!" Ethan yelled, his voice echoing strangely with a depth that only gods would ever hold.

Patrick turned his head and watched Ethan stalk their way. The fire in his hands was the same color as the magic sustaining the spellwork beneath the feet of his followers, rancid and terrible.

Fenrir put himself between them, blocking Patrick's view of Ethan's approach. Ethan's next attack was snapped out of the air by Fenrir, magic breaking apart between Jono's teeth. *"You deserve nothing."*

Patrick knew he couldn't win a fight with a god, even with his dagger. What he could do was try to save Lucien while Fenrir and Jono held the line.

He raised his left hand toward Lucien's face, canting his wrist back, the wound there splitting wider. "Take it freely."

Lucien didn't hesitate to grab his hand and bring Patrick's wrist to his mouth. His fangs sank into Patrick's vein, tearing it wider as Nadine's shield wavered around them. Lucien could walk in sunlight the same way Ashanti could. Daywalkers had a resistance to fire other vampires didn't. Whatever form of hellfire Ethan had hit the master vampire with, Patrick hoped his blood was enough to disrupt the lingering effects and allow Lucien's body time to heal.

It couldn't have been more than half a minute before Lucien took his fangs out of Patrick's wrist. He felt light-headed in a way that would become a problem sooner rather than later, but he couldn't worry about that now. Lucien gripped him by the collar of his jacket and hauled him to his feet. Nadine's shield had cracks on the outer layer that no amount of patching would hold together for much longer, not with Ethan's rage lighting up the fort around them.

"Any time now!" Spencer yelled from the center of the pentagram.

Patrick wrapped his bleeding arm around the infant and stumbled toward where Spencer knelt beside Hannah's ravaged body. Nadine's shield shrank around them as the attacks kept coming from Ethan and the few remaining magic users. Lucien stuck close, weapon raised, as he kept an eye on the threats outside Nadine's shield.

Patrick crashed to his knees beside his twin, staring at Spencer across the horrible, gaping wound in her middle. Spencer was pale-faced, magic crackling at his fingertips. Fatima leaped over Hannah's bare legs and padded to Patrick's side. Her front paws were warm through his wet jeans when she put them on his thighs. Leaning in, she started licking at the blood and other fluid coating the baby girl's tiny feet.

Patrick dropped his gaze to his niece, and his throat seized up when he saw her staring back at him with stormy blue eyes, the aura of a godhead settled in her skin, but draining fast. He juggled her in his arms until she was only cradled in his left despite his wound, the weight of her barely anything at all.

Then he held up the dagger, the sharp tip hovering above his niece's heart, and looked at Spencer. "Tell me where to cut."

Killing his father wouldn't be enough to pay his debt. What he owed was a life for a life, and Macaria was all that Persephone had ever wanted back. But untangling a godhead couldn't be done with mortal magic. That required a godly touch.

Spencer leaned across Hannah's body, gaze a little distant as he reached out one hand, looking not at Patrick but at the edges of souls Patrick knew he'd always been able to see. "I'll show you."

Patrick didn't fight his grip, letting Spencer guide his dagger through the air above his niece. As it moved, ragged threads of light peeled apart from the blade, the embodiment of souls unraveling after years of entrapment in a corrupt bond that should never have been made in the first place. Patrick stared down into his niece's strange eyes and knew she'd never grow up as family.

She'd only grow up to be worshipped.

"I'm sorry, Macaria," Patrick said around numb lips. "For everything."

This wasn't where she should have ended up, reborn in a stolen newborn's body, damaged in ways that should never have happened. Macaria and Hannah deserved a life not brutalized by Ethan's arrogance and cruelty and base desire for something that could never belong to him.

Patrick couldn't undo the past, but he could try to build a future that wasn't Ethan's vision of hell. So he cut and cut and *cut* with Spencer's help, frantically slicing through metaphysical scar tissue as Ethan screamed with fury, kept at bay past Nadine's shields by a god who knew a thing or two about endings.

"Patrick! I can't hold it much longer!" Nadine yelled, her voice breaking from the strain of magical overload.

"Keep going," Patrick urged Spencer.

The dagger passed over Macaria's tiny head, a crown of light glittering softly over thin baby hair. Spencer guided the dagger closer to himself, following the connection to what was left of Hannah in a body gone cold and a mind long since lost to madness.

Nadine's sudden warning shout was full of agony. "*Patrick!*"

Lucien grabbed Spencer by the back of his flak jacket and hauled him away from the blast radius, less quick than he normally would be. Patrick stayed where he was on his knees, cradling Macaria in one hand, his dagger raised in the other to ward off the oncoming attack. Ethan's magic slammed against the golden shield of prayers that erupted from the matte-black blade, the force of the impact making Patrick's arm go numb.

He kept his grip, though, on both Macaria and his dagger.

"This is what I was born for. How *dare* you take it from me!" Ethan spat out, eyes bright with a manic gleam.

His voice had lost the echo that spoke of power. His aura was dimmer than it had been, the torn connection curling and fading at the edges. Patrick had separated what he could of the souls from the godhead, but he knew some still remained within Ethan.

Magic still flowed into Ethan from the spellwork, coiling up his legs to wrap around his body. He'd never stop, Patrick knew. Greed was never satisfied, and Ethan wasn't the god he'd hoped to become, but neither was he fully human, just a living mess of failed dreams that needed to die.

The dagger in Patrick's hands burned like a star, and he could hardly see where Ethan stood through the fire of it. Around them, the Dominion Sect magic users standing on the spellwork started to come out of their trance. Some of those recognized what was happening, and the magic being channeled into Ethan grew more precise, more controlled, as they offered him their strength.

The golden shield remained where it was as Patrick moved his dagger until it pointed at the heart of Ethan's power.

"You don't deserve mercy," Patrick bit out, staring into Ethan's eyes through the brightness. "But my sister does."

He'd never been able to reach her in Salem. He'd never been able to pull the trigger in Cairo. This time, he couldn't afford to hesitate.

This time, Patrick went for the killing blow because it was a kindness long overdue.

He moved with a sureness that ached, aim true. When his dagger pierced Hannah's heart, the world cracked to pieces.

Heavenly fire exploded from the blade, streaking away from Hannah into the pentagram and the spellwork beyond. The rain seemed to slow in its descent, the wind lessening from a howl to a whisper. Everything froze, fate balanced on a precipice.

Ethan's scream was soundless in that void, the magic—the godhead—that could never be his slipping away forever. Because Patrick had come to this fight with two weapons that the gods had given him—the dagger and Jono.

It was Jono who went for Ethan's throat, the shine of Fenrir in his eyes, teeth all his own. Patrick saw a spray of red before Jono dragged Ethan to the ground. The earth shook with their landing, the rumble breaking through the stillness that had settled over everything.

Cold gray fog exploded in the air, the veil covering everything until the only light that Patrick could see was the fire burning around the hilt of his dagger still buried in Hannah's chest. He blinked at it, staring in disbelief at the faintest flicker of light drifting up from Hannah's body. In that weak glow, all he could see was the damaged little girl inside the fractured woman she never got to become flickering in the shine of magic all around them.

"She'll need payment," Hermes said as he stepped out of the veil into the courtyard, the fog parting around him. "The dead always do."

Patrick tipped his head back and stared at Hermes, Macaria squirming in his arms. "Hermes. Please. I can't pay her way."

Hermes arched an eyebrow. "Can't you?"

Patrick opened his mouth to protest that he couldn't, because he had nothing left to offer, but then realized that was a lie. With trembling fingers, Patrick dug into his pocket, biting his lip and hoping—*praying*, for once in his life—that he had what he needed.

His fingers curled around the last gold coin, the one Hermes had left him on that hospital bed over a year ago, and he pulled it free. The obal gleamed against his palm in the dim grayness of the veil, the weight of it impossible to measure.

"Half a payment for half a soul," Hermes said.

Patrick reached out with a shaking hand and placed the coin between Hannah's lips, slipping it past her teeth. Then he gripped the dagger and slid it free of her chest, throat tight as he got to his feet. He sheathed the blade, all the while staring at Hermes over his sister's body and the remnants of her soul.

"What now?" Patrick asked, voice cracking on the question.

Hermes extended his hand, palm up, gaze unyielding. "You come with me."

"*Patrick!*"

Jono's voice echoed through the fog of the veil, and Patrick jerked at the sound of it, wanting to turn and find him.

"Don't look back," Hermes said, the offer of his hand one more choice the gods were forcing Patrick to make. "You can never look back when you follow me like this."

Patrick knew he should ignore Jono's cry, but he couldn't. The soulbond tying them together meant that wasn't possible on Earth, in the heavens, the hells, or, for once, here in the stretched-out emptiness of the veil bridging each world with the ghostly whispers of long-forgotten prayers.

Footsteps sounded in the distance, getting closer. Then a hand —warm and familiar—grabbed his shoulder, fingers holding on tight, as if they would never let go.

"Patrick," Jono said raggedly. "*Stay with me.*"

Patrick didn't blink, his gaze locked on Hermes' face, the god staring at him with that single hand outstretched, fingers beckoning. Hermes tilted his head to the side, faded dyed curls falling across his forehead. The veil was dim all around them, but Hermes' aura washed everything out—everything but the baby Patrick carried in his arms and what was left of Hannah's soul drifting between them like the faintest of witchlights.

Patrick swallowed thickly, mouth dry like desert sand, chilled down to his bones. He licked his lips, felt Jono's grip tighten until his muscles throbbed, and Patrick knew there was no choice here.

There never had been and never would be.

He'd lost that right years ago, a lifetime ago, when he was bleeding at Persephone's feet as he begged her to save him. Because gods never gave anything for free, and Patrick's life and soul had been forfeit when she closed the wound in his chest and held his soul debt in her hand.

"Let me go," Patrick said with numb lips. "Jono, please. You have to let me go."

When Jono spoke, the words came out as if Fenrir had shredded each syllable, but Patrick couldn't hear the god in his lover's voice at all. "*Don't*. Don't ask me to do that."

Patrick sucked in a breath that made his teeth hurt, and his lungs ached from the chill of it. "You can find me again. I need you to find me again."

"*Patrick*. Ethan is dead. He can't hurt you anymore. Just *stay*."

Patrick squeezed his eyes shut, tears pricking at the corners, and when he opened them again, Hermes hadn't disappeared like the god always had in the past. Patrick wanted so badly to turn around, to see Jono's face, but he knew if he did that, he'd be digging their graves for eternity.

"I love you, Jono," Patrick said, the words tumbling from his mouth like a promise, like an anchor—a tether long enough to link them through the veil. "But I have to do this, so I need you to let me go."

Jono pressed up against him, body shockingly warm in the coldness of the veil. Patrick shuddered, head jerking a centimeter to the side before he caught himself. He blinked, still staring at Hermes and the offer the gods were giving him, written in his family's blood.

"*Patrick*."

He wanted to keep the way Jono said his name—like it was the most sacred sound between them—in his heart forever. He wanted everything they'd ever promised each other since the beginning. But he couldn't have it, couldn't keep it, without paying his soul debt first.

"I'll come back," Patrick said, hoping it wasn't a lie, knowing it could be. "I *will*. Find me when I do."

Jono buried his face against the curve of Patrick's shoulder where it met his neck, breath hot against his skin. "You bloody fucking *arsehole*."

Patrick bit down hard on his bottom lip, tasting blood, shaking with the sheer physical need to turn around, hold on to Jono, and never let go. But doing that would mean he'd lose everything he'd fought for over the years, everything he'd ever wanted.

Freedom from the gods.

His life back.

His *soul*.

Because Patrick couldn't live like this—at the mercy of gods—anymore. He only wanted to live for Jono and their pack, in a future not dictated by the Fates.

He wanted to *live*, not just survive like the gods were doing in their endless stretch of immortality.

Jono's lips were warm when they brushed over Patrick's temple, a featherlight kiss that branded him all the way down to his soul. Then Jono pried his hands off Patrick and stepped back. The coldness that took his place felt like winter, and Patrick shivered from the ache of it.

"Say those words to my face when you come back to me," Jono said from behind him, voice ragged and breaking, the heartache in it like a wound that would never mend.

Hermes' mouth ticked up at the corners as he wriggled his fingers. "Ready, Pattycakes?"

Patrick reached for Hermes' hand, holding on tight to the god, trying to remember how to breathe. He stepped over Hannah's body, her soul drifting alongside him, and followed after Hermes deep into the veil, Macaria safe in his arms.

He never looked back.

## 30

Jono stumbled out of the veil into the storm, feeling unmoored in a way he never thought he could. Patrick's grief was thick in his nose and fading fast, his scent washing away from Jono's hands by the rain still pouring down.

"Jono!"

Wade's frantic voice reached him first before the teen careened out of the rapidly fading fog. Jono held out his hands to grab Wade by the shoulders before the teen could crash into him. "Whoa, mate. I'm right here."

Wade's gold eyes darted back and forth, searching the space around them. "Where's Patrick? Patrick!"

Jono tightened his hold on Wade, fingers scraping over red scales pushing up across his shoulders. "He's gone with Hermes."

"What do you *mean* he's *gone with Hermes*? He's supposed to stay with us!"

Jono swallowed around the tightness in his throat, trying to focus past the screaming emptiness at the other end of the soul-bond. Letting go of Patrick had been the hardest thing he'd ever done, but he knew why Patrick had asked it of him. Jono would carry whatever Patrick couldn't if asked, but the soul debt would never be his to pay.

"He's gone to do his duty, but Pat will come back. He always does."

Wade stared at Jono with a painful, betrayed look on his face, mouth opening and closing on words he couldn't say. Jono drew him into a sideways hug, rubbing at his back.

"He's grounded when he comes home," Wade finally said in a small voice, face buried against Jono's shoulder. "I can't—he's an *idiot*. Why couldn't he wait for us? We're *pack*."

"We are, and Pat knows that. But this was something he had to finish on his own."

Jono hated saying that, but all he could see was how Patrick had refused to turn around and face him in the veil, always willing to tear himself apart to save everyone else. Jono would do anything, give up everything, to follow after Patrick, but Fenrir hadn't let him. Some things, the god had told him when Jono had let Patrick go, were always meant to be.

*This is how it begins*, Fenrir reminded him.

*Fuck off*, Jono snapped back.

"I'm kicking Hermes in the balls when I see him next," Wade said. He straightened up and pulled away, scrubbing a hand across his eyes.

"Brilliant plan. I'm all for it."

Jono looked past Wade at the interior of the old fort they still stood in. Ethan's body was in pieces, scattered across the broken pentagram. Jono thought he could still feel the remnants of a soul and a godhead between his teeth. Hannah's body lay at the center of the inactive spellwork, gold glittering between her slightly parted lips. Jono didn't let his attention linger long on her because the world was still cracking to bits around them.

"Sage!" Jono called out, staring across the way at where his dire was holding up Nadine.

She turned her head to look at him, letting out a raspy roar, but didn't move from her protective stance. The ground around them was scorched from dragon fire, half the Dominion Sect magic users nothing more than blackened bodies. Wade had killed a good number of them, and the remaining survivors didn't appear to be too much of a threat from where they lay curled in fetal positions around the courtyard.

"What's wrong with them?" Jono asked.

"Backlash," Spencer said tiredly as he jogged over. "The spell broke, and the power had to go somewhere without Ethan to suck it all up."

"I could eat them," Wade said with a hard glint in his eyes.

Jono shook his head. "That isn't justice."

"Sure it is."

"No."

"*Fine*. So what now?"

"*Now the world forgets.*"

The ghostly, echoing voice from above had Jono snapping his head back. He watched as Muninn and Huginn winged down in a spiral pattern to the courtyard, followed by hundreds of ravens and crows. The flock of corvids settled on the bodies, both living and dead, and began to peck at the skulls.

Jono stared at the way Huginn's beak passed through flesh and bone to come away with *something* held between the raven's beak. "What is that?"

"Memories," Odin said from the fort's entrance.

Jono narrowed his eyes against the downpour as Odin walked toward them, Gungnir held in one hand, the weapon back with its rightful owner. "Of what?"

Odin watched as his ravens accepted the memories from the other ravens and crows, his one good eye shining with the same glow. "We can make the world forget the path Ethan took to this travesty, but we did not want the world to forget a god. No mortal will ever know how Ethan and those that followed him and his ancestors came to this moment."

"Why not just do that from the start?"

"Because Macaria would not have survived, and Persephone's grief would have broken the Underworld. We could not risk a cascade into oblivion."

"So you lot used Patrick to do your dirty work for you, is that it? Couldn't get your own hands messy, yeah?"

Odin turned to look at him, a smile playing about his lips that Jono wanted to punch clean off. "What is a story without its hero?"

Jono shook his head, knowing just how much Patrick had never wanted any of this. "Is it over? Does this mean we won?"

Odin tapped the butt of Gungnir against the ground, the motion sending the ravens and crows darting into the air. Huginn and Muninn flew toward the Allfather, their forms seemingly shrinking until they were small enough to perch on Odon's shoulders. The pair stuck their beaks, filled with all the memories of the past, into Odin's skull, offering up stolen knowledge.

"For now," the Allfather said.

Lucien and Carmen approached, the master vampire's arm slung across her shoulders. Most of Carmen's attention was on her lover, and Jono couldn't hide his wince as he took in the burned half of Lucien's face. The wound snaked down his neck and over his skull, the skin blistered and shockingly red against his normal paleness.

"You need a healer," Jono said.

Lucien bared his fangs, half-burned lips splitting at one corner. "The government can pay for one."

"We're leaving," Carmen said pointedly. "We need to get our people below to the subway."

Lucien didn't dig in his heels and let her lead him to the entrance, back the way they'd come who knew how long ago. Time was fucked all around them, as far as Jono could tell. Sage padded over with Nadine on her back, exhaustion in every line of the mage's body.

"I don't know how much good I'll be if we're still fighting,"

Nadine admitted.

Jono watched Wade nick a trench coat off some bloke lying on the spellwork and wrap it around his body. "Let's go find out who's left."

With Ethan dead and his followers been made to forcibly forget why they had believed in the man, Jono hoped those who'd fought with Ethan and were still alive had left the battlefield.

Jono and what was left of his pack and allies left Castle Clinton behind, heading back to the charred area that had once been a park. Dragon fire had done a lot of damage, but Jono wouldn't hold it against Wade.

They trudged across burned grass, cognizant of the zombies still shambling about, but none of the dead bothered them. Jono's bare feet became muddy in seconds, the rain still coming down but with less intensity than he remembered. Glancing up at the sky past Yggdrasil's branches, Jono thought the storm clouds weren't as low as they had been.

A pair of wolves broke through a line of zombies, racing their way. Jono was desperately glad to see that Emma and Leon had survived and went to his knees so he could wrap his arms around their necks when they arrived, fingers digging into cold, wet fur.

"Real chuffed to see you made it through," Jono said. Emma was the first to pull away, wolf head tilted to the side as she stared at them, and Jono knew when she came up one person short. The mournful sound she made absolutely gutted him. "Pat's alive. He's just…not here, and I couldn't follow where he went."

He'd wanted to, oh, how he'd wanted to. Jono would give anything to be by Patrick's side right now, but a part of him knew his pack and all the ones they were responsible for needed him just as much. Jono needed to make sure everyone was okay, that New York City was still standing, that when Patrick came back, he'd have a home to return to.

Steeling himself to face the aftermath, Jono stood and warily scanned the battlefield arrayed before them on the damaged

Manhattan streets and in the sky. He was prepared to keep fighting but realized after a few seconds that maybe, just maybe, it was truly over.

Hinon and the valkyries laid claim to a sky that was slowly losing its cloud coverage, the reactionary storm receding in the horizon where the veil gave up ground. The demons from before had all disappeared, while ravens and crows filled the air they'd flown through. The dead outnumbered the living on the ground, but Jono didn't see any signs of hunters.

The surviving gods, fae, vampires, and werecreatures who'd come this far with them held their ground, expecting the fight to continue. Jono saw the way the other gods relaxed when they got eyes on Odin, the Allfather impossible to miss, what with the way his godhead shone about him.

The horde of zombies parted, allowing the Morrígan room to approach with the Dagda at her side. Jono's lips curled at the sight of the mayor-in-disguise having finally appeared for battle when the fight was practically over.

"Bloody typical of a politician," he said to no one in particular.

Wade snorted, crossing his arms over his chest. The stolen coat he wore hit midthigh. Marek was still in possession of Wade's rucksack. They needed to get back to Union Square to make sure Marek had survived the fight. They'd left him under Reed's care, and the dragon better have kept him alive.

"Have the memories been erased?" the Dagda asked.

Muninn and Huginn *cawed* raucously before launching themselves off Odin's shoulders. The Dagda's gaze followed their flight path before returning to settle on their group with a power to his stare that made Jono's shoulders twitch.

"They have," Odin promised.

"*I* remember," Wade muttered.

So did Jono, for that matter. Fenrir's laughter was harsh in his mind, trailing after his tired thoughts before settling into words.

*You remember because you will never try to do what Ethan did. That is why we gods chose you.*

The rest of the world would never know the underlying reason for this fight, only the damage done. Jono wasn't sure it was a fair trade.

"What of Macaria?" the Dagda asked.

"She lives," Odin said

"Then it is done." The Dagda's attention settled on Jono, and the god gave a regal nod in his direction. "Your teeth once again rendered an end. You have our thanks, cousin."

Fenrir slipped through Jono's thoughts, guiding his tongue. *"Next time, do not let the telling be written this far."*

"What do you mean *next time*?" Wade protested.

"That is not a promise any of us can give. We gods live to be remembered, and there will be stories of this battle to last us centuries," the Morrígan said.

"The veil is still torn," Jono said, pushing Fenrir aside to speak on his own.

The Morrígan glanced up at the sky where the clouds were slowly pulling back. Jono thought he could see a few stars as the storm swirled around Yggdrasil's branches, the leaves fainter than they had been. Less solid.

Less real.

"Samhain is over. A balance is returning, and we must let it settle," the Morrígan said.

She raised her staff toward the sky. The quartz crystal flashed like a lighthouse beacon, half blinding Jono for a second. When his vision cleared, he could only stare in disbelief at the battlefield around them.

Like a wave, the zombies fell, every soul powering the dead lifting free of their bone and rotting flesh prisons. Souls collided and twisted together in the air, becoming multiple rivers of light that flowed toward the Morrígan's staff.

The sky beyond the buildings surrounding them grew brighter, a false dawn against the fading twilight. Streams of light flowed into the air as millions of souls throughout a veiled Manhattan answered the Morrígan's summons. The shapeless manifestations of life lost streaked like shooting stars through the sky, with only one destination in mind—the staff.

The Morrígan stood as a silent witness to the dead she stole from the battlefield. Her staff absorbed every single soul that had given false life to the dead, the weapon growing brighter in her hand. Jono didn't know how long it took for the Morrígan to lay the dead to rest, but it was far quicker than their efforts ever would have been.

When the last soul disappeared, the glow of the quartz crystal faded as well. The Morrígan lowered her staff, the dead cast aside, hopefully never to rise again on the streets of Manhattan.

"Now what?" Sage asked, having shifted back to human at some point as the Morrígan wielded her staff. Sage had an arm around Nadine's waist, holding the mage up with easy strength.

The Morrígan smiled, an eerie, ancient weight to her gaze as she looked at them. "You live."

The gods all faded from sight, letting the veil steal them away, but the fog of it didn't linger. It recoiled away from where they stood, sliding past the buildings in front of them, wrapping around Yggdrasil and the roots of the world tree, prying it out of the here and now to some other time, some other place.

This wasn't its world, not anymore.

The rain let up, dropping to a hazy sprinkle, as the clouds thinned out above. Sunlight touched the horizon in the east, driving back the dark, washing away the ghosts of the nightmare they'd survived.

Gerard's voice rang through the dawn air like a clarion call. "Jono!"

He followed the sound, seeing Gerard jogging their way, Órlaith keeping pace with him on her steed.

"Communications are back up. Reed is coordinating with our forces in the other boroughs to bring them across the bridges and tunnels. We shouldn't have any problems with the zombies, but I don't know who else is left in the field from the other side," Gerard said.

"Have you heard from Marek?" Sage asked sharply.

"Reed said to tell you he's alive." Gerard's gaze swept the group, a frown settling on his face. "Where's Patrick?"

"He went with Hermes," Jono said.

The understanding in Gerard's eyes was too close to pity for Jono to accept. He looked away, cognizant of the fact he was standing starkers in the street, but wasn't about to go nick clothes off the dead how Wade had done.

"I want to find Marek," Sage said.

Jono understood the quiet desperation in her voice only too well and nodded at her.

"Then we'll do that," Jono promised. "It's over now."

"No," Gerard said quietly with a sureness that came from the long-lived. "It's only the beginning."

Jono tipped his head in Gerard's direction, all his senses tuned to the absence where Patrick should be, and said nothing. The hollow ache in his chest was as much from loss as it was from the emptiness on the other side of the soulbond. He closed his eyes against it, trying to rally himself for the task ahead, choosing to believe in the promise Patrick had been telling him for months and months, as if he'd known how this would end.

*I'll come back.*

Jono would hold Patrick to that vow, and he'd be waiting.

He opened his eyes and stared up Broadway, the Bifröst long since gone. But curving across the sky as the sun rose, pressed up against the last of the rain, was a rainbow spanning the width of Manhattan. It hung in the sky, as if nature herself was apologizing for what magic had wrought.

Jono let it guide him and what remained of his pack into the city they called home, stepping over bodies as they went, with the valkyries flying above to escort them Uptown.

## 31

"ELOISE IS HERE," SAGE SAID AS SHE PEERED OUT THE LIVING ROOM window at the street below the flat.

Jono came out of the kitchen, tea in hand, and took a sip. "She's late."

Sage turned and gave him a pointed look. "Considering the detours she probably had to take from LaGuardia, are you surprised? Half the streets in Manhattan still need to be cleared of the dead."

"The city stinks," Wade agreed before shoving a handful of crisps into his mouth.

"That's not changing anytime soon," Emma muttered from her spot sprawled on the sofa, her head in Leon's lap and her feet in Marek's.

Two weeks since the veil had lifted the day after Samhain and New York City was still struggling to return to normal. The fight inside the veil had damaged the city in ways that would take weeks, if not months or longer, to recover from, to say nothing of the citizens themselves.

When the Morrígan had stolen the souls of the dead, she'd left

375

the bones and bodies behind. As in Paris, the logistics of recovering the dead and figuring out where to bury them was an almost overwhelming task. Jono was just glad it wasn't summer, when the stench of rotting bodies would've made the city near uninhabitable.

That was the most pressing need at the moment, if only for health reasons and to clear the streets for travel. Abandoned vehicles and debris from the battle couldn't be removed until the bodies were gone. Local crews bolstered by the National Guard were working night and day on the task, but crematoriums could only burn so many of the dead at a time.

That hadn't stopped New Yorkers from going about living their lives. Downtown and Midtown had seen the brunt of the battle, but other parts of Manhattan had been attacked as well. Their underlying plan to defend by blocks had meant fewer casualties, but people had still died. Jono didn't know the final number of victims yet because the government was still trying to pin that down. But he'd walked by numerous flyers of the missing, seen mention of many more on PreterWorld and other social media sites.

The only missing person Jono truly cared about was Patrick.

He still hadn't returned from beyond the veil, and there'd been no updates from any of the gods, not even Fenrir. Jono woke up every morning thinking *today*, and every night he went to bed alone he hoped for *tomorrow*. Every day that passed was one more day of loneliness that no amount of working himself to the bone could fix. Jono knew time moved differently past the veil, but waiting was the hardest part.

So he'd thrown himself into rebuilding the werecreature community and making himself available to the government when they came knocking on his door. There was no escaping the fact he and his god pack had been at the center of the battle. Electronics might not have been up and running during that stretch of time when the veil hung over Manhattan, but people talked.

And people prayed.

Hundreds of thousands of people had born witness to gods in battle. Those stories were spreading like wildfire through social media, news interviews, conversations, and written communications for all the world to see. Jono couldn't help but think that's what the gods had wanted in the end—recognition and remembrance. Their names falling from someone's lips once again, their guidance asked for in new prayers.

Jono wondered who Eloise prayed to these days, if it was still Persephone, but he wasn't rude enough to ask. When Sage opened the door to usher Eloise, Madelyn, and Grant inside, Jono merely asked what they'd like to drink.

"Tea is fine, if that's what you're having," Eloise said with a faint smile that didn't quite reach her tired eyes.

"I'll make it," Wade said, heaving himself off the armchair.

"Use the kettle, not the microwave," Jono reminded him.

Wade rolled his eyes. "I did that *once*."

"You've done it at least a dozen times, mate."

"You're lying when you say it tastes different."

"Kettle. Tea."

Wade flapped his hand in Jono's direction. "I could just blow fire on it. That would boil the water faster."

Jono sighed, deciding not to argue further. Wade knew how he preferred tea and would make it correctly, or Jono would know. He turned his attention back to the Pattersons, seeing the sofa had been vacated so the new arrivals could have a place to sit.

Emma walked past Jono to grab her coat where it hung off a chair tucked against the dining room table. "We'll head out. Call us if you need anything."

Jono nodded, going through the motions of scenting Emma and Leon before the pair left. They had pack meetings to oversee, acting as Jono's proxy alongside Sage since he kept getting pulled out of the city for meetings before congressional subcommittees and more private ones at the Pentagon with only Reed to advocate for him. People wanted answers, and Jono could only give them so many.

Everyone wanted *Patrick*, and he wasn't here.

Eloise seemed to realize that, judging by the way her shoulders slumped. Grant patted his mother's hand in a comforting manner.

"He isn't back yet, I take it?" Eloise asked.

Jono shook his head. "I said I'd ring you whenever Pat returned."

"I know. I just…" Her voice trailed off, and she shrugged tiredly. "We buried Hannah last weekend. It would be nice to know we won't be burying him as well."

"Pat promised he would come back. That isn't a promise he'll break."

Jono said it with a sureness that he'd never give up. He tried to impart that in his voice, knowing it came through his scent, even if Eloise and her family would never be able to smell it. Sage could, and she gave him a slow nod of agreement from her spot on the armchair. Marek had taken the floor in front of the chair, leaning against her legs so she could stroke her fingers through his hair.

The pair hadn't left each other's sides since being reunited after the fight. True to Reed's word, he'd kept Marek safe, not wanting to have to explain the death of the seer to the government *and* Sage. Marek had been overseeing PreterWorld from home, having ordered everyone in the company to work remote during the recovery process.

"Did Finley stay in Salem?" Jono asked.

"He's in DC for some meetings on behalf of our coven. We'll join him there tomorrow," Eloise said.

"Won't Congress be mad you'll be a day late?"

"We're meeting with the SOA, actually."

Jono was well aware of her anger toward Patrick's agency, so he wasn't surprised she was delaying that meeting and letting her son handle the initial contact in her stead. "What do they want?"

"We're confirming the timeline for everything that happened in

Salem, starting with my abduction." Eloise pressed her lips together before sighing softly. "I don't like talking about it, but needs must."

"How are you doing with all of that?"

She reached up to tuck a stray piece of pale ginger hair behind her ear. Her hairdo had been slightly disturbed by the wind upon her arrival, the chill outside enough these days that Jono had turned the heat on in anticipation of this visit.

"I'm...okay," Eloise admitted.

"We got her checked out by a healer after the fight in Salem was over. She needs more rest but should make a full recovery," Grant said, offering up more details.

"I'm pleased to hear that," Jono said.

"What about the Salem nexus?" Sage asked.

Madelyn shared a look with her mother before choosing to answer. "The government is insisting they take over control of it. My brothers are reluctant, but Mother and I think it's the right step. We don't have many mages in the coven, and it's clear that the generational wards ultimately failed."

"Knowing now how we were complicit in Hannah's pain isn't something I think I'll ever forgive myself for," Eloise admitted.

Jono shook his head. "The only one who deserves blame is Ethan. You didn't know your granddaughter was still alive. You couldn't have known how he was using her against you."

"Perhaps. But we want to make sure something like this doesn't happen again to our family, or to anyone else's."

Jono couldn't tell her that he didn't think it ever would because of the memories that had been stolen by the gods. Ethan's desires had remained in the global consciousness if the news was anything to go by, but the details of his attempts to turn himself into a god would be forever forgotten. These days, everyone thought Ethan had been after the cumulative power of the nexuses. Jono was fine with everyone believing that god-perpetuated lie.

"Protection of the Salem nexus has been our responsibility for generations. That task has defined our family and coven for so long that I'm worried how we'll be perceived in its absence," Grant said.

"Magic evolves. So must we," Eloise said gently. Grant let out a heavy sigh and nodded at his mother's words.

"Okay, I have flower tea, grass tea, and some black tea that tastes like char, but no iced tea because Jono thinks that's a crime against humanity," Wade called out from the kitchen. "Who wants what?"

Jono sighed heavily and stared up at the ceiling. "I promise we've been teaching him manners."

Madelyn laughed softly, her eyes crinkling at the corners. "I think Wade would get along well with the kids. You'll have to bring him the next time you come visit."

Jono just smiled, not promising anything at the moment. He was bound to New York City when not summoned to DC for the foreseeable future. He had no desire to go anywhere else, not without Patrick. Madelyn seemed to understand that, because her smile became a little wistful.

Jono didn't bother raising his voice when he answered Wade. "Just bring the whole lot."

"How has it been in New York?" Eloise asked after a moment.

"We're recovering. Slowly, but we are."

He wasn't willing to go into details with the Pattersons. As much as they were Patrick's family, none of them were close, despite how much he knew Eloise wanted to be. His pack's ties to them ran through Patrick, and Jono was content to wait until he returned to get to know them.

"All right, I have your *kettle*-boiled water," Wade announced as he came out with mugs and tea boxes stacked on a cutting board in one hand and the kettle in the other, with a trivet hanging from one finger.

He set everything on the coffee table, and Jono gestured for Eloise and the others to serve themselves first as guests.

"Hospitality?" Madelyn asked.

Jono shook his head. "It's fine."

He wasn't going to stand on ceremony, not with them. Madelyn nodded and set about making tea for herself and her mother while Grant did his own. Marek made a mug for himself and Sage, and there was just enough water left in the kettle for Jono's.

"You'll need to refill the kettle for your tea," Sage said, passing it back to Wade.

"That's what the microwave is for," Wade said.

Jono took a sip of his tea and refused to rise to the bait. "Go eat your Pop-Tarts."

"You don't need to tell me twice."

"And put the kettle back on the hob."

Jono could hear Wade puttering about the kitchen as the rest of them enjoyed their tea during a quiet that wasn't as awkward as he expected it to be. Eloise was of a generation where manners were paramount, and she wasn't one to pry into hurts they were all feeling.

"Where are you staying?" Jono asked after the tea was finished and small talk run through.

"At a hotel on the Upper West Side. We were advised to stay clear of Midtown," Grant said.

"It stinks," Wade said from his spot on the floor by the coffee table.

"So we discovered when driving over from the airport."

"It's getting better," Jono said.

Eloise looked at him, mouth curving in a soft smile. "One can only hope."

Jono thought about the promise Marek had made him all those years ago in London. How he'd never have found his pack if he hadn't taken a chance and hoped it was the right choice at the time. He couldn't have known then what was in store for him. He couldn't have known what he'd find or what he'd become.

He wouldn't change it for anything though, and he'd keep waiting until Patrick came home.

"Yeah," Jono said softly, gaze straying to what remained of his pack, finding them looking back at him with love in their eyes. "One can hope."

# 32

PATRICK HAD FORGOTTEN WHAT IT FELT LIKE TO BE WARM AS HE followed Hermes through the veil. "How much further?"

"We're almost there," Hermes said.

"I feel like you said that hours ago."

Hermes hummed in response, never slowing down as he strode through the fog that wanted to cling to them. "Ethan tried to cleave a new world out of the veil, and he failed. The damage wrought makes passing through it more difficult."

"Great."

He bit back everything else he wanted to say, knowing it wouldn't make Hermes go any faster. Patrick knew the longer he spent past the veil, the more time would pass back on Earth. He also knew Hermes didn't care. When Patrick had chosen to take Hermes' hand, he'd known what he risked. That didn't mean he wanted to lose months just because Hermes took the long way around.

Patrick sighed and shifted the newborn in his arms, careful to support Macaria's head. He winced at the throbbing pain in his left arm but didn't let the wound there stop him from keeping her close.

He looked down at the baby wrapped up in his leather jacket, tucked away from the chill of the veil. She stared up at him with gold-brown eyes full of personality and intelligence, her focus eerie in its intensity. He couldn't look at her for long, cognizant of every choice that had resulted in the goddess taking up residence in his niece's body.

He wondered if his niece's soul had ever had a chance to form or if Macaria's godhead had pushed it out how she'd tried to push out Hannah's. A baby was a blank slate, with no personality, and had stood no chance against a goddess who remembered who she was but had no body to call her own. Not until Hannah became pregnant against her will.

Patrick hadn't been around kids very often, babies even less, but he knew no baby was ever this quiet. Macaria wasn't crying, wasn't even squirming all that much, was just a silent presence in his arms with a godhead bleeding through her aura. Ozone lingered in the air around her, growing ever stronger as they traveled through the veil, and Patrick knew he needed to stop thinking of the baby as his niece, because she'd never had a chance to truly exist.

This was Macaria's body now and would be forever more.

Protesting the unfairness of the situation wouldn't change what had happened. Patrick could only move on from the past, no matter how recent it was. Every step he took brought him closer to a freedom that had cost far more than he ever could have realized as a child.

Walking through the veil felt like falling, with no sense of where the ground was. Patrick couldn't see anything through the thick fog that surrounded them. Even Hermes faded from sight sometimes, the god wrapped up in gray nothingness before reappearing. The only constant was the faint glow of what was left of Hannah's soul as it kept pace with them.

Patrick couldn't feel his twin in his soul, the same way he could no longer feel Jono through the soulbond. Whatever lingering connection that might have existed between his sister had been severed with Hannah's death. All that remained was the memory of the child she'd been, the barest structure of a life lost. It had been enough, in the end, to require payment for passage to the afterlife.

Hannah had been alive enough all these years to experience a horrifying, lingering slide into nonexistence, and Patrick knew he'd never forgive himself for that. But she was free now, and he hoped that could give her some peace, even if he'd never find his own over what was done.

Patrick swallowed, dry tongue sticking to the roof of his mouth. He was about to channel Wade and ask how much longer they had left when the fog started to finally thin out. He could actually see the ground rather than just feel it, the soles of his combat boots sinking into black dirt. When the fog finally peeled away for good, he found himself walking beside the River Styx, the cold wind of the Underworld howling through the air.

The full-body shiver that ran through him made his teeth clack together, nearly catching his tongue. Patrick blew out a breath, hunching his shoulders against the wind. The Underworld had always seemed inhospitable the few times he'd visited, and that hadn't changed.

Hermes led him to the edge of the river, and Patrick wasn't surprised at all to see Charon waiting for them at the shore, the ferryman's boat made out of bones ready for them to board. Patrick hesitated, brackish water lapping at the tips of his combat boots.

Hermes, as if sensing Patrick's unease, glanced over his shoulder and tilted his head in the direction of the boat. "You are allowed to ride. Payment was already made."

Patrick steeled himself and waded into the water, struggling a little as he tried to climb on board with a baby held in one arm.

Hermes reached for her, as if to take Macaria from his arms, but Patrick only held her tighter.

"I have her," Patrick said, glaring at the god.

Hermes could say payment was made all he liked, but until Patrick handed Macaria back to Persephone, he wasn't letting her go. Hermes laughed at him, the sound ringing through the dead air, before vaulting onto the boat, making it rock wildly. Patrick scowled and waited until it settled enough in the water to get on board. It took some balancing, but he managed to do it without letting go of Macaria.

Hannah's soul floated over the water to settle in the space beside him on the cold wooden bench, never leaving his side. Charon pushed his pole against the bottom of the river, freeing the boat for the current to take. He steered them deeper into the River Styx, angling the prow downriver rather than across.

The fog of the veil lingered against the water, less thick than it had been in the fringe they'd walked through. The Underworld was a cold, desolate place, and Patrick hunched over Macaria, trying to shield her from the wind. He clenched his teeth together when they started to chatter, wondering if he dared try to set a heat charm again on his leather jacket. The remnants of broken fae magic still lingered on the material, and he was loath to risk Macaria.

So Patrick remained cold on the long ride down the River Styx, staring into the gloom that was ever present in the Underworld. He kept his eyes on the water, wary of the things that swam below the surface, shadows that followed the boat for miles and miles.

The River Styx grew wider as Charon steered them to their final destination. Eventually, Patrick couldn't even see the shore, the fog obscuring it. Macaria shifted in her makeshift swaddle, and Patrick tugged aside the collar some to get eyes on her. She blinked owlishly up at him, her thatch of strawberry blond hair the only color around it seemed like.

"Almost there," Patrick said tiredly.

He couldn't begin to know how long the boat ride was, but the fog began to thin at some point, rolling away from a massive cave that looked as if it was capable of swallowing the River Styx whole. Charon directed his boat toward that darkness, the light in the skull on the prow illuminating their way into the vast tunnel.

The only sound in the dark was Patrick's breathing and the splash of water against the hull of the boat. Charon knew the way, though, and guided the boat with a sureness that came from an eternity of ferrying souls to the Underworld.

A speck of light bloomed in the distance, growing larger and brighter as they drifted toward it. Patrick realized too late it was hellfire, burning in an arc against the end of the tunnel that opened up into a huge cavern. The heat of it was almost scorching after being so cold for so long, driving feeling back into the tips of his fingers.

Patrick straightened up once he caught sight of the welcoming committee standing on a stone ledge the River Styx lapped against. Charon poled the boat closer until the bones that made up its hull brushed against stone. Hermes stood and leaped easily to dry land. Patrick couldn't do the same, not with a baby in his arms, but he wasn't about to ask for help.

He managed to stand and get out of the boat without falling on his ass, but it was a near thing. Finally standing on solid ground, Patrick stared at where Persephone and Hades stood on the shores of their kingdom, watching him with a hunger in their eyes that was all for the infant he carried.

*What did you look like before?* Patrick wondered to himself as he glanced down at Macaria. *Who will you be after this when you find your voice again?*

He had so many questions that he knew would never be answered, simply because Patrick knew better than to go prying into other people's traumas, even when they were so intricately twined with his own. Macaria didn't owe him that, even though she was payment in full of the soul debt he owed Persephone.

"One weapon, as you requested," Hermes said with an overindulgent bow to the rulers of the Underworld.

"Oh, fuck you," Patrick muttered.

Hermes flashed him a smile before stepping aside, allowing Patrick to face Persephone and the end of everything he'd lived for since she'd taken him off that spellwork in Salem all those years ago.

"I brought your daughter back," Patrick said into the cold and the quiet that surrounded them. "I want my soul debt cleared. Tell me it's done. That I've paid up and you don't own me anymore."

He couldn't quite keep the desperation out of his voice and was too tired to really try. The gods would do what they liked, they always had, but he'd played fast and loose with their rules and finally finished what had been asked of him. Persephone owed him his freedom, and Patrick wasn't leaving the Underworld this time without it.

Persephone approached on quiet feet, her gown more traditionally Greek in style than anything she'd worn as of late. Patrick tightened his grip on the baby, not willing to give her up without assurances. Macaria still didn't make a sound, though she wriggled more than she had on the long journey through the veil to this moment. Persephone's gaze dropped to the infant, the love in her eyes impossible to miss.

"You kept your end of the bargain. The terms were met. Your soul debt has been paid," Persephone said.

She stepped closer, reaching not for her daughter like he thought she would but for Patrick. Her hands were warm when they framed his face, tilting his head so she could look him in the eye. Between one blink and the next, her godhead bled through, mixing with Macaria's, until Patrick had to squint to meet her gaze. When he sucked in a breath, all he could smell was spring.

Warmth coursed through his body, the taste of magic on his tongue. The stinging ache in his left arm disappeared, the wound there healed by her touch. All the cuts and scrapes and bruises he'd accumulated in the battle washed away as if they had never been.

"I will remember what your family took from me, and I will remember how you returned it," Persephone said. "I will remember you."

"Please don't," Patrick told her.

She lifted a hand to smooth back his hair, and the touch sent fire lancing through his body. He tried to jerk away but couldn't, standing rigid before her. When Persephone's magic finally fled his body, he felt hollowed out and paper-thin, standing there before the goddess who had dictated the steps of his life for so long.

Persephone pulled his head down so she could brush a kiss over his forehead, the touch soft and almost forgiving in a way, when he didn't think he deserved it. "Be free."

A sound rang in his head, the echo of it making his chest hurt. The scars there from the wound she'd closed up when he was a child ached in a way they hadn't in years, as if all the broken nerve endings were linking to his brain one last time. The heat of the pain made him bite his tongue until it almost bled.

Then it was gone, and Patrick would be lying if he said he felt different, because he didn't. Nothing had changed except his perception, and maybe, finally, that could be enough.

"I'll take my daughter back," Persephone said.

Her arms slid around his, curving around the infant and pulling her out of the leather jacket she was swaddled in. Macaria looked at her with wide, disbelieving eyes, one tiny hand reaching for her mother. Persephone smiled down at her, all the love she was capable of giving there in her face for everyone to see. She let Macaria snag her finger, leaning down to press a kiss to that tiny fist.

"I've missed you so, *κόρη*."

Persephone turned away from him, lifting her head to stare at her husband, who hadn't taken his eyes off them. Hades didn't approach, allowing Persephone to come to him, and Patrick wondered how many years it would take for the goddess to forgive her husband. He wondered if spring would be a year-round season in some other world, some other place, with Hades having to abide in the chill of winter and always be on the outside looking in.

Some part of Patrick wished for that, but he knew winter wouldn't last forever.

Macaria made a soft sound that had Persephone pressing a kiss to her forehead, humming softly. Patrick stared at them, knowing he'd never see his niece again after this. But she'd been gone before her mother died, and what was left was just flesh and bone housing a goddess who'd finally come home.

"What now?" Patrick asked.

Persephone lifted her head and looked at him, every inch a queen and mother in that moment. "Hermes will guide you to where you need to be."

That didn't sound like he was being returned to his pack. Patrick glanced over at the messenger god, seeing Hermes smiling at Macaria. "Back to New York City?"

Hermes shook his head. "Not yet."

"Why the fuck not?"

"Because your twin's passage isn't complete."

Patrick looked at where Hannah's soul hovered between them, glitteringly softly, her brightness almost obscured by the hellfire burning in the background. "I thought she was staying here? I paid her way."

"This isn't where she rests." Hermes headed back to Charon's boat, waving at Patrick to follow him. "Come along, Pattycakes. A heaven of sorts awaits."

Patrick hesitated, wanting to argue, but this wasn't a fight he could win. So he took his prize of a hard-won freedom and followed Hermes to the waiting boat, Hannah's soul beside him. He let all of his family's mistakes be washed away into obscurity by the infant-turned-goddess cradled in Persephone's arms.

<h1 style="text-align:center">33</h1>

New Year's Eve came and went, and January started with a snowstorm that didn't quite make it into blizzard territory. The snow hadn't really let up since it started, results of the reactionary storm that had churned over New York City for days on end at the end of October. Jono had heard from the news and magic users with an affinity for weather magic that the weather was going to take months to return to some semblance of normal.

Wade hadn't stopped complaining about the weather, mostly because Jono insisted he dress appropriately for it.

"I don't need a coat if we're just driving Uptown," Wade groused.

Jono pulled one off the hanger in the spare bedroom's closet and tossed it at his head. Wade had basically moved into the room back in November, and the place was a right mess. Jono made an absent mental note to remind Wade to clean it up later.

"You need to at least pretend to feel the cold."

Wade dragged the coat off his head and scowled at Jono. "I'm fine."

"Wear it, or you're staying put."

Wade yanked it on with a stubborn look in his eyes. "Like hell I'm staying put. I go where you go."

Jono withheld a sigh. He'd stopped fighting Wade on that since well before the Thanksgiving holiday. Patrick's absence was still keenly felt by the entire pack, but Wade had internalized the separation to the point of codependency with Jono. They were still paying rent on his flat elsewhere in the city, but Wade had effectively moved in before the holidays. If he wasn't with Jono, he was with Sage, but he slept in the spare bedroom every night.

Jono, used to falling asleep beside Patrick and having someone else's heart beat in his ear, appreciated Wade's presence, even if he ached for the one he wanted. It had been two and a half months since Patrick had walked away from Jono and into the veil, holding Hermes' hand, and Jono was still waiting.

He would keep waiting and doing their duty as alpha of the New York City god pack until Patrick came back to him, when they could do it together. That didn't mean it was easy waking up every day and going on with his life with half his heart missing.

"Let's go," Jono said.

Wade tucked his hands into his coat pockets and followed Jono out of the flat. Jono had the keys to the Mustang in his hand, the car having been found and towed from near the Brooklyn Bridge at the beginning of December. Jono had been put on the title after Patrick was cleared of murder, so at least there'd been no trouble in retrieving it.

The snowplows had been out, and Jono could smell salt on the air from its use on the road. At least the streets were drivable these days. The last of the zombies had been cleared from them by the end of December, with bodies taken to crematoriums all down the Eastern Seaboard. Of the skeletons commanded by Andras through Ilya, what could be recovered were being repatriated back to Paris for reinternment in the Catacombs. Cargo ships had been commandeered to transport the bones, but it was a lengthy and ongoing process.

Jono wasn't involved with any of that, for which he was glad. He had enough to deal with when it came to the packs under his protection. Thankfully, Sage was a steady presence shoring him up on the days when he could do everything alone and on the days when he didn't want to. Pack was family, and he was grateful for Sage's and Wade's support.

He wasn't quite as grateful for Sage's gentle, pointed needling of what they needed to do as a pack—together—when Patrick wasn't with them.

"We need to expand," Sage said, handing him a coffee from Starbucks. He got a whiff of her scent as she leaned in close, muddled by a new perfume, he supposed.

Jono squinted at the brownstone that belonged to their god pack in Hamilton Heights and hid his frown behind the coffee cup. "You know how I feel about that."

Sage nodded as she pulled a ring of keys out of her purse and easily flipped through them for the correct one. "I know you want to wait for Patrick to return, but politics won't allow us that reprieve for much longer. We have five boroughs and over a hundred packs to rule over. We need more bodies to help us with that. If I'm getting stretched thin, I know you must be feeling worse."

Jono wasn't about to admit to that, but Sage just gave him a pointed look before letting them into a place that still stank of horror beneath the musty air. Oh, the stench wasn't as strong as it had been after Estelle had lost in the challenge ring and they'd claimed the spoils as due their right, but it still lingered. Jono rather thought it always would, or maybe it was the memories for everyone that would never leave.

The brownstones filled the entire block, having stood empty before they'd used the buildings as overflow housing for the packs who'd flown in for the fight and couldn't find decent hotels. Sage had handled all of that, but Jono could reluctantly admit that this was a problem he'd pushed off long enough.

Dust had fallen in a thin layer over everything, the months of disuse showing in the grime and the quiet. They'd closed the buildings up after everyone had left once the fight was over. Jono wasn't sure how the pipes were doing in the cold, but he couldn't smell a water leak anywhere.

Wade lightly kicked the door shut behind him, looking around with curious eyes. "This is a lot of space."

"There's more underground," Sage said.

Jono grimaced at the memory of the challenge ring with its stone seats and blood-soaked floor carved out of the earth below. "We could always turn it into storage."

"You know we can't."

"Right. Just a thought."

They had needs now as the New York City god pack, and that included a place to handle challenges, both to their rule and to the rightful, legal requests that cropped up between packs. For all that Jono wished they could mediate everything to an easy conclusion, he knew that wasn't possible. Not every problem could be solved with words, and sometimes knocking people about until they saw reason was the only answer within their community.

"I don't want to live here. I like my apartment," Wade said.

"You haven't slept in your apartment for months," Sage reminded him.

"I'll sleep there when Patrick comes back."

He said it with a surety that made Jono's mouth twitch into a bittersweet smile of agreement. Wade's belief in Patrick's return rivaled Jono's, and he knew Sage felt the same, but she was also the logical member of their pack, when sometimes, all Jono wanted to do was let his heart rule.

"There are quite a few god pack members who fought with us that have reached out and asked to return to the city and be considered as potential members of our god pack," Sage said as she gazed about the foyer they were in.

"How do their alphas feel about that?" Jono asked.

"As none of them are dires, and none of them are on the outs with their god packs in any way, there's some reluctance, but not outright anger."

"You think it's a good idea."

Sage sighed as she lifted her purse from her shoulder and set it on the credenza in the narrow hallway leading to a living room area. "I think we need to consider it. Fenrir can tell us if we can trust their intentions. He'd know if they're asking because they want to be part of our god pack to do good and not just for the status he brings us."

Because it'd been generations since a god had appeared so prominently within a god pack here. That ceded them power no other god pack currently had. They'd be bloody daft not to use the authority Fenrir provided them to do good by way of the packs within their territory and the ones who had pledged alliances with them.

Besides, Fenrir felt like he was staying. His presence hadn't gone away and the memory of him never would. The aching, burning weight of the god in his soul was something Jono knew he could carry without damage to himself. The soulbond helped with that, but so did acceptance. And one day, whenever Fenrir went away, Jono would live with the absence of him, too.

Wade crossed his arms over his chest. "What about Patrick?"

Jono rubbed his forehead, staring at the floorboards beneath his feet. The brownstone they were in still had its original interior judging by the stained and worn wood. "He'd want us to do what's good for the pack while he's not here."

"He would," Sage agreed.

Wade still looked a bit mutinous. "I want a say in whoever we pick to join."

"Of course. This is a pack decision."

Sage looked at Jono as she spoke, and he could only nod. "No one joins if we don't all agree and Fenrir gives the go-ahead."

Jono had been rather surprised that the god had stuck around after everything. Fenrir was still there in the back of his mind and soul, a presence that made himself known from time to time, but without the sharp need that had colored their interactions over the years. Jono figured killing Ethan had something to do with that.

"I can set up meetings for next week," Sage said.

Jono winced. "That soon?"

"We need more hands on deck. Emma and Leon have their own pack and PreterWorld to oversee with Marek. I don't want to keep leaning on them if we can bring in more pack members. Besides —" Her hand drifted down to press against her abdomen over her coat, a hesitant smile curving her lips. "—I'm pregnant, and there's going to come a point where I can't be racing all around the city to handle pack problems on my own."

Jono stared at her for a couple of seconds, mouth open in gobsmacked silence. Wade whooped and elbowed Jono out of the way so he could—gently—wrap Sage up in a hug. "I'm gonna be an uncle!"

Sage patted his arm, beaming at him. "Yes, you are, but you are *not* feeding my child Pop-Tarts."

"Sure," Wade said with all the blitheness of someone who had no intention of obeying that request.

Jono finally let out a surprised, wonderous laugh. "You're pregnant?"

Sage's smile never left her face. "Two weeks. I know it's really early to announce, but you'd have smelled the change anyway."

He realized it wasn't perfume after all when he'd scented her earlier and could only nod. "I smell it already."

Jono would have to find some way to give his thanks to Eir for the healing she'd done on Sage. He wasn't sure how to get in touch with the valkyries directly, but as far as he knew, Thor still had his bar in Chicago. If anyone could call the valkyries for him, it would be the Norse god of thunder.

Wade's happiness dimmed a little, but he didn't let go of Sage, keeping one arm slung over her shoulders. "I hope Patrick comes back soon. I don't want him to miss this."

None of them did. With Sage's pregnancy announcement, Jono knew he couldn't remain stagnant as they worked toward a future they'd fought too hard for to give up. They needed a firmly established pack to keep their territory and to provide stability and support for Sage's baby.

To do that, they had to put in the work and keep believing that Patrick would return soon. Having a pack was a dream he'd had since first being infected with the werevirus, and Jono wasn't going to give it up now. Because if there was one thing Jono had learned over the lonely weeks of digging out of the aftermath of worldly change, it was that you held on to the truth in the stories like the history they were—and you never let go.

Legends were the building blocks of this reborn world, and Jono still believed Patrick would come back to him. They all did.

He went to Sage and wrapped her up in a hug, breathing in the changed scent of her, knowing he'd do anything to keep her and her baby safe.

"Tell me who you think will be a good fit for our pack," Jono murmured.

She patted him on the back, face tucked against his neck, breathing in his scent the way he was with hers. "Of course."

Wade sidled up close, and Jono freed one arm enough to drag him into the hug, holding on to his growing pack, acutely aware of the arms they were missing.

## 34

GINNUNGAGAP had escaped with minimal damage during the battle all those months ago. Jono hadn't felt the yawning abyss between his teeth since the fight at the Battery. He was sure it had gone where many of the gods had retreated to—somewhere past the veil, out of reach, except in stories. Reachable only by way of prayer.

That wasn't to say the club had been abandoned. Jono knew Lucien had upped the admission price at the beginning of the year and was raking in money. New Yorkers weren't about to let a fight between gods at the end of the world keep them from living their lives.

Vampires had gained a bit more notoriety after the battle, having been seen clearly fighting on the right side for once. Lucien might have a century of freedom to do as he pleased within the United States' borders, but Jono didn't doubt he'd capitalize on the current trend of favorable public opinion toward vampires to cause trouble everywhere.

"I don't know why we have to meet with Lucien," Wade grumbled.

"Pass-through rights won't bargain themselves," Jono said.

"But we *had* pass-through rights."

"And now we're renegotiating them."

Wade muttered something rude under his breath that Jono ignored. He locked the Mustang with a push of a button on the fob and headed for the side door in the alley. It was half past thirteen, and Sage had reminded him twice in the last hour not to miss the meeting. She had a court hearing that afternoon, which was why she wasn't with them, but she'd left explicit instructions on a voicemail that they weren't allowed to start a war with the Night Courts without her say-so.

Wade was just a bit stroppy about that.

Truthfully, Jono didn't want her anywhere near vampires while she was pregnant, so he was fine with her absence. Marek was even worse. Her husband would be happy if she never wanted to leave their home so he could pay people to cater to her every whim throughout her pregnancy. Marek was far more overprotective than Jono, and that was saying something, because Jono felt savage sometimes when people got too close to Sage.

Wade, though. Wade was worse than either of them. Jono had already had a chat with him about how he wasn't allowed to hoard the baby once they were born.

The side door opened before they reached it, Carmen leaning out of the doorway. The hem of her fur coat would've touched the ground if the heels on her boots weren't so neck-breaking high. March was still cold in New York, and she was dressed for winter rather than spring.

Her curly black hair was swept into a thick side braid, while the horns of her kind curved over her skull. One horn ended halfway, broken off during the fight last autumn. She'd covered the jagged end with a silver cap adorned with diamonds. Jono thought it was bloody gaudy, and the silver made his nose itch, but it suited her tastes.

"You're early," Carmen said, her gaze flickering about them before snapping back to Jono. "Still no Patrick?"

Jono shrugged. "He'll be back."

"It's been five months."

"And if it takes five more, then we'll just keep waiting. He's coming back."

Jono tried not to think too much of the passage of time. The snow and sludge still lining the streets helped with that. The winter snows had leveled off, but spring was still some ways off. Jono thought he could see the passage of time in Central Park when he went for a run in the mornings and in the way Sage's stomach had grown some with her unborn child.

"You do realize he's going to have a lot of people to report to once he returns. We'll be one of them."

Jono said nothing to that, well aware that when Patrick returned, the pack would have to share his attention with every level of government still clamoring for answers. Patrick's absence was noted by many, and even Reed had quit calling every day, resorting to a weekly checkup through Wade of all people.

"We're here about the pass-through rights you wanted to discuss. The least you could do is offer us a pint," Jono said.

"We drink with friends, not you."

Carmen still let them step inside. Jono and Wade entered without hesitation, Ginnungagap having long since lost any stigma of fear for them. They followed her into the main level of the well-lit club.

Lucien waited for them at the bar on the ground floor, leaning back against it with both elbows on the counter. Naheed sat on a barstool beside him, handgun resting on the counter within easy reach. A faint bruise was layered over the bite scars on her neck, proof that Lucien had fed and a mark of his favor she always seemed proud to wear.

"Took you long enough," Lucien said.

Jono shrugged, his attention lingering on the wounds Lucien

had sustained last autumn. The left side of the master vampire's face was heavily scarred, pulling at the corner of his mouth, the burn scars cascading down his neck. The damage disappeared beneath the collar of the motorcycle jacket he wore, painful-looking even after the months that had passed.

Jono was honestly surprised Lucien had survived Ethan's attack. He'd expected the master vampire to be a casualty in the end, but Lucien had proven to be a survivor the same way Ashanti was.

Government-paid healers had done their best to render aid to Lucien. In the end, full healing would take time. Lucien might be a daywalker and the last vampire Ashanti had directly sired, but he wasn't a god. He was *something* though, Jono could reluctantly admit these days, because Lucien would never have walked away from that fight with Ethan in one piece. Jono suspected Lucien's degree of closeness to a goddess had aided his survival.

Jono hadn't seen the mother of all vampires since she'd said her goodbyes at the start of the new year and gone to travel the world to reconnect with her children. Ashanti had done her duty by them and won the prize she was after. Her gamble of throwing her support behind Patrick all these years had given her an eternity of prayers, both for herself and her children.

Vampires would continue to thrive now that Ethan's hell would never come to pass. Jono couldn't say he was *thrilled* about that, but his pack would handle the threat they represented, like they always did.

"We aren't late," Jono said, coming to a stop out of reach of Lucien. He would never trust Lucien, and standing more than arms' distance away from the arsehole was Jono's preferred spot to have a conversation.

"Now that you're here, we can get down to business." Lucien's black eyes narrowed some as he stared at Jono. "I hear you're expanding your pack."

"That's not your business."

Lucien smirked, the expression garish against the backdrop of scars. "My Night Court is leaving New York. I have business in South America I need to handle."

"So you're giving up your territory?"

"No. I'm never giving up the Manhattan Night Court."

Jono blinked at him. "You won't be here to claim it."

"You seem to forget how many people are beholden to me. Manhattan is mine and always will be. Whatever we agree to today will hold until I return."

"And if you don't return for a couple of decades?" Wade asked.

Lucien stared unblinkingly at them. "Going to miss me?"

"Not on your undead life."

Lucien shrugged, wrapping an arm around Carmen as she sidled up to him. "I won't be leaving any of my Night Court behind. Where I go, they go, but the territory here belongs to me. Make sure your god pack remembers that over the years."

Lucien's assumption that Jono's god pack would be ruling for a long time was flattering in a way, but they had no guarantee of continued rule.

"Are you leaving behind a proxy?" Jono asked.

"The Night Courts within the five boroughs are proxy enough."

Jono knew from experience the remaining Night Courts weren't to be trusted. It wasn't trust that drove Lucien to appoint them as proxy but necessity. The vampires who called New York City home knew what Lucien had done to Tremaine last year. Jono had a feeling the Night Courts would toe the line for some years before they started testing the boundaries of Lucien's absence.

"Fine. The territory borders and pass-through rights remain the same as previously negotiated."

Jono would keep his word on that, if only because it would provide them leverage down the line whenever Lucien returned. The master vampire couldn't cry foul and go on a killing spree if Jono could prove they'd kept to the terms of the bargain.

He didn't think it would be too much of a problem, at least in the near future. When the werecreature community had fought side by side with the Night Courts, it had produced a wary sort of respect for each other's spaces. He knew it wouldn't last—nothing like that ever did—but it was one less thing to worry about as his god pack settled in for the long haul.

"Tell Patrick I owe him nothing," Lucien said.

"If you go after him when he returns, I'll eat you," Wade shot back.

Lucien laughed, the sound low and raspy as he straightened up. "You can try."

Jono held up a hand toward Wade, and for once, the teen listened to the silent command and kept his gob shut.

"Patrick never owed you anything to begin with, no matter what you both thought. Keep your side of this agreement, we'll keep ours, and you'll have a city to come back to when you're done traipsing about the world," Jono said to Lucien.

The master vampire held still for a long minute, not even bothering with the pretense of breathing. When he finally spoke, the anger Jono expected was missing.

"You know he might not come back," Lucien said. "But I will."

Jono tugged lightly on the soulbond, the ragged end drifting to nothing on the other side where Patrick should be. It'd been months, and the emptiness hadn't changed, but neither had Jono's belief in a promise made.

"Patrick will always come back. When he does, we'll be waiting for whenever you return."

"Not if you're both dead."

"Then *I'll* be waiting," Wade said, showing off his teeth, brown eyes flashing gold.

As goodbyes went, Jono wouldn't lose any sleep over Lucien's absence in New York City. In the end, his pack was staying, Lucien was leaving, and Jono would keep waiting as long as it took for Patrick to come back to him.

## 35

"DID YOU HAVE TO PICK THE ROUTE UP A FUCKING MOUNTAIN TO GET us to Asgard? Couldn't you have picked the shortcut?" Patrick gasped out as he rounded the curve of yet another switchback in the steep road. "They have a rainbow bridge. We could've used that."

Hermes looked over his shoulder, the messenger god not even close to being out of breath. "You should probably look into exercising more. I hear it's good for your health."

Patrick flipped Hermes off before taking a moment to lean against his knees and pant for breath. "Fuck you."

"Your wolf wouldn't approve."

"Fuck you *even more.*"

"Hurry up, Pattycakes. We're almost there."

Straightening up, Patrick pressed his hands to the small of his back and arched his spine to get it to pop. His legs hurt, his feet were sore, and he wanted nothing more than to return past the veil to his pack. Except he'd spent what felt like days walking through the veil after Hermes, only pausing to rest for short periods. It hadn't been enough to get rid of Patrick's exhaustion or the knowledge that every day he spent past the veil, he lost weeks back on Earth.

The only reason he hadn't given up was the faint flicker of Hannah's soul that had never left his side. What he owed her kept Patrick pushing on, so he wiped sweat off his forehead and trudged after Hermes for the gates that led to Asgard.

The mountain they'd climbed towered over a fjord far below. Patrick couldn't see the sapphire waters, hidden as they were by the fog that snaked through the otherworldly inlet. He could still make out the strange, twisted roots that stretched the height of the impossible mountain, ever present in their climb.

When they finally reached the top of the mountain, Patrick was greeted with a regal nod from Thor. Brynhildr, seated astride her pegasus and dressed in her traditional armor as opposed to the motorcycle leathers she was partial to when on the road, offered up a gentle smile.

"Well met, cousin," Thor said.

"Your heaven would've been easier to find if the veil wasn't such a mess. You should do something about that. Maybe have Yggdrasil set down some more roots," Hermes replied.

"What makes you think the world tree hasn't already done so?"

Hermes chuckled, clearly amused by Thor's announcement. Patrick ignored them, tired of the gods and the games they played, no longer obligated to worry about their words and intentions.

He drifted away from their conversation. The small terrace they stood on was covered in vibrant green grass that ran right up against the wall surrounding Asgard and to the cliff's edge that offered up a view of an endless night sky. The jagged shape of mountains reaching for eternity was breathtaking, and Patrick knew he'd never forget the sight of them. Heaven, he supposed, was many things to many people, and here it was a world one step removed from the memories that had once shaped it.

"I hear tell you've paid your soul debt after all these years," Thor said from behind him.

Patrick turned to look at the god, finding the trio had come to join him at the precipice. "I'm done fighting."

Thor raised an eyebrow, then held up his hand, palm up. "If that is the case, then I will relieve you of your weapon."

Patrick hesitated, thinking of Jono, but reached instead for the dagger strapped to his thigh rather than the soulbond. He unsheathed the blade, going through the motions one last time. He stared at the gods-given dagger, watching as silvery words in languages he couldn't read floated across the matte-black blade. A hint of heavenly white fire flickered against the sharp edge before fading away, leaving nothing behind.

The weight of it in his hand came not from metal but from guilt, because a part of him would always remember what the prayers in the dagger had cost. Drawing in a harsh breath, Patrick spun the dagger around one final time before handing it to Thor, hilt first.

"Take it," Patrick said.

Thor's fingers were warm when they brushed against Patrick's palm as he retrieved it. The absence of the dagger had him floundering for a second, panic gripping his chest hard before he shoved it aside. That weapon was no longer his to wield, and he refused to mourn its loss.

Thor turned the dagger this way and that, staring at it with an appraising eye. "I remember when I prayed for this."

"Were your prayers answered?"

Thor tucked the dagger into a metal-lined leather loop on his belt, the cross guard helping to keep it secured in place. "Well enough."

It wasn't praise—it wasn't even a thank-you—but Patrick let the acknowledgment wash over him anyway. He'd made his own road to this moment, and Patrick refused to apologize for the choices he'd made over the years when it came to fighting his family for the sake of all the gods' remembrances.

Patrick cleared his throat and looked at Hermes. "You said Hannah's way was paid."

"I didn't lie," Hermes said.

"So what now?"

When Hermes smiled, it seemed to soften his gaze for once, eyes filled with a grace that brushed up against some kind of forgiveness. "Now you say goodbye."

Patrick stared at where Hannah's soul floated beside him. As he watched, the edges seemed to take the shape of a child for a moment, an afterimage of a life that never got to be lived. He reached for her on instinct, fingers shaking, so close but always so far. Standing there at the cliff's edge, Patrick could only do what he'd always done with his twin sister.

He let her go.

Hannah's soul seemed to contract before disintegrating into nothing but starlight. Patrick's hand closed on emptiness in the space that had always existed between them since that fateful night so long ago.

"I'm sorry," Patrick said through the unholy grief that filled his body in that moment. "I never stopped wanting to save you."

"She knows," Thor said kindly before nodding at what remained of his sister. "Come, child. It is time."

The shimmer of Hannah's soul darted through the air to Brynhildr, who cradled the remnants close to her chest with a careful hand. "I'll guide her home."

"Where are you taking her?" Patrick asked.

"Your twin was god-touched. She died in the battle over her soul." Brynhildr smiled, the gentle curve of her mouth a bittersweet victory for the dead. "Valhalla awaits her."

The pegasus' wings flapped hard in the air, gaining altitude with long sweeps that sent the grass rippling like the sea. They rose into the air, higher and higher, until their passage was obscured by Yggdrasil's branches stretched over the golden city, forever lost to sight.

Patrick opened his mouth, but nothing came out, and everything he'd ever wanted to say to Hannah would stay with him to be said over her grave. In the quiet, beneath an eternal sky, Patrick bore witness to a farewell at the edge of the world, death a companion to the bitter, haunting end.

"Just one more thing, Pattycakes," Hermes said.

Patrick dragged his gaze away from the stars, blinking the blurriness at the edge of his vision to something stronger. "What?"

Hermes smirked, laughter in his voice. "Tell your wolf I said hello."

Then Hermes shoved Patrick off the edge of the world, and gravity caught him tight in its grip, never letting go in the long descent to Earth through the veil. The howling wind stole Patrick's voice as he fell from Asgard into an ocean of regrets found between the roots of the world tree, the water closing over his head and the surface nowhere to be found.

36

THE AIR IN EARLY APRIL WAS CRISP FROM A FADING WINTER, THE smell of spring gaining ground. Slush was melting in the gutters and the sidewalks, on occasion revealing bits of bodies not recovered in the initial clean-up. Luckily the protective wards on Tempest blocked that smell, though they couldn't block Wade when he sneaked inside.

Jono gave him a stern look across the bar counter as Wade scrambled onto a stool beside Sage. "You're not supposed to be in here."

"Yeah, I know, but it's important." Wade planted his elbows on the bar counter, held up his mobile, and pointed at the screen, eyes wide as he stared accusingly at Jono. "What is this?"

Jono glanced at the title of the email showing up and raised an eyebrow. "Your summer classes sign-up confirmation."

"I can see that. Funny how I didn't sign up for any but *somehow* got an email about it."

"Funny how that works," Sage replied calmly as she sipped at her sparkling water. "You're going. You have classes to make up."

"But what about summer break?"

"That's what the weekends are for when you aren't studying."

Wade groaned and let his head fall to the bar counter. "That's so unfair."

"Education is important. We're planning for yours the same way we're planning for our daughter's."

Wade grumbled wordlessly into the wood, clearly not of the same opinion. Sage took education seriously though, and Jono was happy to let her steer Wade where he needed to go in that regard.

The trio of witches seated three spots down from Sage caught Jono's attention, raising their empty drink glasses in a hopeful manner. Jono went to take their next order and bus the empties, going through the motions of working behind the counter on a busy Friday night.

Tempest had turned into the place to be over the last few months. It was no longer just a bar catering to the werecreature community. Coven members, fae, others of supernatural background, and even on occasion vampires could be found walking through the doors. Jono made it a point to welcome everyone. The bar was still considered neutral territory and the place where his god pack handled territory disputes.

Jono and Sage still mostly handled the decision-making in that area, though they'd started delegating more responsibilities to Camilo Rivera, Sahil Agarwal, and Linh Nguyen. The three new god pack members they'd accepted into their god pack after a rigorous interview process had settled in well over the past few weeks. They came with good recommendations from their former god packs, and Fenrir had approved of them, but Jono still worried about what Patrick would think.

The fleeting thought about Patrick came and went, less agonizing than it used to be. Jono didn't spend every moment of the day thinking about his lover, though it had taken time to get to that point. It was going on six months without seeing Patrick's face in person and not in photos on his mobile. People had stopped asking him about Patrick, and he'd gotten used to the pitying looks sometimes thrown his way.

Jono knew Patrick wasn't dead or missing, merely gone to do his duty. He didn't care what the world thought, and neither did Sage or Wade. They'd keep vigil in his absence, but they couldn't stop living their lives. Jono knew Patrick wouldn't want that for them. And while it got lonely, especially at night, Jono got up every morning, ready to face the day.

"Can't I have one summer off?" Wade whinged, finally sitting up.

"Sure," Sage said. "Next year, if you pass all your classes during the normal semesters."

Wade looked absolutely put out and shot Jono a pleading look he refused to succumb to. Jono shook his head. "You know what Sage says goes."

Wade sighed loudly. "I know."

His sulk lasted only about thirty more seconds, because that's when Jono caught the smell of tacos. Leon traversed the crowd in front of the bar, arms held above his head, takeaway bags dangling from both hands.

"I brought dinner," Leon announced.

"We both did," Emma said, squeezing between Sage and Wade. She deposited the largest bag in front of Wade. "We got extra, so you can have this one."

"You're my favorite," Wade said. Then he ripped open the plastic like it was the enemy and dug in.

"And then you need to leave."

"I take it back. The tacos are my favorite."

Emma leaned over the counter and offered Jono a carton, but he shook his head. "Let me finish up a few more drinks, then I'll eat with you."

She set the carton on the counter and passed out a couple more. The smell of meat and salsa filled the immediate area, reminding Jono that lunch had been hours ago. He hurried through making a couple more drinks, the other two bartenders on duty glad for the help. He made a mental note of some of the emptier alcohol bottles that needed a replenish. He'd have to make sure they made it on the order list for tomorrow.

Jono ducked out from behind the bar and slid through the crowd to where his pack was clustered. Linh had arrived in the few minutes he'd been helping customers, and the petite Vietnamese woman flashed him a quick smile from her spot behind Emma. Linh was older than him by five years, but she certainly didn't look it. She'd been the first they'd accepted into their god pack, a weregrizzly who had become a steady, reliable member over the last two months.

"Camilo wanted me to let you know he's running a little late but he'll be here. There's a delay in the subway," Linh said, bright amber eyes reflecting the light in the bar.

"Typical for the subway," Jono said.

"I drove, so if you want me to take Wade home, I can."

"After I finish my tacos," Wade mumbled around a half-eaten al pastor one.

"You can finish the rest at home. I don't want to risk a fine with you being underage. Even Casale can't turn a blind eye to that," Jono told him.

"I can't believe I can fight the denizens of hell, but I can't sit in my pack's bar and share a meal with them."

Jono would've responded to that if it didn't suddenly feel as if he were being stabbed in the chest. Searing pain radiated through his ribs and down his arms and legs. The agony of it had him doubling over, unable to breathe, lungs on fire as the soulbond suddenly snapped into place in a way it hadn't for months and *months*. Frantic voices were a muddled mess in his ears, hands grabbing at him as he went to one knee, still clutching at his chest.

He couldn't breathe, couldn't call out the only name that had a place in the prayers he always said alone.

Then the veil ripped open in the air above everyone's heads, and a veritable waterfall of icy liquid crashed down. Jono breathed in water and coughed hard to clear it from his lungs, ducking his head to try to keep his mouth and nose free of it. Wade's hand wrapped around his upper arm in a bruising grip, keeping him upright as too many others were taken down to the floor.

"Mother*fucker*. I'm going to punch that bastard in the face if I ever see him again."

Jono's heart stuttered out of rhythm in his chest, the sheer joy of hearing that voice in his ears again enough to make him choke on a giddy laugh that came out on a name.

*"Patrick."*

Jono wrenched free of Wade and twisted around. His gaze landed on the figure sprawled on Tempest's floor, ginger hair slicked to his skull, soaked clothes the same as he'd worn back during the fight on Samhain half a year ago.

Jono didn't know he'd moved until he blinked, already reaching for Patrick, desperate to touch, to make sure this wasn't a dream. He wrapped one hand around the collar of Patrick's shirt, hauling him up so Jono could cradle the back of his head with the other and kiss him until it hurt to breathe.

Patrick let out a surprised sound that never escaped their mouths before sinking into the kiss. His hands found their way to Jono's hair, gripping tight, and Jono would've leaned into the touch if he wasn't so focused on trying to breathe for the both of them.

When air became a necessity, Jono broke the kiss with a ragged gasp, pressing his forehead to Patrick's, staring into those green eyes he'd missed so much. "You came back."

Patrick's hands slid down his face to cradle his jaw, fingers shaking. "I told you I would."

Jono nodded jerkily before pulling away enough to look at him. He drank in the sight of the man he loved, searching for wounds and finding none. Patrick stared back at him with a tired smile on his face, looking somehow lighter than he ever had before, as if all that had dragged him down over the years had finally set him free.

"Hey," Patrick said, his thumbs framing Jono's mouth, eyes searching his. "I love you."

Jono didn't think love should ever hurt, but it gutted him right then—the best kind of pain, the ache that said *I'm here, I'm alive, I'm with you.* Jono blinked wetness out of his eyes that he'd blame on the salt water he could taste on his lips.

"I love you too," Jono rasped out before kissing Patrick again and again and again.

"You can stop *anytime* now," Wade said loudly, the rapid tap of his foot against the ground reaching Jono's ears. "It's my turn to hug him."

Jono reluctantly stopped kissing Patrick, loath to let him go, but Wade looked about one second away from tossing Jono aside on his arse if he didn't get his hands on Patrick. Jono let go of Patrick's shirt and grabbed his hand instead, refusing to let go completely. Wade threw himself between them, wrapping both arms around Patrick and squeezing him so tight Jono thought he heard a bone pop.

"I'm so glad you're back," Wade said, sounding almost giddy, which was at odds with how hard he clung to Patrick.

Patrick wrapped his free arm around Wade. The hug went on for nearly a minute before Sage pointedly cleared her throat. "My turn."

Wade wriggled out of Patrick's hold but didn't go far. Sage eased down to her knees beside them, and Jono saw the moment Patrick realized Sage was pregnant. Distress lanced through the bitterness of his scent, and Jono gently squeezed his hand.

"You're pregnant!" Patrick said, reaching toward her stomach and the soft curve there. "How long have I been gone?"

Sage grabbed his hand and pressed it against her baby bump, smiling brilliantly despite the tears in her eyes. "Six months, but that doesn't matter. You're here now."

She folded Patrick into a sideways hug, and Jono could see how gingerly Patrick touched her, a raw look in his eyes now that he knew how much time he'd lost. Sage didn't care, kneeling on the wet ground to hug him as tightly as Wade had. Patrick couldn't hold out against that, and he stopped trying, though his grip in Jono's hand was tight enough to hurt if Jono cared about things like that.

When Sage shifted away, Marek was there to help her to her feet. Jono used that brief lull to stand up and pull Patrick with him. Patrick shivered a little from the cold, and Jono wrapped his arms around him in a tight hug, burying his nose into wet ginger hair, taking a moment to breathe him in and listen to that missed heartbeat.

"Where did you go that I couldn't follow?" Jono murmured.

Patrick's hands dug into his back, a ragged breath gusting over Jono's collarbone. "Hell, then heaven. I brought Macaria home, and then I laid my sister to rest."

"And your soul debt?"

"Paid in full."

The soft confession had Jono holding him even tighter, squeezing his eyes shut. The disbelieving wonder in Patrick's voice came through in his scent as well. Jono basked in the knowledge that the gods could ask for whatever they wanted now, and Patrick could finally say no.

Patrick pulled back with a hard sniff, the wetness in his eyes making the green there brighter. "What did I miss?"

All the words jumbled together on Jono's tongue, and for a moment, he wasn't sure where to start. He just knew he didn't want to let Patrick go ever again.

"I'll tell you when we get home," Jono said.

Patrick's face lit up at that. "Yeah. Yeah, that sounds great. Let's go home."

"I'm going with you," Wade said quickly.

"I'll drive Sage," Marek offered.

Jono nodded, barely listening, refusing to take his eyes off Patrick for longer than necessary. He had an irrational fear that if he looked away, Patrick would disappear again, even though he knew that wouldn't happen here. The tear in the veil had closed, and when Patrick left this time, Jono would go with him.

Sage got everyone sorted, though Jono could see Patrick's confusion at Linh's presence and her deference to Sage. A proper introduction would have to wait until later—so many things would have to wait until later—because right now, Jono just wanted to get Patrick *home*.

They stumbled out of Tempest, Patrick shivering in his soaked clothes as they walked the half block to the car. Wade nicked the keys from Jono's pocket to get the doors unlocked. He climbed into the back seat, and Patrick half collapsed into the front passenger one. The second Jono was behind the steering wheel and pulling into the street, he reached for Patrick's hand, unsurprised to see him reaching back.

Jono kept his eyes on the road for the entire drive back to the flat out of sheer will alone. He still ran three red lights, cut off ten cars, and pissed off more than one taxi driver.

"Next time, I'll drive," Wade announced once they were parked a block away from the flat in Chelsea.

"Did you get your license already?" Patrick asked.

"Nope."

"Then you're not driving."

Jono listened to the pair argue all the way to the front door of the flat, the happiness radiating from both of them putting a smile on his face. Wade kept brushing against Patrick, who didn't mind the encroachment of his space at all. Once they were in the flat, and Patrick was dripping seawater all over the floor, Jono snapped out of his daze.

"Let's get you washed up. You need a hot shower and a change of clothes," Jono said.

Patrick shrugged out of his leather jacket, Wade snagging it with eager hands. "You don't have to tell me twice."

Jono left Wade to figure out dinner with Sage when she arrived while he ushered Patrick into their bedroom's master bathroom. The clothes he wore were filthy, and Jono made the executive decision to bin the lot while Patrick stepped under the hot shower spray to get clean. When he picked up the leather sheath along with Patrick's ruined jeans, he realized it was empty.

"Where's your dagger?" Jono asked.

Patrick squinted through the shampoo suds running down his face, his features a little blurred through the plastic shower curtain. "I gave it back to the gods. I don't need it anymore."

Jono ran a finger along the length of one strap. "So it's really over."

The rattle of the shower curtain being shoved aside had him looking back. Patrick leaned over the tub, beckoning him closer, and Jono went where he was always wanted. Patrick's hand curved over the back of his neck, pulling Jono down into a kiss that was fiercer than the ones they'd shared in the bar. Jono stepped closer, hands resting on slick skin as he let Patrick take what he wanted.

"It's over," Patrick affirmed when he broke the kiss, a weariness to his voice that was for Jono's ears alone.

His scent was a tangle of emotions that filled Jono's nose, and none of it could be sorted right then. Best they could do was take it one day at a time, but Jono was okay with that, because he knew that every morning when he woke up from here on out, Patrick would be lying beside him once again.

They'd face the future how they always had—together.

"Finish up so we can chat," Jono said as he stepped back. "There's loads I have to tell you."

Patrick nodded, a smile lingering on his mouth as he twitched the shower curtain closed again. Jono hummed softly under his breath as he went to retrieve a set of clean clothes for Patrick, the soulbond singing between them.

<h1 style="text-align:center">37</h1>

WASHINGTON, DC, IN MAY WAS MUGGIER THAN USUAL, THE CHANGE linked to the reactionary storms from last year. Patrick knew from experience it would take time for the weather systems to rebalance themselves. He was just grateful the national headquarters for the SOA had air-conditioning.

Sitting in front of the desk that Setsuna used to inhabit and which Priya had taken over was bittersweet in a way. For him, Setsuna's death felt as if it had been yesterday, when in reality for him, it was a month, while for everyone else, it was half a year. The horrific tearing of the veil during Samhain meant Patrick had lost months and months while gone.

He tried not to feel terrible about something out of his control. His pack had managed well enough in his absence, and Patrick knew they'd missed him, but being gone for six months was still a long time. It was even longer for the government.

"I wasn't hiding. I don't see why Congress can't understand that. It's not like this was the first time the veil tore on Earth," Patrick said irritably.

Priya hummed thoughtfully as she flipped through Patrick's

report on her desk. It was incredibly thick and had taken Patrick nearly a week to write up after his reappearance had hit the news and gone viral. Since then, he'd spent just as much time in DC as he had in New York.

"It's the first time you weren't around to issue an after-action report. As you were the lynchpin of everything that occurred, you can understand why Congress has been champing at the bit to complete their investigation," Priya said.

"Our reports weren't good enough?" Jono asked from his spot on the chair next to Patrick's.

He tightened his grip on Jono's thigh, not caring that it wasn't professional to touch each other like this in front of the Director of the Supernatural Operations Agency. He wasn't ready to let go yet, especially after the six hours he'd spent getting interrogated by senators. Patrick's debrief by officers in the Pentagon had happened yesterday, and he was feeling more than a little worn-out. It was his third debrief in as many weeks, and he was honestly tired of it.

"Your reports over the last several months have been acceptable for the most part, but you and your pack aren't Collins," Priya said.

Patrick slumped in his chair, sighing loudly. He'd missed a lot, and something he regretted about his absence was the absolute hell his pack had gone through in the political and military circles. When the earthly powers that be wanted answers, they weren't above harassing people to get them.

Priya closed the report and set it aside, the Eyes Only stamp on the front cover a glaring red against the black text. "As glad as I am that you returned, we do need to discuss your standing within the agency."

He was still technically a special agent, but he hadn't been assigned any case since his return, remaining on paid administrative duty. Considering how many directions he was being pulled in, it was probably for the best.

"Setsuna gave me my badge and gun back last year," Patrick said.

"I'm aware of what her reasoning was for that."

Patrick chewed on his bottom lip, staring at Priya. The last time he'd been in this office, Setsuna had sat behind the desk. The walls had carried her accomplishments, the shelves had held pictures of her life. Now, the space was inhabited by Priya, having officially been appointed to the directorship in Patrick's absence. This space was hers now, and he hadn't realized how much he'd missed what it had been until he'd walked inside and saw what it had become.

"You don't agree with her decision," Patrick said slowly.

Priya didn't blink. "It's very clear that you were integral to winning the fight in Manhattan against Ethan and the Dominion Sect. It is also clear that you were the underlying catalyst."

Jono sat up straighter, bristling. "That's a load of bollocks. You can't blame Ethan's actions on Patrick."

"I'm not. I'm merely stating it was his family which prompted everything that happened. He can't untie himself from that."

"And you don't want the SOA tied to it any more than it already has been, right?" Patrick asked, trying not to sound bitter and failing miserably.

"The SOA is tied to you and what happened no matter what. But the sheer breadth of what occurred and who you associate with means any case you handle will forever have the stigma of bias over it. Any prosecutor worth their salt will ask for a dismissal on the grounds you can't be trusted simply because of the information you've held back over the years."

Patrick glanced at Jono. "Didn't I tell you last year I was going to get fired?"

"I'm not firing you, Collins."

"It sure sounds like you are."

Priya shook her head. "You can't be a field agent, not how you were, but that doesn't mean the SOA won't have use for you. There are other areas your skills can be used in."

"Like what?"

"Your unique position within the preternatural community and the supernatural world lends itself well to rooting out domestic terror threats. You've made inroads with groups we've always had a difficult time accessing."

Patrick frowned, staring at her. "It sounds like you want me working in the Counterintelligence Division. That's still field-work. My bias would still be at issue."

Priya held up a finger. "Not if you're in a supervisory role and if the outreach is done in defense of national security. You've already proven your loyalty in that regard."

"There are still politicians who think I'm a liar."

"And there are more who don't want to see you driven out with pitchforks. Setsuna never wanted that either. What you bring to the table is too valuable to lose."

Patrick managed not to flinch at her words, but it was a near thing. "You mean the alliances my pack claim are too valuable to lose."

"Yes."

At least she didn't sugarcoat the reasoning, but the thought of using the people who had helped them fight against Ethan and the Dominion Sect left a sour taste in Patrick's mouth. "That's a lateral move any way you look at it, and there are a lot of people in the government who will fight you on that placement for me."

"It's a fight we're prepared to take on."

"That's great and all, but I'm not leaving New York. I won't leave my pack."

"I'm not asking you to. I'm just asking you to think about staying on."

He no longer needed to hide behind his badge to survive. Working for the SOA had been a career he'd taken pride in, the same way he'd taken pride in the Mage Corps. While he wasn't sure he wanted to give it all up just yet, he was never going to give up being an alpha of the New York City god pack. He'd had his fill of politics—both the government's and the gods'—and Patrick really just wanted a break. Some time to process everything and heal.

"I will," Patrick said after a pause. "Think about it, I mean."

Priya nodded, looking pleased. "Good."

"It'll be a while before I can give you an answer though."

"Take all the time you need."

"About that. Once I'm finished with Congress and our pack issues have been taken care, I'll be taking a leave of absence."

"Send me the paperwork and I'll push it through when you're ready. I may still need you to be available for congressional reasons if anything comes up while you're on leave."

"Sure, just not when I'm on vacation."

"Oh? Where are you going?"

Patrick couldn't keep the wistfulness out of his voice as he glanced at Jono. "Maui."

---

THE CHERRY blossom trees in the Congressional Cemetery were in full bloom when Patrick laid flowers on Setsuna's grave. The stone monument standing watch over her final resting place was simple in design and had her name carved into the marble, but no one else's. It wasn't her family's plot, only hers, but being buried here in the city she'd lived most of her life in had been her choice.

Priya had told him Setsuna had been cremated after the fight in Manhattan. Her peers had seen her laid to rest according to Shinto practices, body cremated before being placed in an urn that was buried in the ground. A fund had been created to provide fresh flowers once a week for a year after her death, and Patrick already had plans to continue that tradition when the money ran out.

He'd been surprised when, a few weeks back, Priya had given

him a tiny ceramic vial containing a small amount of Setsuna's ashes, a request from those of her family still living that he have something to remember her by for his own shrine. Patrick wasn't much for prayers these days, but the space where Ashanti's altar had once stood was more than good enough for Setsuna's ashes.

He stepped off the grave to return to his spot between Jono and Sage, who had one hand resting beneath her baby bump in an almost unconscious gesture. Wade stood on her other side, fidgeting with the ties on his hoodie. The core of their god pack had been able to travel to DC with him because Linh and the others had stayed behind.

Patrick was still getting used to the new members of their god pack. Admittedly, he'd been a little shocked that their pack had grown in his absence, but he trusted the decisions that had been made. It wasn't like they could remain four people forever, not with the size of the city they had to rule over.

Jono slipped his arm over Patrick's shoulders, pulling him close. Patrick leaned into the touch and let his head rest for a few seconds on Jono's shoulder.

"I miss her," Patrick admitted quietly.

"I know, love," Jono murmured.

He didn't think he would ever miss her the way he did these days, and that made her absence so much worse in a way. He still had nightmares about the night she was shot, and the guilt was always worse after those. But Patrick was talking to his therapist, while Jono was always there to comfort him, and he had his pack. Crawling out of the black pit he sometimes found himself in was getting easier.

Patrick stared at Setsuna's grave for a few minutes longer, thinking about all the things he never got to say to her, wondering if she'd hear them now if he spoke them here. If not today, then maybe the next time he visited DC.

He had time.

"Ready?" Jono asked, rubbing his arm.

Patrick nodded. "Yeah."

They walked away from her grave, the rawness of her passing momentarily soothed by the company he kept. As they headed down the sloped hill for the road, Patrick caught sight of a woman standing beneath the branches of the cherry trees, the gentle breeze shaking petals down upon her.

"Oh, bloody hell," Jono said, scowling.

Patrick didn't know why his pack was bristling at the presence of a stranger whose face he couldn't make out, but then the crackle of ozone pricked against his skin, and he knew.

"Persephone," Patrick said warily once they came to a stop near her.

The Greek goddess of spring smiled, looking happier and brighter than he'd ever seen her before. "Hello, Patrick."

His attention drifted from Persephone to the infant she cradled, Macaria's tiny face turned to look at him. She looked at peace in her mother's arms, the flicker of her godhead burning through her aura, whole in a way it hadn't been while brutalized by Ethan's greed.

"I thought my soul debt was paid?"

"It is. I'm not here to ask anything of you."

"Then why stop by at all?" Jono asked rudely.

Persephone glanced down at her daughter, stroking a finger gently over her chubby cheek. "Because I have one last thing to give Patrick."

"Nope. Patrick doesn't want it," Wade said quickly.

"Wade," Sage said warningly.

He scowled at her, clearly sulking. "No more gods is our pack's motto. We agreed on that last month."

"Hush."

"What is it?" Patrick asked, wanting to get it over with and move on. This time, he wasn't bleeding at Persephone's feet. This time, he had his pack with him. This time, he could say no and survive whatever came after.

"I gave you your life, and you lived it well. We gods gave you the dagger, and you wielded it how heroes do. The only thing left is the wolf."

Patrick went cold, stomach twisting. "You aren't taking Jono."

"I will *eat* you," Wade added, blowing smoke out of his nose.

Persephone chuckled, the sound not quite mocking but close enough. "Oh, fledgling. This is a gift."

"I've had enough of those to last three lifetimes," Patrick said.

Persephone walked over to them, flowers blooming in her wake. "No strings. No debt. This is given freely."

Jono's hand settled against the small of Patrick's back, a grounding touch that helped him stand his ground as Persephone approached. The smell of flowers grew stronger, coating his throat, and he swallowed against the floral taste of spring.

Persephone came to a stop in front of his pack, the smile gracing her face making her look almost human. "We gave you the wolf and bound you together. We have decided you may keep the soulbond, and you need not fear your government learning of it. It is a secret that will be kept by the will of the gods."

"I would've stayed without it," Jono growled.

"We know."

"Why?" Patrick asked, looking for the catch, because there was always something owed when it came to the gods and their machinations.

"Because this is the end the Fates have finally decreed."

And maybe that was true, but it was a costly win no matter how one looked at it. This world was no longer his father's myth, but it was a story Patrick had lived. Going forward, maybe Patrick would be more than a footnote in some long-forgotten history. Maybe he'd be the hero in a cautionary tale, someone who'd survived the trials and tribulations the gods had thrown in his path and gained a future he could live with.

Maybe one day, when he died, he wouldn't be remembered.

Patrick reached for Jono's hand, finding him reaching back. He intertwined their fingers, and the squeeze Jono gave him was a reminder that he'd never let go.

"I don't need a soulbond to know Jono will stay, or to know he loves me, but if removing it is going to hurt how it did when we got it, then I guess we'll keep it," Patrick said.

"So will I," Jono said.

Persephone inclined her head ever so slightly. "May the binding be forever."

She turned to go, the veil already splitting apart behind her, when Patrick said, "Wait."

Persephone paused and looked back at them. "Yes?"

"Does my mother's family still pray to you?"

He hadn't been able to bring himself to ask when he'd spoken to Eloise after he returned from the veil. They were still navigating their familial relationship, and he knew he couldn't move forward without an answer.

Persephone smiled slightly. "There are many prayers that reach my ears these days. So many more people believe in us gods since the fight at the end of the world, but your grandmother's prayers no longer reach my ears."

She walked away and disappeared into the veil, cherry blossoms swirling in the space she left behind. Her words lingered though, and Patrick wondered if that was what she and the gods had been after all along—a life lived through new believers, gods an undying memory, no matter the consequences.

Jono tugged on his hand, drawing him forward. "Come on. We've a flight to catch."

Patrick let himself be led to the road that would take them out of the cemetery, Sage and Wade beside him, finally able to believe that it was well and truly over. That it was *done,* and he could go home.

It felt good, Patrick realized, soul light in a way it never had been before, to finally be free.

# EPILOGUE

Marek and Sage owned in the Makena neighborhood on Maui.

Jono gave a low whistle. "Bit posh, innit?"

"A bit? I think you need your eyes checked."

Patrick got out of the car, the humid heat of Maui in June hanging heavy in the evening air. They'd spent roughly fourteen hours in the air traveling from the East Coast, with a stop in Los Angeles to refuel Marek's private jet, and had finally touched down in paradise an hour ago. Their private chauffeured car had been waiting for them in the hangar, and they'd been driven to the place they were going to call home for the next two weeks.

Sage had taken care of all the logistics for them. Even at six months pregnant, she was a force to be reckoned with. As their dire, she'd cleared their pass-through rights with the Hawaiian god pack. The group of werecreatures weren't werewolves but were*sharks*, and Patrick wasn't keen on getting on their bad side. Luckily, his and Jono's travels hadn't been an issue, despite it taking weeks to extract themselves from work, both with the government and the packs.

But this vacation was long overdue, and Patrick firmly put work and responsibilities aside in favor of hauling their luggage into the mansion. The interior was all dark wood and clean white walls, with huge windows overlooking the ocean on every level. Jono led the way upstairs to the large guest suite, carrying his luggage to the walk-in closet that was probably bigger than their guest bedroom back home.

Sage had coordinated cleaners to come and open up the estate so it didn't smell musty. Patrick left his luggage by the bedroom door, wandering over to the windows. He pulled back the curtain, peering out at the crystal-clear blue waters of the Pacific Ocean lapping against the rocky shore just past the green lawn and gently waving palm trees. The sun was dipping toward the horizon, promising a spectacular sunset.

Paradise never looked so good when he got to share it.

Warm hands settled on his hips, pulling him back against a firm chest. Patrick craned his neck around, seeking a kiss that Jono readily gave him.

"Finally got your vacation," Jono murmured.

"Yeah," Patrick said, half turning in Jono's arms. "It only took forever."

"Sage said she had groceries delivered today. Do you want to eat?"

Patrick pushed against his chest, forcing Jono backward toward the bed. "Maybe in a little while."

Jono's wolf-bright blue eyes went a little dark from lust as he slipped his hands underneath Patrick's shirt. "Is that so?"

"You should probably get undressed."

Jono laughed softly, already stripping out of his clothes. They left a trail of clothes to the king-sized bed in between kisses. By the time Jono hauled Patrick onto the bed, they were both naked. His skin prickled from the cool air in the room, making him shiver, though it was Jono who made him moan when firm fingers wrapped around his half-hard cock and gently stroked him. The friction wasn't something he could handle for long, and he bit at Jono's bottom lip.

"Did you pack the lube?" Patrick asked. Jono was too busy sucking a bruise against the side of Patrick's throat to answer. "Jono."

"In my luggage."

"Go get it."

It took five more minutes before Jono left Patrick to go find the lube. Patrick made good use of the separation by lying on the bed and stroking his cock, enjoying the view of Jono coming and going.

"Menace," Jono said as he settled between Patrick's legs again, fingers already slick and sliding over his balls.

Patrick let his head fall back, allowing Jono to lick his way down his throat. "You're one to talk."

Jono hummed, biting at his collarbone before dragging his teeth gently over scar tissue. "Would rather not."

"Then don't."

They'd done enough talking since Patrick's return, and their partnership was stronger than it ever had been. Patrick could see it in the steady growth of their god pack beyond the core four they'd been for over a year. How there was less friction between the packs under their protection and the remaining Night Courts in the five boroughs. Their alliances hadn't faded after the fight, were only growing, and Patrick knew none of that would be even close to possible without Jono by his side.

"What do you want?" Jono asked as he rolled his hips against Patrick's, their cocks sliding together.

He hissed at the sensation, digging his hands into the sides of Jono's waist, holding him close. "Just you. Only and always you."

Patrick's shields had been down ever since they'd left their apartment, and he knew Jono would get the truth of it in his scent.

After everything they'd gone through, Jono was the one person Patrick would never give up, the one person he would always fight for, because they were better together than they'd ever be apart, soulbond or no soulbond.

Patrick arched his spine when one of Jono's fingers pushed inside him with gentle pressure. He carded his fingers through Jono's hair, mouth dropping open on a moan when Jono stroked his cock, thumb pressing against the sensitive spot beneath the crown.

"Don't know what my life would be like without you in it," Jono muttered against his skin, slipping in another finger.

Patrick blinked, bearing down on the pressure. He curled his fingers over Jono's chin and drew him into a kiss. "I'm not going anywhere."

Because they'd risked it all and won in the end, and their prize was a future that wasn't any of the nightmares that had woken Patrick up over the years. In the end, it was this. It was them. It was warm skin beneath his hands, the feel of Jono pushing into him slow enough to burn. It was the tenderness in Jono's eyes, in his touch, and the wickedness in his smile when he snapped his hips to thrust at just the right angle, hard enough to make Patrick see stars.

Patrick scraped his fingernails across Jono's shoulders, holding him close, the heels of his feet digging into the small of Jono's back. He could feel the way those muscles moved with every roll of Jono's hips, each thrust hard enough to make him lose his breath.

"I'm never letting you go," Jono said, whispering the words into his ear like a sacred promise.

He proved it there, his touch leaving hints of bruises in the shape of fingers on Patrick's hips, marks he'd proudly wear. Patrick could only hold Jono close and open up for him, taking the pleasure he was always so good at giving. Patrick urged him on with hands and voice, fire licking at his nerves.

Then Jono shifted on his knees, pulling Patrick higher onto his thighs, still fucking him with a relentlessness that was almost overwhelming. Patrick slapped a hand against the headboard to steady himself as Jono drove into him again and again, never looking away. Patrick took his own cock in hand, and it only took three strokes before he was coming, spine arching, Jono's hand sliding underneath to hold him there as he ground in hard, cock throbbing deep inside him.

When Jono came, Patrick was already floating in the aftermath of his orgasm, feeling more at peace than he had ever in his life. Jono collapsed on top of him, breathing heavily, and Patrick wrapped his arms around Jono's neck, closing his eyes.

"Now you can make me dinner," Patrick mumbled a few minutes later.

Jono buried his laughter against Patrick's throat, smacking his thigh. Patrick let his legs fall open, allowing Jono to shift back and pull out. Patrick grimaced at the stickiness between his thighs but didn't pull away from Jono's touch as his fingers rubbed it into his skin.

"Shower first, then I'll make you whatever you want."

They eventually made their way out of bed and into the massive bathroom that wouldn't look out of place in a fancy spa. Dinner was a little late in getting started, through no fault of Jono's. Patrick was to blame when he went to his knees in the steam-filled shower, sucking Jono off with a diligence that was rewarded by Jono stroking his cock and fingering him to a release that made him feel like he was drowning, and he couldn't even blame the water.

They ate dinner on the lanai, the sky clear of clouds, and the ocean waves white noise in the dark. When they crawled into bed together, Patrick fell asleep and didn't dream.

He woke the next morning with syrupy slowness, stretching his arm across the bed, already knowing the sheets would be cold. But

Patrick could sense through the soulbond that Jono was somewhere close by, always within reach how it mattered.

He sat up, squinting into the predawn light. Rubbing at his eyes, Patrick yawned and tried to kick-start his brain. He slid out of bed and pulled on a pair of boxers before leaving the bedroom, following the gentle pull of the soulbond to his other half.

Jono wasn't anywhere on land, and Patrick sighed, resigning himself to an early morning swim. He left the coolness of the mansion for the tropical mugginess outside, a gentle breeze curling through his hair. Standing on the lanai, Patrick gazed out over the stretch of grass and the small garden that gave way to the shoreline beyond the cluster of palm trees. He couldn't see Jono, but Patrick knew he was out there in the waves.

He walked across the grass, then picked his way down the rocky shore to where the waves broke against the dark earth. The horizon was turning pink, the gray above lightening to a blue that heralded daylight, but it wasn't quite there yet. Patrick stepped into the ocean, hissing at the chill leftover from the night.

"Jono?"

Patrick was rewarded a few seconds later to the sight of Jono rising from the water some meters away, eyes bright in his face, all slick skin and strong muscle that made Patrick's fingers twitch with the need to touch. Jono smiled in a way that told Patrick he could smell the want on him, but he didn't mind.

"I was going to let you have a lie-in while I swam," Jono said. He rocked a little against the push and pull of the tide but didn't move from his spot.

Patrick rolled his eyes and walked deeper into the water, heading to where Jono stood. "What's the point of vacationing with you if you aren't there with me to enjoy it?"

"I would've come back."

The flip of the promise Patrick had always given first made him swallow. "I know, but I figured I could find you for once."

Jono laughed, carefree in a way he hadn't sounded for too long.

When Patrick reached him, Jono wrapped an arm around his waist, pulling him close until they stood chest to chest. Jono brushed his knuckles over Patrick's cheek, the flash of his teeth easier to see in the growing light.

"You found me, love. You found me when I didn't even know I was lost."

Then he ducked his head, lips brushing over Patrick's with a tenderness that made Patrick never want to let go. He parted his lips, drawing Jono in like air. They kissed there in the waves, feet on the earth with the stars fading above them, Fate some distant promise kept.

"I love you," Patrick said when they parted, meaning the words with everything he had, everything he was.

Jono's smile was brighter than the breaking dawn around them, and Patrick knew he'd carry this moment with him forever into the future that stretched ahead for their pack. Because family was what you made of it, all the ragged bits of an untamed whole, fit together to lean on in times of joy and times of need.

And love?

Love was living, in all its many ways, and Jono had showed him how.

~~~

The Soulbound Universe continues with Resurrection Reprise, a brand new standalone novel releasing on September 1, 2023.

DON'T MISS out on Hailey Turner's steampunk-inspired epic fantasy series, beginning with The Prince's Poisoned Vow (Infernal War Saga I)

. . .
~~~

IF YOU LIKE science fiction romance and are a fan of comics and their movie counterparts, check out Hailey Turner's Metahuman Files series, starting with *In the Wreckage*.

DON'T MISS out on sneak peeks, exciting news, and more! Sign up for Hailey Turner's newsletter to stay up-to-date on her upcoming books.

# GLOSSARY

Short descriptions of words, acronyms and phrases used in the story that weren't readily explained in text. Included as well are character names.

**Abuku, Setsuna:** Witch. Director who oversees and leads the Supernatural Operations Agency.

**Academy:** K-12 school that teaches magic to practitioners of all affinities and designations. All provide boarding options to students.

**Æsir:** Immortals. Principal Norse pantheon of gods.

**Allfather, the:** *See* Odin.

**Áłtsé Hashké:** (Pronunciation: Aht SEH hash KEH) Immortal. Diné (given English name: Navajo) trickster god.

**Andras:** Demon. Ranked as a Great Marquis of Hell. He sows discord in humanity and is in charge of thirty legions of lesser demons.

**Ares:** Immortal. Greek god of war.

**Asgard:** Location. Norse realm of the gods. A heaven.

**Ashanti:** Immortal. Goddess and mother of all vampires. Takes the shape of an Asanbosam vampire out of West African myths.

**Baba Yaga:** Immortal. A supernatural being whose story stems from Slavic folklore. She appears as a deformed or ugly old woman who rides a flying mortar, carries a pestle and broom, and traditionally lives deep in the forest in a house perched on chicken legs. She is sometimes depicted as a child-eating monster. She may choose to help or hinder a person drawn into her path.

**Bailey, Spencer:** Mage. Former combat mage with the Mage Corps, currently a PIA special agent. He is a soulbreaker with the power to put the dead to rest and travels with a psychopomp who takes the form of an ocelot.

**Bifröst:** A burning rainbow bridge between Midgard and Asgard.

**Breckenridge, Gerard (Captain):** Immortal. Current identity of Cú Chulainn. *See*, Cú Chulainn.

**Brigid:** Immortal. Celtic goddess associated with fertility, spring, healing, smithing, and poetry. Spring Queen of the Seelie Court. Daughter of the Dagda and member of the Tuatha Dé Danann.

**Brynhildr:** Immortal. Leader of the valkyries and a shieldmaiden.

**Cailleach Bheur, the:** (Pronunciation: KAI-lach burr) Immortal. Goddess and divine hag. Considered a creator deity and Queen of Winter. Has various Irish and Scottish origin stories.

**Cairbre Nia Fer:** (Pronunciation: KAHR-bre nia fer) Immortal. Unseelie fae out of the Ulster Cycle.

**Carmen:** Succubus. First known recorded appearance was in Venice, Italy.

**Casale, Giovanni:** Human. Chief of the NYPD's Preternatural Crimes Bureau.

**Ceffyl Dŵr:** (Pronunciation: cef-fil dur) A water horse in Welsh folklore. Can evaporate into mist.

**Cerberus:** Immortal. Hound of Hades and guards the gates of the Underworld.

**Cernunnos:** Immortal. A Celtic god generally known as the "horned god." He has horns on his head and is associated with stags, horned serpents, dogs, bulls, and rats. He is interpreted as the god of animals, nature, fertility, travel, commerce, and bi-directionality.

**Charon:** Immortal. Ferryman of the Greek Underworld.

**Citadel:** United States military academy for magic users. Located in Maryland. All Academies across the nation feed into the Citadel. Mages get automatic inclusion. All other kinds of magic users need recommendations.

**Collins, Patrick:** Mage. Former combat mage with the Mage Corps, currently an SOA special agent. Has a tainted soul and crippled magic. Is technically a mage in name only due to a soul wound. Alpha of the New York City god pack he co-leads with Jono.

**Cú Chulainn:** (Pronunciation: ku CULL-ann) Immortal. Celtic god and son of the god Lugh. Member of the Tuatha Dé Danann. Irish warrior. Carries the *Gáe Bulg* in fights. Currently hiding under a mortal identity by the name of Gerard Breckenridge.

**Dagda, the:** Immortal. Celtic god affiliated with life, death, crops, and seasons. Member and king of the Tuatha Dé Danann. Husband to the Morrígan.

***Daoine Sidhe*:** (Pronunciation: dee-na SHEE) Irish term, plural for People of the Mounds. *See,* Tuatha Dé Danann.

**de Vere, Jonothon:** God pack werewolf. Originally from London, England, currently resides in New York City. Alpha of the New York City god pack he co-leads with Patrick.

**DEA:** Drug Enforcement Administration. A US federal law enforcement agency tasked with combating drug smuggling and distribution. It shares jurisdiction with the FBI and the SOA.

**Dire:** A rank held only within a god pack. The moniker is taken from the dire wolf, but has been shortened to account for different werecreature species. Essentially a rank held by a loyal pack member who helps enforce the alphas' orders.

**Dominion Sect:** A shadowy terrorist group consisting of

mundane humans, rogue magic users, immortals aligned with the hells, and other preternatural creatures intent on destroying the veil between worlds so that hell and its denizens can reign on earth. Some members are attempting to steal godheads in order to ensure their hold on power in the new world they hope to create.

**Drekavac:** Originates from South Slavic mythology. (Literally, "the screamer.") An elongated humanoid undead creature.

***Duine Sídhe:*** (Pronunciation: din-na SHEE) Irish term, singular form for fae reference. *See,* Tuatha Dé Danann.

**Einar:** Vampire. Oldest child and second-in-command within Lucien's Night Court. His sire is Lucien.

**Eir:** Immortal. A valkyrie and goddess associated with medicine and healing.

**Erinyes:** Immortal. Also known as Furies. Greek deities of vengeance.

**Espinoza, Wade:** Teenaged fledgling fire dragon. Part of Jono and Patrick's god pack.

**Fae:** Supernatural beings who reside in Tír na nÓg. There are lesser or higher fae depending on their status and species. *See also,* Tuatha Dé Danann.

**Fenrir:** Immortal. Wolf in the Norse pantheon. Patron to a god pack.

***Gáe Bulg:*** Artifact. Cú Chulainn's spear. Translated as "spear of mortal death."

**Ginnungagap:** Primordial void. Belongs to the Norse myths.

**Godhead:** Primordial power belonging to immortals that gives them life. The strength of their power can be altered by worship, or lack thereof.

**God pack:** A pack of werecreatures infected with the god strain of the werevirus. They act as spokespeople for hidden werecreature packs in their territory. They are supported by monetary tithes from the packs under their protection. Very few retain a connection to their animal-god patrons.

**Greene, Ethan:** Mage. Was a double agent formally employed by the SOA. Is currently a mercenary and allied with the Dominion Sect.

**Greene, Hannah:** Mage. Currently a vessel. Spiritually deceased.

**Gungnir:** Artifact. Odin's spear.

**Gwyn ap Nudd:** Immortal. Welsh god and ruler of Annwn. Leads the Wild Hunt.

**Hades:** Immortal. Greek god of the dead and the Underworld.

**Haudenosaunee:** A northeast Native American tribe. Also known as the Iroquois.

**Heimdallr:** Immortal. Norse god of foreknowledge, keen eyesight, and hearing. Called the Shining One.

**Hel:** Immortal. Norse goddess of death.

**Hel:** Location. Norse underworld located in Niflheim.

**Hellraisers:** A US Department of the Preternatural Special Forces team Patrick once belonged to.

**Hera:** Immortal. Greek goddess of women and titular queen of the Greek pantheon.

**Hermes:** Immortal. Greek messenger god and god of trade, thieves, travelers, sports, athletes, border crossings, and guide to the Underworld

**Hernandez, Leon:** Werewolf. Partner to Emma Zhang and co-leader of the Tempest pack.

**Hinon:** Immortal. Haudenosaunee thunder god.

**Huginn:** Immortal. One of Odin's ravens in the Norse pantheon, whose name means "thought."

**Khan, Youssef:** God pack werewolf. Deceased. Former alpha of the previous New York City god pack.

**Krossed Knights:** An organization of hunters that formed in the United States centuries ago. An offshoot of European hunter groups that came out of the Crusades.

**Kū:** Immortal. Hawaiian god of war, politics, farming and fishing. One of the four great gods in the Hawaiian pantheon.

**Ley lines:** Metaphysical rivers of powers that drain into nexuses.

**Lucien:** Master vampire. Was a soldier in William the Conqueror's army before being turned by Ashanti. Currently a weapons and magic trafficker. Is wanted by many governments.

**Maat:** Immortal. Egyptian goddess of truth, justice, wisdom, the stars, law, morality, order, harmony, the seasons, and cosmic balance.

**Macaria:** Immortal. Greek goddess of the blessed death and Hades' daughter.

**Mage:** Highest rank of magic users and the only practitioners who can tap external power from ley lines and nexuses.

**Mage Corps:** Military branch under the purview of the US Department of the Preternatural. Accepts only mages.

**Magic:** Emanating from and powered by a person's soul. Roughly one-quarter of the world's population has magic. Strength varies, with different titles being bestowed depending on a person's magical reach. Casting is divided into defensive wards and offensive spells.

**Medb:** (Pronunciation: may-ve) Immortal. Celtic goddess. Queen of Air and Darkness. Ruler of the Unseelie Court. Member of the Tuatha Dé Danann.

**Mjölnir:** Artifact. Thor's hammer, capable of immense destruction.

**Montu:** Immortal. Egyptian god of war.

**Morrígan:** Immortal. Sometimes depicted as an individual Celtic goddess, or more commonly as a triple goddess, of war and fate. She is particularly affiliated with foretelling of death or victory in battle. Often described as a trio of sisters sometimes given the names of Badb, Macha, and Nemain.

**Muginn:** Immortal. One of Odin's ravens in the Norse pantheon, whose name means "memory" or "mind."

**Mulroney, Nadine:** Mage. Works counterintelligence for the PIA. Is fluent in French and based out of Paris, France.

**Náströnd:** Location. A shore of corpses in Hel.

**Nazarov, Ilya:** Mage. Necromancer who was the former Patriarch of Souls for the Orthodox Church of the Dead.

**Necromancer:** A magic user who can be of any rank. Their magic has an affinity for the dead, allowing them to raise the dead, control zombies, and manipulate the lingering souls of the deceased. Their kind of magic is heavily restricted in use in the United States and in most countries.

**Necromancy:** A family of magic that deals with the dead, usually involving blood magic and sacrifices. Predominately illegal or restricted in most countries.

**Nexus:** Metaphysical lake of power beneath the earth. Usually located in sacred areas or beneath major cities.

**Niflheim:** Location. A Norse realm.

**Night Court:** Vampire group that oversees claimed territory. Headed by a single master vampire. Several Night Courts can exist in the same major city.

**Night Marchers, the:** Spirits. Hawaiian ancestral warrior spirits that are said to rise from their burial sites or the ocean to march to ancient Hawaiian battle sites or other sacred places. Usually visible on nights honoring Hawaiian gods, such as Kū.

**Norns:** Immortals. Norse Fates.

**Odin:** Immortal. Norse god of wisdom, healing, death, knowledge, battle, and the gallows and is the titular king of the Aesir.

**Órlaith:** (Pronunciation: OR-lah) Immortal. Daughter of Ruadán. The Summer Lady of the Seelie Court and heir to Brigid. Cú Chulainn's fiancée within the story.

**Otherworld:** Land of the Celtic pantheon deities, as well as land of the dead, located past the veil. Is more tightly connected to the mortal plane than other mythological worlds. Goes by many different names, and those names can be interpreted as places within it. *See,* Annwn, Underhill, and Tír na nÓg.

**Pearson, Keith (Sergeant):** Human. Soldier in the Hellraisers.

**Pegasus:** Winged horses favored by valkyries.

**Peklabog:** Immortal. Slavic god of the underworld who guides the souls of the dead. He is associated with fire, water, snakes, and earthquakes.

**Persephone:** Immortal. Greek goddess of the Underworld and springtime.

**PCB:** Preternatural Crimes Bureau. A PCB is usually found only in the police departments of major metropolitan areas in the United States. The PCB in New York City is headed up by a Bureau Chief. The five Detective Boroughs within the NYPD all field detectives specializing in preternatural crimes through the PCB. The PCB has jurisdiction throughout the five boroughs and its own detachment of cops that work in homicide, narcotics, major crimes, and CSU. The PCB is one of the least manned departments in the NYPD due to the type of cases it handles.

**PIA:** Preternatural Intelligence Agency. PIA is a national-level foreign intelligence organization overseen by the Secretary of Defense directly through the USDI. The PIA's intelligence operations extend beyond the zones of combat, and approximately half of its employees serve overseas at hundreds of locations and US Embassies in many countries. The agency specializes in collection and analysis of preternatural-source intelligence, both overt and clandestine, while also handling American military-diplomatic relations abroad. The agency has no law enforcement authority. (Equivalent to CIA)

**Psychopomp:** Creatures, spirits, angels, or deities that appear in many religions and take many forms. Responsible for guiding newly deceased souls from Earth to the afterlife, whether a heaven or hell. Are used most commonly with necromancy and other magic that has an affinity for souls or the dead.

**Quetzalcoatl:** Immortal. Aztec god of wind and wisdom. Can take the form of a feathered serpent.

**Ragnarök:** A series of events and great battles that will bring about the destruction and annihilation of the Norse gods. An end-time myth.

**Reed, Noah:** Fire dragon. Currently hiding in human form as a three-star Army general who oversees the US Department of the Preternatural.

**Santa Muerte:** Immortal. *Nuestra Señora de la Santa Muerte* (English translation: Our Lady of Holy Death), commonly shortened and referred to as Santa Muerte. A personification of death associated with healing, protection, and safe passage to the afterlife.

**Seelie Court:** Court of the spring and summer fae.

**Shields:** Ward. Defensive magic used for protection on a large or small scale.

**Shiva:** Immortal. Hindu god of destruction and one of Hinduisms principal deities.

**Sleipnir:** Immortal. Eight-legged horse ridden by Odin.

**Sluagh:** (Pronunciation: SLOO-ah) Spirits of the restless dead. Aligned with the Unseelie Court.

**Spells:** Offensive magic.

**Spriggan:** Lesser fae.

**SOA:** Supernatural Operations Agency. SOA is the domestic intelligence and security service of the United States that focuses on magical and preternatural crimes and terrorism. Employs human, preternatural and magically affiliated people to field positions for domestic defense. (Equivalent to FBI)

**Sorcerer/Sorceress:** Second-highest rank of magic users and moderately more common than mages but are outnumbered by witches and wizards.

**Soulbond:** A binding of two or more souls to tie people together for magical needs. Illegal under the laws of all governments.

**Srecha:** Immortal. Slavic dual goddess of fate who appears as a beautiful woman that spins a golden thread. She bestows positive welfare on chosen recipients. When depicted as misfortune, she is known as Nesrecha and appears as an old woman with bloodshot eyes.

**Takoma:** Vampire. Master vampire of the Seattle Night Court.

**Taylor, Marek:** Seer. CEO of PreterWorld, a social media platform geared toward the preternatural and supernatural community. His patrons are the Norns.

**Taylor, Sage:** Weretiger. A Diné lawyer who works for the fae law firm Gentry & Thyme.

**Tezcatlipoca:** Immortal. Aztec god of obsidian, jaguars, war, strife, night sky, and the night winds.

**Thor:** Immortal. Norse god of thunder, lightning, storms, oak trees, strength, the protection of mankind, hallowing, and fertility.

**Threshold:** Ward. Applied to a hearth and home for protection to keep out negative magic, spirits, and demons.

**Tiarnán:** Member of the Tuatha Dé Danann. Carries the title Lord of Ivy and Gold.

**Tír na nÓg:** (Pronunciation: TEER-na-nog) English translation: Land of the Young. A place in the Otherworld past the veil where the Tuatha Dé Danann and lesser fae reside.

**Tisiphone:** Immortal. A Greek Erinyes.

**Tremaine:** Master vampire. Deceased. Headed up the former Manhattan Night Court. His maker was Lucien.

**Tuatha Dé Danann:** (Pronunciation: TOO-ah de-danan) Celtic pantheon of gods. They are considered high-status fae.

**Underhill:** Another name for the Otherworld.

**Unseelie Court:** Court of the autumn and winter fae.

**US Department of the Preternatural:** Employs all manner of magically affiliated and preternatural people for military service. Active duty combat mages are seconded to the Army, Navy, Air Force, and Marines and are required to go through BTC and joint training.

**Valhalla:** Location. A majestic hall beyond the veil in Asgard ruled over by Odin. Warriors who die in battle spend eternity there waiting for Ragnarök.

**Valkyries:** Immortals. A host of female riders who choose who live and die in battle. They guide the dead to either Valhalla or Fólkvangr.

**Veil:** The metaphysical barrier between Earth/mundane plane and other worlds/dimensions/planes, such as Faerie, versions of hell and heaven derived from myths.

**Walker, Estelle:** God pack werewolf. Deceased. Former alpha of the New York City god pack.

**Wards:** Defensive magic.

**Warlock:** Most common rank of magic users. On par with witches.

**Werecreatures:** Humans who are infected with the werevirus. Can change form into various animalistic shapes. Werecreatures are either infected later on in life or are born with the disease.

**Werevirus:** An incurable disease that makes those who are infected change into monstrous beasts. Created by an ancient Roman mage, the werevirus was one of the first recorded instances of magically created biological warfare introduced into society. People are born with the werevirus or become infected through intercourse or blood. Two strains exist: a normal strain and a god strain. The god strain has stronger magical properties which can cause the infected to be susceptible to an immortal patron.

**Wild Hunt:** Supernatural and ghostly hunters who steal souls. Aligned with Gwyn ap Nudd.

**Witch:** Most common rank of magic users. On par with warlocks.

**Wizard:** Second most common rank of magic users.

**Yggdrasil:** Norse world tree that connects the Nine Realms.

**Zeus:** Immortal. Greek god of thunder and titular king of the Greek pantheon.

**Zhang, Emma:** Werewolf. Alpha of the Tempest pack.

**Zombie:** An undead creature consisting of either a skeleton or fresher corpse. They can only be raised by necromancers. Zombies are powered by black magic and souls pulled from the afterlife beyond the veil.

# AUTHOR'S NOTES

This final Soulbound book was years in the making. I can't begin to tell you how many times I started and stopped Patrick's story over the years, always coming back to it, because this was a story my brain just would not let go of or give up on.

As a writer, you always have that one idea that will take root and never let go until you get the words out. That was me with Patrick and Soulbound. This entire series was my love letter to mythology and legends and the histories, oral and written, that we all keep. I spent so long trying to give Patrick the story he deserved, and when I typed the last word in *A Veiled & Hallowed Eve*, I knew it was finally over for good, and I'm proud of what I accomplished.

I can't thank you, the reader, enough for joining me on this journey through the book of my heart that ended up as a seven-volume series. Thank you for loving Patrick and Jono and their pack as much as I do. Thank you for the messages and fanart and joy. Thank you so very much for saying *yes* when the gods came calling.

My personal thanks to the following:

Nora Sakavic, who was there from the very beginning and never let me give up on telling this story.

Leslie Copeland, for helping me make my words better and putting up with my insanity.

Lily Morton, for never letting me go the Dick Van Dyke route. You know I love you for all that you do.

May Archer, for always cheering on my mad ideas and laughing with me through the hard times.

Bear, for your patience and all that you do to make my books look so nice.

I would be thrilled and grateful if you would consider reviewing *A Veiled & Hallowed Eve* on Amazon or Goodreads. I appreciate all honest reviews, positive or negative. Reviews definitely help my books get seen, so thank you!

Cover design by AngstyG LLC.
Professional Beta Reading by Leslie Copeland: lcopelandwrites@ gmail.com
Edited by One Love Editing
Proofing by Lori Parks: lp.nerdproblems@gmail.com
Proofing by Jenni Lea at LesCourt Author Services

# CONNECT WITH HAILEY

Keep up with my book news by signing up for my newsletter and get the free Soulbound prequel short story *Down A Twisted Path* and several free Metahuman Files short stories while you're at it.

Join the reader group on Facebook: Hailey's Hellions

Visit Hailey's website: www.HaileyTurner.com

Like Hailey's author page

# OTHER WORKS BY HAILEY TURNER

**M/M Science Fiction Military Romance:**

Captain Jamie Callahan, son of a wealthy senator and socialite mother, is a survivor.

Staff Sergeant Kyle Brannigan, a Special Forces operative, is a man with secrets.

Alpha Team, the Metahuman Defense Force's top-ranked field team, is where the two collide and their lives will never be the same.

## Metahuman Files

In the Wreckage

In the Ruins

In the Shadows

In The Blood

In The Requiem

In The Solace

## A Metahuman Files: Classified Novella

Out of the Ashes

New Horizons

Fire In The Heart

**M/M Urban Fantasy**

## Soulbound

A Ferry of Bones & Gold

All Souls Near & Nigh

A Crown of Iron & Silver

A Vigil in the Mourning

On the Wings of War

An Echo In The Sorrow

A Veiled & Hallowed Eve

## Soulbound Universe Standalones

Resurrection Reprise

**LGBTQ+ Epic steampunk-inspired fantasy:**

Welcome to Maricol, where the land will kill you, kinship turns the gears of war, and burning the dead lest they come back to life is the only way to survive.

## Infernal War Saga

The Prince's Poisoned Vow

The Emperor's Bone Palace

## Infernal War Saga Novella

An Emporium of Hearts

**Contemporary gay romance**

Short stories previously published in the Heart2Heart Charity Anthologies.

From the Heart: A Short Story Collection

**Audible**

All of Hailey Turner's books are available in audiobooks. Visit Audible to discover your next favorite listen.

Hailey Turner Audiobooks

Thanks for reading!

www.ingramcontent.com/pod-product-compliance
Lightning Source LLC
Chambersburg PA
CBHW022018300726
48970CB00003B/950